ALL THESE MONSTERS

ALL THESE MONSTERS

BY AMY TINTERA

HOUGHTON MIFFLIN HARCOURT
BOSTON NEW YORK

hmhbooks.com

The text was set in Fairfield LT Std.

Library of Congress Cataloging-in-Publication Data
Names: Tintera, Amy, author.
Title: All these monsters / by Amy Tintera.
Description: Boston : Houghton Mifflin Harcourt, [2020] |
Summary: Seventeen-year-old Clara runs away from home to join
a vigilante monster-fighting squad, only to discover that sometimes
the most dangerous monsters are where you least expect them.
Identifiers: LCCN 2019011416 | ISBN 9780358012405 (hardcover)
Subjects: | CYAC: Monsters—Fiction. | Social media—Fiction. |
Dating (Social customs)—Fiction. | Family violence—Fiction. |
Racially mixed people—Fiction. | Hispanic Americans—Fiction.
Classification: LCC PZ7.T493 Al 2020 | DDC [Fic]—dc23
LC record available at https://lccn.loc.gov/2019011416

Manufactured in the United States of America
DOC 10 9 8 7 6 5 4 3 2 1
4500794928

Part One
RUN

1

THE BAG SLAMMED INTO MY BODY, AND I HIT THE MAT WITH A grunt. I flipped over, scrambling to my knees as I tried to find the weapon that just flew out of my hand.

Four claws appeared at my throat. A loud buzzer sounded.

Dead.

I flopped back on the mat, letting out an annoyed huff of air. That was embarrassing. I didn't even make it thirty seconds that round.

"*You have one more life,*" the voice on the intercom said. "*Do you want to take a break first?*"

I got to my feet and turned to where a large, skeptical man named Bubba watched me through the window. I considered telling him to forget about the last life. Surely I'd humiliated myself enough for one day.

I shook my head. "No, I'm fine."

Bubba made a face like, *wow, she's an idiot.* I was very familiar with this expression.

He pressed a button on his computer, and the practice dummy retracted, squeaking as it zipped along the track mounted to the ceiling.

I put my hands on my hips as I took a deep breath. Four lives, and I died within two minutes each round. I really was an idiot. Bubba was a good judge of character.

"You sure you don't want the body pads, Clara?" Bubba asked over the intercom. *"You took a pretty big hit just now."*

"No." I shook out my shoulders. "I don't need pads." Pads were for football players. I'd never had padding to protect me from a hit.

"The girls usually take the pads," he said. *"Especially . . ."* He didn't finish his sentence. He didn't need to. Especially the girls who didn't look tough. Especially the girls with their dark brown hair in French braid pigtails and breasts that were made to hold up dresses, not jump around fighting monsters. I really shouldn't have been doing this in a regular bra. *Sorry, boobs.*

"I don't need pads," I said again.

"All right. Ready?" Bubba asked over the intercom.

"Yeah."

"Sword." Bubba sounded like he'd lost what little faith he had in me.

I grabbed my sword from the mat. It wasn't actually a sword, just a plastic tube that looked like it belonged on a vacuum cleaner. It had a light on the end that glowed green if I hit a weak spot. I'd only seen it light up once, briefly.

The buzzer sounded, indicating that I had five seconds to prepare. I tightened my grip on my vacuum attachment.

There were four practice dummies hanging from the ceiling, but I'd picked a level one session, so only one jolted away from the wall. It was made out of a large punching bag with plastic arms attached, complete with four-inch claws at the end.

It looked cheap, and stupid. Until it started moving.

The dummy flew at me, metal screeching as it zoomed forward. It was made to approximate a real scrab, and it moved incredibly fast.

Claws sliced through the air. I stumbled backward, the mat squishing beneath my feet.

The dummy's body swung side to side as it raced along the track, claws outstretched. I ducked beneath its arms and darted around it. I'd clearly surprised it, because it took a second for it to swing around.

I jumped forward, thrusting the sword at its neck. I saw the green light, but only for a second. I hadn't put enough force behind the weapon for a kill shot.

I barely pulled my hand back in time to miss getting dinged by plastic claws. I spun and ran, ready to swerve and surprise it again—

The bag slammed into my back, sending me crashing into the wall. I hit it so hard that I could have sworn the wall shook. That was going to leave a bruise.

"*Whoa, are you—*"

Bubba's voice cut out as I jumped away from the wall and dashed around the dummy. It swung to face me, all ten claws stretching for my face. I launched at it, throwing my sword into its neck as hard as I could.

The sword glowed bright green. The dummy's arms dropped. A pleasant dinging sound echoed through the room.

I won. I killed it.

"*Congrats, darlin',*" Bubba said over the intercom. He didn't actually sound all that happy for me. *"You sure can take a hit. Last guy in here cried after round two."*

I blew my bangs out of my eyes. I could definitely take a hit. One of my few talents.

And I could kill a dummy pretending to be a scrab one in five times.

I watched as the dummy retracted. If I'd had more money, I might have asked Bubba to give me another full set of lives. I wanted to pound the vacuum attachment into that fake scrab until it was thoroughly dead.

"Meet me up front," Bubba said.

The dummy took its place at the back of the room, and I dropped my sword into its charger on the wall.

I walked out of the simulation room and down the hallway to the front desk. Bubba's Combat Training and Games wasn't much to look at, inside or out. It was a squat, windowless building on the side of the highway, the kind of place that might be the last thing you saw before you died. The front room consisted of a few metal chairs, a desk, and walls covered in flyers advertising various services.

European Vacation Special
Buy 5 defense classes for the family and get 2 free!
Weapons, Armor, and Guns
What works, and what doesn't. Free book with class!
Florida Beach Tips
Learn to spot scrabs in the sand.

The last one was a couple years old. There hadn't been a scrab sighting in Florida for a long time. They were rarely spotted anywhere in North America these days. It had been three months since the last one, in South Carolina, and the National Guard had shown up almost immediately to whisk it away.

Bubba must never have removed old flyers, because I spotted a bunch of old stuff—the announcement requiring Texas high school students to take combat class instead of gym, a seminar discussing scrab origin theories, even a newspaper article from 2013 about the attack in New Orleans, with a photo of President Obama standing amongst the wreckage. The walls were more history than advertising.

"All right, Clara," Bubba said as he walked through the door and sat down at his desk. He pushed aside a coffee mug. "That'll be twenty."

I dug the bill out of my pocket, flattening it with my hand against the counter before handing it over. Bubba whisked it into a box in the top drawer of the desk. I swallowed as I watched it disappear. With the exception of a few quarters, that was all the money I had. I'd been saving that twenty for months.

The television mounted on the wall above my head was silently playing the news, and Bubba glanced up at it. The words *Grayson St. John* and *Elite Fighting Squad* scrolled across the bottom of the screen, beneath a photo of three scrabs standing over a destroyed food cart in Beijing. The scrabs looked a bit different depending on the region—in Asia they were large, typically six or seven feet tall, with enormous bodies covered in spikes. They ran on all fours and mostly used their massive mouths full of fangs to fight. Scrabs in Europe and the UK fought on two legs and made better use of their front claws. North American scrabs were a mix of both, but everyone said ours were smaller and kind of sluggish compared to the rest of the world.

I wondered which version Bubba had modeled his dummy after.

"You thinking of joining?" Bubba asked.

"Uh, I don't know." I was too embarrassed to say yes.

He squinted at me, running a hand over his dark beard. "You got any special skills or anything?"

"No." I tilted my head. "Well, maybe. Is surviving a special skill?"

"I guess?" Bubba said it skeptically, probably thinking of my four deaths he'd just witnessed. But Bubba didn't know. Not really.

"Yeah, I've got that, then. Not dying. That's what I'm good at."

2

I HAD TO TAKE TWO BUSES TO GET HOME. THE SECOND ONE WAS crowded, and I pressed my body into a corner, face-to-face with a poster of Beyoncé selling makeup.

My phone dinged repeatedly in my pocket, but I didn't pull it out. My news alerts hadn't stopped since last night. The same headline was everywhere—on the phones around me, rolling across the small television screen mounted to the wall of the bus behind the driver. GRAYSON ST. JOHN ANNOUNCES INTERNATIONAL FIGHT SQUAD.

Grayson St. John would have beaten that fake scrab five out of five times. The people trying out for his fight squads probably could have done a level one course with their eyes closed.

The bus screeched to a stop. I squeezed around a guy staring at his phone and stepped off.

Sweat rolled down my back as I trudged down the sidewalk. It was May, in Dallas, which meant it had already been summer for a month.

Fridays were always lively in my neighborhood, even with the heat. The Brown boys whizzed by on their bikes, a taco truck at the end of the block had several customers, and Mrs. Gonzalez sat on her porch, wearing her leather shoulder holster over her loose blue dress. Her gun sat against her hip, clearly visible to anyone who walked by. She'd moved here from New York City several years ago, after the scrab attack in Midtown Manhattan, and she spent all day, every day, on her porch with her gun. Some of the neighbors reminded her that she'd moved here because there had never been a scrab attack in Dallas. She'd showed them the scar on her leg—twenty-four stitches—where a scrab had swiped its claws across her flesh. We all left her alone.

A few girls I went to school with were gathered around a car in the street, one of them on the ground, pulling a flat tire off the wheel. The girl sipping a large fountain drink, Adriana, caught me watching them and smiled, lifting her hand in a wave.

"Hey, Clara!" Her nails were so bright pink that I could see the color from across the street. Adriana's hair and makeup were always perfect—she'd been the one to teach me how to put on eyeliner.

I waved back and walked a little faster.

All the eleventh-grade girls in my neighborhood were friends, except for me. I'd hung out with them until middle school, when it had become clear that they were the smart girls, the girls who would get scholarships and spend years voluntarily going to school after the required portion. It would be a miracle if I even finished high school. I just made them uncomfortable, so I came up with excuses not to hang out with them until they stopped asking.

I turned the corner and headed for the first house on the left. It was small, one-story, white, with bars on the windows that were ostensibly for our protection. The path to the front door was covered in weeds. The lawn always went to hell when Dad was gone.

Inside, the television was on, the local news playing to our empty faded blue couch. Paintings hung at strange spots on the walls, like someone had slapped them wherever or had a very odd design sense. In reality, they covered bad patch jobs or holes that had never been fixed. The most recent addition was a brightly colored painting of Texas that hung crooked at my eye level.

I found Mom in the kitchen, frantically stirring something in a bowl, flour dusting her black T-shirt. Mom did everything frantically, like someone was chasing her while she was mixing. I didn't know if it was an acquired behavior or if she'd always been that way. I'd have put money on the former.

She noticed me standing at the entrance to the kitchen. A crease appeared between her eyebrows. I was a constant source of worry, or disappointment, or concern. Never quite figured out which.

"What are you making?" I asked.

"Your school called," she replied.

My phone dinged in my pocket. In the other pocket was a summer school schedule confirming what we all already knew—I was an idiot. I swallowed as I pulled the paper out.

"Two classes, mija?" Mom said, stirring so hard batter splattered across her shirt. "You failed *two* classes?"

"I could never figure out what the physics teacher was talking about. It never made any sense to me. Even after lots of studying," I added, which was a total lie. I never studied. How did you study something that made absolutely no sense? Was I supposed to stare at the book and hope it all miraculously clicked one day?

"And English?" Mom asked. "How do you fail English? You like to read."

Not the kinds of books they made us read in class. I shrugged.

She stopped stirring and let out a sigh so heavy the neighbors probably heard it. "You were supposed to get a job this summer."

"I know."

"You were supposed to help me." She gestured with both arms to nothing in particular. I was supposed to get a job to help her pay the bills so she wouldn't break down and call Dad again. It was our deal.

"Maybe I should just get a GED," I said.

"No. Absolutely not."

"I'm not going to college anyway. What does it matter?"

"You are not dropping out of high school."

"Then I'll get a job on nights and weekends. You worked in high school."

She gave me a look that clearly said, *You're not me*. I wasn't her. I'd never wanted to be, in most ways.

The front door opened, and my older brother stepped inside. Laurence had an expression that clearly said he wished he'd stayed gone longer. It was his usual expression.

"I'm flunking out of high school," I said.

"Oh." There was no surprise in his tone.

"You are not flunking out. You're going to summer school," Mom said.

Was physics suddenly going to make sense in summer school? I was going to fail, again, and we'd have further confirmation of my stupidity. It had been well established since first grade, when the teacher sent a note home to my parents saying I was unfocused and kept hitting the other kids when I got frustrated. I was nothing if not consistent.

But no one ever asked *why* I was unfocused, or why I had so many absences, or why hitting the other kids seemed like a good idea. So I fell further behind, and I never found a way to catch up. My teachers got used to disappointment. We all did.

"Just don't call Dad," I said. "We can figure this out." I looked at Laurence, hoping for help, for a sudden reveal that he'd found a new job after getting fired from the last one.

Laurence seemed uncomfortable, like he always did when anyone expected something of him. He was happiest slipping through life invisible, which should have been difficult, at six feet tall with the build of a former football player. But he managed it most of the time. He could move like a ballerina on a spy mission whenever he detected a potentially awkward situation.

"My buddy has a line on a job," he finally said. I didn't try to hide my surprise. Laurence so rarely came through with the good news I hoped for.

"It's in Oklahoma," he finished.

Right. There was the Laurence I knew. Perpetually disappointing.

"You're moving to Oklahoma?" Mom abandoned her mixing and gaped at my brother.

"It's a good job," he said apologetically. His gaze met mine, and he quickly looked away.

If I were being reasonable, I'd say I couldn't blame Laurence for wanting to leave. He was twenty years old; he was supposed to move out on his own, not hang around to help support his mom and little sister. Objectively, he was allowed to have his own life.

In reality, I resented him. I wanted to ask him to stick it out for one more year, because surely—*surely*—I could figure out a way to escape when I was eighteen.

But I said nothing. I'd never been able to ask Laurence for anything. My brother and I barely spoke at all.

"When?" Mom asked.

"Next week," Laurence said.

Mom nodded. "Call your father and tell him." She paused. "And let me speak to him."

My heart sank.

I retreated to my bedroom and didn't listen to Laurence's and Mom's conversations with Dad. I didn't need to. I'd heard it a dozen times. Mom always kicked Dad out, and she always asked him to come back.

This was my fault, anyway. It was my fault for thinking this time would be different just because Dad put my head through a wall. If he'd put only a tiny bit more muscle behind it, he could have killed me. Mom had lost it, screaming at him to get out with such ferocity I was surprised she didn't damage her vocal cords. The world was still tilted as I listened to her throw his clothes out the window, and Dad was gone before I'd fully regained consciousness. But the horror of that incident had faded, like it always did. It was naïve to think otherwise.

And it was my fault for not being able to pass classes that, honestly, weren't even that hard. My school was regularly ranked at the bottom of Dallas public high schools. Failing at my high school was a truly embarrassing feat.

My phone dinged again, and I finally pulled it out. The top news alert was in all caps. **GRAYSON ST. JOHN POSTS RECRUITMENT VIDEO.**

I clicked on it.

Grayson sat in front of a white background. He was a blond man in his early twenties, and handsome in a way that was almost unappealing. He was so good-looking that he'd circled right back around to ugly.

His blue eyes sparkled as he smiled at the camera. He was well lit. Grayson St. John was no stranger to the camera. I'd heard of the dude for the first time two days ago, and I'd already figured that one out.

"Hello, friends," he said. *"I'm Grayson St. John. You've probably heard of my father, the former CEO of St. John Technologies, Gregor St. John. Our company provides weapons to soldiers fighting scrabs in the US.*

"I'll get right to the point. I'm going to go kill some scrabs. My father died in Prague trying to fight these things, and I'm not going to let his death be in vain. He wanted Congress to act, to send any kind of help, but they've just voted—again—to stay out of the fight overseas. Parts of Europe and Asia are under constant siege, and I don't know about you, but I'm tired of sitting here while people die. Our government has closed its borders, and our president has repeatedly said that America must come first. Well, I say screw that, and I know many of you agree with me.

"We're forming fight squads. Training and weapons will be provided. You don't need a military or police background, just a desire to help, though if you're one of the young people who received combat training in school, we'd love to have you. We have cutting-edge technology that helps us track scrabs, and we'll be partnering with local law enforcement or military wherever we are. Most fighting will be hand-to-hand, so please have some skill in that area.

"We'll cover all your expenses, and you'll get stipends that increase every week you spend with us. And because they said I have to set a minimum age, you have to be sixteen.

"We do value your safety, so we're holding tryouts to make sure you're equipped to fight. If you live in America, tryouts will only be held in Los Angeles and Atlanta, but we've chartered buses from several major cities to help you get there. Everyone else, there's a list of cities around the world where our trainers will be holding tryouts. If you pass, you will be assigned to a team, and we'll pay for your transportation to Europe or Asia.

"Call the number on our website, and we'll get you sorted. We won't be paying for any return airfare if you change your mind, so please be sure before you hop on that plane."

He leaned closer to the camera. "More information at the link. Please contact us even if you don't have a passport. We're working it out. I hope you'll join me, friends. We can be better than our government."

The video ended, and I lowered my phone. I understood suddenly the kinds of people who were going to show up in Atlanta and Los Angeles — a few thrill seekers, sure, but mostly do-gooder types. Humanitarians and charity workers and the sort of people who went to foreign countries to build schools for orphans.

Not me, basically. People probably didn't join just because they were flunking out of high school and they were scared of their father. Those sorts of people simply ran away from home. I saw them living on streets, popping into the church a few blocks over for a free meal and a shower. Some of them looked like they were doing fine. Some of them didn't.

I knew my place. It was here, trying to make ends meet with my mom, or it was with the street kids, or it was in one of the group homes a few of my grade school friends were always cycling through. It wasn't in Europe, fighting monsters because I had a burning urge to save people. The only person I wanted to save was myself.

Not to mention, just setting foot in Europe was a terrifying prospect, much less *going there specifically to fight scrabs*. You couldn't even tell when they were approaching, because they dug elaborate tunnels underneath the ground for travel. They'd spring up in heavily populated areas, like they were hoping to inflict as much damage as possible. And they did.

Scientists were still unsure about their intelligence levels, but they were pretty sure that all scrabs had the same goal: destroy. Human, animal, plant, building—it didn't matter to a scrab. If it was in their way, they demolished (or ate) it. It was like they were trying to clear the Earth of every obstacle until they were the only thing left.

And I didn't want to spend every waking second worrying about the ground beneath my feet.

A knock sounded on my door, and Mom pushed it open. I knew what she was going to say before she opened her mouth. Her face was determined, but a little abashed.

"I spoke to your father," she said.

My stomach dropped to my feet. "OK."

"He's really sorry."

"OK."

Mom pressed her lips together like she did when she was trying not to cry. "Clara, please don't be like that."

"Like what?"

"It's been hard around here without your father. I can't . . ." She gulped. "And now you're flunking out of high school and Laurence is leaving. I can't do this by myself."

She couldn't. Mom wasn't able support us, not on a cafeteria worker's salary. And she'd never been good at being alone. It was the mortgage, or a busted pipe, or a broken-down car, or just loneliness, but it always ended the same—asking Dad to come back.

"Please, try to act happy that he's home," Mom said.

I plastered a huge fake smile on my face. "How's this?"

"Please try, Clara. He's sorry."

He was always sorry. There were holes all over the house that he'd been sorry about later. *Sorry I kicked a hole in the cabinet while we were fighting. Sorry I threw the doorstop through the window after I had a bad day at work. Sorry I put Clara's head through the wall.*

Mom was looking at me like she was expecting an answer. Like I was still a ten-year-old girl who would tearfully agree with her—Dad was sorry, and things would get better.

"Sure, Mom," I said dryly.

"He'll apologize to you. He promised."

"I can't wait. I'll treasure every moment."

Mom didn't know how to deal with sarcasm, so she just pretended she hadn't heard it. "There will be plenty of cake," she said, and left.

3

DAD WOULD BE HOME AT SIX.

I trudged out of my bedroom at 5:58. It would be worse if I ignored him.

The painting of Texas had been set straight. I hated it, and I wasn't sure if it was because it covered the hole made by my head or simply because it was Texas. I despised this state, even though I'd never visited the forty-nine others. The only place I'd ever been was Guanajuato, Mexico, to visit Mom's family. Tía Julia paid for plane tickets for just Mom and me two years ago, and then tried to convince Mom to stay once we arrived. I'd been in favor of it. I loved the city, with its brightly colored buildings and streets so narrow you couldn't drive cars most places. I could step out of the house and get lost in the winding roads.

No one walked in Dallas. I could walk to the bus, which would take me through miles of suburbs and into the city, and I still wouldn't have seen most of the Dallas–Fort Worth area. It was too big. All of Texas was too big. It made it too hard to escape.

Mom was in the kitchen again, stir-frying like her life depended on it. Laurence brushed past me and raised his eyebrows as he looked at the meat and vegetables over Mom's shoulder.

"Is Dad going to like that?" he asked.

"I'm using the sweet sauce he likes." Still, worry crossed her face. It was risky, trying a new recipe. Dad enjoyed barbeque and burgers and fried Americanized Chinese food.

Mom took me to a ramen restaurant once, for lunch, just the two of us. *Let's not tell your father,* she'd whispered in my ear as we left, because Dad was the sort of man to get angry about noodles.

The television was on, the news blaring, and Laurence walked into the living room and flopped onto the couch. My eyes drifted to the screen.

"We have reports that three thousand people have already signed up to join Grayson St. John's team," the male anchor said.

He had two guests on the program with him, and the blond woman shook her head.

"Who are these people?" she asked the anchor.

"From what we've heard, they're mostly young people, and they're from all over the world."

"It's been suggested that some of them were rejected from the military in their countries," the blond woman said.

"That's just speculation at this point," the anchor said. *"And some are too young to even join the military, since the minimum age for these teams is only sixteen. But St. John has made it clear that the training will be rigorous, and they won't accept people who aren't fit to fight."*

I swallowed. *One in five.* Was that fit to fight?

I looked away from the television and caught Laurence staring at me. The thing about quiet people was, they were always watching. And listening. And noticing things I'd rather they didn't notice.

"Those idiots are going to get themselves killed," Mom grumbled.

"I think it's brave," Laurence said quietly, still watching me.

Outside, a car door shut.

Mom frantically wagged her hand. "Turn that off, turn that off."

Laurence grabbed the remote, and the television screen went black. I pressed both arms to my chest, my left hand tightly clasping my opposite wrist. It was all I could ever think to do to protect myself.

There wouldn't be any danger immediately—Dad was always on good behavior at first—but my body didn't know that. It had been trained to tense up at the mere mention of Dad.

The door opened, and he stepped into the house. Dad was well over six feet tall, with shoulders so wide he sometimes had to turn sideways to go through doors. He'd been good-looking in his youth. Now he always looked like someone had just spat in his tea.

Dad's eyes skipped over me, standing in the middle of the living room, to Laurence, perched awkwardly on the edge of the couch. I wondered what it was like to live in Dad's world, where everyone shifted things to your liking. At work, did he walk into rooms and wonder why it wasn't quiet, neat, and full of nervous energy?

Mom's face lit up as she stepped out of the kitchen to kiss Dad on the cheek.

Why anyone would get excited to see Dad was beyond me, but I guessed Mom had found something to like about him. They were opposites in appearance (Dad: white, blond, built like a line-backer; Mom: Latina, olive skin, brown hair, short and thin) but alike in other ways (love of football, hatred of crowds, an impressive ability to completely ignore reality).

I, thankfully, took after Mom, except taller and with more curves. I had serious curves, the kind everyone liked to comment on. *Those are birthing hips, mija,* Tía Julia said. *That is an ASS,* a random guy at 7-Eleven said. *That shirt makes you look like a whore,* Dad said.

My boobs looked great in that shirt. I wore it several more times, until it mysteriously vanished one day.

"Laurence," Dad said, clapping him on the shoulder. Laurence clearly wanted to disappear. "You think about what I said?"

Laurence nodded.

"And? Dallas is a lot bigger than Tulsa. You can't find a job here?"

Laurence shook his head.

"What's there to do in Oklahoma anyway?"

Laurence shrugged.

"It's just a construction job," Dad said. "It'll be over in a few months. What are you going to do then?"

It took my brother a moment to answer, and when he did, it was with a sigh, like being forced to actually say something was tiresome. "I guess I'll find a different job. Or move somewhere else."

A look crossed Dad's face, like he was both surprised and dismayed. "I don't know where you think you'll go," he muttered.

I realized suddenly why Dad was trying to convince Laurence to stay. He wasn't going to miss him; Laurence could barely muster up the energy to be marginally polite to Dad. There was no love lost there.

Dad was scared that his son would be better than him. Dad had never been anywhere. He grew up a few blocks from where we lived now. He visited Austin once with Mom and declared it "terrible." He was a plumber, a job that only required travel within the Dallas–Fort Worth area.

Mom had him beat; she was born in Mexico and immigrated here with her parents when she was six years old. She'd traveled around the southwest states and Mexico a lot in her early twenties, before she met Dad. Maybe I even had him beat, with my one trip to Guanajuato.

Dad shifted his attention to me. He laid a hand on my shoulder. I tightened my fingers around my wrist. "Clara." His voice shook with emotion. "I'm so sorry about losing my temper."

I'd never understood the phrase *losing my temper*. It was never lost. Dad kept his temper with him always. He managed to hide it from everyone—from his coworkers, his friends, from the cops I'd called once, only to have Mom tell them I was a liar. He could keep a grasp on his temper in all those situations, so that meant he chose to free it at home. He hadn't lost anything.

"I hope you can forgive me," he said.

His face was open and sincere. He thought he meant the apology. He didn't. He always did it again, and you can't be truly sorry for something if you turn around and do the exact same thing, repeatedly.

He stared at me anxiously. I was expected to be a bottomless pit of forgiveness. No matter what he said, what he did, I had to forgive or I was a horrible person. Everyone forgave Dad. Those were the rules.

I broke the rules last time. No forgiveness. He flew into a rage within two hours of returning home, because he said I was being rude to him.

There was no reason to believe that this time would be any different. Mom was widening her eyes at me, silently asking me to play nice. The smart thing to do here was to force a smile and say I understood. *Yes, Dad. It's fine that you called me a moron and bashed my head into the wall. It's OK, even though I know you'll do it again.*

I said nothing. I was not a bottomless pit of forgiveness; I was a screaming ball of resentment. There were two options here — silence or hysteria. I chose the former, always.

Dad's contrite look faded. His jaw twitched. His apology only applied if I accepted it. I didn't think apologies were supposed to work like that.

He turned on his heel and grabbed his bags. "There's something wrong with that girl," he muttered to my mom. I'd heard him say it before. *Do you think she has feelings at all?* he whispered once to Mom, with an actual edge of concern in his voice.

I had feelings. He just didn't like any of the ones I had for him.

Dad deposited his bags in the bedroom and returned to join Mom in the kitchen. He wrapped his arms around her waist from behind, and she smiled as she leaned into him.

She loved him. It defied all common sense and logic, but she really did. And it made me feel like a crazy person that I didn't. Was I overreacting? Did I expect too much? Was this how fathers were, it was just that no one talked about it?

I had loved him once, as a kid. I remembered the feeling of relief when he was happy, the certainty that *this time* would be different. I was sure that if I was good enough, everything would be fine.

But there was no such thing as *good enough*. It was embarrassing how hard I'd tried, looking back now. I never wanted to be that dumb again.

"Clara." My name was disappointment on Dad's lips. He stepped away from Mom, his hand lingering on hers a moment. I watched the way their fingers clung to each other for a few extra seconds before splitting apart.

"We need to talk about your grades," he said.

Mom's demeanor completely changed. Her shoulders tensed, her eyes going a little wide. She was still trying to be good enough.

"She got an A in history and combat class!" she blurted out. "I should have mentioned that before."

"That's great about history, Clara." Dad smiled at me. I didn't return it.

I'd liked history this semester. We studied recent history, up to the first scrab attack in Scotland. That's how they got their name—the first sighting was in Scrabster, Scotland.

I'd never even known how they got the name until Ms. Watson took us through their history and the various conspiracy theories about their origin and how they ended up in the US. She'd made a strong argument that someone must have smuggled a few into the country and lost control of them. Scrabs could reproduce, so she reasoned that all our scrabs could have come from just one male and one female brought over from Europe or Asia.

"What do you think went wrong in English and physics?" Dad asked.

"I'm dumb. I failed. As expected."

"You're not dumb," Laurence said. I threw him an annoyed look. There was no need for lies just to make me feel better.

"Spare us the pity party," Dad said. "You just need to focus on studying, not . . ." He trailed off, because he had absolutely no idea what I liked to do. I'd been marathoning all eight seasons of *Game of Thrones* when I should have been studying for my physics final.

"Boys?" I guessed.

"Exactly." He held out his hand. "Your phone, please."

I peered at Mom. He gave me a concussion, and the first thing he did upon returning was *punish* me?

Mom twisted a towel in her hands and swallowed.

"Come on," Dad said, opening and closing his fingers.

I stared harder at Mom.

"Clara, maybe it's better if you don't have any distractions this summer," she said quietly.

Behind Dad's shoulder was a framed picture of a stream, and I couldn't remember which hole it covered. I didn't know if it was the time he punched it in a rage about something Mom had done, or if it was the time he'd hurled a chair at the wall when I came home late. I wondered if, one day, I'd forget what the painting of Texas was covering up. Would I be like Mom, who swore up and down that Dad hadn't been aiming that chair for my head? I already wasn't sure if I had really ducked, because she so adamantly claimed it didn't happen. How long until my reality bent the same way Mom's did?

I dug my phone out of my pocket and put it in Dad's outstretched hand, but my eyes stayed on Mom.

She looked away.

4

After midnight, when Mom and Dad were asleep, I slipped out of my room and into the backyard. I sat on the edge of the porch, feet in the grass. It was early enough in the season for the weather to be pleasant this late, almost cool now that the sun was gone. In a few weeks it would be miserably humid every hour of the day.

France probably had better weather. It was a terrible reason to run off to fight scrabs, but I'd always hated the summer. I hadn't even known that other places were cool at night, even in the summer, until I visited Mexico.

The door slid open behind me, and fear gripped my chest so intensely that I couldn't breathe until I turned to see that it was just Laurence. I let the air out of my lungs slowly.

Laurence had something square tucked under his arm, and he used his elbow to keep it steady as he lit a match and held it to the cigarette in his mouth. He hadn't noticed me yet, sitting at the far edge of the porch.

"Laurence," I said.

He jerked like I'd startled him and almost dropped whatever he had under his arm. He adjusted it and tucked his lighter in his pocket.

"Hey," he said, blowing out a breath of smoke. "What are you doing out here?"

"Nothing."

He watched me for a moment, like he was debating saying something. Laurence's words were never an accident.

He settled for silence and strode across the yard to where an old drum sat on top of two concrete blocks. He removed the lid.

"The neighbors hate it when you do that," I called.

"Life's full of disappointment." He peered inside the barrel, then grabbed the matches from his pocket and lit one. He dropped it in and added leaves until smoke began to rise.

I stood, dead grass crunching under my feet as I walked to him. He took the square object out from underneath his arm and dropped it on the ground. It was the painting of Texas.

He slammed his foot down on it, cracking the wooden frame. He picked it up again, another crack echoing across the yard as he folded it in half. He dropped it in the barrel.

I stopped next to him, watching the black smoke curl up from the fire. "Didn't like that painting?"

"You kept staring at it."

He said the words to the barrel, not meeting my gaze even when I turned to him. The flames lit up his expressionless face in the darkness. I said nothing, because sometimes if you waited, Laurence would finally choose the right words.

"They should have to look at that hole," he said after a silence so long the flames were almost gone, leaving nothing but smoke. He tossed his cigarette butt in with it. "He almost killed you. They should have to look at the evidence."

Mom would just buy another one—that painting was ten dollars at Walmart—but I didn't say that. I didn't say anything, because the words *he almost killed you* were vibrating through my brain. Laurence had never acknowledged the danger I was in out loud.

"I'm going to stay," he said. He pulled a pack of cigarettes from his pocket, shook it, and sighed dejectedly. He tossed the empty pack in the barrel.

"Why?" I asked, even though the answer seemed obvious. Obvious, but unexpected.

He met my gaze and shoved his hands in his pockets. "Unless you're leaving too, I'm going to stay."

"I didn't ask you to protect me," I said.

"I'm going to do it anyway," he said.

You've done a terrible job so far, I didn't say.

"Unless you're leaving?" It was a question this time.

"What about the job?"

He shrugged. "There will be others. Dad can feel smug, at least."

The wind shifted, blowing smoke in our faces, and we both stepped back, in opposite directions. I stared at him through the smoky haze; his eyes fixed on a point at the other side of the yard. When I looked, there was nothing.

I wondered if there would always be an excuse not to go. Maybe Dad had planned to leave when he was twenty. Maybe there were jobs in Oklahoma or road trips planned but never taken. A different life plotted but never lived.

I thought of the street kids at the church, the group home I could be placed at with one phone call, of Grayson St. John and beating a scrab with a plastic vacuum attachment. There were good reasons not to do all of them, to stick with the danger I knew. It would be so easy to get stuck forever.

"Can I borrow your phone?" I asked.

Laurence handed it over without question and then turned and walked back inside.

I went to the website. I pressed my finger to the phone number. I was actually doing this.

"What's up? You got the Grayson St. John fight squad hotline."

The man who answered the phone sounded like he was having the best day of his life. I scurried to the far corner of the yard, as far away from the house as I could get.

"Um, hi," I said quietly. "I'm Clara. I'm interested in joining?"

"That's awesome. I'm Victor."

"Uh, yeah," I said.

"Where are you?" Victor asked. "Did you look at the list of charter buses on our website?"

"Yeah. I'm in Dallas."

"Perfect. You'll go to Atlanta. So here's how it'll work. I'll get some details from you—age, race, gender, current address, combat background, all that jazz, and you'll be all set to try out when you get here. Do you have a passport?"

"Yes."

"Perfect. We're asking that you bring that with you to Atlanta. If you pass, you won't be returning home before going to Paris. Do you have any questions?"

"Um." *What are my chances of dying? Have I lost my mind? Are you people sure you know what you're doing?* "It's not a problem that I'm only seventeen?"

"Nope. As long as your parents are cool with it, we're cool with it."

"How are you going to know if they're cool with it?"

"I'll email you a consent form. Just have a parent or guardian sign it and bring it with you or email it back. You'll need to include their phone number too. We'll call to follow up."

There was no way that Mom or Dad would sign a consent form.

But there was also no way for anyone on the St. John teams to know if I forged the signature and put Laurence's number down instead. He never answered his phone anyway. And his outgoing voicemail message just said *"leave a message if you want, but I don't check them."*

"Cool?" Victor said.

"Cool," I said. "Where will we be going? If I make it, I mean."

"I can't answer that one. Certainly not the US, but other than that, it depends on where your team is assigned. You'll all start in Paris, but we'll have teams in the UK, certain parts of Europe, and China."

"OK."

"And be aware that the US government is extremely skeptical of what we're doing, and they are monitoring our activities very closely. The NSA is probably listening to us right now." He raised his voice a little. "What's up, NSA? How's the weather over there?"

I laughed, then quickly covered the phone so they couldn't hear it. Maybe you shouldn't laugh at the NSA.

"But most importantly, we need you to understand that this is a one-way ticket. We won't pay for return tickets until you've been with us for at least a year. You'll have to get back to the States on your own if you want to leave before that, and plane tickets to the US are outrageously expensive and hard to come by these days. Once you're there, it will likely be very hard to get back."

That might have been the most appealing reason to do this so far.

"Why don't I get some information from you while you're thinking about it. We're gathering info on everyone who calls us. Voluntary, of course. And keep in mind that our buddy at the NSA is getting it all too."

"Sure," I said, suppressing another laugh.

"Full name? First, middle, last."

"Clara Rivera Pratt."

"Gender? This one's optional, if you'd rather not answer."

"Female."

"Race?"

"Hispanic and white."

"I don't know if I can click more than one . . . Oh, I can! Perfect. Date of birth?"

He asked a few more questions and hummed as he inputted my info. I gripped the phone, wondering if I'd lost my mind.

"The Dallas bus leaves tomorrow at ten a.m.," Victor said. "If you miss it, you can find your own way to Atlanta, but we can't help."

"Tomorrow?"

"Sorry, it's after midnight, isn't it? I mean today. Saturday."

Keys clicked on a keyboard. "So what do you think, Clara? Should I sign you up?"

I looked at the house. It was dark except for the small barred window of Laurence's bedroom. It wasn't a bad house. There were worse ones in the neighborhood.

Mom always liked to point out how things could be worse. We could be homeless, or run out of food at the end of every month, or we could have been born in the UK or Europe, where scrabs attacked constantly. We might get slapped around occasionally, but there was always someone who had it worse.

But this felt like the worst. The things that my mom had decided to accept were as bad as it could get for me. This house with the man who was allowed to terrorize us, over and over, was the worst thing I could imagine.

Victor had remained quiet, even though it had been at least thirty seconds since he'd asked his question.

"It can't be worse than this, right?" I whispered.

I thought he'd laugh, or make a joke about how fighting scrabs was no picnic. Instead, he let out a breath of air that sounded like agreement. "Yeah," he said. "I know what you mean."

5

AFTER A FEW HOURS' SLEEP, I STUFFED MY BACKPACK WITH clothes, underwear, and my sneakers. The confirmation email Victor sent me said to pack lunch and snacks, but when I checked the kitchen late last night, the only snacks I found were some very brown bananas. Mom didn't keep the pantry well stocked when Dad was away.

I could live without food for a day, but I really wanted my phone. Dad would cut off the service as soon as I disappeared, but I could still use it with Wi-Fi. I slipped out of my room and walked to Mom, putting on my best pitiful face.

She smiled at me. "Morning, mija."

"Good morning." I sat down next to her. "Do you think I could have my phone back, just for a few minutes? I want to text my friends and let them know why I'm not responding to them. They're probably worried."

She patted my leg and smiled. Mom didn't know I had no friends. "Your father is still asleep, so I don't see why not. I'll go grab it. Just be quick, OK?"

"Sure. Thanks." Mom never seemed to care about whatever rule or punishment Dad had doled out. She was perfectly happy to be on my side, as long as Dad never found out.

She disappeared into their bedroom. The television was on, the news playing at a very low volume.

"And St. John issued a statement saying he would abide by all UN rules regarding scrabs," the anchor said. "It is currently illegal to transport any part of a scrab, including blood samples, and any scrab kills must be immediately reported to local authorities so that the body can be disposed of properly. St. John says he will ensure that all recruits abide by these rules.

"But the Monster Defense Group continues to criticize St. John for his plan to take inexperienced Americans overseas. The private security firm pointed to their own training program, which is rigorous and highly competitive, and they claim that St. John will simply cause chaos and get people killed."

"They're not wrong," the blond woman next to him said. "MDG is a fairly new company, but they gained several new high-profile clients recently after providing protection to Taylor Swift while she was on tour in Europe, and a lot of people have been impressed by their methods and training. If St. John is so determined to help, he should have just applied to join MDG."

"St. John has actually been highly critical of MDG," the anchor said. "He pointed out that MDG's protection services are extremely costly, and that MDG doesn't fight scrabs unless it's to protect a client. This seems to be St. John's main goal—he's mentioned several times that he disagrees with the decision to pull all US troops out of scrab-infested countries."

"Well, he's in the minority there," the blond woman said.

"You think so?"

"Yes! The president campaigned on a promise to put American interests first, close our borders, and let our troops focus on keeping the US free of scrabs. Our military is already stretched incredibly thin, and we can't spend resources in countries that, frankly, haven't done enough to combat the scrab problem themselves."

Mom returned with my phone and plunked it into my hand. I jumped to my feet, gave her a quick smile, and darted back to my room. I'd hoped to get Laurence to drive me to the bus station, but he was still asleep, and I needed to get out of the house before Dad woke up. I had just enough quarters for the bus tucked into my backpack anyway.

I slipped my phone into my pocket, slung my backpack over my shoulder, and took one last glance at my room. My purple comforter had been picked out by Mom, my desk was Dad's old one, every poster on my wall was put up knowing that Dad would see them. The room had never really been mine.

I put my hand on the doorknob.

"Good morning, baby."

I froze. Dad's voice was close, from the hallway. He'd just walked out of the bedroom.

Mom murmured a reply. They both laughed.

I turned, pressing my back to the door. I'd have to make a run for it. Dad wouldn't be able to catch me if I made it out of the house. Running was one of the few things I was good at.

I gripped the straps of my backpack. Deep breaths. I could do this.

I opened my door and stepped into the hallway. Mom stood in the kitchen. Dad was sitting on the sofa. I'd have to pass right in front of Dad to get out. He hadn't noticed me yet, and I walked as quietly as possible, hoping he wouldn't see me until the last possible second.

My phone dinged in my pocket. *Shit.* I should have silenced it. Dad's gaze shifted to me.

Danger.

"Why do you have your phone?" he asked. He stood, doing a quick survey of me. "Where do you think you're going?"

In the kitchen, Mom was silent. She would never own up to it. I didn't want her to.

I just stared at Dad. There was no explanation, lie or truth, that would make this better. Nothing ever made it better. I was done trying.

I darted around Dad, dodged the edge of the couch, leapt over the coffee table, swerved—

And a hand grabbed me. Dad grabbed my arm so hard I was lucky he didn't pull it out of its socket. I yelped and tried to twist away. He held tighter, using his other hand to dig into my pocket.

"What is so important that you need . . ." He trailed off as he turned my phone to peer at the screen. His face went red.

"You signed up to fight scrabs?" Dad yelled.

"What?" Mom gasped. "No, Clara wouldn't do that."

"It's right here, you moron," Dad said, throwing the phone at Mom. "They're texting her confirming she's headed to Atlanta today."

"What do you care?" I said evenly.

Dad actually had the nerve to look insulted. Like I was supposed to believe that whatever it was that he felt for me was love.

Then he was pissed.

He slammed me against the wall—not hard enough to leave a dent this time, which was good, since we were down one painting.

"Are you stupid?" Dad spat out the last word.

"Clara, that is far too dangerous." Mom pressed a hand to her heart. I didn't even try to suppress an eye roll. She had the decency to look ashamed. We both knew it wasn't any safer here.

"Do you want to die? You will DIE." Dad's rage was barely contained in his body. He was shaking with it. Mom started to cry.

I hadn't realized that Mom and Dad were so concerned with my well-being. I was skeptical, to be honest. I wasn't sure what it was that had them so upset, but it seemed unlikely that this display was all about my safety.

"You are not going," Dad said through clenched teeth.

I tugged harder against his grasp, but he was too strong. He was holding my arm so tightly that it was hard not to cry out. It would leave a bruise.

He dragged me in the direction of my bedroom. I eyed Laurence's door. He slept like the dead.

I screamed. I tried to avoid hysterics with Dad—it was just used against me—but I needed whatever distraction Laurence could provide. Him simply emerging from his room might be enough for me to bolt.

Dad used his grip on my arm to hurl me into my room. I stumbled and hit the ground on my knees. The door slammed shut behind me.

"I'm protecting you!" he yelled. "That idiot will get you killed!"

I dove for the handle, but Dad must have been holding it shut.

"Veronica, get me that rope from the back."

I froze. He was locking me in. I could handle Dad pounding the shit out of me before I made my escape, but if he made me miss my bus, it was all over.

I sank back on my heels, an unexpected blast of terror shooting down my spine. I'd been so scared to go, but now, faced with the possibility that I *couldn't* go, I wanted to scream again. Tears pricked my eyes.

"What the hell is going on?" Laurence's voice was right outside my door. My head shot up, and I wiped at the tears that had spilled down my cheeks. *"Did you lock her in?"*

"Don't touch that," Dad said. *"I said don't touch that!"*

"Get off me!" Laurence yelled, followed by a grunt.

I tried the doorknob again. It twisted this time, but the door caught on something when I tried to push it open. Dad had tied it shut.

"Get off of—Veronica, are you going to help me here?" Dad yelled.

I heard more grunts, followed by another yell from Dad. He was bigger than Laurence, but my brother was apparently putting up quite a fight.

"You want your sister to go get herself killed?" Mom screamed.

More grunts.

I stared at the door. It wasn't anything special—just a standard, white plywood door you'd find in any home. It wasn't all that sturdy.

Why was I just sitting here? What if Dad knocked Laurence out? It wouldn't be the first time.

I looked around the room. Shockingly, I didn't keep anything in my room that would help break down a door. That was bad planning on my part.

I looked down at my boots. Those would have to do.

I scooted closer to the door. I lifted my feet up. I slammed them against the wood.

Pain rippled up my legs. I ignored it and slammed my shoes against the wood again.

"What is that?" Dad yelled.

Footsteps ran down the hallway. *"Clara?"* It was Mom.

I kicked the door again. The wood splintered. A victorious thrill raced down my spine.

"Clara, stop!" Mom screamed.

I kicked the door harder. I kicked it until a piece of wood began to split off, then I grabbed it and pulled it away. I bashed my boots against it a few more times. Another piece. The hole was finally big enough to crawl through.

I grabbed my backpack and threw it out first. Then I crawled through, hands first, then shoulders, then hips (barely), legs, and I was out.

I jumped to my feet and scooped up my backpack. Mom stood pressed against the wall, horror and astonishment on her face.

I turned to the living room. Laurence had Dad pinned face-down to the ground. Blood poured from Laurence's nose, and he was breathing heavily, but his face broke into a smile when our eyes met.

"Run, Clara."

I darted out of the hallway and across the living room. I flung the door open and dared a glance back at Laurence. Dad was struggling with all his might, wriggling and squirming on the ground.

I slammed the door shut behind me. My feet hit the pavement, my backpack bouncing as I ran. Dad's screams faded behind me.

Part Two

TEAM LOSER

6

I RAN ALL THE WAY TO THE BUS STOP, AND THEN SPENT THE entire ride peering out the window, heart pounding as I searched for Dad's car. It never appeared. Tears pricked my eyes. I wasn't sure if it was relief or fear.

I'd done it. I was seriously *volunteering* to fight scrabs. I took in a ragged breath.

I spotted the Grayson St. John bus as soon as we pulled into the station. A white sign taped to the back said RECRUITS, and a few people were in line to board.

My bus let me off at the end of the parking lot, and I gripped the straps of my backpack as I walked across it. A couple nearby was saying goodbye, the guy with a bag slung over his shoulder, the girl sobbing. He said something that didn't seem to comfort her in the least.

Everyone had boarded the bus except for a balding man holding a clipboard. Another bus screeched to a stop behind me.

"Atlanta for tryouts?" he asked.

"Yeah."

"Name?"

"Clara Pratt."

He scanned his sheet and crossed something off. "You're a minor? I need your consent form."

I dug the forged consent form out of my bag and handed it over. He barely glanced at it before slipping it in a folder. I bit back a smile.

"You by yourself?" he asked.

"Yeah."

"Perfect. I have one more spot on this bus. Hop on."

I gripped the straps of my backpack and stepped onto the bus. A sea of faces stared at me.

Probably about 70 percent of the bus was male. And they were mostly big guys, with broad shoulders and muscles. A few had military-style haircuts. The women were all older than me, probably in their twenties and thirties, and some of them looked like they were also no strangers to the weight room.

People were talking and laughing, like they already knew each other. Were we supposed to enlist with friends? Or were they bonding in that way normal people did when they met someone with similar interests?

The only open seat was in the back, next to a girl about my age with pale skin and dyed black hair. She peered at me, didn't appear to approve of what she saw, and turned back to the window.

I walked down the aisle and sat down, backpack in my lap. The girl wore leggings, an old white T-shirt, and, notably, handcuffs. They weren't attached, a chain dangling from each wrist, like they'd been cut off.

It was jewelry. Probably.

She caught me staring and raised an eyebrow.

I quickly looked away.

|\|/|

"Hey."

I turned at the whisper from across the aisle. We were five hours into the twelve-hour drive to Atlanta, and so far I'd spoken to no one.

It was the tall, ridiculously attractive Asian American boy seated in the row across from me. He had tousled black hair, long, lean limbs, and a smile like he'd never been so happy to see anyone as he was to see me. He should have been modeling skinny jeans, not joining an elite group of monster hunters.

"Were those handcuffs on her wrists?" he whispered, his gaze cutting to where my seatmate had disappeared into the bathroom.

"I think they're jewelry? I hope?" I said softly.

He tilted his head back as he laughed. He had the sort of laugh that put normal people at ease. The guy in front of him actually looked back and smiled just at the sound of it.

"I'm Patrick," he said, extending his hand to me.

I shook it. "Clara."

He leaned closer, gesturing for me to lean in as well. "Do you get the feeling we're on the wrong bus?"

I laughed softly, relieved he felt the same way. "Yeah. Everyone seems kind of . . ."

"Intense? Yeah. This guy next to me?" He glanced over his shoulder as if to confirm the large bearded man next to him was still asleep. "He went to Belgium last year with friends to chase down scrabs. Just for kicks. One of them stuffed a scrab head, shipped it back to himself, and hung it on his wall."

"Wow. That's . . ."

"Illegal?" he guessed.

"I was going to say intense, but that too."

His eyes skipped over me, though not in a sleazy way. It was hard to describe how some men simply surveyed you, and others were obviously mentally running their hands all over your body. You just knew.

"You didn't run off to Europe to chase scrabs for fun, did you?" he asked. "I guess I'm making assumptions because you look young."

"No, you're right. I'm seventeen. No time for trips to Europe yet."

"Eighteen. Are you done with high school?"

"I mean, it wasn't done with me, but I ended the relationship anyway."

He laughed. "I can respect that. I mean, I did well in school and everyone loved me, but not everyone is so lucky."

"And you're so modest about it too."

"Modesty is overrated. I'm great, honestly. Just wait until you get to know me." He leaned out of the aisle as the handcuffed girl exited the restroom. I stood so she could slide back into her seat.

Patrick grabbed a black messenger bag from the floor and flipped it open to reveal snacks—chips, cookies, nuts, a few sodas, even some sandwiches packed in plastic bags. He noticed me watching him, and I quickly looked away.

"Did you forget snacks?" he asked.

"Yeah," I lied.

"Here. Do you like peanut butter? My mom packed me enough for five people."

He held out one of the sandwiches and a bag of chips. I could see why everyone loved him.

"Thank you," I said, taking the sandwich. My stomach had been rumbling for hours. In fact, he may have heard it.

I unwrapped the sandwich and took a bite. Patrick passed me a soda, and I smiled at him as I took it.

"So why'd you join?" he asked.

I chewed slowly, considering how to answer that question. "The fame. The glory."

"Well, of course."

"What about you?" I asked, hoping he wouldn't notice that I hadn't given a serious answer.

"Well, I was always complaining about the government's policy to close our borders and not help overseas. I marched and protested and yelled at my dumb friends until they were smarter. So when the opportunity came up, I couldn't really say no. What was I going to do, make my Facebook picture a solidarity ribbon again and *not* join? I mean, come on."

"Sure." I was surrounded by badasses and do-gooders, as expected. I was going to be the only loser who joined just to put an entire ocean between her and her family.

"Are you from Dallas?" I asked.

"No, Austin, but Dallas was the only Texas bus. My boyfriend drove me." He rolled his eyes like he'd just remembered something annoying. "*Ex*-boyfriend. He said he couldn't be in a relationship with someone if he was scared for their life the whole time."

That sounded reasonable to me. "That sucks."

"Meh. Clearly I can do better." His phone dinged, and he pulled it out of his pocket. A smile twitched at his lips. He typed something and glanced over at me. "Are your parents freaking out too?"

"A little bit."

"My mom's been texting me every twenty minutes."

I popped a chip in my mouth. "I guess it's good I don't have a phone." I'd really wanted it, but now I wondered if Dad would have kept the service on for the sole purpose of sending me mean texts. He loved dropping terrible shit on me randomly, probably just to ruin my day.

Patrick's eyebrows knitted together. It was weird not to have a phone, and I realized too late that I probably shouldn't have admitted it. He looked from my five-year-old backpack, dirty and frayed at the edges, to my scuffed combat boots. Judging by his perfectly fitted jeans, the expensive laptop I'd glimpsed earlier, and the designer label on his messenger bag, he'd never spent a second of his life wanting for anything.

"Were they OK with you coming?" I asked before he figured out how to ask why I didn't have a phone. "Your parents?"

"Sort of." A sheepish expression crossed his face. "So . . . Yeah, I'm just going to tell you this story. Why not." He laughed. "I'd been planning to come out to my parents for a while. I figured they kind of knew, especially my mom, but I thought I should do it, like, officially."

"Sure."

"But then this happened, and I figured . . ." He lifted both shoulders, making a face like *I don't know.* "I could just do both at the same time."

"What?" I asked with a laugh.

"I wasn't sure how they were going to take the gay news, so I decided to just immediately follow it up with the scrab news. And then they'd be so distracted by me running off to fight scrabs in Europe that they wouldn't care at all about me being gay."

"Smart."

"Thank you. So I walked in, and I said, 'Dad, Mom, Grandma—'"

"Jesus, your Grandma was there too?"

"Well, she lives with us, so she's always there. I said, 'Dad, Mom, Grandma, I'm gay. And also I've signed up for Grayson St. John's fight squads.'"

"How'd they take it?"

"Oh, it worked perfectly. They barely even reacted to me being gay." He pointed one finger at his face. "Master of avoiding conflict here. I think that one was my proudest moment."

"How out are you now?" I asked, even though I suspected I knew the answer. But I was the sort of person who liked to keep her secrets, and I didn't want to go around spilling other people's. "With everyone here, I mean." I gestured around the bus.

"It's not a secret. Please tell everyone so I don't have to do it," he said.

I smiled. "Got it."

His phone dinged again, and he rolled his eyes as he pulled it out of his pocket. "She only made it three minutes." His face shifted into surprise when he looked at the screen. It was a happy surprise, the kind that made his lips curve up. He typed something and glanced over to see me watching him.

"My dad this time," he said. He was still smiling as he returned his phone to his pocket. He looked at me quickly, like he'd just remembered something. "Do you want to use my phone to call your parents? Or anyone?"

"No, thank you." I wanted to check on Laurence, but I didn't have his number memorized. I'd have to email him later.

"Your parents were mad?" he guessed. It was the guess of someone who had a good relationship with his parents.

"I'm pretty sure they think I'm crazy," I said lightly.

"We're not crazy. We're brave. We just have to keep reminding people of that." He grinned.

"Sure," I said with a laugh.

Brave. I'd have to keep reminding myself of that, actually.

7

IT WAS DARK WHEN WE ARRIVED IN ATLANTA. WE WERE SURrounded by tall buildings on all sides, lights twinkling in the darkness. A billboard advertised the new Apple Watch: NOW WITH SCRAB SENSOR! There were a lot of people on the streets, even at this hour. We must have been downtown.

The bus was starting to come alive, people stretching and checking their phones as they woke up. The girl beside me rubbed a hand across her eyes.

"The Centennial Park Memorial is on your left!" a male voice called from the front of the bus.

I turned to look. We were driving by Centennial Olympic Park, the site of one of the worst scrab attacks in the US. Hundreds had died. The images on the news had showed destroyed fountains, bodies lying in the grass, a statue in pieces.

The memorial was built about a year ago, a plain stone tower that listed all the names of those who had died there. It was faint in the darkness, partially hidden behind a tree, but I could make out the flowers, stuffed animals, and crosses that surrounded it.

The overhead lights clicked on as we neared the end of the street. We jerked to a stop.

When I stepped off the bus, the first thing I noticed was the sign on the street corner. I'd never seen one in person before.

Scrab sighting?
Dial 911 or
Text SCRAB to 911
SEEK SHELTER

My fingers tightened around the straps of my backpack as I looked down at the pavement. I'd never been in a city with a scrab threat before. There could have been one beneath my feet right at that moment, waiting for the right time to attack.

No wonder so many people had fled the East Coast cities. Half the residents of Florida never went back after the initial attack and evacuation in the summer of 2010, and I certainly couldn't blame them. Dallas might have been one of the most expensive cities in the country, but at least we'd never had to deal with scrabs.

I tried not to think about it. If I spent too much time dwelling on scrabs, I might remember that I'd signed up to go to Europe, where there would *definitely* be scrabs beneath my feet.

I found Patrick standing next to a large roller bag. The bus driver was still unloading bags, and Patrick didn't do a good job of hiding his surprise when I walked right by the pile of suitcases with only my backpack.

The balding man who had checked us in in Dallas stood near the bus, gesturing wildly as he talked on his phone.

"Yes! A full bus from Dallas!" he said. "And there's a second one about half an hour behind us. What are they supposed to do, sleep in the streets?"

"That doesn't sound good," Patrick said.

The man listened for a moment. "Yeah, all right. Tell Grayson

I'll send them over." He lowered his phone and cupped his hands around his mouth. "Recruits! There's room for thirty of you at this hotel." He pointed to a group of guys standing near the door. "You guys can stay here. Everyone else—you're going to the Hyatt. It's a short walk that way." He pointed behind me, and then began walking, gesturing for us to follow him.

"Well, at least we don't have to sleep in the streets." Patrick grabbed his roller bag, and we followed the other recruits down the sidewalk. People turned to stare. They must have heard we were coming.

A homeless man stood across the street, belongings at his feet, and he held his sign up higher as we passed. THE END OF THE WORLD ALREADY HAPPENED, YOU MISSED IT.

We approached an intersection, and the walk signal changed to a flashing hand as Patrick and I drew closer. The recruits in front of us made a run for it, leaving the two of us behind.

"Let's just wait," Patrick said as the hand went solid and cars began speeding past. He pointed. "The Hyatt's right there."

I looked up at the buildings as I waited for the light to change. Atlanta wasn't really that different from Dallas. Big buildings, wide streets, cars everywhere, homeless people sleeping on benches. It was sort of disappointing.

The walk signal lit up, and we crossed. The recruits had disappeared around the corner, into the Hyatt, but the balding man was standing with a shorter man at the end of the street, pointing to us.

Our side of the street was otherwise empty, except for a boy in a black leather jacket.

He caught my attention right away, leaning against a white car parked on the street, because it was too hot for a jacket. A faded purple backpack rested by his feet, and he had one ankle casually crossed over the other, like he was waiting for something. His eyes skipped over Patrick and landed on me, catching me watching him. He winked.

I heard a clattering noise behind me, and I turned to see Patrick's phone bouncing off the sidewalk.

"I've got it." The boy reached down and scooped up the phone, extending it to Patrick with a smile.

"Thanks," Patrick said, taking it and examining it for cracks.

The boy gave him a friendly slap on the arm. "No problem." As he said the words, he easily slipped Patrick's wallet out of his back pocket. I barely saw the flash of leather before it disappeared into the boy's jacket.

The thief grabbed his backpack, jumped off the sidewalk, and began walking—at a brisk pace, but not a run. He hadn't noticed me watching him. Patrick started toward the hotel again, oblivious.

"Hold this." I threw my backpack at Patrick and broke into a run. I wasn't letting this thief rob Patrick, who was maybe one of the nicest people I'd ever met. Shit like that was supposed to happen to me, not him.

I darted between the parked cars and into the road. The thief was still walking, apparently oblivious to me following him.

I reached for him. I grabbed a handful of his jacket.

I was crazy. What if he punched me in the face?

Wouldn't be the first time.

He jumped, clearly startled, and tried to twist out of my grasp.

I kicked the back of his knee, and he let out a yelp as he fell to the ground.

I launched at him before he could scramble to his feet. He squirmed beneath me, rolling over as he tried to throw me off. I sat on his stomach and shoved my forearm into his throat.

He wheezed as his body went limp beneath me. Panic crossed his face. He lifted both hands in surrender.

I pulled back, surprised at how easily he'd given up. He probably could have tossed me off, if he really tried. He was at least six inches taller and outweighed me.

"What the hell's wrong with you?" he gasped as I removed my arm from his neck.

"Uh, Clara?" Patrick's shoes appeared next to us. "Is there a problem?"

I dug my hand into the thief's jacket pocket and grabbed Patrick's wallet. I held it out to him.

"Oh, crap," Patrick said, patting his pockets. He took the wallet, peering from me to the boy I still had pinned to the ground.

"Get off me," the thief said, squirming.

I climbed off him. He got to his feet and did a quick scan of the area, probably checking for cops. He spotted something behind me and rolled his eyes.

"Wonderful," he said.

I glanced over my shoulder and found Grayson St. John, in the flesh, jogging toward us. He had a big smile on his face. That smile wasn't just for the cameras.

"Please tell me you're one of my recruits," Grayson said breathlessly as he stopped next to us. He was shorter than he appeared on camera, maybe only an inch or two taller than me, and I was five foot six.

It took me a moment to realize he was talking to me. "Oh. Yeah, actually."

Grayson's smile widened. "Awesome."

An emotion I'd never experienced rushed through my veins. Pride? It was strange to be in a place where tackling someone was cause for praise.

"Edan," Grayson said to the thief. "I'm glad to see you came back. Less glad that you're pickpocketing my recruits."

"In my defense, I didn't know he was a recruit," Edan said. "I thought they'd all gone inside." He gestured at Patrick. "And come on. Look at him."

"Hey!" Patrick did a quick scan of his own body. "What's that supposed to mean?"

"You're carrying designer luggage, dude. Your jeans have been tailored for you." He pointed to Patrick's ankles. "You look like a rich kid on your way to a party in the Hamptons."

Patrick lifted one foot. "It's just good sense to have your jeans tailored. They last for years."

"That's true," Grayson agreed.

Edan looked at me with an expression I could only describe as *rich people, huh?* I ignored it. I didn't want to trade any looks with this thief. We were not the same.

"You guys go ahead and get checked in," Grayson said, clapping Edan on the shoulder. "I'm going to talk to Edan here."

"I'm going to decline that offer, thank you," Edan said, ducking out of Grayson's grip.

Grayson grabbed him by the back of the neck and easily kept him in place. Edan muttered something that made Grayson laugh.

"Should we call the cops or something?" Patrick asked, still clutching his wallet.

"I'd prefer we didn't, if you don't mind," Grayson said. "He's harmless."

"I am not. How dare you?" But Edan said the words with a trace of humor, a grin spreading across his face.

I would have known that boy was trouble even if I hadn't just seen him rob someone. He was super hot, and he knew it. He had thick brown hair that was a bit longer on top and still looked great after being tackled. When he smiled, one side of his mouth rose higher than the other. It was the smile of someone who was definitely plotting the fastest way to screw you. In more ways than one, maybe.

"Put your wallet in your front pocket," Grayson said to Patrick. "I'm Grayson, by the way."

"I know. Patrick." He shook Grayson's hand.

Grayson stretched his hand out to me.

"Clara," I said.

He clasped my hand briefly. "Nice to meet you. I'm glad you guys are here."

"I'm glad to be here," I said. It was the understatement of the century.

8

IN THE MORNING, I REMEMBERED.

I woke at six a.m., panic crawling through my veins, and I remembered why I'd never left before. Mom and Laurence.

I lay in bed for a few minutes, my brain cycling through every worst-case scenario. Dad could have seriously injured Laurence. He could have thrown my phone at Mom's head and hit his target this time. I'd never protected Mom and Laurence any more than they'd protected me, but there was a certain amount of safety in maintaining the status quo. We all worked our hardest to keep Dad at the lowest possible rage levels.

Until I'd blown everything up.

I tossed the covers off with a shiver. I'd turned the a/c down too low last night, and the room was dark and chilly. The bed across from me was untouched, even though I'd been told I'd have a roommate.

The phone and the mini bar had been removed from the room to avoid racking up extra charges, so I'd have to find a phone somewhere else. Maybe I could ask in the lobby.

I showered and threw on the least wrinkled clothes in my bag —jeans and a gray Wonder Woman T-shirt—and slipped out of my room. We didn't need to be at the other hotel for the welcome session for two hours, and the lobby was far quieter than it had been last night. A group of men in suits milled around the front desk, and two women stood near the doors, holding paper coffee cups.

I approached the front desk, and a woman with a name tag that said JAN smiled at me.

"Do you have a phone I could use?" I asked.

"Sure thing, hon. There are courtesy phones around that corner." She pointed to my right, in the direction of the restaurant.

"Thanks." I walked around the corner to find three phones on the wall. I picked up one and dialed the only number I knew by heart—Mom's.

She answered on the third ring. "Bueno?"

Mom didn't answer the phone in Spanish unless she knew it was one of her sisters. Or if Dad was sitting beside her, and she knew there was only one person who would call her from a Georgia number.

"Hi, Mom."

"Hola, Julia. Cómo estuvo tu viaje?"

"The trip was fine. I'm here."

She then said something I didn't understand, her words too fast.

"The only word I understood in that sentence was *crazy*," I said.

She made an annoyed sound.

"Well, whose fault is that? You should have taught me Spanish when I was little, like my cousins." It was Dad's fault, since he didn't want Mom to teach me and Laurence. He probably thought we would talk shit about him right in front of his face. (We would have.)

"I said that you have lost your mind, and you need to come home immediately, before you get yourself killed." Mom's words were hushed now, probably spoken from behind the door in her bedroom.

"I just called to see if you're OK," I said.

"If I'm OK—mija, I am very much not OK. Have you been watching the news? They say this Grayson man is a fanatic who's going to get you all killed."

"I met him yesterday, he didn't seem like a fanatic, whatever that means." Maybe a little too willing to brush off robbery attempts, but otherwise normal. "How is Laurence?"

"Your brother is gone. He packed his bags and left maybe an hour after you."

I didn't realize how much tension I was holding in my body until I let it out. "Really? He's OK?"

"He's fine."

"Can you give me his number? I don't have it memorized, and I left my phone there."

She let out a sigh but rattled it off for me. I found a pen but no paper, so I wrote it on the inside of my wrist.

"I know you don't believe this, but your father is worried sick about you. He would have jumped in his car and stopped you at the bus station if Laurence hadn't held him back."

I felt another surge of affection for Laurence.

"Maybe you won't make the cut." Mom sounded hopeful now. "Are there a lot of people there?"

"Yes. Mom, I should go. I just wanted to check on you." I didn't want to think about what I'd do if I didn't make it. Apparently they'd hired the buses for a round trip, so we had a free ride back if we didn't make it. The thought was terrifying.

"You're dropping out of high school, then?" Mom asked, undeterred.

"Seems so." I blew out a breath. "Don't be afraid to leave if it gets bad, OK? I know it's scary, but sometimes it's worse to stay."

She was silent.

"OK. I don't know when I'll be able to call again. Just . . . assume I'm fine if you haven't heard from me." That assumption could easily be wrong, but it seemed like the kindest thing to say. "Bye, Mom."

She was still silent, and I waited a few seconds before hanging up the phone. I took a couple shaky breaths before picking it up again and dialing Laurence.

It went to voicemail, which was no surprise. Laurence rarely answered his phone for people he knew, much less a strange number.

"Hey," I said after the beep. "It's me. I just wanted to let you know that I made it to Atlanta. And I wanted to say, um, thanks. For . . . you know, tackling Dad." I laughed softly. "I don't have a phone, but I'll try to email you if I make it. And I'm going to put you as my emergency contact, which means you get my ashes if I die. You can do whatever you want with them. Just don't take them back to Texas." A group of people behind me burst out laughing, and I cupped my hand around the phone. "Anyway, that's it. Thanks again." I hung up the phone, letting my hand linger on it for a second.

There wasn't anything more I could do for Mom. She'd had

the opportunity to leave Dad—so many times—and she never took it. She wasn't stuck, especially now that both her kids were gone. She had family in Mexico and a few friends in Dallas who would be willing to help. We'd both made our choices, and I wasn't responsible for hers.

I knew this, but still, the panic lingered. I could bury it deep down, but it was always there, a tiny reminder that part of me was always dreading the day that Dad killed her.

But I'd lived with a tiny bit of panic my whole life. It wasn't so bad.

We'd been instructed to pick up our welcome packets before the session this morning, so I followed the signs that said RECRUITS. Two long tables were set up on either side of the large room, one with the sign LAST NAMES A–M and the other for the rest of the alphabet. I walked to the latter table. A harried woman sat surrounded by boxes, tipping her head back as she drained a huge cup of coffee.

"Name," she said, slapping the cup down.

"Clara Pratt."

"P . . . P . . ." She stood, shifting boxes with her foot as she searched for the right letter. "Oh, P! There it is." She grabbed the box and plunked it on the table. "Sorry. We're not organized yet." She dug around and whipped out a blue folder with my name on it. "The schedule is in there, along with all the info you need about the program if you're selected."

I opened it and glanced at the schedule, hoping to find something about a meal. But it wasn't much of a schedule at all:

DAY ONE

9am–10am — Welcome Session

11am–6pm — Tryouts

DAY TWO

10am–3pm — Tryouts *no lunch break

DAY THREE

8am — Team Announcements — BE READY TO
    LEAVE IMMEDIATELY

"Are there any meals?" I asked without looking up from my folder.

"Yeah, you'll get a lunch break. You can bring something or buy food at the hotel."

My heart sank. I snapped the folder closed.

"They told you meals would be on your own for tryouts, didn't they?" the woman asked, alarmed. "It should have been in the first email you got."

That sounded familiar, now that she mentioned it. I'd skipped over it while reading about bringing snacks for the bus. I hadn't considered how many days that would be without food.

"Oh, yeah, they told me," I said, trying to sound casual. "I was just wondering, since it's not on the schedule." I didn't want her pity, and I could go a few days without food. Humans could survive, like, two or three weeks without food. I could do a couple days.

She didn't appear totally convinced, so I turned on my heel and quickly walked out of the room.

|\ | / |

I hid in my room until eight thirty. It took about ten minutes to read through the information in the folder (which could be summed up as YOU'RE PROBABLY GOING TO DIE, AND WHEN YOU DO, IT'S NOT OUR FAULT), and I spent the rest of the time flipping through the television channels, doing my best to pretend that my stomach wasn't growling. I would have savored that peanut-butter-and-jelly sandwich Patrick gave me on the bus if I'd known it was going to be my last meal.

Patrick was waiting for me outside, like we'd planned. A short boy with dark wavy hair and glasses stood next to him. He held a blue folder, label facing out. It said *Noah Cohen*.

Behind them, a digital billboard changed from an ad for a sports drink to a picture of a man in a suit standing in front of the American flag. Words were printed next to his face:

THE MONSTER DEFENSE GROUP
PROFESSIONAL
SAFE
AMERICAN

"Clara!" Patrick waved when he spotted me. "This is Noah, my roommate."

Noah extended his hand to me. He had an unremarkable face, the kind that didn't provoke much of a reaction either way. Thin and a bit pale, he was the sort of boy I'd expect to be at home playing *Call of Duty*, not joining a scrab hunting squad.

"Patrick was nice enough to let me go over with you guys since I'm awkward and alone," Noah said. His smile was big and friendly, and I thought that he was probably never alone for long. I could see why he and Patrick hit it off.

"Plus, I told him that you'd protect us on the way over," Patrick said.

"I heard you tackle thieves in a single bound," said Noah.

"Only the really inept ones."

"Yeah, he wasn't the greatest thief, was he?" Patrick said as we started walking.

"He was great at the actual stealing part, it's his getaway that could use some work," I said.

Noah filled me in on his life as we walked to the other hotel, gesturing wildly when he got excited (eighteen years old, from Asheville, North Carolina, his parents thought it was great that he was joining). He cut off suddenly in the middle of telling us he'd deferred NYU for a year to do this.

"Whoa," he said suddenly.

I followed his gaze. The front of the hotel was swarming with reporters and people holding signs. Protestors? Supporters? It was hard to tell.

Security guards were keeping the crowds away from the doors and had created a path for us to walk through.

"Excuse me! Where are you guys from?" a reporter called. Patrick replied, but I kept walking, my eyes catching on the signs.

TRAITORS, one said.

"DO NOT WITHHOLD GOOD FROM THOSE TO WHOM IT IS DUE, WHEN IT IS IN YOUR POWER TO ACT"—PROVERBS 3:27, another said.

THE MONSTERS ARE HERE, said another. I wasn't sure if that one was supportive or not.

The biggest group of protestors stood a bit apart from the others, singing a song and swaying to the rhythm. Most of them held signs, the same ones I'd seen on the news several times: THE VISITORS ARE NOT OUR ENEMIES. STOP SCRAB MURDER. PEACE WILL SAVE US.

They were members of the Worshippers of the New Gods, a cult that thought the scrabs were aliens sent by god to cleanse the earth. They worshipped the scrabs and argued against any type of violence against them.

A man with a KEEP CALM AND KILL SCRABS sign walked up to the Worshippers, yelling something at them. I turned away and ducked into the hotel.

The lobby was absolutely stuffed with people laughing and chatting. A security guard was pushing a reporter and her cameraman toward the exit.

We followed the signs to the ballroom, which was huge, easily seating a thousand people, and already over half full. Rows of chairs faced the front of the room, where an elevated platform was set up with a microphone.

The room practically vibrated with excitement. Chatter and laughter echoed all around me. Four huge men with military-style haircuts passed us, talking loudly and fist-bumping each other.

"Let's sit there," Noah said, pointing to a row in the middle of the room that was empty except for an auburn-haired boy.

Noah skipped ahead without waiting for our reply, and plunked down right next to the boy. He looked up, clearly alarmed, and then glanced at the completely empty rows in front of and behind him. He was light-skinned and freckled, with a long, thin nose.

"Hello, I'm Noah," said Noah, either oblivious or choosing to ignore the boy's *why are you sitting next to me* face. I slid into the seat next to Patrick.

"Archer." He spoke so softly that I wasn't sure I'd heard him correctly.

"Archie?" Patrick asked.

"Archer," he said, a little louder.

"People probably call you Archie, though, right? Like the comic?"

"No." He paused for a beat. "Or, I'd rather they didn't."

Patrick was clearly trying not to laugh. "Got it. Archer it is."

"Archer from . . ." Noah prompted.

"Ohio. Outside Springfield."

"Never been," Noah said. "Like I said, I'm Noah, from Asheville, that's Patrick, and Clara. They're both from Texas."

"Austin," Patrick said, because people from Austin didn't think they were actually part of Texas.

Noah opened his mouth and then abruptly snapped it shut. His eyes widened.

"Is that Madison St. John?" His tone was almost reverent.

A blond girl in impressively high heels was striding toward the microphone at the front of the room. She wore a pristine white dress, the kind that always seemed hard to walk in to me. Couldn't take big steps in a skirt that tight.

Her shiny hair fell over one shoulder as she leaned into the microphone. "Excuse me," she said sweetly. The room immediately quieted. "If you could please take your seats, we'd appreciate it. Move all the way into the center of the rows. We'll be starting in five minutes."

"Is she related to Grayson?" I asked, watching as she walked away from the microphone. Three-fourths of the room was watching her. The whole world tilted in the direction of Madison St. John. She pretended not to notice.

"Yeah," Noah said, looking at me strangely. "She's his younger sister. You don't know who Madison is?"

"I didn't know who Grayson was until a couple days ago."

He looked even more baffled. Archer leaned over and peered at me like maybe I was making a joke he didn't understand.

"But . . ." Noah typed furiously into his phone, then flipped the screen to face me. "Seriously?"

He'd typed *"Madison St. John tabloid."* The screen was covered in tabloid covers featuring Madison in various poses. Madison walking out of a coffee shop with a man in sunglasses and a headline that said MADISON AND JULIAN: BACK TOGETHER? Madison and Grayson smiling above the words AMERICAN ROYALTY. Madison in sunglasses and messy hair, still looking like a supermodel, the headline reading MADISON ST. JOHN'S WILD NIGHT.

"Huh," I said. "I didn't know they were famous."

"Really?" Patrick said with a laugh.

"I've never kept up with celebrity stuff. What were they famous for before this?" I asked.

"Being rich?" Noah lifted his hands in a shrug.

"And hot," Patrick said. "And hanging out with celebrities. I'm surprised they never had their own reality show, honestly."

"There's still time," Noah said. He paused. "Assuming we don't all die."

"Reality television execs everywhere wait with bated breath," Patrick said.

More people filed into the room, until almost every seat was full and the noise in the room had reached alarming levels. I was relieved to see that there were far more women than had been on my bus — probably sixty-forty men to women. Our group of four was definitely younger than most of the people around us. The man sitting on the other side of me had an impressive beard and was at least in his late twenties.

The room quieted as Grayson St. John strolled through the door, hands slid into the pockets of his perfectly fitted black pants. Everyone was on their feet suddenly, thunderous applause echoing through the ballroom. I stood and joined them. I supposed he deserved a standing ovation, since he got me out of Texas.

Grayson had an easy smile on his face as he waved to the cheering crowd. He and Madison both looked exactly as one would expect someone with the last name St. John to look. They were both slim and blond, the sort of white people you'd find playing golf and saying things like *we're going to the yacht club with the Vanderbilts later, dear.*

Madison walked to the microphone first, Grayson standing back a bit.

"Hello," Madison said into the microphone. More cheers.

"Thanks for coming," Madison said, then stopped and smiled. Everyone laughed, even though it wasn't really funny. "I won't take up too much of your time. I'm here to introduce my brother. And to let you know that the rumors are true—I'm joining the recruits."

"YEAH," someone yelled. Laughter and cheers followed.

"So if you have any doubts about your ability, just look at me." She swept her hand down. "Do I look ready to go off to battle?" More laughter. "If I can do it, anyone can."

I hoped that became our official slogan. *If we can do it, anyone can!*

"But you're not here for me. Without further ado, my brother, Grayson St. John." Madison stepped back from the microphone, and Grayson took her place. We stood up and clapped again, in case he hadn't felt enough love the first time.

"Thank you," Grayson said with an embarrassed laugh as the applause began to die down. We all took our seats again. "I appreciate that. I've mostly been hearing that I'm an anarchist traitor these days."

"They're idiots!" someone yelled.

"Thank you. Agreed." He smiled. "Just a note, you can feel free to film this and post it wherever. All our activities will be public. We don't have anything to hide."

A few people whooped. Several phones popped up in the front few rows. Noah whipped his out as well.

"First of all," Grayson began, "welcome. And thank you so much for coming. I was worried when I put the call out that I'd only get a few hundred people. But I'm proud to report that as of today, we've had almost ten thousand people volunteer."

My mouth dropped open as everyone cheered. I wasn't the only crazy one, it seemed.

"We have tryouts happening in Los Angeles, Beijing, Paris, London, Berlin, Bangkok, Warsaw, Madrid, Sydney, and a few more I'm forgetting," Grayson said. "We'll be partnering with teams all over the world. The response has been incredible. Thank you."

More applause. "So let me tell you what you can expect if you're put on a team. This is a completely voluntary program. You are under no obligation to stay. But you will receive a stipend at the end of every two weeks of service. The stipend increases every week you serve. But let me be clear. This will be very dangerous. There are easier ways to make money. If you decide to walk away and just call this a free trip to Atlanta, I won't blame you."

He pointed to the men in blue shirts lined up against the wall. "These are your team leaders. We lost five guys a month ago when we went to Germany to finalize battle strategies. Five well-trained guys died fighting these things." His face was serious. "Please understand what you're getting into."

The room had gone silent. I drew in a slow breath as I regarded the team leaders. One tall, thin man had a long scar down his face, straight through his right eye, and I wondered if it was glass. Another man wore a knee brace, angry red claw marks poking out from the edges.

"But if you choose to stay, you'll be part of something special," Grayson continued. "This is your opportunity to actually take action. I don't know about you, but I'm tired of sitting around complaining. I'm tired of watching our government make excuses for not helping people. I'm tired of watching them turn away from suffering."

A few people murmured their agreement.

"Congress says it's too risky to send Americans overseas to fight scrabs. But I'm of the opinion that we are plenty strong enough if we partner with people from other countries. We don't have to leave them to do this alone." He pointed at us. "It won't be easy. In fact, it will probably be the hardest thing you've ever done. But together, I think we can kick some serious scrab ass."

The room exploded with cheers, and he paused until they died down. "So, the particulars. We're doing two days of tryouts. There should be a name tag with a number in your folder. Please attach that to the back of your shirt. We've rented out a few gyms, so you'll need to take the bus over. They'll be waiting in front of your hotel. We'll evaluate you, then you'll be divided into teams based on your native language and abilities. You'll have an experienced team leader who will be in charge of your training, then your assignments. The length of training depends on how quickly your team progresses. But don't expect more than six weeks."

Terror unfurled in my chest. I'd be out fighting scrabs in *six weeks*? Less, maybe?

"Jesus," Patrick muttered.

"Americans under the age of twenty, you can expect less, since you were required to take combat classes in school. All meals and lodging and transportation will be covered while you're with us," Grayson said. "You won't need to spend a dime. But don't expect high-class accommodations. We've rented a sports complex in

Paris for training, and it won't be nearly as nice as the rooms you're in now. We've set up cots, and many of you will be sharing a room with at least twenty people. The schedule will be brutal occasionally, but I also hope we'll have some fun." He smiled. "Are you guys ready to get started?"

Cheers erupted all around me. It sounded like we were ready.

9

Buses were waiting in front of the hotel, and they took us to a large building with a sign that said BOXING, MARTIAL ARTS, TRAINING. We filed inside and through a lobby packed with workout clothes and fancy sports drinks for sale.

The gym consisted of several different large rooms, and the men in blue shirts took us through them quickly. There was a boxing ring, a room with bags hanging from the ceiling, and a huge area that had been set up with different stations, military boot camp style.

"One fifty to two hundred with me!" a tall, bulky man called. He stood in the corner of the boot camp room.

I was number 187, so I walked to him, taking a deep breath to calm my nerves. It was starting to sink in that there was a real chance I might not be good enough to join. *One in five.*

"Hey, I'm Wallace," the man said. He was one of those guys who was so muscular it almost appeared painful. Was it comfortable trying to sleep on all that hard muscle?

He also had four long, thin scars across both arms that had clearly been made by claws, and he was missing two fingers—the pinky and ring—on his left hand. I swallowed as I balled my own fingers into fists.

"We'll be moving fast," Wallace said. "Get used to it. We're going to get into the fight as quickly as possible, so there's no time for coddling. And before we get started, I'd just like to remind you that you're free to leave whenever you want. No one's keeping you here." He held up his left hand to show off his three remaining fingers. "This isn't a video game. This is real life, and trust me, fighting these things is no joke."

His eyes skipped over the group, like he thought we might take the opportunity to run right now.

"Good," he said when no one moved. "We're scheduled to do running first today, then the obstacle course, then boxing, and back to the obstacle course at the end."

"Oh, god," a voice beside me whispered. It was a short, pretty girl with light brown skin and black hair tied into a high ponytail. She wore a bright pink T-shirt that said NORTH HILLS CHEER on it. "I've never boxed before." She looked at me like I might be able to fix this.

"I haven't either," I said. She chewed on her lip like that didn't make her feel better.

"Tomorrow you'll go to the shooting range for target practice," Wallace continued. "And you'll do some hand-to-hand combat to see how you'd do actually fighting a scrab. We're giving you lots of opportunities to show your stuff, and also the chance for each of us to evaluate you. I'll be your point of contact for the next two days, but all the team leaders will be rotating through, watching you. Just do your best. It's not a competition."

It was definitely a competition. No one said *it's not a competition* unless it was.

"All right, let's get going." Wallace clapped his hands together and started walking toward the exit.

"Right." The cheerleader next to me let out a huge breath. "No problem. I can do this." She had a hint of a Southern accent.

"For sure," I said.

She flashed me a smile. I could see why she was a cheerleader. She had a smile that was impossible not to return. I glanced at the paper pinned to the back of her shirt as she followed Wallace. *Priya Mehta 153.*

We walked outside, where Wallace explained that we'd be running around the building, which they'd mapped as a little under a quarter of a mile for one lap.

"You won't be running on a track fighting scrabs," he explained. "First lap is half walk, half slow jog. Then we'll really get started."

I swallowed down a wave of nerves. Like Priya said. *No problem. I can do this.*

By the end of day one, my body felt like one giant bruise.

The running was fine, as expected, but the boxing portion consisted of getting repeatedly pummeled by a tall girl who giggled every time I fell. They paired me with two other girls, with even more disastrous results.

The obstacle course was a tire run (OK), hurdles (less OK), a net climb (bad), monkey bars (fail), and a rope climb (total fail).

I hobbled back to the bus and sank into a seat. My body was weak and heavy, and I was pretty sure I was starving, but it was hard to tell at this point. Everything sort of ached. I closed my eyes. Maybe if I just slept until tomorrow, I wouldn't even care.

Someone dropped into the seat next to me with a giant sigh.

I opened my eyes to see a boy with dark hair leaning his head against the seat in front of him. His tag said *Edan Pearce 102*.

Edan. That was the name Grayson called the thief who tried to rob Patrick.

Edan turned and straightened with a start. He was missing his leather jacket, instead wearing a gray T-shirt and black track pants. He had several tattoos down his left arm, and at least one more poking out from the sleeve of his other arm.

"Seriously?" I said.

"Seriously what?" One side of his mouth lifted like something was funny.

"You're trying out?"

"Well, I didn't just do that shit for fun."

The bus jerked away from the curb, and he put a hand on the seat in front of him. His throat bobbed as he swallowed.

It wasn't really a surprise that Grayson didn't disqualify people because of a little criminal activity. Though it did make me wonder where he'd draw the line, if he drew one at all.

"Why?" I asked.

Edan turned to me again, lifting an eyebrow. He had truly impressive eyes—green, with a hint of gray—and I could just imagine him leaning closer to a girl, batting his lashes as he slipped her wallet out of her purse.

"Why'd you join?" he retorted.

I shrugged. "Why not?"

"I mean . . ." He started ticking the reasons off on his fingers. "Death, dismemberment, the fact that the US government hates us—"

"OK, I really—"

"The possibility of lifelong PTSD, we have to share a room with twenty people, the food is probably going to be terrible—"

"I don't—"

"We're headed off to exercise *all day* for weeks, and I don't know about you, but I hate exercising. We don't—"

"It was rhetorical," I said loudly. "Jesus."

"Just pointing out the facts." The bus hit a bump, and he grabbed the seat in front of him like it was going to save him. "Will you switch seats with me?"

"What?"

"Switch seats with me. I may need to puke out the window."

"What? Really?"

"Yes, I get motion sick." He jumped out of his seat and gestured for me to move. I quickly slid out and glanced around for a different seat. It was a totally full bus. I gingerly sat down next to Edan again, hugging the edge in case vomit came flying in my direction.

He pushed the window open and leaned his forehead against it, the breeze ruffling his dark hair.

"Better?" I asked.

"Yes. Thank you. The air helps."

I watched him until I felt safe I wasn't about to see his lunch. "Why'd you join, then? If we're all going to die and be dismembered."

"There are worse things to do, I guess."

I hadn't given him a real answer either, so I couldn't exactly complain about the one he'd just offered up.

The bus hit another bump, and Edan took in a sharp breath.

"I hate buses," he said. He was sitting very still. "And cars. And anything that moves. Well, except the subway. The subway isn't as bad, for some reason."

"Plus good opportunities to rob people on a subway," I said.

"Sometimes I took it just to get places." His lips twitched like he might smile, but he seemed to think better of it. He focused on a spot outside.

"How is the subway different?"

"I don't know. The movement is just different, you know?"

"No. I've never been on a subway."

His eyes flicked to me like this was weird. "Where are you from?"

"Dallas."

He made a face like he didn't like Dallas.

"What?" I asked.

"Nothing. It's just, *Texas*."

"What's wrong with Texas?" I wasn't sure why I was defending a state I didn't even like.

"It's *Texas*. You know what I mean."

I did, but I decided it was best to pretend I didn't. I crossed my arms over my chest and looked away. My stomach growled loudly, and I lowered my arms over it, hoping he hadn't heard.

"Thank god," Edan said when the bus jerked to a stop in front of the hotel. We filed off, and he shakily walked to a pillar and leaned against it, taking several deep breaths.

I scanned the parking lot for the other buses. One was pulling away, another letting off the last of its passengers. I was hoping to run into Patrick. He would definitely buy me dinner if he realized

I had nothing. Even a granola bar would be amazing at this point. It had been over twenty-four hours since I'd eaten, and I'd just spent eight hours running around and climbing ropes and making poor attempts at punching people.

But I didn't see him. We must have been one of the last buses to arrive. I didn't even know his room number. I could ask at the front desk, but that seemed too pathetic. I didn't want to show up at his door begging for food.

One more day. I hadn't been the worst one today at the gym. I'd seen one boy get knocked over by his own punching bag. Twice. The cheerleader I met at the beginning of the day could barely throw a punch. I had a shot at making it, provided I didn't screw up too badly tomorrow.

I took one more glance around for Patrick, then sighed in defeat. Edan was still against the pillar, his eyes following me.

"You look lost," he said.

"I'm fine," I lied. I trudged into the hotel. I'd just sleep. I only had to make it one more day.

10

IN THE MORNING, I REGRETTED NOT BEGGING PATRICK FOR food. I woke up weak and shaking, my muscles screaming from yesterday's tryouts, and it took more effort than usual to shower and get dressed.

I'd never gone this long without food. I'd gone almost a full day once, when I was too scared to leave my room after Dad threw one of his tantrums. But I'd snuck into the kitchen that night and eaten several leftover tamales.

Maybe I understood a little what Mom meant when she said things could be worse. Her parents didn't have much when they immigrated to Texas, and she'd mentioned fishing the last can of beans out of the cabinet at the end of the month more than once. Mom knew what it was like to go hungry, and for her, it was worse than a life of fear with Dad. I didn't agree, but I could sympathize. A little.

There was a mini convenience store on the first floor of the hotel, and I slowed as I approached it, eyeing the granola bars near the cash register. The cashier was distracted, peering at her phone. If I was quiet, I could dart inside, grab the granola bar, and run back out before she turned around.

I sighed as I noticed the security bars on either side of the entrance. The hotel was bustling with recruits, and I couldn't imagine anything more embarrassing than fleeing from a convenience store as the alarm blared, granola bar clutched in one hand.

I trudged past the store and outside.

"Hello, Tex," a voice said as I walked toward the bus. Edan fell into step beside me. The asshole was eating a fucking granola bar.

"I will tackle your ass again if you call me that one more time." Hunger had made me a bit grouchy.

"Such hostility so early in the morning." He sounded amused.

I shot him a look I hoped conveyed that I was seriously considering tackling him. His smile faltered, and he disappeared from my side.

I glanced around for my bus. They'd split us up differently this time—I'd found a paper slipped under my door this morning, with the number 8 on it, and a note saying we'd been put into specific groups today.

Bus eight was at the front. I walked to it and lumbered up the steps. It was almost full, and I spotted two familiar faces immediately—Noah and Patrick.

"Hey!" Patrick smiled and waved. I managed a weak smile as I plopped down in the seat across from him, next to a thin Black boy with glasses. "We were looking for you last night. I thought maybe you went to bed early."

"I did." I eyed the area around Patrick, searching for his messenger bag full of snacks. Nothing.

"Same. My everything hurts." He arched his back and winced as if to prove it. His eyes caught on something at the front of the bus. "Is that the guy who tried to rob me?"

"Yeah, he's trying out." I crossed my arms to hide my shaky hands.

"Good thing I left my wallet at the hotel," Patrick grumbled. I leaned back in my seat and closed my eyes, my brain too focused on hunger for conversation. Luckily Patrick seemed preoccupied with Edan.

The bus took us to a shooting range. SHOOT-EM-UP INDOOR/ OUTDOOR SHOOTING RANGE, the sign said. I'd never even held a gun before, despite Texas's reputation as a gun-happy state. Mom and Dad never owned one, thank god.

We only had three team leaders with us today, all male. Was there even one female team leader? I'd yet to see one.

One of the guys — the one who looked the youngest — waved to get our attention. "Hey, I'm Julian." He pointed to the Latino guy to his left. "This is Andy." He pointed to the white guy on his right. "And Liam. We're evaluating you today. First thing — who here has shot a gun before?"

Several hands went up.

"You guys go with Andy." About ten people broke away, leaving forty or so of us behind. Julian put his hand out, cutting us in half. "Everyone on this side, come with me. The rest of you are with Liam."

I was on Julian's side, so I followed him into the building. He stopped in the lobby, which had lots of posters of guns and several signs about safety. I liked the one that said PLEASE DON'T PLAY WITH YOUR GUN IN THE LOBBY. IT MAKES PEOPLE NERVOUS.

"We're going to do a very brief safety and shooting lesson, and then you guys will fire a few rounds," Julian said. "We're going to have sharpshooter teams, so this is just to see if we should consider you for one of those. I'm going to need you to listen carefully to everything the employees tell you today. Remember, you already signed a form saying it's not our fault if you get shot." He grinned, and a few people laughed nervously.

"I'm going to be bad at this," a girl whispered. I glanced over to see a redhead glancing nervously at a girl about my age. She had long light brown hair, impressive winged eyeliner, and an expression like she was so incredibly bored.

"Well, you should try your best, because the sharpshooter teams are the best," the bored girl said.

"They are?" The redhead was worried now.

"Yeah. Sharpshooters are the best, then the elite ground teams are second, and then the regular ground teams are the worst. Those are the ones they don't care if they die first." The bored girl twisted a piece of hair around her finger. "That's what I heard anyway."

I turned away. I didn't care what team I was on, as long as I made one.

An employee named Angela took us through some basic safety procedures, gave us a short lesson on how to load and shoot a gun, handed out safety glasses and earmuffs, and escorted us into individual booths. We were doing a practice round first, then we'd be judged on how well we hit the man-shaped targets in front of us.

The gun was heavier than I was expecting, and my hands were still shaking a little as I lifted it and aimed at the target. I tried to will my body still. I only needed it to cooperate for the rest of the day, and then I'd swallow my pride and ask Patrick for some food.

The people around me started firing, so I took a deep breath and squeezed the trigger. The recoil wasn't terrible, like Angela had said, but I still didn't like the way each shot seemed to vibrate through my body. I felt unsteady on my feet by the time I'd emptied the chamber.

The paper man zipped along the track and stopped in front of me. I'd hit it three times, none of them within the white numbered circles.

Clearly I was not cut out for the sharpshooter team.

Angela reloaded my gun for me, and a new target appeared at the end of the lane. When he zipped toward me after I was done, I realized I'd done even worse this time. Two shots. One was almost inside the outermost circle, though.

Julian walked into my booth, glancing from me to the target. He'd been handsome from a distance, but up close he looked like a movie star. He had clear, perfect skin and dark brown eyes that seemed to smile even when his lips weren't. His short, dark hair had a bit of red in it, and it fell right back into place when he ran a hand through it.

He was staring at me like he expected something of me, and I felt heat rise in my cheeks.

"What's your number?" he asked after several awkward seconds.

"Oh." I turned so he could see it. "One eighty-seven."

He wrote something down on his clipboard, glancing back at the target as if to confirm I only hit it twice.

"Not so great, huh?" I asked with a nervous laugh. I pressed my lips together, wishing I'd kept my mouth shut.

He smiled at me. "It's fine. First time." He took a step out of my booth. "You can go get on the bus. Just leave the gun there."

I quickly walked out of the booth, eager to put some distance between me and Julian. My face still felt warm. I didn't know if he was really that hot or if I was getting delirious from lack of food.

"How did I not even hit it once? Not even *once?*" An angry voice drifted out of the booth. I glanced back to see a tall, muscular blond boy with a pinched face glaring at Julian like he was at fault.

"Don't worry about it," Julian said evenly. The boy flushed.

Outside, I spotted two news vans with the bus, and a reporter held out a microphone to someone I couldn't see. I leaned to peer past the cameraman.

Madison St. John. She wore workout clothes, the expensive kind that hugged her perfect figure. Her blond hair was pulled up in a ponytail and she wore a full face of makeup.

"Of course, I'm thrilled to be here," she gushed to the camera. "I'm so proud of my brother, and I totally believe in what we're doing."

"The White House issued a statement today condemning this program as dangerous and disorganized. They've urged people not to join. What's your response to that?"

Madison smiled wider, her ponytail swinging. "Well, they're certainly entitled to their opinion, but we believe in what we're doing. We know our results will speak for themselves."

The reporter signaled for the cameraman to stop filming, and she thanked Madison. Madison nodded and enthusiastically shook her hand. She drew the attention of everyone in the immediate area with that bright smile.

I turned away, too hungry and annoyed for that much bubbliness. Noah and Patrick weren't on the bus yet, so I sank into an empty seat behind the handcuffs girl who'd been on my bus from Dallas. She was still wearing the handcuffs.

The bus took us back to the gym we'd been at yesterday, and I suppressed a moan when the team leaders informed us we'd be doing the obstacle course again, three rounds. It was probably to see how we performed when exhausted and sore, but I was willing to bet that everyone else was at least somewhat well fed.

I got in line behind Patrick to start. He promptly fell on his face while doing the tire run. I'd be lying if I said it didn't make me feel a little bit better.

By my third round on the obstacle course, I was dragging, my heart beating faster than normal for this level of exercise. I stopped at the net climb and put my hands on my hips, trying to catch my breath.

"Move," a voice said from behind me. A shoulder roughly bumped against mine, and I stumbled, barely staying upright. It was the blond boy who hadn't hit the target even once. He had a friend with him, pale and freckled and currently inspecting me in an obviously sleazy way. He sort of grimaced, like he didn't appreciate what he saw. His friend snorted.

"Keep it moving over there on the net climb!" a team leader

called. The boys moved away from me and started climbing. A few feet away, Julian watched us and marked something on his clipboard. Wonderful.

I slipped off the very first bar of the monkey bars, and by the time I hit the rope climb, I felt like I was about to pass out. I swallowed hard.

"That's all right." Someone patted my back. "Why don't you go get some water and sit down for a minute?"

Tears filled my eyes, and I didn't turn around to see which team leader had said it. I didn't need to further this humiliation by letting them see me cry.

I sat down against the wall next to a Black girl with a pink headband, her curly hair pulled back in a ponytail. She didn't look nearly as tired as I felt. The white, red-faced boy a few feet away looked like he might hurl at any moment, though.

"You all right?" the girl asked as I slumped down and leaned my head against my knees.

"I'm fine." My stomach growled loudly, and she gawked at it, alarmed. "I'm just a little hungry."

"They have some protein bars and stuff up front," she said.

I shook my head. "I don't have any money."

She dug into her pocket. "Well, I was about to eat mine, and I don't need the whole thing." She tore open the package and broke the bar in half, then held one half out to me.

I took it slowly. "Oh, my god, *thank you.*"

She reeled back a little, clearly startled by that level of gratitude for half a protein bar. "Yeah, sure."

I ate the bar in three bites. I was still hungry when I was done, but at least my hands had stopped shaking.

"Thank you," I said again. "I'm Clara."

"Laila." She polished off her half and hopped to her feet. "Good luck."

"You too."

The last portion of tryouts was an actual scrab fight. They didn't have a setup like at Bubba's, so a few team leaders had to be our scrab stand-ins. Julian stood in the middle of the boxing ring with Liam, who had fastened fake claws onto either arm. He wore a helmet and a bulky pad strapped to his chest.

"These"—Julian held up one of Liam's arms—"are not sharp. We've rounded the edges, so he's going to whack you with them. We're going to have real versions of these for our recruits on certain ground teams." He gestured at us. "Number one thirty-eight, let's start with you."

The freckled asshole who'd leered at me earlier stood and ducked under the ropes to enter the ring. His tag said *Hunter Ward 138.*

"We're not giving you fake weapons because we don't need you beating us to hell with them," Julian said. That got a few laughs. "Tap the weak spots. He's wearing pads, but there's no need to hit him hard. We're just seeing how you move." Julian climbed out of the ring. "This is going to be quick, because we have a lot of you to get through." He made a *sit* motion with his hands. "You guys can sit while you wait."

I sat cross-legged on the ground. The boy next to me leaned back on his hands, legs stretched out and crossed at the ankles. His light brown curly hair was a mess, like he'd just rolled out of bed after a particularly rough night.

Cheers rose up from the other room, where another group was doing the same thing as us. Noah and Patrick must have been with that group, because I didn't see them.

In the ring, Liam took a swipe at Hunter, which the latter easily avoided.

"Yeah, get it!" the boy with messy curls next to me yelled. He leaned forward as he clapped so I could see the tag on his back. *Andrew Dorsey 155.*

Hunter dodged Liam twice more before the team leader pinned him to the ground with his claws.

"Next!" Julian called.

I was one of the last people to go. Liam was a bit slower now, wiping his forehead with the back of his hands and nearly poking himself in the eye with a rounded claw.

"Try to tap him on the neck," Julian called. "Have at it."

That was the cue to go, and I darted forward, fists raised. Liam knocked my first swing out of the way.

I stepped back, ducking as he tried to swipe at me. This was easier than Bubba's, which was only slightly comforting. Bubba had crafted his dummies to be like the real thing. This was just a tired guy with some plastic strapped to his fingers.

I ducked again, barely missing the claws.

"Good," Julian called.

A victorious thrill raced up my spine.

The feeling didn't last long. Liam faked left, and I didn't realize it until the claws on his other hand swiped across my neck. I stumbled and landed on my butt. Dead.

"Next!" Julian called.

I shakily got to my feet, ducking my head for fear that the tears pricking my eyes would suddenly spill over. I took my seat as another recruit stepped into the ring.

Dad's voice rang in my ears — *you will DIE* — no matter how much I tried to push it out. I didn't want him to be right. I didn't want him to be so right that I didn't even make a team.

I wanted to prove him wrong.

11

I LEANED MY HEAD AGAINST THE BUS WINDOW, SLUMPED IN MY seat as we made our way back to the hotel. I was replaying training in my head, trying to remember if I'd seen people who were worse than me. There had been a few. I saw one guy fall flat on his face after trying to throw a single punch. The curly-haired guy had knocked several people over while trying to work with a spear.

My stomach growled loudly, and I closed my eyes briefly. The protein bar had somehow made me hungrier. I wasn't sure I even had the strength to get out of this seat. I lived here now.

Julian stood and faced us as the bus jerked to a stop. "Is there a Clara Pratt on this bus?"

I blinked, surprised, and slowly raised my hand. "Yeah, I'm here."

"Come with me a sec."

I stood, ignoring the protests from my body. I gripped the edge of a seat as I stepped into the aisle and took a moment to steady my shaking legs.

I couldn't think of any good reason why a team leader would want to see me. Were they letting everyone who had been eliminated know tonight? I swallowed down mounting panic as I made my way off the bus.

Julian led me into the hotel, pausing for a moment in the lobby like he wasn't sure where to go. He headed into one of the meeting rooms, the one where I'd picked up my folder. It was nearly empty now, only the tables and a few empty boxes left.

"So." Julian pulled out his phone as he turned to face me. "We got an email from your father. He says he did not sign a consent form, and he wants you home right away. And no one answers at the number you gave us."

My body went cold. I couldn't feel my feet on the ground anymore. I realized suddenly that the air conditioner was really loud in this room. I could hear it buzzing.

"We're sort of in a gray area with you guys who are minors," Julian continued. "The army started letting seventeen-year-olds sign up without parental consent after the first scrab attacks in the States, but we're not the US military, so . . ." He looked at me sympathetically. "We have a bus to Dallas leaving tomorrow at noon."

The world tilted and my legs gave out. I crashed to the carpet as a sob escaped my mouth. I was crying. Not pretty, sniffling crying, but choked sobs and tears streaming down my face.

"Hey, it's OK," Julian said, his tone alarmed.

I shook my head, because it was not OK, and I did not appreciate him telling me it was. He didn't know how hard it had been for me to escape. How proud I'd felt for getting out. If I let Dad yank me back now, I'd never get out again. Not in one piece, anyway.

"How long until you're eighteen?" he asked. He knelt down next to me on the ground. "Maybe you can call him and talk to him?"

I let out a short, angry laugh and lifted my head to meet his gaze. He was obviously startled, maybe by my tear-soaked face, or maybe because I looked like I wanted to murder someone. "I'm not calling him."

"OK." I liked how he didn't try to press the issue. "But I'm going to have to put you on that Dallas bus tomorrow."

I shook my head. "I'm not getting on that bus." Even if they wouldn't let me on a team, I wasn't getting on that bus. I didn't care about my growling stomach, or the fact that I had no money and no place to sleep after tonight. I wouldn't go back.

Uncertainty flickered across Julian's face. It wasn't normal for a girl to be this hysterical about the prospect of going home. The wheels were already turning in his head, trying to figure out what I didn't want to go back to. If I said it, if I told him the truth, he might let me stay.

But I'd never found quite the right words for that, so I held out my left arm and placed the fingers of my right hand on each of the four round bruises that Dad had made a few days ago.

"I'm not getting on that bus," I said again, holding his gaze.

I moved my fingers, and he stared at the spot where they'd been. He looked at me and then quickly away.

He grabbed his phone from the floor and swiped at it.

"Oh no, I deleted it." He swiped a few more times. "Too bad, I seem to have deleted it from my trash as well. I guess I never got it at all."

Relief flooded my veins, and I had to blink away a fresh round of tears. I wiped my hands across my cheeks and smiled at him.

"Thank you."

He returned the smile. He had a heavy, dark brow that made

him look like he always had something serious to say, but his smile was sweet, almost innocent.

I pushed my bangs out of the way with an embarrassed laugh. "I guess I don't even know if I made it, right?" The humiliation was starting to break through the panic. I was on the ground. My eyes were probably red and puffy. I'd just told him my darkest secret.

"Wellll . . ." His face broke into a grin again. I wished my nose would stop running. "Don't tell anyone I did this." He tapped on his phone a few times. "I remember you from the sparring, I'm pretty sure you . . . Yep. You're in."

I let out a short laugh. The world was tilted, and I wasn't sure I'd heard him right. Maybe I'd passed out and was dreaming of a world where I was going to put an ocean between me and Texas. "Seriously?"

"Yes. Actually, Grayson has you marked on here." He squinted at his phone. "Oh! You're the one who jumped Edan outside the hotel."

Honestly, I didn't mind that this was how people knew me. There were worse things to be known for.

I laughed again. My body felt about a hundred times lighter. "Yeah, that was me."

"He made a note that you were in, unless you did really horribly at the tryouts. And you didn't do really horribly."

"Only a little bit horribly?" I wiped the last of my tears away.

"Only at shooting. No guns for you."

"I'm good with that."

"You were assigned to my team, actually. I'm taking one of the young teams." He smiled at me. I didn't think I would mind being on his team at all.

He jumped up, offering me his hand. I took it and let him pull me to my feet.

The world went black around the edges, and I stumbled, bumping into his shoulder.

"Whoa." He grabbed both my arms, which I was pretty sure was the only thing keeping me from falling back to the floor. "Are you OK?"

"Yeah." I blinked until the world came into focus again. Julian was staring at me, brows knitted together. The smile was cute, but maybe the concern was cuter.

No, that was not what was important right now. Growling stomach. Fainting. Priorities.

"I just didn't eat today . . . Well, a nice girl gave me half a protein bar but . . ." I shook my head, my thoughts finally falling back into place. My legs felt solid on the ground again.

"All you ate today is half a protein bar?"

"And I didn't eat anything yesterday, so . . ." I laughed to hide my embarrassment. There was just no way this interaction could get any worse at this point.

"What?" His concern was growing. "Why wouldn't you eat anything yesterday?"

"I don't have any food. Or any money to buy some." I said it evenly, like I didn't want to dig a hole in the ground and stick my head in it.

"Oh my god. You could have told—" He cut himself off. "I was about to order an obscene amount of Chinese food for some of the team leaders. You're having some."

I wasn't even going to pretend to protest. "Thank you."

"I'll need to pick it up because they don't deliver, but I'll run you up to my room real quick first. You can wait there."

"Your . . ." I let my voice trail off. His room? I desperately wanted food, but I was not in the habit of following strange guys into their hotel rooms. Even if they were one of Grayson's team leaders.

"Oh!" His face lit up with understanding. "Right. Sorry. I should have said. Some of the guys are already up there. And Grayson and Madison are headed that way too. So it won't just be us."

I smiled, relieved that he understood my hesitancy. "Great."

He steered me to the door, his hand on my arm like he was afraid I might swoon again. We took the elevator up to the top floor, and he led me around the corner to the last door. He swiped his card and pushed it open.

"After you," he said with a smile.

I stepped inside. It was a suite, with a little living room and kitchen area, the door to the bedroom ajar to my left. Two vaguely familiar men were in the kitchen area, both typing furiously on their phones. Team leaders. They looked like most of Grayson's team leaders—muscular, early twenties, white, shoulders tense like they expected something to jump out at them. The one with shoulder-length brown hair tied back in a ponytail glanced up at me and did a double take.

"Can I use your bathroom?" I asked Julian quietly, very aware that my eyes were probably red and my cheeks splotchy.

"Sure. It's through the bedroom." He pointed. "I'm going to order the food. Anything you want? Or don't like?"

"I don't like seafood," Ponytail said. He seemed to be deliberately avoiding my gaze, in that way guys did when they didn't know how to handle a girl's tears.

"Wasn't talking to you," Julian said, rolling his eyes and throwing a smile my way. The guy made a face at him.

"I eat pretty much everything." Especially right now.

"One of everything, got it." He grinned as he pulled his phone from his pocket.

I walked through the bedroom and into the bathroom. The damage wasn't quite as bad as I thought—my mascara was waterproof, and I wasn't wearing eyeliner today—but my eyes were red and puffy, and I had pink splotches on my cheeks.

I splashed some cold water on my face and fixed my ponytail. It was obvious I'd been crying, but I'd just have to live with it.

I emerged from the bathroom to find the two leaders on their way out of the room. Ponytail held the door open with one hand, peering from his phone to Julian.

"They're all down at the bar. You sure you don't want to come?" he asked.

"Nah, I'm starving. Tell them I ordered plenty of food if they want to come up later," Julian said.

"He's too young anyway," the other team leader said from the hallway.

Ponytail laughed. "Right. I forgot you're a baby."

Julian shot him a mildly irritated look. Ponytail moved away from the door, and Julian caught it before it closed, flipping the latch so that it stayed propped open. I felt like it was done for my benefit, and I smiled at him when he turned back to me.

"Grayson and Madison are on their way." He walked to the kitchen counter and pulled tea bags out of two mugs of water. He let them drain, and then, oddly, popped them in the freezer.

"I ordered the food," he said. "It's too early for the dinner rush, so it should be fast."

"Thanks." I slid my hands into my pockets, trying to appear less awkward than I felt.

"Sit," he ordered, pointing at the couch.

I lowered onto one of the cushions, tucking my leg beneath me. My body nearly groaned in response. I was so hungry I'd barely noticed how tired and sore I was.

"You did a good job at sparring today." He leaned against the counter next to the refrigerator, cocking his head as he examined me. I felt like a puzzle he was trying to put together. "You had combat class in high school?"

"Yes."

"Did you graduate early?"

"No." I pretended to be fascinated by the magazine on the table in front of the couch. "I have one more year. I figured I'd take the GED later. If I don't die, I mean."

He let out a short laugh. "Sure. Stay alive first, GED second."

"How did you get to be a team leader? Do you know Grayson?"

His eyebrows lifted, like he was surprised. "Uh, yeah. Our families have been friends for a long time." He said it like I should have already known this.

A headline floated through my memory—MADISON AND JULIAN: BACK TOGETHER?—and I realized that I probably should have known exactly who he was.

Also, it made perfect sense that he dated a girl who looked like Madison.

He opened the freezer and took out the tea bags he'd put in there a couple minutes earlier. "Perfect, they're cool." He walked toward me. "Lie down."

"Why?"

"My mom used to do this when her eyes were puffy. Lie down."

I did as he ordered, stretching my legs out and letting my head fall back on the pillow.

"Close your eyes," he said. He gently placed a tea bag over either eyelid. "There. Just stay like that for about ten minutes."

"Seriously? Tea bags?" I reached up, moving one of the tea bags to the side so I could see him.

"Yes. My mom swears it works. Something about the caffeine. And she would know. She cries a lot." He gently pushed my hand away and replaced the tea bag.

"Why does she cry a lot?" I asked.

"She's just . . . prone to hysterics." He laughed a little. "But this is helpful, right? I was going for helpful."

"Very helpful. Thank you." One of the bags started to slide off my eye, and Julian caught it before I did. He was perched on the edge of the coffee table, right next to me, and he leaned over and moved the bag back into place. The tips of his fingers brushed against my forehead, sending a jolt of electricity up my spine. I felt exposed suddenly, lying on his couch unable to see him. I didn't know what to do with my hands.

"Did you join alone?" His voice was a little softer. His fingers lingered on my forehead for longer than necessary before disappearing. "Any friends come with you?"

"No, just me."

"You must have been scared."

I was more scared at home, but I didn't expect him to understand that. "So where are you from?" I asked.

"New York."

Right, because he knew Grayson and Madison.

"You're in college?" I guessed. "Or you were?"

"I did one semester at Columbia before I left to help Grayson plan all this." I heard the table creak. "Will you be OK for a few minutes? I'm going to go grab the food. It's just across the street."

"Yeah, I'm fine."

"OK, I'll be back." Footsteps padded across the carpet, and then the door opened and closed.

I left the tea bags on for a few more minutes, then tossed them and took a look in the mirror. Honestly, my eyes were a bit better.

When Julian returned, he had three huge bags of food. He heaved them onto the counter.

"I thought you were kidding about ordering one of everything," I said.

"Well, not *everything*." He put the bags on the counter. "But one of everything that sounded good. Grayson may be small, but that guy can put away some food." He started unpacking the boxes and handed one to me. "Here, have a dumpling now. I'm worried you're going to faint again."

I took it without argument, and Julian offered me chopsticks and a fork. I took the latter, speared a dumpling, and took a bite. I had to restrain myself from stuffing the whole thing in my mouth.

Julian took one for himself and cocked his head as he chewed. "Eh. OK."

I took another bite. "It's the best dumpling I've ever had."

A smile spread across his face, but his face still held a hint of worry. I didn't feel any relief about telling him about Dad. Was I supposed to? Was this supposed to feel good? It just felt like Dad was still in control, forcing me to share things with strangers that made me look weak instead of strong. He was still on my back, dragging me down.

Julian opened the other boxes, revealing an assortment of meats and rice and noodles. He handed me a paper plate and we loaded them up and sat on the couch. I dug into the orange chicken.

The door swung open, and Grayson stepped inside, dressed in black pants and a button-up shirt, his tie loosened around his neck.

"Hey," he said to Julian. "Did you—" He stopped when he spotted me on the couch. "Hello."

It was not exactly a friendly *hello*. It wasn't unfriendly, but it was clearly a question, directed at Julian. Grayson's eyes slid between us.

"You remember Clara," Julian said. "I asked her to come eat

with us, as a thank-you for beating up Edan." He grinned at me. "I've always wanted to do that."

"I didn't beat him up. I just . . . tackled him a little." I returned Julian's smile, relieved at his easy cover-up.

"She scared the shit out of the poor guy," Grayson said, typing something into his phone as he talked.

"The poor guy shouldn't rob people," I said. Julian laughed.

Grayson snorted. "Can't argue with that."

"Also I told Clara that she made it," Julian said.

Grayson made an exasperated noise. "Julian, you're not—"

"She promised not to tell anyone!" Julian interrupted.

"I won't," I said quickly.

"Act surprised tomorrow when you get your letter," Grayson said.

"My roommate never showed up, so there's no one around to see it anyway."

Grayson piled food on his plate and sat on the other side of the couch. "Perfect." He shoveled food into his mouth with chopsticks in one hand and held his phone in the other. "Julian, I need you to sort out these ground teams they keep messaging us about. You took the best notes."

"I'm getting to it." Julian took a bite of an eggroll.

"Julian."

"I'm getting to it! It's only"—he twisted around to peer at the clock on the wall—"four o'clock. Give me, like, thirty minutes. I'm going to eat, and Clara's going to tell us all the gossip."

I looked up in surprise. "Gossip?"

"Yeah. What are the other recruits like? How's the mood?"

Grayson lowered his phone. He was interested in the gossip too, apparently.

"Oh, um, I don't know," I said. "People seem excited, I guess. I haven't hung out with people much. Except Patrick."

"Patrick?" Julian repeated.

"Yeah, we met on the Dallas bus. He's really nice. Most of our bus was older people, so we connected."

"I'm sure he didn't mind connecting with the pretty girl," Julian said, one side of his mouth lifting. Grayson looked at him sharply.

I tried not to react to the fact that he'd just called me *pretty*. I focused on scooping up a forkful of fried rice. "Well, he's gay, so I don't think he was thinking about that."

"Oh," Julian said. Was he relieved? I was probably imagining it.

"Patrick said he joined because it was the right thing to do, to help people," I said. "I sort of thought that's why most people joined."

Grayson smiled. Julian grabbed his phone. "Patrick . . ."

"Choi."

Julian scrolled through something on his phone. "Choi, Choi . . ."

"Do *not* tell her if he made it," Grayson warned.

"I won't! I was just checking my notes." Julian put his phone back on the table and waited until Grayson returned his attention to his plate. He shot me a grin and a thumbs-up.

I quickly ducked my head to hide my smile.

The door opened, and Madison St. John blew inside, changed from the perfect workout clothes I'd seen earlier into shiny black leggings and bright green crop top, three-inch heels on her feet.

"Those fucking motherfuckers are still outside, and I swear to god, Grayson, I am not"—her eyes skipped over me—"in the mood today. I will lose my shit if I have to do another interview. Who is that?" She said it all in a rush, and it took me a moment to realize the last part referred to me.

"Clara, Madison," Julian said, with a hint of annoyance. "Madison, Clara."

She planted her hands on her hips and turned her attention back to Grayson without acknowledging me. "Did you hear me?"

"The people three doors down heard you, Maddie."

"I'm not talking to those bastards again today."

"Fine."

She winced and stepped out of her shoes, shrinking considerably. She was only a couple inches taller than me, maybe five foot eight. "These fucking things are killing me."

"Why are you dressed like you're going out to the club?" Julian asked.

"I invited a few people over to my suite." She speared a piece of beef from a carton and popped it in her mouth.

"We have to be up early in the morning," Grayson said in a warning tone.

"I'll sleep on the plane."

"Did you call back the *Times* reporter?" Grayson asked.

"No. What did I just say about interviews?"

"Call him back, please."

"No, I shan't."

"He has a deadline. And the MDG spokesperson has given him about ten quotes calling us insane mercenaries."

"MDG does know that they're also kind of mercenaries, right?" Madison said. "This seems like a pot calling the kettle black situation."

"Perfect. Call Bill and tell him that. We need to get our side out there. Just one more, Maddie."

She rolled her eyes. "I'm so tired of all these goddamn reporters." But she dug her phone out of her pocket and angrily poked at it. She held it up to her ear. "Hi, Bill!" Her tone changed drastically, switching to the perky tone I'd heard at her interview earlier today. "Sure, I can give you a quote." She walked into the bedroom and shut the door behind her.

"Don't mind her," Julian said. "She's not very friendly on her best days, much less when she's had to talk to reporters all day."

"She's friendly!" Grayson said. "It's just buried deep down."

"Deep, *deep* down," Julian said.

The bedroom door opened again, and Madison stuck her head out, still on the phone. "Julian? Can you come talk to Bill a minute?"

He jumped up. "Sure." He had to pass by me on his way, and he reached his hand out like he was going to put it on my shoulder, then seemed to think better of it. I might have tensed without even realizing it. I cursed my stupid traitorous body.

He tucked the hand into his pocket, a hint of embarrassment crossing his face. God, he was even cuter when he was nervous.

He disappeared into the bedroom, leaving me alone with Grayson. I took another bite of chicken. My stomach had filled up faster than usual, and it was close to bursting. I put the plate on the table in front of me.

"Do you think everyone is like Patrick?" I blurted out. "I mean, they joined because they genuinely want to do the right thing."

Grayson barked out a laugh. "No."

"No?" I repeated, surprised.

"Of course not. Does everyone join the military because of a burning desire to defend their country? No. That may be part of it, but they're also thinking about free college and health care and everything else that comes with serving in our armed forces."

"True."

"That's not why you joined?" Grayson asked.

"Uh, well . . ." I tugged at a string on the end of my shirt. "I'm not sure I joined for the right reasons."

"This isn't *The Bachelor*. There are no right reasons."

I laughed and met his gaze again. His eyes made him seem less intimidating than I'd expected. They were blue, like always, but the screen had never captured how kind they were. Maybe it was intentional, a way to put people at ease, but he looked at me like he genuinely cared what I thought.

"What was your reason?" he asked.

"I just wanted to escape." The words came out quietly. "I wanted to get away from home."

"There are a lot of other ways to get away from home," he said.

"Yes. But this takes me overseas, and there's a stipend . . ." I shrugged, embarrassed.

"You think everyone has noble intentions for everything? Half of the reason I'm here is to prove everyone wrong."

"Prove everyone wrong about what?"

"About me. About the technology my company invented. About my entire generation. People think we don't care about anything."

"But I bet the other half of your reasons are noble."

He lifted one shoulder. *Yes* was the obvious answer.

I thought of Dad, who never considered that I'd join. Who said *you will DIE* with such conviction, like it was the only possible outcome.

"It's not such a bad reason," I said. "Proving everyone wrong."

Grayson smiled. "No, it's not."

12

I FOUND A LETTER UNDER MY DOOR THE NEXT MORNING. I ripped it open.

Congratulations, Clara Pratt!

You've been assigned to American team seven.

Please be in the ballroom by eight a.m. with your luggage.

I grinned. Even though I'd known, it felt good to see it in print. It was real. I was going to Paris.

At seven fifteen, room service knocked on my door.

"I didn't order anything," I said to the haggard man.

"There's a note," he said. "It's paid for. Can I just put it on the desk?"

I stepped back so he could put the tray down. He practically ran out of the room. I grabbed the note that sat next to the tray.

Congrats, newest member of team seven.

—Julian

I lifted the plate covers to find eggs, bacon, sausage, toast, potatoes, and even a stack of pancakes. There was juice and water and an assortment of butter, syrup, and jam. He'd ordered the biggest breakfast on the menu.

A smile spread across my face. It was sort of embarrassing, this giant sympathy breakfast, but it was also incredibly nice. I was hungry again, and I'd had no idea where my next meal was coming from. I left Julian's room not long after my conversation with Grayson, and I'd declined Julian's offer to take some leftovers with me. Madison had been watching me, and something about her piercing stare made it too embarrassing to leave the room with a pile of Chinese food paid for by Julian.

I sat down and dug into the food, tucking Julian's note into my pocket. I ate as much as I could, then shoved my clothes into my backpack, leaving my room key on the bed, as we'd been instructed.

I headed downstairs in a packed elevator. Everyone around me must have made it, because the energy was almost palpable. The guy next to me kept smiling.

"Your team leader is holding your number!" a guy yelled as we stepped off the elevator. "Please go join him!"

I stepped into the ballroom. I was early, only a handful of people milling around all the team leaders holding signs with numbers. I searched until I found Julian holding 7. He was watching me, and a smile spread across his face as our eyes met. I felt my own lips twitch up as I walked across the ballroom.

"Welcome to team seven," he said.

"Thank you for the breakfast," I said quietly.

"You're welcome." His gaze caught on something behind me.

I turned to see Patrick walking toward us. He grinned and flipped his paper around so I could see **AMERICAN TEAM SEVEN** on it.

"You're team seven?" he asked. I nodded with a smile.

"Welcome," Julian said, extending his hand. "Julian Montgomery."

"Patrick Choi," he said, shaking it. He stepped closer to me. "Noah's on this team too."

He pointed at Noah, who was making his way over to us.

More people trickled in, and the members of team seven introduced themselves as they wandered over. I'd met or noticed them all yesterday. They must have grouped us into potential teams after the first day.

There was a trend taking shape. We were all young.

And, well, we were not great.

Team seven was:

Me. I had no illusions about my abilities.

Patrick. He had a mark on his forehead from where he'd fallen flat on his face yesterday.

Noah. Admittedly, I hadn't seen Noah in action during try-outs, but nothing about him screamed *badass*.

Archer (not Archie). He'd mysteriously acquired a black eye since I'd met him at orientation.

Dani, the girl from the Dallas bus wearing handcuffs. She might have been pretty good, actually.

Priya, the cheerleader who couldn't throw a punch to save her life.

Gage, the boy who hadn't shot the target once and yelled at me on the obstacle course.

Hunter, his buddy, who had leered at me.

Andrew Dorsey, the boy who couldn't work a spear.

Laila, the girl who gave me half her protein bar. She was tiny —barely five feet tall.

Zoe, the bored girl with perfect eyeliner who explained which teams were bad yesterday and now seemed horrified.

Madison St. John, who joined us by announcing she had "the fucking worst hangover."

And Edan Pearce, the thief who threatened to vomit on me.

Patrick looked around as we formed, then across to the other American groups. They were cheering and slapping each other on the back. There was one team, all men, all white, who seemed exceptionally pleased with themselves. Another American team was also all men except for one woman—a tall girl with short hair.

"I think we're the loser team," Patrick said under his breath. He was obviously trying not to laugh.

"We're the bad team, aren't we?" Priya whispered.

"Ugh, this is so embarrassing," Zoe moaned.

"Shut up," said Gage.

Patrick threw his head back with a laugh. "Team Loser, unite!"

I laughed. No one else looked amused.

Part Three

ENGAGE IN COMBAT AT YOUR OWN RISK

13

It was noon when we arrived in Paris. I didn't sleep at all on the plane, but I felt wide awake, my stomach jumping around in anticipation.

We piled off the plane, and I followed the other recruits through the airport. Patrick fell into step beside me, covering his mouth as he yawned.

All the signs in the airport were in several different languages, including English. I saw three of the same sign as we walked to customs, like they really didn't want people to miss it.

YOU ARE ENTERING A SCRAB HOT ZONE CITY
PLEASE BE ADVISED:
Scrabs usually attack in population-dense areas.
This includes all tourist areas.
You will hear a rumbling noise about ten seconds
before they appear.
If you see a scrab, find shelter until the police and/or
the French National Guard arrive.
Engage in combat at your own risk.

People stared as we went through passport control. A couple in the EU line whispered to each other as they watched us line up, not even trying to hide their bafflement. Those expressions clearly said *those people are crazy.* I got the look several more times before I cleared customs.

The team leaders led us in the direction of something called RER, which ended up being a train.

"Thank god," someone muttered from behind me. It was Edan, still looking a bit airsick and wearing his black leather jacket again. Like me, he only carried a small backpack. It occurred to me that maybe he wore the jacket because he had no place else to put it.

We got off at a crowded train station, only to be immediately led to the subway. The team leaders held their hands up in the air so we could see them.

"Off, recruits!" someone yelled as the subway came to a stop.

I stepped off the train and headed up the stairs behind Patrick. I caught a glimpse of the sky as we climbed. It was clear and blue, the sun shining, but it wasn't nearly as hot as Dallas. The air was crisp and fresh instead of humid.

I took the last step and stopped. Cars buzzed by on the street, and a woman said, "*Pardon,*" as she stepped around me. I moved away from the subway exit.

A café with a red awning was directly in front of me, with chairs lined up on the sidewalk and a little round table between each of them. The chairs all faced out—at me—instead of at each other, and the two men sitting at a table stared at people as they walked by. The French weren't subtle about their people watching, it seemed.

The streets were narrow and lined with cars, and I was

surrounded by buildings, though they were only about six or seven stories high. Nothing like the tall buildings of Dallas and Atlanta.

There was a giant hole in the sidewalk on the other side of the road. It had been roped off, and I watched as two women walked around it, laughing and barely glancing at it.

No one in the area seemed particularly scared. I'd thought that perhaps everyone in Europe would be terrified, rushing from place to place and trying to get to higher ground as fast as possible. I'd heard that daily life was mostly the same here, but I hadn't quite believed it.

"Clara."

I turned at the sound of my name. Patrick pointed to where the other recruits were walking, following the team leaders.

"You OK?" he asked.

"It seems so normal, doesn't it? You wouldn't even know that there are thousands of scrabs here."

He looked left and then right. "No. I guess you wouldn't."

"Ugh, this is the ugly part of Paris," Madison said, walking past me. "It's going to take us forever to get to the city center on the metro."

I peered down the tree-lined street. This was the *ugly* part of Paris?

We turned a corner and trekked to the huge sports complex at the end of the road. Outdoor tracks, rugby fields, and tennis courts were visible as we approached. A group of about thirty people were on the rugby fields. They waved at us.

A man dressed in blue, the word POLICE printed across his

back, approached Grayson. *"Bonjour,"* the policeman said. Grayson steered him in the direction of the rugby field.

"The French teams have already started training," Julian explained. "And we're coordinating with the French police. You'll work with them soon." He held the door open for us, his gaze catching on mine. My cheeks heated.

I quickly became fascinated with the ground. I could *not* form a crush on Julian. We were here to fight monsters, not date. He would probably think I was ridiculous if I started batting my eyelashes at him like I thought I was still in high school.

Besides, if the tabloids were to be believed, he was dating Madison. Which, of course he was.

"Team seven!" Julian called. "Your rooms are on the third floor, labeled with your names. Change into your workout clothes and then meet me in the small gym on this level." He pointed to the back of the complex. "It's that way."

I climbed the stairs, glancing around as we walked. Julian had said earlier that the complex had been a popular spot for boxing and martial arts before it closed a few years ago. I glimpsed several rooms with mats and other equipment as we walked inside and down the hallway.

My name was on a door around the corner, the last one in the hallway. I'd glimpsed rooms with at least twenty cots, but there were only six names on the door. All the girls of team seven:

Clara Pratt
Priya Mehta
Madison St. John

Zoe Hughes
Dani Russell
Laila Williams

I opened the door to find a small room with six cots, a pillow and blanket on each one. I dropped my backpack on the cot closest to the wall.

Priya walked into the room and dragged her huge roller bag to the cot across from mine. She looked from her bag to my backpack. "Teach me your ways," she said.

I laughed. "Did you pack your entire wardrobe?"

"I thought I narrowed it down, but apparently not."

The other girls filed into the room, and I glanced around as I dug through my bag. Madison had the cot next to me, and she was scrolling through her phone instead of getting dressed. Zoe was stripping down. Dani ducked out of the room, clothes pressed to her chest so she could change elsewhere. Priya dug through her suitcase, clothes scattered all over her cot. Laila was already changed, and she laughed with Priya as she held up one of several dresses hanging out of Priya's suitcase.

My chest tightened, and it took me a moment to identify the emotion. I missed my room, even if it had only been a tiny step above a prison. It was a private prison, at least. I'd never slept in the same space with anyone, and I'd always liked that I could retreat to my bedroom when I wanted to be alone. The bathroom was probably my only option for privacy here. I changed as fast as possible.

"Are you putting on makeup?" Laila asked. I glanced over to

see she was talking to Zoe, who was now perched on the edge of her cot, squinting into a compact.

"I sure am," Zoe said, swiping mascara on her lashes. "Our team leader is super hot, and I look like death after that flight."

She did not look at all like death. Her eyeliner was still impressively perfect, actually.

"Are we allowed to date team leaders?" Zoe asked, reaching into her makeup bag. "Because Julian is the hottest guy on the team, for sure."

"Uh, isn't Julian already taken?" Priya asked, her eyes sliding to Madison.

Madison tossed her phone aside and stood. "No."

I tried to ignore the way my heart leapt.

"We've never been a couple. Officially," she added.

The word *officially* made my heart sink right back down. Zoe's expression soured as well. Madison pretended not to notice. She pulled off her shirt, revealing a flat stomach and a lacy bra that would not adequately hold my boobs up at all.

"And no, you are not allowed to date team leaders," Madison continued. "Grayson was very clear about that. All his team leaders are dudes, and he doesn't want any of the girls feeling uncomfortable."

Zoe squinted like she was trying to find the loophole. I tried to ignore my growing sense of disappointment.

"I think it's Edan, personally," Priya said quickly, clearly sensing the awkwardness.

"What's Edan?" Madison asked.

"The hottest guy on the team."

I wrinkled my nose.

"What is that look?" Zoe asked. "You don't think Edan's hot?"

"No, he is," I said. "But he seems like the kind of guy who'd sneak out of your bedroom in the morning and later you discover a twenty missing from your wallet."

Priya tilted her head back dramatically. "Stop it. You're just making me want him more."

"That's what does it for you?" Laila asked. "A guy who robs you?"

"I like the bad boys. Those tattoos! And the eyes. And the hair. And the everything."

I finished lacing up my sneakers and stood, glancing at Madison. She was now wearing a bright pink tank top and black pants and little to no makeup. She was just as pretty without it.

She caught me watching her, and I quickly looked away. I edged closer to Priya and Laila. "Are we ready?"

We walked back downstairs. All the doors had been labeled, and we passed TRAINING ROOM 1, CAFETERIA, and BIG GYM until we found SMALL GYM. Blue mats were laid out across the floor, and boxes of gloves and headgear were pushed against the wall. One of the French-speaking Canadian teams was already there, using half of the room.

Some of the guys on team seven were waiting. Patrick waved. Archer didn't appear to notice that we'd arrived. Noah stood with Andrew—no, Dorsey, he'd told us to call him by his last name—and held his phone up to record something as they laughed.

"That was great," Noah said, lowering the phone. "Thanks."

"I don't know about great," Dorsey said, ruffling his hair. "Maybe we should do it again."

"Nah, I edit them a little so you all look good." He jerked his thumb at Archer, who was watching the Canadian team practice. "I'm going to need to do his intro again, though. No salvaging that one."

It took Archer a moment to respond, like he hadn't realized Noah was talking about him. He blinked. "I said hello."

"And literally nothing else."

Archer just stared at him. Patrick made a sound like he was trying to cover up a laugh.

Noah slid his phone into his pocket as Madison bounced to a stop in front of him. "What are you doing? Edit what?"

"I—I have a YouTube channel," Noah stammered, his cheeks pink. "I was introducing everyone in the group."

"But not me? Why not me?"

"No, you too, of course, I, um, I just hadn't gotten around to . . ." His voice trailed off as he dug his phone back out of his pocket, almost dropping it twice in the process.

"How's my hair?" Madison smoothed it with her hand.

"When does her hair not look perfect?" Zoe grumbled under her breath.

Julian walked into the room, followed by the rest of the boys on the team and Dani. Hunter's gaze quickly found me and then quickly found my breasts. I turned away, crossing my arms over my chest. Laila saw me do it and rolled her eyes in his direction.

"OK, I'm going to be the one to ask since everyone else is chickenshit," Madison said, pointing to the handcuffs on Dani's wrists.

"Do you need help getting those off? Because I know where they keep the machetes."

Dani blinked, clearly startled to find that Madison was talking to her. Her lips twisted into something that was almost a smile. She used two fingers to snap the handcuff open.

"It's jewelry," she said.

"Oh, that's too bad," Madison said with a disappointed sigh. "I was looking forward to that story."

Dani actually laughed at that, revealing a small gap between her two front teeth. I caught Laila discreetly rolling her eyes again, and I suppressed a smile.

"All right, guys, we're diving right into training today," Julian said. "I know you're tired, but we've decided on only two weeks of training for this team, so we're going to be moving pretty fast."

"Two weeks?" Priya squeaked, echoing my thoughts.

"You all had combat training in school," Julian said. "We think two weeks should be enough to get you ready for some simple stuff. You'll continue training after we go out there."

"But we're the bad team," Zoe said.

"You're not the bad team," Julian said quickly.

"Uh, we're not great," Zoe said. "No offense." Archer looked kind of offended.

"You're not a bad team, you're a young team," Julian said. "Everyone is eighteen or under."

"How old are you?" Gage asked.

"Nineteen."

"How are you qualified to do this?" Gage asked.

Julian's eyebrows lifted a little. "Sorry?"

"Why are you a team leader? What's your background? Besides being Grayson St. John's best friend."

An awkward silence fell over the team, but Julian smiled.

"I actually helped Grayson build all of this from day one," he said. "We spent the past six months putting together training and battle plans. And Grayson and I used to take daily combat classes together, in addition to what we got at school, so I'm pretty skilled at fighting myself." He nodded at Madison. "Maddie too. She could be a team leader, but she declined."

Madison leaned back on her hands. "I don't appreciate being given responsibility."

"I am qualified to train you guys and develop our battle strategies," Julian continued. "But it's true that I'm not that much older than you, so please feel free to come talk to me anytime. I know that for most of you, this is your first time away from home. I'm here for whatever you need."

His eyes flicked to me for a second, a smile briefly crossing his lips. I returned it.

"Let's get going, then. We're doing a couple days of basic hand-to-hand, and then we'll move to working with weapons and armor. Teams of two today." Julian patted his pockets. He frowned and then made a deeply annoyed noise. "Dammit, Edan!"

"What?" Edan's wide-eyed innocence looked genuine. So it probably wasn't.

"Whatever, keep it. I remember."

"Are you sure it's not in your sock? I feel like it's in your sock." Edan pointed. A piece of paper was sticking out of Julian's sock. Priya giggled.

"Dammit, Edan, how do you even . . ." Julian trailed off as he grabbed the paper. He glared at Edan and shoved it in his pocket. "Noah, you're with me, Patrick and Priya . . ." He trailed off as he regarded us. He glanced from me to Gage.

"Yo, no," Gage interrupted.

"Sorry?" Julian asked.

"I'm not sparring with her. I saw her at tryouts. I need to be with a dude who can actually fight."

I flushed. Gage smirked at me in a way I knew well—daring me to say something back but certain that I probably wouldn't. He was the kind of guy who liked publicly embarrassing people (and I bet he enjoyed doing it to girls the most).

Julian opened his mouth to respond.

"I saw you at tryouts too, and you were flat on your ass most of the time," I said evenly. "At least I stayed standing most of the time."

Someone snorted loudly. Priya giggled.

Gage's nostrils flared. He muttered something under his breath and stuffed his hands in his pockets. His face was red.

"Did I ask for your opinion?" Julian spat out the words with such hostility that I didn't recognize his voice for a second.

The team went completely silent. Across the room, the Canadians paused their practice to stare.

"This isn't high school gym class." Julian's voice was still loud, but a little calmer. "You don't get an opinion, you don't get detention if you're rude. If you can't take this seriously, you're off the team. Are we clear?"

We could be kicked off our teams? What were we supposed

to do if that happened? I didn't have any money for a return ticket —would I just be stuck in France forever?

Gage swallowed and nodded. I didn't think he had a plan if he was kicked off either.

The Canadian team leader called something to Julian in French. Julian replied, also in French. I didn't think it was very nice, because the other team leader widened his eyes a little like, *Wow*, and then turned away.

I pressed my arms to my chest and grasped one wrist. This angry version of Julian made me nervous.

He let out a sigh, rubbing a hand across the back of his neck. The anger drained from his face. "Sorry," he said to us. "I don't mean to be an ass, I just want you guys to be safe. It's on me if you get killed out there, you know?"

I let go of my wrist, the tightness in my stomach loosening. I hadn't considered how much pressure it was to be a team leader. And Julian was leading a team that was both the youngest *and* the worst. I'd probably yell at us too.

"It's cool, I'm in favor of not dying," Patrick said lightly. Most of the team laughed, and I saw the same understanding on their faces. We weren't in high school combat class anymore.

Julian smiled. "Gage and Hunter, team up. Clara and Edan."

He rattled off the rest of the pairs, and asked us to spread out on the mats. Then he caught my eye, and a small smile spread across his face. Was I blushing? I was probably blushing.

I turned away to see Madison watching me like she was considering the best angle to tackle me from.

Officially. She and Julian were never *officially* together. Maybe I was stepping into something complicated between them.

I avoided her gaze as I took my spot across from Edan on the mat.

"This is just sparring, like you did in combat classes," Julian called. "Pull your punches. I don't want any broken noses today."

I strapped on my headgear and gloves. Edan did the same. He bounced on his heels and then turned in a circle, shaking his arms out.

"What are you doing?" I asked.

"Warming up."

Beside me, Patrick grunted as Priya elbowed him in the stomach.

"Whoops, sorry," she said with a giggle.

"Are you ready?" I asked Edan.

"Yeah. You can go first."

I planted my feet and lifted my arms. I drew back, preparing to throw my first punch. He quickly stepped to the side as I let it fly, leaning back to easily miss my fist and watch it sail past his face.

"Edan, block it, don't run away," Julian called with a sigh that clearly said he'd been expecting this from Edan.

"I didn't run. I saw it coming from a mile away, so I just moved aside." He swept his arms out dramatically to show how he'd avoided my slow swing. I flushed.

Julian's gaze flicked across the gym, distracted by something. "Gage, why are you punching Hunter in the ear?" He walked away from us.

Edan took his spot across from me and raised his gloved hands. He jerked his head, beckoning me forward without meeting my eyes.

I swung again. He leaned to the side, avoiding it by a mile again. I threw another one right away, aiming for his side this time, and he skittered away from that one too. He was really fast. You'd have to be, in his line of work.

"You're supposed to block," I said, swinging again because I hoped he'd be distracted by my voice.

No luck. He ducked the punch.

"I'll block when you actually get close to landing one," he said.

"Julian just said that's not what you're supposed to do." I swung again.

"This is"—he ducked my swing again—"how I intend to avoid"—he leaned way back out of my reach—"scrabs, so Julian" —he jumped to the left, my fist almost grazing his cheek—"can suck it."

I lowered my arms, letting out a sigh of defeat. Around us, other members of the team grunted as their gloves connected with bodies.

"Clara, keep trying!" Julian called.

I sprang into action immediately, taking a big step forward and swinging right at Edan's face. He blinked, clearly startled, and stumbled backward. My glove barely grazed his nose. Well, at least I sort of made contact.

"Some warning would be nice," he said, an edge in his voice.

"You're the one who wasn't paying attention."

He didn't move back onto the mat. He was still avoiding my

gaze, his eyes flicking all around the gym and to the floor. He swallowed. He was nervous, I realized with a start.

"I'm not going to hurt you," I said. It came out more exasperated than reassuring. Maybe this was why Julian had paired me with him. The guy was clearly more scared of me than I was of him.

"Why do you say that like it should be obvious?" he asked.

"Because Julian told us to pull our punches."

"Within the first forty-eight hours we knew each other, you jumped me and threatened to 'tackle my ass—'" He made a motion with his hands that was probably supposed to be quote marks, though the gloves hid his fingers. "So forgive me if I don't trust you."

"You don't trust *me*?"

"Nope."

"Guys, hold on," Julian called, addressing the entire team. "Let's pick up the pace here. I want to see fists flying. Watch me and Noah for a minute." He nodded at Noah. "I'll block."

Noah lifted his fists. He was lightly muscular, I realized as he lifted his arms. The kind of muscular that wasn't for show.

He launched at Julian. His fists flew through the air so fast I wasn't sure how Julian was even blocking them. He was incredibly quick, punching and dodging as Julian attempted a few hits.

"Holy shit," Dorsey said under his breath.

Noah ducked as Julian swung at him, and Julian lost his footing and hit the mat. I hadn't even seen how Noah made him stumble.

"Like that," Julian said with a grin, breathing heavily. Noah held out a hand to help him to his feet.

"Noah was put on this team to keep us all alive, wasn't he?" Patrick asked from behind me.

"Yep," I said. "He definitely was."

14

AFTER TRAINING, WE WERE USHERED TO THE CAFETERIA FOR a dinner of barely warm chicken and limp salad. At the back of the cafeteria, workers dressed in black ran frantically in and out of a door, carrying huge trays of food or stacks of dishes.

I sat across from Noah and Patrick, who were excitedly talking about Noah's YouTube subscriber numbers. They were exploding, apparently. Dorsey, Hunter, and Gage were at the end of the table. To my left, Zoe and Dani laughed at something Madison said. On my right, Priya was trying to explain just how huge high school football was in Alabama to Laila and Edan, both of whom seemed dubious.

I was in the middle of all the conversations, but part of none of them. I was watching them form their friend groups, and I didn't have one. That always happened to me. It was part of the reason I stopped being friends with Adriana and the other girls a few years ago. Every time we hung out, I'd look around and realize that they were all better friends with each other than they were with me. Even when a new girl joined the group, she immediately found a place. I would watch it, wondering how on earth it happened. How did normal people just bond like that? How did they meet someone and just start sharing things? I couldn't do it. I didn't know *how* to do it.

But everyone else did, apparently. Even *Dani* had found a place with Zoe and Madison.

I glanced at Patrick. I'd been relieved to have a friend on the team, but he was clearly already better friends with Noah. Only Archer was also alone, across from Gage but obviously in his own world. That guy was weirder than me, at least.

I realized that Noah was watching me. His gaze cut to the team members on either side of me, and he seemed to recognize that I was left out. Great. That wasn't embarrassing at all.

"Clara, I need your phone number," he said, picking up the phone next to his empty plate. "Yours is the only one I don't have."

"I don't have a phone," I said, using the edge of my fork to drag a soggy piece of lettuce across my plate.

"You don't have a phone?" Priya asked, leaning past Laila to peer at me.

I shook my head. "I . . . forgot it."

"You *forgot* it?" Noah repeated, like this was the strangest thing he'd ever heard.

"Uh, yeah," I said, already regretting this lie. Why didn't I just say I couldn't afford one? That was technically true. My parents had bought that phone for me. Without them, I couldn't afford anything.

Why had I lied at all? Why hadn't I rolled my eyes and said, *My dad took it as punishment?*

Because that invited questions. Questions I didn't want to answer. I didn't care about protecting Dad, but I cared about protecting myself. And I wasn't interested in answering those questions.

Noah blinked at me, and I realized that silence had stretched out for a beat too long.

"Let's get out of here," Priya said quickly. "I need a shower."

"Me too," Noah said, and everyone rose from their seats.

No wonder I couldn't make friends. I'd successfully made everyone feel awkward in three seconds flat.

I sighed as I grabbed my plate and walked across the cafeteria to dump it in the bin. I followed a few steps behind Noah and Patrick as we exited into the hallway.

"Hey. Clara."

I turned at the sound of the soft voice to see Julian standing at the edge of a dark hallway. He jerked his head, indicating for me to come to him. I did, suddenly very aware that I hadn't had a chance to shower or change since training. I was still in my work-out clothes, my hair in a sweaty ponytail. I self-consciously ran a hand over it.

Julian slid his hands into his pockets as I approached him. He was smiling, but it was the kind of smile that hinted at embarrassment simmering underneath. A paper bag sat on the floor next to his feet.

"Dinner wasn't that great, right?" he said.

"It could have been worse."

He laughed. "I like that attitude. We're still working out some kinks. But I thought that maybe you'd be interested in dessert after such a terrible dinner?"

"Dessert?" I repeated.

"Yeah, I . . ." He trailed off as he grabbed the paper bag from the floor. "I have a problem with sweets. They're my weakness."

He held the bag a little higher. "Especially macarons. Do you like them?"

"I've never had them," I said, flustered. This almost felt like he was asking me out on a date.

His eyes widened a little. "You have to try them. Come with me. Save me from myself."

I nodded with a laugh. He glanced at the recruits still filing out of the cafeteria, and then gestured for me to follow him down the dark hallway. We walked to the back of the building and out a door that Julian propped open with a rock.

He plopped down in a patch of grass. Across the field, a group of guys sat on the ground, surrounded by bottles of something that was probably alcohol. They laughed loudly, apparently oblivious to our presence.

Julian took a box out of the bag and opened it to reveal rows of multicolored macarons.

"You got a lot," I said with a laugh.

"I told you I had a problem." He held it a little closer to me. "Please."

"Any flavor in particular I should try first?" I asked.

"Maybe chocolate? Always a safe choice." He pointed to a brown one, and I plucked it from the box.

I took a bite. It was soft, and incredibly sweet.

"Wow," I said.

"Right?" He reached into the bag and handed me a water bottle.

"Thanks."

"You did good today," he said as I polished off the first macaron. He extended the box to me, and I took a pink one.

"Right," I said with a snort.

"You did! Don't let Gage get to you."

"No, he didn't," I said. "But a lot of them are better than me. Most of them, actually. And I kind of . . ." I trailed off, and he looked at me expectantly. "I don't really fit in with them," I said.

Relief washed over me, sudden and unexpected. I'd never had anyone to talk to about this. Or anything. Mom, with her relentless (unjustified) optimism, did not count.

"Why not?" he asked.

"I don't know how to talk to them, I guess. I don't know how to talk to anyone. And I feel like there's no entry point. They talk about school or cheerleading or social media. I don't even have an Instagram. Or Snapchat."

"Seriously?" He sounded more impressed than surprised. "Why not?"

Because I had no friends. Because after I stopped being friends with Adriana, it was depressing to constantly see pictures of my former friends hanging out together. Because no one followed me, except a couple kids from school who I barely knew. Because Dad screamed at me about a picture once, saying I was *asking for it.* My social media accounts were just another way for him to keep tabs on me, and part of me still felt that way. I didn't want him to have access to any part of my life.

"I never had that many friends," I said, trying to keep my voice light. "Sort of depressing to be snapping and have no one watching it."

He winced, like he felt so much pity for me that it physically hurt.

"And I don't have a phone anyway, so it wouldn't matter if I did," I said quickly, to cover up my embarrassment.

"Why didn't you have many friends?" he asked.

"I just never . . . fit in, I guess."

He nodded, and was quiet for a moment. "I never had that many either," he said. "Grayson and Madison's dad was good friends with my dad, so they came built in. But Grayson is older than me, so I was always kind of alone at school. Especially in high school, after he graduated."

"He's . . . how old is he?"

"Twenty-two. Three years older than me. I never got along with kids my own age. Maybe because Grayson was always around, but my mom says that I seemed to hate being a kid, even from a very young age. She said I was resentful."

"How so?"

"I resented that no one would take me seriously because I was young. And she's right, honestly. I remember looking up at adults laughing at me, not even in a mean way, just like because they thought I was cute, and I was so *angry* about it." He laughed. "I was an old soul, I guess. My father had no patience with children, even his own. *Especially* his own."

I cocked my head, silently asking for him to go on.

"He's not a bad guy," Julian said quickly. "Not like—" He cut himself off abruptly.

"My dad," I finished for him. "It's fine, you can say it."

"He never hit us or anything," he said, a little gently. "But he's very busy, and the stress of his job bled through to us at home, I guess. I can't blame him for it."

I could blame him for it, but I didn't say it. I wasn't here to tell Julian how to feel about his own father.

"Anyway, he didn't understand children, and he expected me to act like an adult most of the time. So I did. And it was frustrating when other adults treated me like a kid, because I didn't feel like one, on the inside." He turned to me, his gaze soft. "It's the same with you, I think."

"I wouldn't say my parents treated me like an adult."

"Sure they did. Your dad hit you, and it sounds like your mom didn't protect you. You don't treat a child that way."

"That's . . . a really good point."

He leaned a little closer to me, until our shoulders touched. "So it's not surprising you have trouble connecting with people on the team. You're older than them. You've always been older than them."

I smiled at him, warmth flooding my arm where he was barely touching me. His face was only inches from mine, a distance that we could close in a second. A distance I could close. But I'd never kissed a guy first. I'd only kissed two guys, total, and they'd both made the first move.

Laughter sounded from across the field, and Julian jumped, taking a quick glance at them like he was worried about being caught doing something wrong. The guys in the middle of the field were walking away, disappearing around the side of the building. Quiet settled in between us as their voices faded.

Were we doing something wrong? This sort of felt like a date, which was against the rules, according to Madison.

He held out the macaron box to me again, not meeting my eyes. I took one.

"Thanks for keeping me company," he said, a little quietly.

It seemed weird that he would thank *me* for that. I'd spent all day surrounded by people, but this moment, with just him, was the least alone I'd felt all day.

"Thank you for the macarons," I said. My voice was barely above a whisper, and I hoped my tone conveyed that I was expressing gratitude for more than dessert.

His gaze met mine again, his lips turning up a tiny bit. He understood.

15

I WAS STIFF AND SORE THE THIRD MORNING OF TRAINING, AND I winced as I descended the steps to the ground floor of the sports complex. Priya bounced ahead of me, jumping over the last two steps and turning around with a grin.

"Just run through the pain," she said. "It helps."

"I really doubt that."

"I did five summers at cheer camp. I know what I'm talking about."

I lifted an eyebrow.

"Don't give me that look. Cheer camp is no joke."

"I'm sure it's not." I took the last step and followed her through the door and into the hallway. Given that Priya seemed to be in much better shape than I was, I could definitely believe that cheer camp was no joke.

Laughter and talking echoed from the cafeteria as we walked toward it.

"What did you do in high school?" Priya asked. "Wait, no, don't tell me." She tapped her chin as she considered. "Newspaper."

"No." I looked at her strangely. "Your high school had a newspaper?"

"Yeah. It was just online, but we had one. My friend wrote for it."

"Huh."

"Rugby?" she guessed again.

"I'm not even totally sure what rugby is." I reached for the cafeteria door. "It's nothing."

"Nothing?"

"What I did in high school. Nothing." Unless staying alive counted as an activity.

"Oh."

We walked into the cafeteria, which consisted of rows of long tables and plastic folding chairs, most of which were occupied. Hundreds of people filled the large, noisy room. There were the American teams (about half of us went to France. The other half went to Beijing after they realized they had more recruits than the Paris complex could accommodate), and the Canadian and Mexican teams. The French teams were here as well, though some of them had been sent to another facility in Marseille for training. Teams from Senegal, Botswana, and Kenya had arrived yesterday as well, and I spotted a few of them at a table. The training was mostly divided by language, and we were an English-, French-, and Spanish-speaking facility.

The table in the back had steaming pots of food on it, and we headed to it. I piled some eggs, toast, and fruit on my plate, then walked across the room to where team seven was sitting. I slid into the empty seat across from Patrick. Noah was on one side of him, a girl I didn't know on the other side. She was Black with chin-length straight black hair and large square glasses.

"Really?" she asked Patrick. She had a British accent.

Dorsey plopped down in the seat next to me.

"Nope, I don't date guys who smoke. Strict rule," Patrick said. "Clara, this is Naomi. UK team nine."

"Nice to meet you," I said. I eyed Patrick. "Who smokes?"

"One of his many admirers," Naomi said, gesturing vaguely to her left.

"I don't have *admirers*," Patrick said with a laugh.

"Uh, yeah, you do, and you know it," Priya said as she and Laila joined us. Patrick shrugged like maybe he really did know it.

Priya extended her hand to Naomi. "Priya. Nice to meet you. I thought all the UK teams were in London."

"Yeah, they are, but they sent some of the bad teams here," Naomi said.

"That's why I invited her to sit with us," Patrick said. "They're the British version of Team Loser."

"Would you stop calling us that?" Zoe snapped. She sat on the other side of me.

"Where's the rest of the team?" I asked Naomi.

She gestured to her right. A girl with long purple hair approached a table and roughly shoved a teenage boy wearing a baseball cap. He said something, and everyone laughed.

"They're a young team too," Noah said, glancing at Zoe. She nodded her approval.

"Young, loser, whatever," Naomi said. "If we do all right in training, we can go back to the UK. That's what our leader said, anyway."

"You definitely want to go back to the UK," Noah said.

"I mean, if you want to die, sure," Priya said.

I stopped with my toast halfway to my mouth. "Is it bad there?"

"Yeah, it's bad," Naomi said, looking at me like I was an idiot. I ducked my head.

"They say the UK scrabs are the worst," Patrick explained. "But there's some disagreement."

"There's no disagreement," said Naomi.

"There are more of them," Laila said.

"And they're smarter," Naomi added.

"Debatable," Patrick said. "How do you measure scrab intelligence?"

"Talk to me after you've been to London, mate," Naomi said.

"No. Thank. You." The drawn out words came from behind me, and I turned to see Madison. "Julian wants us in the gym."

I shoved another bite of eggs in my mouth, got up from the table, deposited my tray in the dirty dish bin, and followed the team to the small gym.

Julian stood in the middle of the floor, breathing heavily, like he'd already started working out. He used the bottom of his shirt to wipe his face, flashing us his abs. He worked hard on those abs. Those did not happen by accident.

He caught me watching him as he lowered his shirt. One side of his mouth quirked up. I quickly looked away. I hadn't been alone with him since the macarons two nights ago, and I was trying to pretend that I wasn't sad about it.

Julian's eyes flicked to Noah, who was holding up his phone like he was taking a picture.

"Noah, what are you doing?" Julian asked wearily.

"I'm taking video of you. Everyone loves you. On YouTube, I mean. They want to see more of you."

"Everyone loves—" Julian's lips had started to turn up in a smile, but he cut himself off with a shake of his head. "No. Put the phone away. We're training, not filming videos for YouTube."

"They only love you because they don't know you," Madison said, twisting a lock of hair around her finger. She was always saying vaguely mean things to Julian, like she was trying to get a rise out of him. Or at least get him to pay attention to her. It was a strange way to flirt with someone.

He ignored her. It was true that everyone on YouTube loved him. I'd seen the comments. He was already kind of famous for being part of the New York rich people scene or whatever, so I guessed it made sense that he was the most popular team member.

It made me feel kind of stupid for having a crush on him, though. Everyone had a crush on Julian. I glanced at Madison again. It did make me feel a little bit better that he seemed to have zero interest in her. He never played along or let her get under his skin.

"OK, guys, we're—" Julian stopped suddenly, a flash of annoyance crossing his face. I followed his gaze to the far gym wall, where Edan was lying flat on the ground, holding a book over his face. "Edan!"

"What?" He glanced over and spotted us all standing around Julian. "Oh." He hopped up, bringing the book with him.

Like me, Edan didn't seem to be bonding with anyone else on the team. Wonderful. Edan and Archer. I was in such great company. The thief and the weird kid who never talked.

"Did you eat?" Julian asked Edan, a bit wearily. "You all had instructions to eat before eight a.m."

"Yeah."

Julian gave him a look like he didn't believe it.

"I did! It was just really early. I can't sleep. I'm jetlagged, I guess."

"Fine," Julian said. "But you need to get your body used to this time zone. No naps. You're sluggish, and I won't have you dragging down my team. I won't hesitate to give you the boot if I think you're endangering your team members." He turned to us. "That goes for all of you."

A burst of panic shot through my veins. If nimble, agile Edan was *sluggish*, then what was I?

"We're splitting up today to work on different things," Julian said. "Laila, Hunter, Priya, and Zoe—you guys go work with Grayson on blades. Madison, Noah, Patrick, and Dani—you four go do drills with the Canadian teams in the big gym. Gage and Archer, you guys stay here with me and Dorsey. I want to work out with the bags. Edan and Clara, sparring room."

I bit back a moan. This was my third time being paired with Edan. Honestly, I wanted to be paired with someone slower. The guy just darted away from every punch I threw and then gave me a smug look. It was incredibly annoying.

Julian clapped his hands. "All right, let's go, guys. Grayson is picking which teams to send to the UK soon, and I'd like for us to be on that list."

The team began filing out of the room, and Julian jogged to me, his fingers brushing against my arm briefly. He always touched me when we were close, just barely. It sent shivers up my spine every time.

"This is your last day sparring with Edan," he said. "You're going to work with Laila starting tomorrow. I think she'll help you improve."

I swallowed a surge of panic at the word *improve*. I knew I was one of the worst on the team—Dorsey and I seemed to be competing for that spot, actually. And it certainly didn't help that I looked like a graceless idiot when paired with Edan. Yesterday I'd thrown a punch, missed him by at least six inches, and then fallen flat on my face. It was so embarrassing that even Edan took pity on me and wiped the smug expression from his face for a few minutes.

"OK. I'm sorry, I—"

"Don't apologize." He put a hand on my arm and took a step closer to me. Warmth spread across my skin from his touch. "I know Edan is . . . challenging." His eyes drifted to the door, where Edan was on his way out.

"I guess it could be worse," I said. "I could be getting my ass kicked. He just avoids everything. He's like a fox."

Julian's face scrunched up in obvious distaste. I hadn't figured out how he and Edan knew each other in New York, but it didn't seem like their relationship was particularly friendly. They barely spoke to each other. Clearly it was only Grayson and Edan who had been friends.

Julian slowly let go of my arm, letting his fingers brush my skin as he stepped back. "Just one more day with Edan. He's fast, at least. That's good practice for you." His lips curved into a smile, and I tried not to stare at them. I failed. He noticed. Heat rose up my cheeks.

I attempted a smile before turning away. Madison passed by

me, one eyebrow raised. I'd never met someone who could convey so much hostility with just an eyebrow.

I quickly walked out of the gym and headed toward the stairs. The sounds of training were all around me—grunts from the room to my left, where the Senegalese teams were sparring, the Argentinian teams shouting orders outside the building, and I caught a few words in Spanish from one of the Spanish-speaking American teams leaving the cafeteria. The teams from Mexico followed them out. Luis, of Mexican team three, waved when he spotted me. He'd been friendly since he learned my mom was from Mexico. I waved back and opened the stairwell door.

I'd mostly avoided the Spanish-speaking American teams. And the Mexican teams. It was awkward to explain that, yes, I was Latina and my mom was from Mexico, but no, I didn't speak Spanish. I could understand a little if you spoke really slowly, which was just embarrassing. It made me feel like I didn't actually belong with them, like I wasn't supposed to claim that part of my identity if I didn't speak the language.

I climbed the stairs and walked into the sparring room to find Edan waiting, standing on the mat with two sets of gloves at his feet. He pushed a hand through his dark hair, giving me a glimpse of the tattoo on his left inner forearm—a tree. It was huge, taking up nearly the whole space from his wrist to his elbow, a mess of a twisted limbs and roots.

I thought that maybe it was rude to stare at someone's tattoos, so I'd only gotten brief glimpses of Edan's. I couldn't tell what was poking out from his right shirtsleeve, but I could read the words *way leads on to way* looping around his forearm. No idea what that meant.

He had a lot of tattoos for someone who was only eighteen. I suspected he must have started before he was legally allowed to get them. He didn't seem like much of a rule follower.

"Thanks," I said as he handed me a set of gloves. I stuck my hand inside one and tightened the strap around my wrist. "Can you try to block a few instead of just running away this time? And return some punches? I don't care if you hit me hard."

He scrunched up his face.

"What does that mean? Is that a no?"

"I just don't think that's helpful. You need to speed up, so you should keep trying to hit me. There's no point in me hitting back."

"You need to train too."

"Eh, I'm fine on sparring."

"I don't need you to coddle me."

"I'm not." He rolled his eyes, causing a burst of annoyance in my chest. I got the impression he liked being partnered with me as much as I enjoyed being partnered with him.

"Julian said we'll have new partners tomorrow," I said. "So you'll be with someone on your level soon."

"Why do we even have to keep sparring? We're fighting scrabs, not people. It's a whole different thing."

"The basic techniques are the same. And like you said, some of us need to get faster. We didn't all train by lifting wallets from unsuspecting people and then bolting."

"You're very secure in the knowledge that you're better than me, aren't you?" Edan asked.

"I don't think I'm better than you."

He pointed to my face, turning his finger in a circle. "Yes you do. You have a judgy look."

"I do not have a judgy look." I tried to plant my hands on my hips, forgetting that I was wearing boxing gloves, and succeeded in basically punching myself. Edan snorted. I flushed.

"Fine. But in my defense, most people would judge you for robbing Patrick. Or for robbing anyone, for that matter. You're a criminal. I mean, not a good one, but still a criminal."

He reeled back like he was actually insulted. "Rude."

"You're seriously mad that I called you a bad criminal?"

"I'll have you know that I am very skilled at lifting wallets. You wouldn't even notice if I took yours."

"I don't carry a wallet."

"Well, you should start."

"So you can rob me?"

"I'd give it back."

"Hard pass."

He rolled his eyes again, leaning his head back for extra emphasis.

"We should do this," I said, banging my gloves together. I pointed to his. "Put yours on."

"Can we not and say we did?"

"No."

"Why? Because if Julian finds out, you won't be his favorite anymore?"

Heat crawled up my neck. "I'm not his favorite. I'm, like, one of the worst ones on the team."

"God, you're a terrible liar. You're his favorite, and you know it. That's why you swing your ponytail back and forth every time he comes near you." He looked left to right in a quick, exaggerated motion. "Like this."

"I do not do that."

He kept swinging. "Hi, Julian."

"Would you—"

"Look at my ponytail, isn't it bouncy?"

"I have never—"

"What's that? You want to touch my ponytail? Oh sure, go ahead."

I snapped my mouth shut. Julian had touched my hair yesterday. It was at the beginning of training, after I'd almost fallen going over a hurdle. I'd caught myself before crashing to the ground, and Julian had asked if I was OK. He'd put his hand on my ponytail and then my neck, which was a strange and unexpected place for him to touch me. I'd barely been able to stammer out a *yes*. Just thinking about it again made my stomach flop around happily.

"See?" He looked smug. "You're his favorite."

"Can we just do this, please?"

"Fine." He reached for his gloves, and then stilled suddenly. "Did you hear that?"

"What?"

A scream saved him from having to answer. It was distant, maybe outside.

Edan and I bolted for the door. I threw it open and ran to the end of the hallway, where a window overlooked the front of the sports complex and the street.

Scrabs.

There were at least twenty of them, and several more burst up in the middle of the road. A car swerved and crashed into a traffic sign. People were running in every direction. The tables and chairs of a nearby café were scattered all over the sidewalk.

Dread uncoiled in my stomach. Video and pictures had never done them justice. They were so much more terrifying in the flesh, even from a distance.

They weren't huge—they weren't all that much bigger than a very muscular, very tall person—but they looked *solid*. Like you could hit them with a bulldozer and they'd barely blink. They actually had a lot of similarities to us—two eyes, one nose, two ears, a mouth, ten fingers and toes. A lot of conspiracy theorists were convinced that scrabs were some kind of science experiment gone wrong.

But that was where the similarities ended. Their skin had a grayish hue to it, some very light, others a darker shade, and even from this distance I could see how impenetrable it was. It was more like armor than skin. And they had long, sharp claws coming from every finger and toe.

Plus, they were so *fast*. I'd known, objectively, that they were, but I'd still sort of pictured them lumbering about, swinging wildly in every direction.

And some of them did look disoriented—one was repeatedly pounding a table into the ground, like it was super angry at that particular piece of furniture.

But most of them moved swiftly toward their targets— humans. Three of them even seemed to be working as a team, closing in together on a woman and tackling her to the ground. I swallowed hard.

"Look, the French teams," Edan said, pointing.

All the French teams were streaming out of the sports complex, armed with machetes and guns. A few Kenyan and American teams followed.

"Do . . . do we find a weapon?" I asked dumbly. My hands were shaking. Would I even be able to hold a weapon?

Edan's phone buzzed, and he pulled it out of his pocket. "No." He turned the screen so I could see. It was a text message from Julian.

TEAM SEVEN, STAY PUT. I MEAN IT. SEEK SHELTER.

"We're just supposed to watch?" I tried not to sound too relieved. The French teams were engaged in an all-out battle with the scrabs in the street. Gunfire echoed from below.

"I guess so."

Suddenly, a crash.

Then a roar.

Edan and I whirled around.

"Is that—"

"Oh shit," Edan said.

16

THUMP THUMP THUMP. THE SOUND WAS GETTING CLOSER. I EYED the stairwell door.

"Can they climb stairs?" My voice wobbled.

Edan grabbed my arm and pulled me back into the sparring room. He swiped at the door, but it didn't close all the way.

A scrab smashed through the stairwell door and was quickly followed by three more. They crashed down the hallway, galloping on all fours, moving almost in sync. Their claws clicked against the floor as they ran. One opened its mouth, revealing huge, sharp teeth.

The scrabs flew past the sparring room without spotting us. I took a tiny, silent step back.

"Are there real weapons in here?" Edan whispered, looking around. There was nothing but boxing gloves, punching bags, and some dull sparring blades. Those wouldn't cut human skin, much less a scrab's.

"No," I said. Were we actually going out to fight those things? Right. That's what we did. It was part of that whole *monster hunter* description.

"I think they're next door," I said, fighting down every impulse in my body that said *hide*. "I saw Grayson putting them back in the closet after he showed them to us."

Screams sounded from somewhere in the complex.

"We should try to get to them, right?" Edan said. "Julian told us to stay put, but I don't think he realized they would come in—" He abruptly stopped talking as another scream ripped through the building. It sounded like it was coming from below us, on the first floor.

"Yes," I said. Hiding wasn't an option. Half the teams were outside. The *good* teams. We had to help the other recruits.

I slowly pushed open the door again and peeked out. No scrabs. Just a trail of blood.

Edan and I stepped into the hallway. I walked as quietly as I could, jumping at a roar that sounded a little too close for comfort.

The door to the storage room creaked as I opened it. Edan sucked in a breath, his head snapping to where the scrabs had disappeared at the end of the hall. It was still empty.

The room was full of boxes, with at least a hundred spears in a clump against the wall. I grabbed two and handed one to Edan. The first box I opened was full of daggers, each of them in its own sheath. My pants didn't have pockets (thanks for nothing, women's clothing designers), so I tucked the handle into my waistband.

It didn't feel like nearly enough. There was supposed to be armor and formations and a plan. This wasn't supposed to happen, not yet.

Edan grabbed one of the daggers and slipped it into his pocket (showoff). He looked just as nervous as I was.

"Do we follow them?" I asked, pointing. I could hear human screams and scrab roars from that direction.

"I think we should."

We walked down the hallway, sidestepping the splatters of blood. I realized I didn't know if scrab blood was red. There was no way to tell if it was human blood or not.

We turned the corner.

A scrab flew through the air.

I gasped as it crashed into Edan. He yelled. The scrab pinned him to the wall with the claws of one arm. It smelled like dirt and blood and something sour.

I lifted the spear. Neck. Upward thrust. We'd practiced this yesterday, and Julian had said, *Good job*.

I drove the spear into the scrab's neck. My fingers brushed its tough, prickly skin, and I had to repress the urge to immediately snatch my hand away.

I tried to push the spear upward, but the scrab howled and spun around to face me, making me lose my grip on it. The scrab reached up and yanked the blade out of its neck. Blood poured from the wound. It *was* red.

The knife slipped easily out of my waistband, and I was surprised to find that my hands were only shaking a little.

A spear rammed straight through the back of its neck and out the other side, splattering blood across my shirt. Edan grimaced as he held tight to the end of the spear.

The scrab had the worst scream. It was more animal than human, the sort of sound that made your blood curdle because you knew something just died.

It staggered backwards and slumped to the floor. The spear cracked in half as it hit the ground. Edan scrambled closer to me.

"Thanks," I said breathlessly. I returned my knife to my waistband.

"Yeah, you too." Four holes were poked into the left shoulder of his shirt, where the scrab stuck its claws in. Blood dripped down his arm.

"On your left!" someone screamed nearby. A scrab roared.

I heard the click of claws on the floor before it rounded the corner. I reached for the spear protruding from the dead scrab's neck and yanked it as hard as I could, stumbling as it came loose.

Edan ducked the scrab's claw as it swiped at him, and then jabbed his knife into its side before skittering away. He was nimble and fast, just like in practice. Even more so now, like the adrenaline pushed him to be better.

The scrab yelped as Edan drove the blade in, but it wasn't a kill shot. He took advantage of the momentary distraction to deliver a kick straight into its stomach.

I jumped forward and plunged the spear into the scrab's neck. Upward thrust. Harder this time.

I must have hit its vocal cords, because only a squeak escaped its mouth. I tried to keep a grip on the spear, but it broke off inside the scrab's neck as it slumped to the ground. I tossed the broken handle to the ground.

"Oh shit, oh shit, oh shit!" Dorsey burst through the stairwell door, shoes slipping on the tile. He flailed and nearly fell, catching himself with one arm. He shot up and broke into a run, leaping over the dead scrab sprawled out on the floor. I suddenly understood why training included jumping over hurdles.

"I stabbed it, and it barely slowed down!" Dorsey yelled as he passed me.

The scrab flew around the corner, dripping blood from a wound on its side.

Dorsey skidded to a stop, looking from the spear in the scrab's throat and back to me. "Where did you get those weapons?"

I pointed. "Closet. That way." He took off.

I pulled my knife out of my pants. Edan stood next to me, bloody knife gripped in his hand.

"We should do that dive thing—what did Julian call it?" I asked. The scrab was running straight toward us, a little slower than the others had. The wound was slowing it down.

"Team dive," Edan said.

"Right. I'll dive."

He looked at me quickly. "You sure?"

"Yeah, I can take a hit."

He nodded once, either because he believed me or because there was no time to argue. The scrab had nearly reached us.

It ran for us, claws outstretched. I waited until the last possible moment before diving to the ground on all fours, then covering my head with my hands as I braced for impact.

The scrab crashed into me, its legs buckling as it lost its balance. It landed with a thump. I scrambled to my feet.

Edan drove his spear into the back of the scrab's neck. It thrashed, screamed, and then stilled.

"You all right?" Edan asked, watching as I rolled my shoulders. That would leave a bruise.

"I'm fine." I pointed to where blood was dripping down his arm. "You?"

"I can't feel it. I think it's the intense panic." He grinned. He must have been really good at hiding his panic.

Footsteps sounded behind us, and I turned to see Dorsey running toward us with four machetes, two gripped in each hand.

"Oh, you got it," he said breathlessly. He leaned against the wall, breathing heavily. "Damn. I barely outran that thing."

Edan pointed to where a piece of broken wood was sticking out of the Scrab's side. "Did you do that?"

"Yeah. Broke a chair leg. It was all I could find." He held up his machetes. "I brought one each for you guys."

"And two for you?" I took one.

"Hell yes, two for me. I'm not going anywhere without a weapon after this." He held his two blades up in front of his body. "You guys ready? It's bad down there."

"Wait, weren't you with Julian in the boxing room?" I asked. "Does no one have weapons down there?"

"No, I saw a bunch of people down there with weapons. But I left for a minute to refill my water bottle, so I wasn't with Julian when they came." He broke into a jog. "Come on."

Edan and I followed Dorsey to the end of the hallway and down the stairs. He skidded to a stop as he pushed open the door on the first floor. I stepped around him.

The lobby was covered in dead scrabs. I counted ten—no, twelve. There was a giant hole in the middle of the floor where they must have entered the building.

And Madison was walking through the dead bodies, bloody machete in hand, looking like she was ready to kill twelve more. She wiped the back of her arm across her forehead, smearing blood across it.

A scrab leapt out of the stairwell on the other side of the room, launching its body at Madison.

She swung the machete, hitting the scrab on its side. It screamed as she slid the blade out. She ducked as it swung at her, and then sliced the machete across its throat. It slumped to the ground.

"What the fuck is going on?" she yelled.

Noah emerged from the stairwell behind the scrab. He was breathing heavily and carried his own bloody machete.

"Did you get all of them?" Madison asked.

"Not even close," he panted. "Get ready." He pointed to us. "Move away from that door. I drove them to the other end of the hallway, and they're probably coming down now."

We scrambled away from the door. I whipped around to face it, machete poised to fight.

A scream sounded from my right. A recruit flew out of the small gym and smashed into the wall. Dani and Hunter flew around the corner. Dani had a machete, Hunter a gun.

"We're all going to die," Dorsey said.

"You are, at least," Madison said.

He shot her an incredulous, horrified look.

"Move back more, dumbass," she said. "You're so close to the door that they'll crush you as soon as they open it."

He still looked insulted, but he took several big steps back.

"If you die, I apologize for calling you a dumbass," Madison said.

"And if I don't die?"

"Then I meant it."

Noah actually laughed. My heart was beating too fast for laughter.

The stairwell door banged open.

They piled out, one after the other. I counted six before I had to stop counting because one was flying toward me.

"Duck, Clara!" Noah yelled from behind me.

I dropped into a squat. The scrab flew over my head.

I jumped to my feet. A scrab trailed out the door behind the rest, blood dripping from its neck. It opened its mouth and roared, giving me the best view yet of its teeth. I tried not to think about how it could easily rip off my arm if I got it between those teeth.

It swiped at me. I ducked. It took another try, and I grabbed its arm. Its flesh was prickly and just as hard as it looked, more like a shell than skin. I shoved it out of the way as I sliced the blade of the machete across its neck. It stumbled backward, hitting the door and crumpling to the ground.

I quickly turned to find the rest of the team midfight. Dorsey screamed as he tried to stab a scrab with both machetes at once. Hunter shot off a round at it. Madison kicked a scrab in the chest.

Noah was pinned to the ground, and I jumped forward, aiming my blade for the scrab's side. I drove it in. It screamed, and Noah kicked it off and scrambled to his feet. He was completely covered in blood, and from the look of it, none of it was his.

"Oh, that's gross," he said, wrinkling his nose as he pulled his shirt away from his body. He grinned at me. "Thanks. You're not bad with that thing." He gestured at the machete I was holding.

"She's pretty good with a spear too," Edan said as he stepped away from the scrab he'd just killed. They were all dead. Dorsey slumped against the wall and let out a string of curse words.

I looked down at the blood on my machete. A cheer rose up from the back of the building.

"I think we got them all," Noah said. His gaze snagged on something behind me. Julian and Grayson were running toward the front doors, recruits trailing after them.

Dani's handcuffs rattled as she shook blood off her blade. "Hey, did you guys see—"

A scrab burst up from the ground and pieces of concrete went flying. Dani's eyes widened as she stumbled backward.

Its claws were in her chest. The machete slipped from her hand.

I gasped and shot forward as the scrab pulled its claws from Dani's body. Blood stained her shirt.

The scrab whirled away from me, and I reached for Dani. She swayed out of my reach. Out of the corner of my eye, I saw Hunter raise his gun. Shots rang out.

"Hunter, no!" Madison yelled.

Dani crumpled to the ground. The scrab jerked as bullets pelted its thick hide.

Something sharp hit my arm, and I yelped. It left a trail of fire on my skin. I blinked, my grip on my machete slipping.

The scrab lunged at me.

17

NOAH MOVED SO QUICKLY THAT I DIDN'T REALIZE HE WAS IN front of me until I saw his machete in the scrab's neck. It made a choking sound before it hit the ground.

I blinked as I took an unsteady step backward. Blood dripped down my arm, and I wasn't sure why. Had the scrab scratched me?

Grayson shot across the lobby and skidded to a stop in front of me. "Where did it go in? Is she the only one hit?"

Madison surveyed the team. "I think so."

Grayson carefully pushed up my shirtsleeve. Blood dripped from a gash.

"Is that a *bullet wound*?" I asked incredulously.

"It's just a scratch," Grayson said with a sigh. "Jesus, that's lucky." His gaze drifted to the ground, the relief on his face disappearing.

Dani. Her head was turned away from me, blood seeping out of the holes the claws had made in her chest. She was dead.

I gasped and looked away. I swayed on my feet, and Grayson quickly grabbed my arms to steady me.

Panic crawled up my stomach. Grayson's hands tightened around my arms, like he could tell. I took a shaky breath and squeezed my eyes shut like that would block out the image of the dead body now seared into my brain.

"What the hell is wrong with you?" Julian yelled. My eyes

popped open. Julian yanked the gun from Hunter's grasp. "You're not cleared for guns!"

"Yeah, but it was an emergency, and—"

"You just shot one of your teammates!" Julian pointed at me. "You could have killed her!"

"I didn't mean to! She should have stayed out of the way if she didn't—"

"Get your shit and get out," Julian spat. "You're off my team."

"What?" Hunter's face went red. "You can't do that. I was just trying to—"

"I don't care what you were trying to do. Get. Out." Julian said the last two words through clenched teeth.

"Edan, are you injured too?" Grayson asked quietly. My breathing was ragged, and he still had one hand on my elbow. My other arm was starting to burn where the bullet had hit.

Edan had one finger hooked into the neck of his shirt, peering at his shoulder. "Yeah. I don't think it's too bad, though. One got me with its claws."

"Come on. You're both going to medical." Grayson gently steered me away from the lobby.

We passed more dead scrabs on the way to medical in the back of the building—in the hallway, in the doorway to the cafeteria, a piece of one outside a restroom. The door to the small gym was open, revealing several members of team five standing amongst a bloody mess.

Medical was a midsized room that had been converted into a doctor's office. There were ten cots lined up, half of them with privacy curtains. Various supplies in plastic containers were open and spread out everywhere. Dr. Walsh, a volunteer from Kansas, shook his head at two recruits standing in front of me. One was bleeding from a wound on his head.

"No, he needs to go to the hospital. All head injuries go to the hospital. Take him to the front, there's a van leaving soon."

The recruits turned and brushed past us.

"Dave, I think these two just need stitches. Can you take a look?" Grayson asked.

"Yes, sit." Dr. Walsh gestured at the cots.

I sank onto one. Edan took the one next to me.

"Make yourself useful." Dr. Walsh thrust a bottle into Grayson's hands. "Clean his injury while I do hers."

More recruits streamed into the room as Dr. Walsh began cleaning my arm. I blinked at them, the noisy chatter making my head spin. All I could think about was the pool of blood around Dani's body.

We were on day three of training, and we'd already lost a team member.

"I'll be right back to do your sutures," Dr. Walsh said. "I need to examine this guy real quick. OK?" He gestured at a man cradling his arm against his chest. I nodded.

"Clara?"

I looked up to see Julian pushing his way through the crowd. He rushed forward and knelt in front of me. "Are you all right?"

"I'm—I'm fine," I stuttered, startled by the open affection in his expression. I could still see his face when he was yelling at Hunter. So full of anger I thought he'd burst.

He leaned closer to inspect my wound. "I thought you and

Edan might have locked yourselves up in the sparring room," he said. "I wouldn't have blamed you."

"We didn't sign up to hide," I said, with far more confidence than I actually felt. But saying the words out loud almost made them feel true. I took a slow breath, my heartbeat slowing a little.

A smile broke across his face. "No. You certainly didn't. But I'm sorry. I should have been there. It didn't occur to us that you guys wouldn't be safe in the building. We didn't even realize what was happening in here until we'd killed all the scrabs outside."

"I think there were more outside, anyway," I said. "They needed you out there."

"I know, I just wish I'd been here. For the whole team," he quickly added. "We had plans for how to introduce you guys to battle. It wasn't supposed to be like this, on your own, scrambling for weapons." He paused, and his next words were a little softer. "But I would have liked to be there for you."

My face warmed. "You'll be happy to hear that I did a pretty good job by myself. So did Edan."

"I am happy to hear it." He glanced at Edan. He was sitting alone on the cot, Grayson nowhere to be seen. Julian grabbed the curtain and pulled it closed, shielding us from view. He took a seat next to me, so close that our shoulders pressed together.

"Hunter's gone. He's packing his bags now."

"It was an accident," I said. I wasn't sure why I was defending Hunter. Maybe because it was the truth.

"An accident that could have been prevented if he'd followed the rules. We only assign guns to certain recruits for this exact reason. I should have been there," he said again, and I wondered if part of his anger at Hunter was because Julian was mad at himself too.

With Hunter gone and Dani dead, team seven was down two members. We were eleven now. I shuddered.

"You don't have to stay with me," I said. "I know you probably have a lot of things to take care of."

He opened his mouth and then closed it. It took him a moment to find the words.

"Do you want me to go?" he asked quietly.

Before I could answer, he took my hand, lacing our fingers together. The pain in my arm completely faded. All I could feel was his warm hand in mine, the gentle way he brushed his thumb across my skin.

"No," I said, my voice barely a whisper.

He leaned in closer to me. "There's this rule," he said softly. "About us dating our team members."

"I know." My heart thumped frantically as he tightened his fingers around mine. His other hand landed softly on my jaw.

"But I was never very good at following rules." He was even closer now, eyebrows lifted just slightly like he was asking a question.

The smile that I couldn't stop was clearly my answer, and his own lips turned up before he pressed them to mine. It was a slow kiss, almost careful, like he wanted to memorize every second of it. I leaned closer when his lips barely left mine. Our second kiss was far less careful. It left me breathless, the noise around me fading away.

When he pulled away, we were both smiling.

18

THE FINAL DEATH TOLL FOR THE DAY WAS SIX—THREE FROM American teams, two from French teams, and one from a Canadian team. Three more recruits decided to leave after the dust settled.

The reality of actually fighting scrabs must have been too much.

Grayson gave us all a pep talk after they left, claiming that we all did an amazing job and he was proud of us.

The media saw things differently. Most of the headlines were something along the lines of ST. JOHN'S RECRUITS ATTACKED AT THEIR OWN FACILITY, CASUALTIES REPORTED. CIVILIANS ALSO INJURED OR KILLED.

It did not make us look great. Granted, we'd only had three days of training, but no one seemed to care about that.

It was evening, hours after the scrab attack. My arm was stitched up and bandaged. We'd spent the afternoon helping the French authorities load the dead scrabs into trucks for disposal and trying to clean up the complex a bit. Now I sat on my cot, watching as Priya carefully folded Dani's clothes and tucked them into her suitcase. Grayson had asked us to pack up everything to send back to her parents.

I imagined my mom receiving my backpack in the mail. She'd

probably hide it from Dad so it wouldn't set him off. Even in death, I would be the cause of his rage.

I took in a shaky breath. I hadn't known Dani that well, but the room felt empty now. I couldn't stop thinking about how she smiled when she talked about her handcuffs.

Priya zipped up the suitcase and dragged it into the hall-way. When she returned, Julian was behind her. He lingered in the doorway, a small smile crossing his lips when our eyes met.

"You can all have the rest of the night off," he said, addressing everyone in the room. "I just told the guys. The team leaders are meeting with the French police tonight, and I'm not going to make you train this evening after everything. Get some rest." He took a step back. "Clara, can I have a moment?"

"Sure." I got to my feet and followed him out of the room.

The door closed behind me and he turned. His expression mirrored mine: a mix of hope, sadness, embarrassment, and exhaustion.

"Um, so—" he began, and then abruptly stopped as a door banged open at the end of the hall. He looked left, then right. "Let's . . ." His voice trailed off as he walked to a door a few steps down and pulled it open. It was a closet, empty except for an ancient broom propped up against one wall. He jerked his head, indicating for me to follow him inside.

I did, and he began to close the door, but it was suddenly very dark. His laugh was a huff of embarrassment as he pushed it open a crack, letting light back in.

"Sorry," he said. "There aren't a lot of places to be alone here."

"Are we . . ." I didn't finish the sentence. I wanted to say, *Are we a secret?* but I didn't know if we were a *we.*

"What?" he asked quietly. His fingers touched my arm and made a slow path down to my hand.

"Is this a secret?" I asked. My voice sounded funny. I couldn't form words properly with him doing that to my arm.

"I thought it might be weird for you, with the rest of the team," he said. "Honestly I think Grayson's rule is stupid. We're both fully capable of making our own choices. But I understand if you don't want the team to think I'm favoring you."

That was a good point. Plus, there was Madison to think of. We were team members, and flaunting my relationship with Julian would probably make her hate me.

"Maybe it is best if we don't say anything right away," I said, and then felt stupid. We'd kissed *once* and I was already planning a long-term relationship. "I mean, assuming you wanted to . . . if we were going to . . ." I trailed off, my cheeks hot.

Julian grinned, his arms circling my waist. He pressed his lips to mine.

"You're cute when you're nervous," he said when he pulled away, and then kissed me again.

I wrapped my arms around his neck, letting my fingers weave into his hair. He kissed like someone who'd had a lot of practice, and I did not mean that as a criticism.

A soft buzzing noise sounded from his pocket, and he sighed as he pulled away.

"I have to go," he said. "Grayson's waiting for me."

I nodded, my body still humming from his kiss.

He reached for the door, then seemed to change his mind. He wrapped his arms around me again, pulling me into a hug.

He briefly pressed his lips to mine again as he pulled away, then pushed open the door. He peered down the hallway before stepping out of the closet. I followed, shutting the door behind us.

"I'll see you later," he said, and looked over his shoulder once as he walked away. I bit my lip to keep from grinning like an idiot.

When I returned to my room, Priya was standing near her cot, observing the other girls. Zoe was glued to her phone. Madison was staring into space, twisting her hair around her finger. Laila was on her stomach on the floor, sketching something in a notebook. My smile faded as my gaze drifted to Dani's empty cot.

"Let's get out of here," Priya said.

Madison snapped to attention. "What?"

"Let's get out of here. We haven't even had a chance to see Paris. Let's go see the Eiffel Tower before we die. Julian said we could do whatever we wanted tonight. Clara, are you up for it?" She gestured to my bandages.

"Yeah, it's no big deal. Just a scratch."

Laila looked up from her notebook, one eyebrow cocked. "Getting shot is no big deal?"

"I mean, it just grazed me. Does that count as getting shot?"

"I think you can count it."

"Laila, grab those beers we bought," Priya said. "Clara, get dressed. You can tell people you got shot and saw the Eiffel Tower for the first time all in the same day."

"Usually you need to be in America to see major historical landmarks *and* get shot in the same day," Zoe said.

I shed my sweats and pulled on jeans and a T-shirt. I zipped a hoodie over it and followed the other girls out into the hallway. We walked to the end of the hallway, where the boys of team seven were staying. It was a bigger room, with at least twenty cots. Clothes and food wrappers littered the floor. It did not smell great.

Three guys in the middle of the room laughed loudly, and in the far corner, an angry dude yelled into his phone. Noah and Patrick were hunched over a laptop on the floor, and Gage stomped around the room, lifting up suitcases and peering underneath blankets. Edan was on his cot reading, apparently oblivious to the madness around him.

"Where's the rest of team seven?" Priya asked from the doorway. None of us stepped inside. A shirtless bearded man regarded us and scratched his stomach.

"Dammit, Edan!" Gage yelled, grabbing something from beneath a pile of clothes. His phone was clenched in his hand as he whirled around. "Stop stealing my shit!"

"I have no idea what you're referring to, Gage." Edan calmly turned the page of his book and peered around it at Priya. "They're in the lounge, I think."

"Get them. We're all going to the Eiffel Tower. Meet us downstairs in five minutes. Bring snacks and alcohol if you want." She walked away without waiting for an answer. Edan hopped up, leaving his book on his cot.

I followed the other girls to the lobby. Priya and Laila talked softly to each other, and Madison showed Zoe something on her phone. I was alone, a few steps behind them. It didn't feel quite so bad, now that I maybe had Julian.

Still, it didn't feel great. I slid my hands into my pockets and tried to look like I enjoyed being left out.

The boys appeared in the lobby a few minutes later. Besides Edan, Dorsey and Archer had suffered minor injuries — Dorsey had shallow scratches on his arm and Archer had a bandage on his ear. Gage and Patrick were unharmed. Patrick still seemed a little terrified.

"Do we actually know how to get to the Eiffel Tower?" Patrick asked, gripping the straps of his backpack.

"Yeah, we can take the metro," Madison said. "I grabbed some passes from Grayson." She handed one to each of us, then led us outside and across the street to the subway stop.

We took the subway to a second station, where we had to change lines. People stared at us as we piled onto the second train. We must have seemed suspicious, eleven American teenagers traveling together. Maybe they could tell we were part of Grayson's squads.

I stood next to Madison on the second train, watching as Edan looked from her to a man wearing a black cap a few feet away. Edan reached out, pushing Madison's purse so it was in front of her body. Madison frowned at him.

"Pickpocket," Edan explained, jerking his head at the guy.

"Oh. Thanks." She put a hand over her bag.

Madison squinted at the man, who had turned away from us. "How can you tell?"

"Just a guess," Edan replied. He caught me watching him and quickly looked away. The guy probably reminded him of himself.

At our stop, I followed the rest of the team out of the train, up the stairs, and onto the street. It was a clear, cool night, a light breeze ruffling my hair. We were in a touristy part of Paris, the streets full of people taking pictures and carrying bags of souvenirs. I'd heard that tourism in Paris was way down, but it looked like plenty of people still came. Most of Europe had a scrab problem, so maybe a trip to Paris didn't faze most people from this continent.

The Eiffel Tower came into sight as we walked. People were sprawled out on the lawn in front of it, some with picnic baskets or bottles of wine. There was a hole in the middle of the lawn, blocked off with cones.

We sat down on the ground, and Laila and Patrick pulled beers out of their bags and distributed them.

"No thanks," I said when Laila held one out to me. I'd never tried alcohol. There had never been a moment in my life where I would have felt comfortable being a little fuzzy. I needed to be sharp, and ready to defend myself, always. Now was no different.

Edan also declined a beer. So did Dorsey and Gage, but they were sharing something from a bottle.

Laila grabbed a beer for herself and moved the bag so it was behind her. It was a canvas tote covered in hand-painted flowers.

"I like your bag," I said. "Did you paint it yourself?"

"Oh, yeah." She glanced back at it. "I was just messing around one day."

"That's just messing around?" Archer asked, eyeing the elaborate flowers, the bright colors and the butterfly near one of the handles.

"Laila's an artist," Noah said. "I linked to some of her shops in my last video. Someone clearly wasn't watching."

Archer ducked his head sheepishly. I also hadn't seen it, but maybe I got a pass as the only member of the team without a phone.

"It's just some totes and prints and stuff." Laila smiled as she played with the top of her beer can.

"You all right?" Zoe asked Edan. He was gingerly touching the bandage poking out of the neck of his shirt.

"Yeah, it's fine." He lowered his hand.

"It didn't mess up one of your tattoos, did it?" Priya asked.

"No, I'm just as beautiful as usual, thank you for asking."

"Look how many views you got on that last video," Madison said, tilting her phone so Noah could see.

His face went red. "I know."

"He was refreshing it, like, every five seconds before we left," Patrick said.

"Did you post a new video?" Dorsey asked. He pulled his own phone out and then sighed, returning it to his pocket. "I keep forgetting I don't have service here."

"Yeah, there's a new video," Noah said.

"It's really good," Madison said. "He got some footage of the dead scrabs and some recruits after fighting and cut it all together."

"I try." Noah tried to sound nonchalant, but his cheeks turned even redder. He avoided Madison's gaze. "I'm thinking of getting a small camera that attaches to my uniform, so I can get footage of us fighting when we get out there. I just need to find a little body camera."

"You can put it on your list," Madison said.

"What list?" Noah asked.

"Grayson's going to put recruit wish lists online next week. A lot of people have asked how they can help, and he knows that sometimes people don't like just sending money, because they don't know where it's going. So he's going to do wish lists, where people can buy what we want, and send it to us with a note."

"Oh, that's nice," Zoe said.

"Thank god," Gage said, talking around the cigarette he was lighting. "I'm running low on cigarettes."

"You will not be allowed to ask for alcohol or tobacco," Madison said.

"What is even the point, then?" Gage blew smoke up into the sky.

I watched the smoke disappear, considering what I wanted. A phone, though that seemed like too much to ask for.

"Did Grayson already contact Dani's family?" Laila asked quietly.

"Yes," Madison said, reaching for her beer.

We were quiet for a moment. I'd barely known Dani—all of us barely knew her—but my throat closed up anyway. Who would be next? Julian? Patrick? Me?

"No one's thinking of quitting, are they?" Madison asked, peering at us. Her eyes stopped on Zoe.

"Fuck no, I'm not quitting," Gage said. "I've barely seen any action."

It took Zoe a moment to realize Madison was looking at her. "What? Me? Why would I quit?"

"I was just asking. I heard you complaining that Julian left us alone in the complex."

Zoe flushed. "Well, he should have stayed with his team. The other team leaders did."

"I wasn't arguing," Madison said.

"I'm not quitting." Zoe drew her knees up to her chest, throwing an arm across them. "It's not like I . . ." Her usual annoyed mask fell away as she searched for the words. "I don't have anywhere to go if I quit. Most of us can't even afford the plane ticket home." She glanced at Madison, because we all knew she could take a private jet back to the US if she wanted. "But even if I could get home, my parents just got a divorce. My dad moved in with his slut girlfriend—"

I winced inwardly at the word *slut*, especially the way it came out of her mouth. It was a dagger, one she had used many times.

"And she hates me," Zoe continued. I could sort of guess why. "And my mom and my little sister moved into this tiny apartment with my grandma, who, I'm sorry, is the total worst."

Dorsey barked out a laugh. "Your grandma is the worst?"

"Yes. People are always talking about their grandmas like they're out there making cookies and knitting or whatever, but my grandma is super mean."

"My grandma does not knit," Laila said.

"Mine does," Dorsey said.

"My grandma yells at people," Zoe said. "Me, specifically. So, no, I'm not quitting." Her last sentence was directed at Madison and had a bit of an edge to it. Madison held both her hands up in surrender.

"Noah, what are you doing?" Laila asked with a laugh. I looked at Noah to see his head tilted way back, his mouth open as he stared intensely at the black sky.

"The abyss is staring back," he whispered.

"What?" Zoe asked.

"The abyss. I'm staring at it, and it's staring back."

"What is he talking about?" Dorsey grabbed the can in front of Noah. "You didn't even drink half of this yet. You're a lightweight, dude."

"It's Nietzsche," Laila said. "What's that quote . . . ?"

"It's something like, he who fights monsters should make sure he doesn't become a monster himself," Madison said. "And if you stare long enough into the abyss, the abyss stares back."

"Yes," Noah said, pointing in Madison and Laila's direction without looking away from the sky. "They know." He leaned back so far that he lost his balance and ended up on the ground.

"You can't become a scrab," Dorsey said. "They're not zombies."

"He didn't mean literally," Laila said. "Nietzsche died, like, a hundred years before actual monsters showed up."

"Well, I clearly slept through that day at school," Dorsey said, taking a swig of beer.

I lifted a shoulder, because I must have too. Neither the quote nor the name sounded at all familiar. Dorsey noticed and gave me a crooked smile.

"I think you slept through most days at school," Gage said. Dorsey punched his shoulder.

Madison flopped down on her back next to Noah. "How do I get the abyss to stare back?"

"I don't know. It just happens." Noah swept his arm at the sky dramatically.

Priya lay down on her back, and then Edan, then me, and soon we were all on our backs, except for Dorsey and Gage, who were apparently too cool.

There weren't any stars visible, since we were in the middle of the city. Maybe that was what Noah meant by *abyss*. It was mostly just hazy blackness.

I put a hand behind my head. My left arm burned a little as I moved, and I shifted it away from the ground.

"What is that expression?" I heard Priya ask.

"I'm just really happy that I'm not at home right now," Archer said softly.

"Seriously," Dorsey agreed.

I smiled.

19

ON DAY SIX OF TRAINING WE HAD WHAT GRAYSON CALLED "AN informational session." Julian called it a "shit's getting real session."

"If you're going to quit, it'll probably be after this session," he said, hands on his hips as he peered down at us. We were in the small gym, where we started every day.

"I mean, we already fought scrabs," Edan said. "I think if we were going to quit, it would have been two days ago."

Julian shot Edan an annoyed look. Edan sort of had a point, though. I didn't think that Grayson telling us how scary scrabs were was going to be worse than watching one kill Dani.

"Please give Grayson your full attention in the session," Julian said. "People already don't take you seriously because you're the teenage team. Don't give them more ammo."

People didn't take us seriously? Beside me, Laila seemed startled as well. Dorsey and Gage exchanged a look.

I stole a glance at Julian. He still seemed annoyed. He wasn't great at showing his sweet side to the rest of the team. I felt like I knew a completely different person sometimes.

"All right, go," Julian said. "Be ready to do the obstacle course right after."

Julian's gaze lingered on me, and I waited as the rest of the team filed out of the gym. The door banged shut, leaving us alone.

"Everything OK?" I asked.

"Yeah." He tugged at his lower lip. "I was too harsh with them, wasn't I? I keep worrying that if I'm not tough, they'll just totally ignore me, because I'm barely older than you guys. And if they ignore me, they could end up dead."

"No, that totally makes sense," I said. "Better for them to think you're the bad guy than to get eaten, right?"

"Yes." He looked relieved. "I've become my father." He let out a short laugh.

"How so?"

"He was always saying the same thing to me, that he wasn't my friend and he was tough for my own good. I get it now. Don't tell him I said that," he added with a smile.

"My lips are sealed." I wondered if he thought I might actually meet his father one day. The idea made a thrill of excitement race up my spine. We'd just started . . . whatever we were doing (dating? hanging out? kissing?), but I liked the idea that he thought we might be more one day.

"You should go. I don't want to make you late." He tugged on the edge of my shirt, pulling me closer so he could press his lips to mine. I smiled at him when we pulled apart, then turned to walk out of the gym and down the hallway.

Mexican team three was leaving the big gym, and Luis stopped when he spotted me.

"Um, you . . ." He paused for a second while he searched for the English words. He gestured to my arm. "You were shot?"

I was famous for getting shot. Lovely. "I was. But it's fine. Just a scratch. No es gran cosa."

He smiled, giving me a thumbs-up before jogging to catch up with his team. I headed into the small gym. Several teams were already there, sitting on the ground facing the back wall. A laptop and projector had been set up behind them.

American teams one and two (the all-male teams made up of a bunch of beefy dudes) were at the front, talking and laughing. The one with shoulder-length blond hair peered over his shoulder at me. We'd met yesterday, when he'd randomly introduced himself in the cafeteria. Jeff. He was at least thirty.

His eyes lingered, a smile spreading across his face. I looked away.

"Creeper," Zoe muttered under her breath as she sat down next to me.

"You met him too?"

"I sure did. If you ever see me talking to him, please come rescue me immediately."

"Same."

"Deal."

More teams filled in the area around us. Madison scooted over to one of the Canadian teams as they sat down. They all greeted her like they'd already met.

I glanced around at my own team. I felt like I'd barely gotten to know them, much less buddied up to other teams.

"All right, guys, let's get started." Grayson strode across the gym. The American team one leader, Jayden, took a seat at the projector. Everyone around me quieted immediately.

"I know that most of you have already seen scrabs up close and personal, so some of this may be redundant, but we want to make sure you have a full picture of what we're dealing with," Grayson said. "Plus I know that there is a ton of information on the internet about these things, so I just want to separate fact from fiction for you guys.

"But before we start, a quick reminder—it's against UN rules to keep or transport *any* part of a scrab. That includes teeth, eyes, and blood. Scientists are still studying these things, and they've regulated the transport of samples for a reason." He fixed us with a hard stare. "I've heard that some recruits took trophies from their kills, and I can't have that. The French police will be here later to collect anything you may have . . . forgotten. You can drop it off, no questions asked. Got it? Good."

He gestured at Jayden, and a photo of a scrab appeared on the wall behind him. It was standing in the middle of a street, an overturned trashcan at its feet. It had spikes on its back and small horns that protruded from either side of its head.

"A team leader in Beijing took this photo," Grayson said. "This is what a lot of the scrabs in Asia look like. They have spikes on the plates of the back. The entire back is basically impenetrable."

The image changed to a more familiar scrab. Grayish skin, fangs, incredibly long claws. It was dead, half its body in a hole in the ground. Killed while it tried to come up.

"You know this one," Grayson said. "This is what you'll usually see in Europe, basically until you get to Russia, where you'll see a mix of these and the Asian scrabs. As far as we know, anyway. We can't get accurate information out of Russia, and we don't have any teams there." The image changed again. Another scrab, with spikes, though they were much smaller. More like little knobs.

"This was taken near Moscow in 2013. So they could look like that in Russia. But it's unlikely that Russia will open its borders anytime soon, so that's just for your information."

The image changed back to a familiar scrab. A *very* familiar scrab.

"Oh shit," Priya breathed behind me.

It was the one that had killed Dani. It was sprawled out on its side on the concrete floor of the lobby, soft underbelly exposed.

Grayson walked closer to the wall and pointed to the scrab's back. "Some people call these areas of scrabs *skin*, but they're technically plates. See how these big squares all connect together? And these smaller clusters around its neck and down its side? Those are basically the scrab's armor. Most of them are bullet-proof, or very close to it." He pointed to a dent in the plate on the scrab's neck. "See this? That's where a recruit's bullet ricocheted off the plate and hit another recruit."

Several people turned to look at me.

"There's a reason you have to be cleared to use guns," Grayson said. "Wildly shooting at a scrab will only result in human casualties. You only take the shot if you have a very clear line to its soft areas." He pointed to the neck and underbelly. "We use blades like machetes because they're safer for nearby civilians, and you can pierce the plates with a very sharp blade in some spots. The plates on the head often aren't as tough, but not always. I personally like to stick them in the neck, underneath the chin. There usually aren't any plates there, and if there are, they're softer. This all goes for baby scrabs, too. Don't be fooled by the small size of newly born scrabs. They have all the same plates, and they are not like other baby animals. They will rip your face off if given half the chance."

A new photo popped up. Beside me, Zoe jumped. The scrab in the image was in a tunnel, its mouth open wide to reveal every fang.

"So you've seen how the scrabs come up from the ground," Grayson said. "They construct elaborate networks of tunnels at truly amazing speeds, given their size. They work together to do this. I know you guys have probably heard that most of the tunnels in the US were discovered and filled in, but I assure you that is a lie. They construct backup tunnels. They construct backups for their backups. There is no way that our military already found *all* of them. I'm hopeful that the scrabs are nearly gone in the US, but if they're not, they will still have plenty of ways to get around. We should be prepared."

I thought of Mrs. Gonzalez, sitting on her porch every day with her gun. She was certainly prepared, though considering what Grayson had just told us, she was more likely to accidentally shoot herself or a neighbor than a scrab.

"We use drones to monitor scrab activity in several countries, including this one," Grayson said. They capture scrabs above-ground, and we have some equipment that tracks their movements underground too. All the data goes into a program that analyzes their movements and tells us where they will appear next. It's similar to what the US government uses to monitor terrorists. Ours is more advanced, though, if you want to know the truth." He looked proud. "And it's pretty accurate. So understand that when you're assigned to a hot spot, there is a very good chance you will see action. The military tries to cut them off before they get to populated areas, but they can't track them all. The ones that attacked us here slipped through unnoticed, and we'll need to be there when that happens again."

A hand in front shot up.

"Yeah, Mike," Grayson said.

"MDG has been saying that their equipment is better than yours. Is that true?"

"No," Grayson said, without hesitation. "They also have ways of monitoring scrab movement, but ours is much better."

"Did you ever consider partnering with them?" Mike asked.

"We did. They turned us down. They have no interest in fighting scrabs outside the US, except while protecting their wealthy clients."

Another hand shot up. "What do you think about the consumer-grade scrab sensors? Like the Apple Watch? Are they any good?"

"Eh, they're fine," he said. "The Apple Watch detects scrabs about fifty percent of the time, which is better than nothing. Feel free to use one if you want, but we'll always be relying on my tech first."

The image behind Grayson changed again. It was a city grid, yellow lines like a bus map squiggled all over it.

"This is Paris," Grayson said. "The yellow lines are the scrab tunnels we know about, or suspect to be there. They are often dug out again as soon as workers can fill them in. Pay attention to the signs announcing subway closures when you're out and about. The scrabs will often use the existing tunnels, which, I'm sure you can imagine, causes some problems. Also, be cautious of any red signs you see in front of buildings—it means that a scrab dug a tunnel underneath it and they're still checking structural integrity." The image changed again, the yellow lines at least doubled, so thick in places they all seemed to run together.

"This is London," Grayson said.

"Damn," Noah breathed.

"Some of you will go to London after training," Grayson said. "If we think you're ready. As you can see, London is no joke."

"I hope we go," Noah whispered.

Priya craned her neck to give him a truly baffled look. "Do you see that map? I want to stay here. Where there are fewer scrabs. And lots of croissants."

"The croissants are good," Noah conceded. "But London! They have . . . What do they have in London?"

"Death," Edan said. He had one elbow propped up on his knee, his chin cupped in his hand. "And fish and chips."

"And rain," Laila added.

"Death, rain, and fish," Noah said with a grin. "I'm in."

20

Two weeks of training went by quickly, and without another attack in our area. We spent twelve-hour days sparring, mastering weapon techniques, and doing physical conditioning, but I still wasn't sure I was ready to go *looking* for scrabs to fight.

Julian disagreed. He said we were ready. We were joining some teams today in hot spots. Part of me hoped that Grayson's software wasn't as "scarily accurate" as he claimed it to be.

I put my arms through my new sports bra and tugged it down. We'd been given uniforms, and they included a plain black sports bra for the women.

I pulled down harder on the bra. It didn't help. I had a serious underboob problem.

"Is it just me, or are my boobs trying to escape?"

Priya bounded across the room, clapping a hand over her mouth when she caught sight of my chest. She giggled. "They're totally trying to escape."

Zoe stood up from her cot, completely dressed. She'd easily slipped on the sports bra a few minutes ago.

Our uniform consisted of black cargo pants, an optional light-weight black jacket, and a gray T-shirt with a small emblem on the left side. It was the St. John Technologies logo—an interlocking *S* and *J* that looked a little like a broken infinity symbol.

"OK, I have to ask," Zoe said. "Are those things real?"

"You think I would do this to myself on purpose?" I exclaimed.

"I mean, they're really nice, so yes," Priya said. "But I assumed they were real. They suit your body type."

"They don't suit this sports bra, that's for sure."

"Do you want me to go grab you a bigger size?" Priya asked.

"This was the biggest one they had."

The door opened, and Madison stepped inside, her eyes flicking to me and then to my boobs. "This is why men shouldn't be in charge of ordering bras."

"Did Grayson do this to me?" I asked.

"He sure did." She tugged the neck of her shirt aside, showing the strap of a pink sports bra that definitely wasn't part of our uniform. "Just wear your own. They don't fit my boobs right either."

"Why do they care what bra we wear anyway?" Priya asked.

"Grayson was trying to be helpful, believe it or not. He thought that if the women on the teams *had* to wear a bra to fight, he should issue them one."

"I mean, that's nice, but . . ." I gestured to my breasts.

"Yeah," Madison said dryly. "He ordered them before I had a chance to give some input. At least I caught him before he ordered tampons. You should have seen the horrible generic ones he chose."

I pulled off the too-small bra and put on my own. At least the rest of the uniform fit well.

Zoe opened our door to reveal Patrick, hand poised to knock.

"Good timing," he said, lowering his hand. "Are you guys ready? I'm supposed to deliver the message that the Australian teams have arrived."

"Are we supposed to go say hi to the Australian teams or something?" Priya asked.

"You should at least go take a look at them," Patrick said. A smile twitched at his lips. "Trust me."

Priya and Zoe giggled and quickly scurried out of the room. I stepped into the hall with Patrick.

"Lots of good-looking guys on the Australian teams?" I asked.

"Oh yes. And women. Most of the guys on team seven are already down there." He raised an eyebrow at me as we walked to the stairwell. "No interest?"

"I'll say hi later." I tried to keep my voice casual. Julian and I might have only stolen a few moments together the past couple weeks, but we were definitely . . . something. Something that made it weird to go gawk at hot Australians.

We walked into the big gym to find only Edan with Julian. They both sat on the floor, a bit apart from each other, not speaking.

Julian's face lit up when he spotted me. "Hey. The uniforms look great. Is the rest of the team dressed?"

"Yes, but there are Australians," Patrick said. He glanced down at his phone. We still had ten minutes until we had to report.

"Right," Julian said. "Clara, do you want to come with me to get weapons together?"

"Sure."

"Patrick, Edan, you guys stay here until the whole team arrives, then bring them to the weapons room. And make sure everyone has a metro pass. From here on out, you should never be anywhere without your metro passes and weapons."

Patrick nodded. Edan didn't look up from his phone.

I followed Julian out of the gym, and we walked down the hallway and turned a corner. Julian came to an abrupt stop, glancing around like he was checking we were alone. "I have something for you." He reached into his pocket and pulled out a phone.

I peered at the screen, but it was dark. "What?"

"It's a phone," he said with a laugh.

I blinked. "You got me a phone?" It looked brand-new, and like it was probably a recent model. It would have cost at least several hundred dollars. I'd never had a new phone before. I always got Mom's hand-me-downs.

"You're the only person on my team without a phone," he said. "I need a way to get in contact with you. Especially now that you guys are going to be out there in the city. What if you get separated from everyone?"

"But . . ." I looked down at the phone as he pressed it into my hand. I didn't think I should accept such a huge gift, even if I desperately wanted it. And I didn't know what it meant—was he giving it to me just because of our relationship?

"You really need it. I've been messaging the whole team, and you're not getting any of them. What if you hadn't been with Edan when the scrabs attacked? You wouldn't have even known that I messaged everyone to stay put."

"Oh." I flushed. Had the rest of the team had been talking about how I didn't have a phone? Maybe they were all best friends at this point, messaging each other every hour of the day. "I'll pay you back. After I get my first stipend."

"Don't worry about it. I actually went ahead and put this phone on my plan, so you have international data and minutes. I think a couple other members of the team still don't have new SIM cards, so you can let them use it too, if you want. Think of it as a team phone."

I knew he was just trying to make me feel better about being the only loser without a phone. I smiled, my cheeks warm. "Thank you." I stepped forward, slipping my arms around his neck and giving him a kiss.

"You're welcome." He kissed me again, then pulled away just a little bit. "You know you can ask me for help, right? If you ever need anything. You're not alone here."

An unexpected lump rose in my throat. He didn't need to say it—Julian was the only reason I didn't feel completely alone here—but it still felt nice to hear it out loud.

No one had ever noticed me the way Julian did. I'd spent most of my life wishing Mom and Laurence would notice more and that Dad would notice less. I didn't know what to do with this person listening to me and giving me things like food and a phone to try and make my life easier. I couldn't remember anyone ever trying to make my life easier. Mostly it felt like people wanted me to go away so I'd stop reminding them of their failures.

I rose up on my toes, tightening my arms around his neck as I kissed him. I didn't even care if someone saw us. Just yesterday I'd caught one of the Canadian team leaders making out with one of his team members behind the building. That rule was clearly flexible.

Julian smiled at me as he pulled away.

"Maybe you should mention this to Grayson," I said. "Us, I mean."

He looked pleased. Maybe it also felt like a step forward to him. "OK. I will."

He kissed me again, and then we made our way down the hall to the weapons room. It was just a large closet where most of the weapons (except for guns and explosive devices) were stored. We had spears, machetes, Tasers, axes, swords, and a club of Grayson's own design, which had very sharp blades coming out from all sides (I didn't understand how we were supposed to transport that one, but I kept that to myself). My favorite was the baton with a hidden sword inside. It looked like a regular baton until you pulled it apart to reveal a twenty-inch blade. The handles screwed together, making it so that you could swing the sword far away from your body. I also liked the ax that folded up sort of like a huge pocketknife.

We also had lightweight armor available to us, all of which was optional. I liked the leather arm coverings, which were like fingerless gloves that stretched up to your elbows. They helped prevent scrab claws from piercing the skin.

Grayson stood over a chest of machetes, and he glanced up as we walked in. "Oh good, you're my last team. What are you guys taking?"

"We'll need machetes, batons, shields, and shoulder harnesses," Julian said. "I think stun guns too. They should get used to the weight of carrying them."

Grayson nodded, then pointed to a box in the corner. "Clara, you want to count out twelve shoulder harnesses?"

"Sure." I walked to the box and began pulling them out, piling them up on the shelf next to me.

"Julian, your mom texted me again," Grayson said. "Call her, will ya?"

Julian rolled his eyes at Grayson. I wondered if he didn't get along with his mom. All I knew about her was that she cried a lot.

The door opened before I got a chance to ask. Edan stepped inside.

"I thought you were waiting for the rest of the team in the gym," Julian said, clearly annoyed.

"Patrick's still there. I figured I'd grab stuff for the two of us before the rush."

I handed over two shoulder harnesses.

"How's the shoulder?" Grayson asked.

"It's fine. Pretty much healed."

Julian held out two sheathed machetes, but pulled them back when Edan started to reach for them. "You remember the weapons safety we went over yesterday?"

"Yes," Edan said with an impatient sigh.

"It's not a joke, dude. You could seriously hurt someone with this."

"I'm aware. I'll put them straight into the harnesses." He opened and closed his fingers, waiting.

Julian put the machetes in his hand, then the batons and shields, jaw twitching like he was angry. Grayson gave him two Tasers, and Edan disappeared through the door.

"Is he doing OK?" Grayson asked.

"He puts forth the bare minimum amount of effort," Julian

said, which was a little unfair. Edan was actually one of the best on the team; he just ignored most of what Julian said.

"He did manage to fight off the scrabs last week, though," Grayson said, his voice perky. "So that's encouraging."

"I guess," Julian said. "I'm not sure why I was elected to babysit Edan."

Grayson glanced at me, clearly uncomfortable that I was witnessing this conversation.

"She's fine, she doesn't like him either," Julian said.

"You guys weren't friends in New York?" I asked. I'd been waiting for an opening to ask that question. "I thought you hung out."

"*Hung out* is not the right term," Julian said with a snort. "Grayson met him doing volunteer work at one of the drop-in centers for homeless kids. Took pity on him."

"I didn't take *pity* on him," Grayson said quickly. "I saw him a lot. We became friends."

A few things about Edan clicked into place — wearing the black leather jacket in hot weather, his tiny backpack, even the pickpocketing in Atlanta. I didn't want to excuse it, but I couldn't help but think of how I'd considered swiping a granola bar from the store when I was starving. Maybe Edan hadn't wanted to ask for help either.

Grayson was watching me like he could see the wheels turning in my brain.

"Could you keep that to yourself?" he asked quietly. "About how I met Edan? I don't know if he wants people to know. He deserves a fresh start, if he wants one."

Julian sighed loudly. "Not everyone deserves a fresh start."

I avoided his eyes. The word *pity* was vibrating in my brain, making me uncomfortable. It was a mean thing to say. It positioned Grayson as a rich jerk looking down on the little people. It made Edan sound pitiful. The word cast insults in all directions, and I wondered if Julian had done that purposefully.

You're not alone here. His words from a few minutes before echoed in my brain. He probably hadn't meant for it to sound so harsh. Knowing Julian, he was super nervous about his team going out for the first time today. He seemed to have a bad habit of lashing out when he was nervous and then immediately feeling bad about it.

"Julian," Grayson said in a warning tone. He returned his attention to me, waiting for my reply.

"Of course," I said. "I won't say anything."

We were assigned to the Montparnasse area for our first day. Julian led us through the subway and up the steps, and we exited in the middle of a busy intersection. Cars zipped by, and the sidewalks were crowded. It was eleven a.m. on a Wednesday, a normal workday for most people.

"Remember what we talked about," Julian said, walking backwards so he could face us. "Stay out of people's way. Be polite. You're free to talk to people if they approach you, but please don't approach them. Don't leer at women or catcall."

"Yo, why are you looking at me when you say that?" Gage asked.

"I'm looking at all of you."

We walked to a median in the middle of the intersection, where bikes and scooters were parked. Directly across from us was a department store and a huge skyscraper. On all other sides were bars, restaurants, and shops. Even a McDonald's.

And Grayson's teams were everywhere. I spotted a French team and a couple Mexican teams standing in front of the department store. An American team below a sign that said HIPPOPOTA-MUS. Teams down the street in both directions, too far away for me to see who they were.

"Stand here, near the bikes," Julian said. He pointed to the other side of the median. "Or over there, in between those trees. Just leave a big pathway in the middle for people to walk through."

"So we just stand here?" Dorsey asked.

"Yes, you just stand here," Julian snapped, suddenly angry. "Were you listening when we detailed what missions would be like?"

"I was just asking. Damn," Dorsey muttered.

I squinted through the sun at Julian. I couldn't really blame him for being short with us today. He was so nervous that it was practically radiating off of him. It was our first day on a mission, and if the number of teams in this area was any indication, Grayson expected scrabs.

"I'm going across the street for a minute," Julian said, pointing to the French team. "You guys hang out for a sec. You can sit if you want, as long as you're not in the way."

I leaned against one of the bike racks as I watched him dart across the street. Edan wandered to the other side of the median. Dorsey and Gage pulled out their cigarettes.

"Man, I forgot my lighter," Gage said, patting his pockets. "Dorsey, you have one?"

"Mine stopped working yesterday."

"Here," Priya said, holding a pink one out to him.

"Do you smoke?" Gage asked, taking it from her.

"No. You just never know when you might need to light something on fire, right?"

Dorsey barked out a laugh. Gage stopped with the lighter poised in front of his cigarette and gave Priya a look like perhaps he had severely underestimated her.

"You can keep it, I have plenty more." Priya tilted her head up to the sky. It was sunny and clear. "I hope this is a boring day."

"That is highly unlikely," Madison said. "This part of the city has been hit often, and Grayson has ten teams just in the immediate area." She peered at something behind me. "I wish the scrabs would take out that skyscraper, honestly. It's super ugly."

Nearby, a woman with a stroller spotted us, stopped dead in her tracks, and then turned and ran in the other direction.

"Wow," I said with a laugh.

"The news has been telling people to leave if they see us in an area, because it probably means a scrab attack is coming," Noah said, and I realized he was talking to his phone camera.

Right. We were the crazy ones who stuck around. Several other people seemed in a big hurry to leave the area, but others were ignoring us, sitting at the outdoor tables in front of cafés or pausing to text.

"That's, like, the fifth one," Priya giggle-whispered to Zoe. I followed their gaze to where Edan was leaning against a tree, one foot propped up on the trunk. He had his sleeves rolled up, his tattoos more visible than usual. He tugged on the wrapping of a small piece of candy, his hair failing in his eyes.

"Fifth what?" I asked.

"Girl checking him out," Priya said. She nodded to a group of girls across the street, maybe a couple years younger than us, casting very obvious glances in his direction. Edan was pretending not to notice.

He tugged harder on his candy. Maybe he really hadn't noticed.

"Is that . . ." I squinted at the tattoo on Edan's right shoulder. "Is that a Hufflepuff crest?"

"Yeah, it is," Priya said approvingly.

Laila leaned closer to me, following my gaze. "I have never found that boy more attractive than I do right now."

"Ugh, being in Hufflepuff is embarrassing," Zoe said. "I don't know why you'd tattoo that on your body."

"You shut your mouth about Hufflepuff," Priya said. "We are lowkey the best house."

Zoe widened her eyes like she disagreed. She took another look at Edan. "He really is super hot, though, isn't he?"

Priya made a sound of agreement.

Edan's hand slipped off the candy, flew backward, and he whacked himself straight in the nose. The watching girls giggled.

"And so smooth too," I said dryly.

Archer was staring straight ahead with a frown, and Priya said something to him I couldn't hear.

"I have a bad feeling," he said quietly.

Behind me, tires screeched. Edan straightened. I whirled around.

Down the street, about a block away, two black vans came to a sudden stop. Grayson bolted out of the first one, recruits pouring out after him.

Grayson yelled something in French before switching to English. "RUN!" he yelled. "IF YOU'RE NOT A RECRUIT, RUN!"

21

At first, everyone in the area froze. Then they were all in motion at once—running, bumping into each other, dropping shopping bags on the ground.

"That way!" Grayson yelled to the civilians. He said something in French, and then pointed in our direction. "Go that way!"

"Oh shit," Noah breathed.

The French team across the street ran to Grayson. Julian was halfway between him and us, shouting something to him.

There were still no scrabs. Not that I could see.

"Guys, we need—we need to be getting ready," Noah stuttered. He grabbed his weapons pack off his back.

He was right. I grabbed my own pack and pulled out my leather armor. I strapped the first one to my left arm with shaking hands. It covered from just above my elbows all the way down to my fingers, with straps beneath to keep it in place. It was hard to secure with one hand, especially when I was trembling.

"I'll do that one," Zoe said, grabbing the right one. I gave her a grateful look as she quickly strapped it into place.

I pulled out my baton and unsheathed it to reveal the blade. I touched the handles of the two machetes sticking out from the harness on my back. I could grab them quickly, if I needed. I also had a Taser attached to a belt on my waist that would briefly stun the scrabs.

"Julian!" Madison yelled.

"Do you feel that?" Priya said.

Rumbling. The ground was moving beneath my feet.

Julian was still in the middle of the street. He opened his mouth like he was going to yell something.

A scrab sprang up from the earth.

Dirt and rocks flew through the air, obscuring my vision for a moment. When it cleared, all I saw was the scrab where Julian used to be. It bellowed, showing off a mouthful of fangs.

And then they were everywhere. They exploded up from the ground one by one, so many I lost count. They were all covered in dirt. One only a few yards away had bugs crawling all over its dark gray skin.

Screams sounded from every direction. I heard gunfire.

The scrab directly in front of me lunged, and Madison took a swing. Laila shot her Taser, and the scrab convulsed.

"Where did—"

"Behind—"

"HOLY SHIT!"

A body flew over my head. The recruit hit the ground, motionless.

Claws swiped through the air and I gasped as I stumbled backward. The scrab was charging me, black eyes fixed intently on my machete.

Patrick rushed at it from the side, blade pointed at its neck. The scrab threw his arm out. Patrick went flying.

I ducked as the scrab aimed its claws for my face again. I scrambled across the ground and popped up on its other side, thrusting my blade into its side as hard as I could. It screamed.

"Clara, move!" someone yelled. I darted away. A shot rang out. The scrab screamed again, blood pouring out of its neck.

"Cuidado! SCRAB!" I whirled around to see the ground starting to come apart beneath Dorsey's feet. A member of one of the Mexican teams was yelling at him from a few yards away.

I yanked Dorsey's shirtsleeve, pulling him out of the way just as the scrab burst up. We both stumbled, and he hit the ground. The scrab took off toward the Mexican team. The guy who had been yelling pulled a second machete from his pack. His team was immediately at his side, weapons poised.

"Thanks," Dorsey said as I extended a hand to help him up.

I watched as the Mexican team easily took out the scrab. It hit the ground with a *thud,* and they turned away from it, practically in unison. They stuck close together as they ran away from it. They had clearly practiced staying together in battle.

Where was *my* team?

The area immediately around me had cleared out some — it looked like most of the scrabs were down the street where Grayson had been. Recruits ran in that direction. Civilians ran opposite. A lady bumped my shoulder as she went, blood dripping from the claw marks across her chest.

I spotted Edan a few yards away, spear in one hand, baton in another. He swung his baton at a scrab's belly. He missed. It swiped at him. Edan easily ducked it. Behind him, a different scrab, this one with blood on its fangs, spat out what was left of the person it had just torn apart. My stomach turned over.

"Come on!" I yelled to Dorsey as I took off. The scrab behind Edan had its gaze on him. It lunged.

Edan noticed in the nick of time, hitting the ground and scrambling away so that the two scrabs ended up swiping at each other instead. They both spun to face Edan.

I shot forward, surprising the bloody scrab. My blade slid across its belly, and it lurched forward, front claws hitting the ground. Dorsey darted in from the side and stuck his machete into the scrab's neck. It slumped lifeless to the ground.

The other scrab was dead too. Edan pulled his spear from its neck, his gaze catching mine.

"Thanks," he said breathlessly. His eyes widened suddenly, and he grabbed my waist with one hand, spinning me away from something I couldn't see. With his other hand, he thrust his spear into the air.

The scrab batted it away. It slipped from Edan's hand and clattered to the ground. I dove forward, reaching for the Taser on my waist. I aimed and fired.

The scrab jolted. Edan grabbed his spear, darted right under the scrab, and thrust it up. He scampered away as the scrab started to fall.

"Damn, that dude is fast," Dorsey breathed.

A crash made all three of us jump. Half a block away, two scrabs had just tipped a car over. Another scrab fell on top of it, shaking from the Taser darts in its chest. Grayson sprang forward, swinging his bladed club so hard the scrab's feet left the ground.

Edan took off down the street, Dorsey and me at his heels. We had to dart around bodies, both human and scrab. I swallowed as I passed a dead recruit missing several limbs.

A French team was fighting a scrab not far from Grayson, and I watched as three members used their blades at once. They were also sticking together, fighting as a team. Julian hadn't mentioned us staying together during battle.

I took a quick look around, hoping to catch a glimpse of him. That scrab had popped up so close to him. Had he been killed?

"That one!" Grayson yelled, pointing at something down the street. He was talking to us, I realized. A scrab ran down the street toward the French team, limping slightly. Edan had already taken off.

I ran behind him, skidding to a stop when he did. The scrab lumbered toward us, showing its mouthful of fangs as it roared. I gripped my baton tighter.

"You go for the belly, I'll go for the neck," Edan said. I nodded.

The scrab's feet left the ground as it dove for us. I darted to one side. Edan went to the other. I thrust my blade forward. Its claws swiped my arm above my armor, and I gasped at the sudden pain. I tightened my grip on my baton, plunging it forward until it tore into the scrab's belly. A spear went straight through its neck. It crashed into the ground face first.

Edan stood on the other side of the scrab. His eyes flicked to my arm. Blood oozed from claw marks.

"It's just a scratch," I said, wiping the back of my hand across the sweat on my brow. I turned to look for another scrab.

It was quiet, I realized. The roars had stopped. On the other side of the street, Grayson pulled a blade from a scrab he'd killed. There were three more in his immediate area, sprawled on the ground, blood seeping out of their wounds.

There were dead scrabs everywhere. I counted at least twenty, just on this street. And up ahead, at the intersection, I could see several more.

But there were way more human bodies. Dead recruits up and down the street, blood staining their uniforms and spilling onto the asphalt. A few yards away, a man pressed down on his badly bleeding leg, several people surrounding him to help.

"Where's the rest of team seven?" Edan said. His voice sounded strange.

"I don't know."

Sirens sounded in the distance. Grayson stood amongst the bodies, both hands in his hair. He was searching for something. He finally found it, his face practically crumpling with relief. I turned to look. Madison. She was covered in blood, holding the handle of a machete that had somehow lost its blade. She tossed it aside and gave Grayson a tired thumbs-up.

"Team seven!"

I whirled around. It was Julian, in the middle of the intersection where I'd last seen him. He was OK. Blood covered his hands and arms, and his shirt was torn down the middle, like he'd narrowly escaped claws, but I didn't see any injuries.

"I said *I don't know!*" he yelled at an American team leader next to him. The man's shoulders sagged, and he quickly walked away. "Team seven!" Julian yelled again. He didn't see me and Edan. We started toward him.

As we entered the intersection, I saw recruits headed to him from all sides. Relief coursed through my veins as I spotted them. Priya, breathing heavily. Patrick, holding a hand to his bloody head. Noah, covered head to toe in blood and grime. Laila, gingerly touching bloody scratches on his neck. Gage, Archer, Dorsey, Madison—all alive.

Julian was counting as we approached him. His eyes finally met mine, and he let out a huge breath of air. No one had ever looked that happy to see me in my life. I would have smiled, if I hadn't been trying to ward off a panic attack.

"Ten," Julian said, and then counted again. "We're missing one. Who are we missing?"

"Me."

I turned to see Zoe trudging toward us, the knees of her pants dirty but otherwise unharmed. I wondered if she hid instead of joining the fight. She stared at the ground.

"Jesus." Julian pressed the palms of his hand to his forehead. "You all made it."

"You don't have to sound so surprised," Dorsey said dryly.

"Look at this." Julian gestured to the bodies around us. "It's a miracle."

Patrick wrapped an arm around my shoulders and gave me a squeeze. "I thought you were gone for a minute there."

"Me too."

"I think . . ." Julian closed his eyes for a moment, like he was gathering his thoughts. "I think we're going to have to help with these bodies. But let's move to the side for a minute while the paramedics grab the injured."

We followed him back to where we'd started, the median with the bikes. There was a big hole where the scooters had been. We clustered together on the other side, near the trees.

Medics ran out of ambulances and onto the street. Julian examined the cut on Patrick's head, then inspected a wound on Laila's arm. He stopped in front of me.

"How bad is that?" he asked quietly.

I blinked. "What?" I remembered suddenly that a scrab's claws had caught my arm. "Oh. No, it's fine. Just a scratch." The pain felt dull and far away. My brain was buzzing.

He nodded, but didn't move right away. His arm moved toward me, then dropped back to his side, like he'd thought better of it. We were surrounded by other recruits, and so far, we'd kept our relationship secret.

He took a step back. "You guys can sit," he said to the rest of the team. "Relax a minute." He scanned the area. "I'll be back." He headed in Grayson's direction.

I sat down on the curb and examined my arm, which was starting to burn as the panic wore off. Four angry claw marks ripped into my skin. I touched the edge of my fingertips just below each one.

"That was some shit," Dorsey said, after several minutes of silence.

Priya let out a semihysterical laugh and roughly wiped tears off her face. Gage was trying to light a cigarette, but his hands were shaking too badly. Archer reached over and took the lighter from him, flicking it to produce a flame. Gage gave him a grateful look.

"This is the darkest timeline," Edan said. "I want a different one."

"No way," Noah said. "I read science fiction. The Nazis always win in the other timelines. I'll take the monsters."

"That's a really good point," Edan muttered. "Second darkest timeline."

"Agreed."

Silence settled over the group again, until I broke it. "We should have stuck together." My voice was too quiet, and I could tell that Laila and Archer, on the other side of the group, hadn't heard it. I cleared my throat. "We should have stuck together."

"Yeah, a lot of the teams were working as a unit," Noah said. "I think it's a better strategy."

"I don't know, we all made it," Patrick said. "Maybe we're OK as is."

"What's the point of having a team if we all run off and do our own thing?" Noah asked. "Besides, like Julian said, it's a miracle. I don't know about you guys, but I almost died, like, three times. I think some of this is just dumb luck."

"Same," Edan said.

"Same," Laila said. "I don't know about dumb luck, though." She touched the cross around her neck.

"I'm only alive because Clara pulled me out of the way just in time," Dorsey said, shooting me a smile. "So I vote we stay together next time."

"Agreed," Madison said.

"Together, then," Noah said. "I'll tell Julian that's what we want to do."

We were quiet again.

22

GRAYSON ST. JOHN FIGHT SQUADS DEFEATED IN PARIS
Massive casualties call training methods into question.

The news reports about our first battle were not kind.

The UK squads had encountered some scrabs, as had teams in Beijing and Tokyo, and they'd suffered some casualties, but not like us. We'd taken failure to a new level.

I slipped my phone (the team phone?) into my pocket and headed for the door. The rest of the girls on team seven were still sleeping. Their alarms would go off soon, but I'd woken up early, hungry and still vibrating with terror from yesterday.

I walked down the hallway and descended the stairs to the ground floor. I could hear the murmured sounds of people talking behind closed doors, but the complex was mostly quiet, everyone still asleep or in their rooms. As I passed through the lobby, I saw some of the Australian teams outside, doing yoga on the grass.

I pulled open the door of the cafeteria. It was empty, except for Grayson. He sat on the floor in the back of the room, knees bent, his head down. Next to him were several large paper bags.

The door banged closed behind me, and he looked up with

a start. His eyes were red, and he quickly wiped his hand across them.

I hesitated, taking a step back. Was it kinder to pretend I hadn't noticed him crying and just leave? Or should I stay?

"I bought croissants." He gestured to the bags. "If you want one."

I started across the cafeteria. If he wanted me to leave, he wouldn't have offered me food.

"Everything OK?" I asked, even though I knew it wasn't. I didn't know what else to say. I barely knew Grayson.

He leaned his head back against the wall and let out a long sigh. "I bought croissants to apologize for getting everyone's friends killed. I'm the worst."

I sat down next to him, pulling my knees up and wrapping my arms around them. "We knew what we signed up for. You didn't sugarcoat it."

"I know, but . . . it could have gone better. To put it mildly."

"Maybe," I conceded. "But you did this to save people, right? The civilian casualties were much smaller than usual. The news reports mentioned that too."

"Yeah, they were. It was mostly my people who died."

"And we signed up for that."

"I know. It's just . . ." He looked at his phone, on the ground beside him. "I have so many calls to make today. I want to call all the families personally, and I don't know what to say. We came up with a script months ago, and now it seems like not enough. Not nearly enough."

"Some of them might be grateful you cared enough to call

yourself." Certainly not all. My dad would just scream and tell Grayson he was an idiot. I was glad that I'd only put down Laurence's number as my emergency contact.

I touched the phone in my pocket. Maybe I should text him. I hadn't contacted Laurence since I left him a message when I was in Atlanta.

"Do you regret it?" I asked, after a long silence. "Doing this?"

"No," he said immediately. "I believe in what we're doing. I just wonder how long people are going to stay with me if this keeps happening."

"Well, I'm not leaving," I said. "If that makes you feel better."

He smiled. "It does, actually."

"You know, when we were sitting there yesterday, after, no one was talking about quitting," I said. He turned to me. "We were talking about what we could do differently. How we could improve and work well as a team. For some of us—like me—this is the first thing we really chose to do on our own. The first thing that I could maybe be good at. I don't want to quit just because things are hard. And I think most of my team feels the same way."

"You are good at this. Your whole team is."

"We try. And I didn't even get shot by a fellow team member this time! That's improvement, right?"

He laughed. The cafeteria door opened, and Julian walked in, his eyebrows shooting up as he found us. Maybe he was surprised to find Grayson laughing.

"Hey," he said, walking to us. His gaze held mine for a few extra seconds. "What's going on?"

"Clara was making me feel better." Grayson got to his feet and offered me his hand.

"Yeah?" Julian regarded me curiously, then looked down at where Grayson was still holding my hand. He squeezed it gently before letting it go. "How is my girlfriend making you feel better?"

I looked at Julian quickly. I didn't know what to respond to first—the fact that he'd called me his *girlfriend,* or that his words seemed angry, even if he'd said them calmly.

Grayson rolled his eyes, punching Julian on the shoulder as he walked past him. "If you'd stayed gone just a couple minutes longer, I could have stolen her away for sure."

It was a joke, and one side of Julian's mouth lifted, but I still caught a flash of anger. I wondered if they'd fought over a girl before.

I guessed that meant that Julian had told Grayson about our relationship, and it was fine. I should have been relieved, but I felt off kilter instead, like I'd missed something important. Maybe I should have asked Julian to talk to Grayson together.

"I need to go talk to Jayden," Grayson said, swiping at his phone screen. "Clara, have a croissant. And tell other people to help themselves when they come in. Julian, come find me after you eat? We need to discuss your team's next assignment." He shot me a smile before walking away.

"He seems to be in a better mood." Julian watched as Grayson left the cafeteria.

"You know I would never . . ." I didn't finish the sentence. I felt a flash of annoyance that I had to say it at all. He really thought I was interested in Grayson?

"Oh no, I know," Julian said quickly. "I was just giving Grayson a hard time. I talked to him, by the way. Obviously. He's cool."

"He wasn't mad about us breaking the rules?"

"Nah, those rules were just to keep the creepers at bay."

He took a step closer to me. His fingers brushed my wrist, and then the back of my palm, and then he intertwined our fingers together. I sucked in a tiny breath.

"You called me your girlfriend," I said quietly.

"I did. Is that OK?"

I tried not to smile too widely. "Yes."

The cafeteria door opened again, and the Australian teams that had been doing yoga burst inside. They were followed by Madison, whose gaze immediately went to our intertwined fingers.

"I need to tell them to put out breakfast," Julian said. He let his fingers drop from mine very slowly, his fingertips lingering on mine for an extra second, like he didn't want to let go quite yet.

"I'll put out the croissants," I said. Madison was still staring at me with a sour expression on her face. I pretended not to notice.

I grabbed the paper bags and pulled out the boxes of croissants, opening one and leaving the rest stacked on the table. I snagged one for myself and moved out of the way as more people trickled into the cafeteria.

The chefs wheeled in steaming pans of eggs and potatoes, and I filled my plate and joined a few members of team seven who had wandered in. Priya and Archer sat side by side, Zoe across from them. Madison sat with one of the Kenyan teams, her hand resting on the back of one of the guys. He leaned down and stole a quick kiss.

I tried to hide my smile. If she was involved with someone else, maybe she'd stop hating me over Julian.

"Is Madison dating that guy?" Zoe asked as I slid into the seat next to her.

Priya leaned over to see. "Looks like it. She has good taste."

Archer peered up at Priya. He cocked his head, a smile playing on his lips.

"I was just stating a fact." Priya bumped her shoulder against his. Archer's smile widened as he ducked his head into his chest.

Patrick slid into the seat next to me. "Good morning."

"Dammit, Edan!" Gage's voice rang across the cafeteria. Archer laughed, choking on his eggs.

I turned to see Gage pulling a boot out of the brown paper bags I'd discarded in the corner. He was wearing the other boot, and he hopped on one foot as he tried to put it on.

"I have no idea why your boot is there, Gage," Edan called innocently from the food line. Gage flipped him off.

"Why does Edan keep taking Gage's stuff?" Zoe asked.

"Because Gage is a dick and it makes the rest of us laugh," Patrick said.

"Plus he thinks it's funny to punch Edan in the face with nearly full strength during practice," Noah said as he sat down next to Priya. "Julian hasn't put a stop to it, so I think this is Edan's revenge."

"Edan could just punch him back," Zoe said.

"I don't think that's his style," Noah said. It certainly wasn't. Edan barely threw any punches at all, and when he did, they were weak. I couldn't imagine him fighting with Gage. I'd been with Priya the last few days, and I hadn't noticed Edan and Gage paired together.

I polished off my breakfast as the team leader at the door called for us to wrap it up. I grabbed my tray and dropped it in the bucket near the kitchen.

Julian had instructed us to meet him in the big gym today, and I followed Zoe and Archer that way. Edan, Patrick, and Noah trailed behind me. Patrick smiled at something Edan said. It didn't seem like there were any hard feelings about the attempted robbery.

Zoe and Archer stopped suddenly outside the gym door.

"That's bullshit, Grayson." It was Julian's angry voice. I took a step forward and stopped when Grayson and Julian came into view. Grayson was holding the door open just a bit, giving us a glimpse inside the gym. It was empty except for them.

"We need people out there, and I think your team is a good choice," Grayson said.

"Nests can have *hundreds* of scrabs," Julian said. "We're not equipped to handle that."

"Of course you are. Your team came out of yesterday with zero casualties. And three of your members are cleared to use guns and explosives."

"Most of our teams are weak, Grayson, including mine. Look at what happened yesterday. We need to take a few days. Rethink things. They're going to get *massacred* out there."

"Things will be less intense in the country. And I personally think our teams did a hell of a job at that battle." Grayson clapped Julian on the shoulder. "I'm not sending you guys alone. Have a little faith."

Julian said nothing in reply. Grayson pushed the door the rest of the way open, caught us all standing there, and winced.

"Sorry, guys, you shouldn't have heard that. Julian's wrong. You're all doing great work, and you're prepared for this." His eyes caught mine for a moment, and he gave me a small smile before turning to walk away.

We trailed into the gym. Julian was typing furiously into his phone. He looked up at us and sighed. "We're being sent outside the city to hunt nests. The scrabs make temporary nests for sleeping and reproducing. You learned about it in session, right? They move constantly, but if we can find them, it will be a big help. It's not such a bad assignment."

His anger at Grayson directly contradicted that statement. We all stared at him.

"Outside the city where?" Zoe asked.

"Some small towns around Paris. Just a few hours away. But we will need to leave the complex. You guys are leaving this afternoon, and I'll follow tomorrow morning. Pack your bags."

23

I WALKED DOWN THE STAIRS LATE THAT AFTERNOON, MY BACK-pack and weapons pack slung over my shoulder. I pushed open the door to the lobby to find Madison standing in the middle of it, alone.

The door slammed shut behind me, and I winced. I'd been hoping to sneak through without her noticing me. But she turned and immediately spotted me. I offered a weak smile and made a beeline for the front door.

"Clara," she called.

I stopped and slowly faced her. "Yeah?"

She closed the distance between us, her boots squeaking on the tile floor. She was dressed in the same uniform as me, but she'd tied her shirt at the bottom so that it pulled tight across her stomach. Her blue eyes looked extra bright in the late afternoon sun streaming in from behind me. I wished I'd spent a little more time on my makeup.

"Listen," she said with a sigh like she was annoyed that she had to speak to me. "It's about Julian."

Out of the corner of my eye, I could see the hole in the ground where a scrab had shot up a couple weeks ago. I wished another one would pop up right now. I would take a scrab over this conversation any day.

"What about Julian?" It came out more annoyed than I'd intended. I'd been trying not to sound nervous.

"You guys are, like, together?" she asked.

"Yes."

"OK, I just think you should know that he can be kind of intense in relationships." Her words were clipped, almost angry.

"What do you mean?" I asked.

"He falls pretty hard. If this is your first relationship, I think you should be careful."

"I've dated guys before," I said defensively, even though that was barely true. I'd dated two guys, one for a few weeks, the other for two months. I wasn't sure either qualified as a *relationship*. They hadn't been anything like what I had with Julian.

"Whatever," she said with a hand wave. "He just gets jealous, from what I've seen."

"*He* gets jealous?" The words popped out of my mouth before I could stop them.

She raised one eyebrow with even more hostility than usual. "What is that supposed to mean?"

My pulse pounded in my ears. I wished I'd kept my mouth shut. "I just think that maybe it's been hard for you to see the two of us together," I said slowly.

"Please," she said, too forcefully. I looked at her skeptically, and she flushed. "Whatever, I'm just saying that I know Julian better than you do."

I waited for more, but apparently she simply wanted to remind me that she and Julian knew each other well. "Uh, OK?" I meant to sound annoyed this time.

"You know what? Never mind." She took a step back. "I was just going to warn you that Julian can be a raging jerk on occasion, but you can figure that one out for yourself." She stomped away, throwing the door open with too much force.

I waited several seconds before following her out the door. *Raging jerk.* That seemed sort of unfair, especially given how she treated Julian. If she'd acted the same way in a relationship, I honestly couldn't blame him for snapping back.

And I could totally believe that he got jealous occasionally, especially after what I'd seen with Grayson in the cafeteria. But who didn't get a little jealous at times? *I* was jealous of Madison's previous relationship with Julian. Now I wished I'd been nice to Madison long enough to find out what had happened between them.

I found team seven on the curb, minus Madison, who had thankfully disappeared.

Grayson stood in front of a black SUV, keys in hand. "Do any of you know how to drive a standard?"

"Yeah, I do," Patrick said.

Grayson tossed him the keys. "Six of you can go with Patrick. There will be a van along in a few minutes for everyone else. And drop your bags over there. They'll arrive right after you." He pointed to a couple French team leaders piling luggage into a van.

I dropped my backpack off, keeping my small weapons pack with me since we'd been instructed to always have it nearby. It had the sword baton, a small machete, and a first aid kit in it.

I climbed into the last row of the SUV. Priya and Archer joined me in the back, and Laila and Noah took the first row.

Noah immediately pulled out his laptop and began editing video. Edan was in the passenger's seat next to Patrick.

"What is that?" Laila asked, pointing to the box at Noah's feet.

"Our body cameras." Noah nudged it with his foot. "I put them on my list and someone got *six* for us. I'm going to see if I can get a few volunteers to wear some starting tomorrow. They're really small."

"I'll wear one," Laila said.

Grayson handed Patrick a map through the window. "I marked it on the map. It's not hard to find the campsite. You're just going to go straight on this road for a while." He pointed to the map, and Patrick nodded. He handed the map to Edan, who immediately handed it back to Noah.

"I can't look at it while the car is moving," Edan explained.

"See you guys soon," Grayson said. Patrick shifted the car into gear.

"Wait!" Priya said. She was typing furiously on her phone. "I need the Wi-Fi for just, like, ten more seconds. I'm running out of data, and my mom is freaking out after yesterday. She keeps checking to see if I'm still alive." She typed a few more words and pressed Send. "OK, I'm good."

I pulled my phone out of my pocket as the SUV started moving. I never texted Laurence. Was he worried I was dead? Grayson hadn't released all the names of the deceased recruits yet, and the massacre was all over the news.

I tapped the messages icon and punched in Laurence's number. I'd memorized it after Mom gave it to me, but I hadn't used it yet.

I typed out a message.

Hey, it's Clara. I'm fine. Not dead yet.

Knowing Laurence, he hadn't read the news in days and was totally clueless anyway.

A reply popped up almost immediately.

Thanks for letting me know.

A few seconds went by before the next message popped up.

Is this your new phone number?

I typed a response.

It's sort of a shared phone, but you can reach me here. Do me a favor and don't give the number to Mom or Dad.

Sure.

A brief pause again before his next message.

Maybe text sooner next time. I was freaking out a little over here. That Noah kid hasn't even uploaded a video yet.

My eyebrows shot up. I couldn't imagine Laurence *freaking out*. It probably wasn't a visible emotion from the outside. I was surprised he'd admitted to it at all.

A hint of a smile crossed my face.

You watch Noah's videos?

Yes. He's not dead, is he?

No. He's working on it now. I'll text you sooner next time.

Thank you.

"What are you smiling about?" Priya asked, glancing at my screen. "Is that Julian? Are you guys really a thing?" Both Laila and Noah turned to look at me.

"No," I said, slipping the phone back in my pocket. "I mean, no, it's not Julian. But yes, we are a thing."

Noah widened his eyes slightly, like he didn't like the news of me dating Julian. Priya clearly expected more. I guessed she wanted to know who I was texting, if not Julian.

"It was my brother," I said.

"You have a brother?" Patrick asked.

"I thought you were an orphan," Noah said. "Or in foster care or whatever."

"What? No. Why did you think that?" I frowned in confusion, and realized that everyone in the SUV, except for Patrick, was looking at me. Even Edan had twisted around in his seat, his face curious.

"Because you've literally never said a single thing about your family," Priya said. "I asked you once if you missed your parents, and you looked at me like I'd grown a second head."

Right. I had done that. I'd been trying to make the words "of course!" come out of my mouth, but they'd gotten stuck. Julian had shouted out an order, and I'd used it as an excuse to run away.

"Also Patrick said you were," Laila said, pointing to him.

Patrick rounded his shoulders. "I said *maybe*. It was just a guess."

"I've never been in foster care," I said. "I have an older brother. And a mom and a dad."

Priya's expression was curious. Laila was trying to catch her eye, and she shook her head once, just barely, like she was trying to tell Priya to leave it.

Had they been talking about me? Why was Laila trying to make Priya stop asking questions? Had I given something away? Neither of them knew enough about my life to put all the pieces together, but maybe they suspected. Girls always knew things. It was part of the reason I stopped being friends with Adriana and the others.

"Noah, you better be telling the world that our whole team made it," Edan said suddenly. "Do you want to interview me? I'll tell them how awesome I was."

"You already have a very loyal fan base." Noah pressed a key on his laptop. "Let's keep them hanging for a week."

"You have a loyal fan base?" I asked.

"I do not appreciate that surprised tone." Edan put both hands on his chest. "I'll have you know that there's an entire Tumblr dedicated to how cute I am."

"No there's not."

"Yes there is," Noah said, like he was trying to suppress a laugh. "And they've gotten excited in the last few days, because one of Edan's ex-girlfriends posted something about how he was a great guy."

"Are you sure it was actually his ex?" I asked.

"I also do not appreciate that skepticism," Edan said. "I am delightful, and all my ex-girlfriends will confirm it. Except for that one who said she hoped someone pushed me in front of a train. She maybe wouldn't have nice things to say."

I snorted, and then thought of Madison. She certainly didn't have nice things to say about her ex. It was normal, maybe.

"And there are several Tumblrs dedicated to how cute Noah is," Edan continued.

Noah's cheeks went red. "There are a bunch of fan sites for all of us. Clara, you have no online presence. Can you at least get on

Instagram? Post some selfies. Make the people happy. There are a few people from your high school commenting on stuff, but who knows if they even really know you."

I looked at him with a start. "What are they saying?"

"Nothing bad," he said quickly. "Just that you mostly kept to yourself, you were good in combat class . . ." He trailed off.

"What?"

A short silence followed. My heart jumped into my throat. I couldn't imagine what anyone at my school could possibly know about me. I barely spoke to anyone.

"Someone said you failed some classes," Laila finally said. "Which is no big deal," she quickly added. "Half of our team dropped out of high school."

"Like me," Archer said. Everyone in the back of the SUV turned to gawk at him. We did it every time he spoke, quietly waiting for him to say more. He just blinked and looked out the window.

"I dropped out sophomore year," Edan said. He was facing the road again.

"Why?" Priya asked.

"I had better things to do."

I clicked on the Tumblr app and searched for my own name. It was true—there were several Tumblrs dedicated to team seven. Lots of screenshots from Noah's videos. Old photos of several members—Priya smiling at the camera with her cheer squad; Zoe doing duck face into the camera with some girls at the beach; Edan sitting on a stoop, both hands cupping his chin, a huge grin on his face.

The only pictures of me included a school portrait from ninth grade and a few shots from middle school. Those must have come from Adriana or one of her friends. We smiled outside a movie theater, waved at the camera from in front of a river.

Noah had caught me swinging a machete one day in practice, and someone had made a gif set out of it.

teamsevenfans

How to be a badass, featuring Clara Pratt.

kylorensuckssss

This girl is literally the most mysterious person on the planet. Are we sure she isn't a spy? I wouldn't put it past my government to send some spies.

beeboopaloop

Is she Latinx?

anniehatesyouallTX

She went to my school. She's not a spy, she's just quiet. I think she was super Christian or something.

hellyeahmonsterfighters

Swinging that machete for Jesus!

I barked out a laugh.

"What?" Priya asked.

"I'm not religious."

"Oh yeah, I saw that one," Noah said. "I was wondering."

I glanced back down at the phone. According to Tumblr, I was a super Christian who failed her classes and/or a spy.

No one really knew who I was, which had once seemed like a good thing. Now it felt like the world was crafting a narrative for me. Like they had a story prepared if I didn't tell it myself.

Priya looked at me expectantly.

"I'm not a spy," I said with a smile.

Patrick laughed. "Thank god."

"And I am Latinx. My mom is from Mexico. My dad is white and from Texas. And they're both assholes, so I don't keep in touch with them."

On the other side of Priya, Archer nodded like he understood. I was pretty sure everyone knew less about Archer than they did about me. I had that going for me, at least.

"But your brother isn't an asshole?" Priya asked.

I shook my head. "No, he's all right."

"Good." She smiled.

Patrick took us out onto the highway, then to a two-lane with crops on either side. We drove for a long time, the sun sinking lower in the sky.

"Noah, are we supposed to turn at some point?" Patrick asked.

Noah looked up from his phone with a start. "Am I supposed to be navigating?"

"Yes!" Patrick said with a laugh.

"Oh. Well, um . . ." He unfolded the map and squinted at it. He flipped it every which way. "I can't even tell which way is up."

Laila leaned over to look at it. "I don't know how people used to read these things."

"Someone give me their phone," Patrick said. "I left mine in my bag."

Noah made a face like he didn't want to give his up.

"Here," I said, suppressing a laugh as I passed my phone to Noah. "Use mine."

"Thanks." Noah opened the maps app and typed in the address Grayson had written on the map. He handed the phone to Patrick, who stuck it in the cup holder.

"Well, we went way too far down this road." Patrick slowed and made a U-turn.

"Sorry," Noah said. "I got distrac—"

The ground exploded in front of us.

"Holy shit!" Patrick swerved the SUV, narrowly missing the scrab that had just sprung up out of the earth.

Another one smashed up from the ground. It was massive, one of the biggest scrabs I'd ever seen. At least seven feet tall.

Two more ran at my window.

"Just hit them!" Priya yelled.

"I think that will do more damage to us than the scrab." Patrick hit the gas hard. The car lurched forward.

"Another one!" Edan yelled, pointing to where a crack was starting to appear on the road. A scrab sprang up and roared.

Patrick turned the wheel so quickly the vehicle spun out of control. I gripped the back of the seat in front of me as we swung in almost a full circle and veered off the road. The SUV bounced and jerked as we soared into the short, bushy green crops on the side of the road.

Something smashed into my side of the car, and I yelped as we bounced again. A scrab roared at the window as it slammed its body against my door.

"Go, go!" Laila yelled.

To my right, a scrab galloped at us on all fours, teeth bared.

It hit the side with a crunch of metal and glass. The car slowed. *Thump thump thump.*

"I think they got the tires!" Patrick grimaced. The car continued to slow.

"We're going to have to get out," Edan said. I grabbed my pack and pulled out my baton, popping the top off to reveal the blade.

Patrick swerved around the scrabs, and we bounced forward a few yards.

"Ready?" he asked. I saw the fear in his eyes as he glanced in the rearview mirror.

I looked over my shoulder. Scrabs came for us from all directions. There were six of them that I could see.

"Ready," Priya said.

The car screeched to a stop. I pushed the door open and dove out, nearly losing my balance as I tried to keep a grip on my baton.

A scrab galloped straight toward me. Its mouth was open, fangs bared and spit flying as it ran.

I swung as it approached, my injured arm screaming in protest. Missed. I ducked as it swiped its claws, pressing one hand to the ground as I slashed my blade across its belly. It screamed and lurched backward. I'd made a really deep cut — best I'd ever done — and blood poured out of the wound. It hit the ground with a *thud.*

I turned to find two more dead scrabs on the ground. Patrick and Archer fought another one together. Laila and Priya each were fending off one. Laila's hit the ground, dead. Edan was a few yards away, swinging his blade at a scrab. He kept stepping back as it came closer, putting more space between him and us.

Two more scrabs galloped toward him. Edan paused for half a second before bolting.

I took off, pumping my arms as I ran as fast as I could. One of the scrabs caught up with Edan, and he whirled around, swinging his machete. Another dove at him from the side, and he barely managed to dodge its claws as he swung his weapon at them.

"Hey!" I yelled as the third scrab closed in. It snarled as it spotted me. It gave up on Edan and headed for me.

I skidded to a stop. The scrab snarled as it looked down at me. Its black eyes focused on the blade in my hand. I swung it.

With my other hand, I grabbed the machete sticking out of my pack. The scrab batted my baton away. It leaned down, fangs bared.

I sliced my machete across its neck. Blood splattered across my clothes.

Thud. I spun around to find Edan. One scrab was dead, the other injured, blood dripping from its neck. Edan swung his machete, trying to finish it off.

It swiped away the weapon. Edan froze for a moment, reaching for something in his pack. Another knife, maybe. There was nothing.

He took off, the scrab chasing him. It was slower than usual, dragging its right leg as it ran. I bolted after them.

I yelled at the scrab, but it kept pursuing Edan. We ran until my lungs started to burn — I was flat-out sprinting — and the scrab began gaining on Edan. We burst through a patch of trees. I cast a frantic glance over my shoulder, but I'd lost sight of everyone else.

We ran straight into a patch of houses, and my stomach clenched as I waited for the screams of the occupants. But as we got closer, I realized they were all long abandoned, the windows smashed, doors swinging open. One small home was missing part of its walls in the front and back of the house, like something had smashed straight through it.

Edan darted inside that one. Probably looking for a weapon. It was what I would have done, since it was becoming clear he couldn't outrun the scrab.

It crashed into the house. I pushed myself as hard as I could, running until I thought my lungs might burst. I skidded into the house.

Edan had a frying pan, and I watched as he slammed it into the scrab's face. It stumbled back, disoriented. Edan hit it again. I darted around an old rickety table, blade pointed at it.

A second whack on the head just made it mad. It stalked forward, opening its mouth like it was trying to roar. Only a squeak came out. Edan must have sliced its vocal cords.

Edan tried to swing again, but the scrab blocked it, charging at him and grabbing his foot. Edan went down, hard. He screamed as the scrab lunged at him.

24

I DARTED FORWARD AND YANKED THE SCRAB BY THE ARM, SLASH-ing my blade across its neck. It made a horrible choked noise and toppled to the ground.

Edan looked from me to the scrab. He was still on the ground, gasping for breath.

"Holy hell, Clara. Thank you."

I nodded, switching my machete to my left hand as I offered him my other one. He got to his feet, wincing as he peered down at his leg. A bloody claw stuck out from his pants.

"Ew, is that lodged in your skin?" I asked.

"It sure is." He grimaced as he limped forward. Something behind me made his eyes widen. He stopped.

I quickly turned. Scrabs. Dozens of them in the field behind the house. They were climbing out of several holes in the ground, one after the other. Several were on their feet, faces pointed in the direction we'd come from. Distantly, I heard someone call my name. Tires screeched. It sounded like more than one car. Someone stopped to help, maybe.

Edan grabbed my arm. He was pressed against the wall, and I did the same.

"What do we do?" I breathed. I looked down at the claw

protruding from his skin. I wasn't sure how fast he could run with that in his leg.

It didn't matter, anyway. We couldn't outrun dozens of scrabs, even at full strength.

"Did they see us?" Edan whispered.

I leaned forward a tiny bit and dared a glance at the scrabs. A few took off in the direction of the yell we'd just heard. At least fifty remained.

"I don't think so." I leaned back against the wall, my eyes darting around the room.

"Hide?" Edan guessed.

I nodded. "Until they leave." With any luck, everyone else in the SUV was still alive and would come with reinforcements. I reached for my pocket.

"Shit."

"What?" Edan asked.

"I left my phone in the car. Do you have yours?"

"Yeah, but it doesn't have cell service. I just use it with Wi-Fi." He looked at the broken chair in the corner. "I get the feeling they don't have Wi-Fi here."

"Can't you call nine-one-one even without service?" I asked.

His face lit up, then fell. "I don't know what the French equivalent of nine-one-one is. They really should have covered that in one of our sessions."

I heard a rumbling noise suddenly, different than the one I was used to. This was more like a stampede. Edan went pale.

On the other side of the house, a group of at least fifty more scrabs were coming over the hill. They ran aboveground on all fours.

I searched desperately for a hiding spot.

There was a door open a few feet to my left, and I edged closer to it and turned the doorknob. I braced myself as it opened, waiting for a creak or for a mouse to scurry out, but it was quiet. It was a small closet, empty except for a few hangers dangling from the rack. I jerked my head at it. Edan nodded.

The scrabs were getting closer.

I darted inside the closet as quietly as I could and sank to the ground. Edan stepped in after me, pulling the door shut very slowly so that it didn't make a sound. He squeezed down next to me.

It was pitch-black in the closet, and there was barely enough room for us to sit side by side. Our shoulders were pressed together, and I could feel his body moving up and down with his breath. I could smell his shampoo when he turned his head. I could also smell scrab guts. Their blood was splashed across my pants.

The rumbling grew closer. We were both so still that I felt dizzy in the darkness.

Then, I heard it. *Click click click.* Claws on the wooden floor. The sound was everywhere. The entire house was full of scrabs.

The dizziness grew more intense, and I realized suddenly that I might be about to die. The fear had been there, in the back of my mind, every time I fought a scrab, but the threat felt incredibly real at the moment.

I reached out, finding Edan's wrist first, and then his hand.

He was not the person I would have liked to be holding hands with in my last moment, but I had to make do with what I had. He gripped my hand tightly.

One of the scrabs snorted. They were so close I could hear them breathing. I held my own breath. My heart pounded so loudly in my ears I felt sick.

I heard more clicking noises, and then a sound like someone was eating. Like flesh tearing. Then, more.

My stomach turned. Were they *eating* that dead scrab? I had no idea that they ate their dead. I pressed my free hand to my mouth.

This was *not* how I wanted to die. I didn't want this to be the last thing I heard. I squeezed Edan's hand so hard I could feel his bones grinding together.

The scrabs finished in a matter of minutes, and their claws clicked against the wood again and then disappeared. Silence descended on the closet.

Neither Edan nor I moved for at least twenty minutes. I dropped his hand as my heart rate began to slow and let myself relax against the wall. Our breathing evened out, his shoulder still and warm against mine.

"Should I look?" he finally said, his voice barely audible.

I nodded, and then realized he couldn't see me. "Yes," I whispered.

The door opened a crack, dim light flooding the closet. The sun had almost completely set.

Edan leaned forward a little, and then quickly back.

"They're still in that field," he whispered. I caught him wincing as he slowly shut the door. "And they're not all asleep yet. It looks like some of them went underground, but there are a bunch up there still. I think we should wait a couple more hours."

Darkness closed in on us again as the door clicked closed. I fumbled for my pack, my shoulder bumping into him.

"I have my first aid kit," I said, still not daring to speak above a whisper. Scrabs couldn't hear high-frequency sounds as well as we did, so it was unlikely they could hear our voices even at a normal volume. Still, a whisper seemed safer. "You want me to pull that claw out for you? It's going to get infected."

He hesitated. "OK."

"I don't have to, if you want to leave it."

"No, just do it. Please."

"Can we use the flashlight on your phone for a minute? I can't see anything."

He shifted a few times until a bright light clicked on.

"Thank you." I grabbed the antibiotic wipes, ointment, and all the bandages I had. I wedged them against the wall and my thigh. I leaned forward to examine his leg, and he shifted the light to it.

I tugged up his pant leg to reveal where the claw was stuck. It wasn't a huge piece, but there were three puncture holes around it, blood seeping out of them.

"OK, you can't scream," I said, glancing back at him. He nodded and clapped a hand over his mouth.

"On three. One . . . two . . . three." I yanked the claw out. He made a very soft muffled noise, and his body jerked. I carefully nudged the claw into the corner by his other foot.

I grabbed the wipes and swiped them over the whole area,

then used one to put the ointment on. I covered what I could with bandages, though we didn't have quite enough.

"That should do it for now," I whispered, pulling his pant leg over the bandages. I settled back down next to him.

"Thank you," he said softly.

"You're welcome."

We sat in silence after that, the light beneath the door fading completely. An hour passed, which I only knew because Edan checked his phone once, then peeked out the door again.

"Still a couple moving around," he whispered.

"What if they don't all sleep at the same time?"

"Then I guess we're stuck in here forever. Hope you don't have to pee."

"Edan."

"What?"

"I'm serious. What are we going to do if they don't sleep soon?"

"What do you say we revisit that in a few hours?" His voice was barely a whisper, but it was steadier than mine. "It's only nine. Let's save panicking for like . . . four a.m. Four a.m. seems like a good time to panic, right?"

I didn't know whether to be relieved or annoyed that he was being so flip. But his composure did make me feel like I should be calm too. We wouldn't accomplish anything by panicking.

"I'm sorry I got you into this," he said.

"It's not your fault," I said quietly. I couldn't reasonably blame him for a scrab attack.

"Well, it's my fault that I tried to outrun a scrab. I took an entire class once about how that doesn't work and what to do instead."

"With Grayson? Julian said he'd seen you training with Grayson in New York."

"Yeah, he took me along pretty often. He'd go after volunteering at the drop-in center, so he'd bring me along if I was around."

"The drop-in center?" I asked, even though I knew what it was.

"I heard that Julian told you how I met Grayson."

"Right. Sorry."

"It's fine." He paused. "I know Grayson said not to tell everyone, but I don't care. It's not a secret."

"That you were homeless?"

"Yeah."

"Have you told other people on the team?"

"Patrick. But the two of you are the least gossipy people I've ever met. If I ever do have secrets, I'm telling the two of you. No one will ever find out."

"You and Patrick are friends now, huh?"

"I think so." His voice changed, like he was embarrassed. "I apologized for robbing him. He was very nice about it."

"Patrick's nice about everything."

"True. But I—"

"What?"

"I don't want to sound like I'm making excuses."

"You can tell me. There's, like, a fifty percent chance we're going to die tonight, so you might as well tell me now."

"Thanks, that makes me feel better."

"Any time."

He let out a breath of air that was almost a laugh. "I'd just spent all my money getting down to Atlanta. Grayson didn't even know I was coming, I hadn't seen him in a few months. I ate all my snacks on the bus ride down, so I was hungry, and you know how they didn't feed us at tryouts."

I really did.

"I couldn't bring myself to ask Grayson for help, because I knew he was busy, and I hate asking him for anything. He always gives me way more than I asked for, and it just makes me feel like shit, you know?"

"Yeah," I said softly.

"I don't mean that to sound bad. He has good intentions. It's just that if I'd told him I had no money for food, he would have handed me a hundred-dollar bill. And I know that it makes, like, no sense to turn around and rob people instead, but at least I figured things out myself, you know? Does that sound stupid? It probably sounds stupid."

"No, it doesn't sound stupid," I said. "I get. I really get it, actually. I didn't have any money or food at tryouts either. I practically fainted on Julian the last day."

"Seriously?"

"Yeah. I didn't know anyone, and I couldn't bring myself to beg someone for food." I thought of that convenience store, of the granola bar I'd considered stealing. I would have, if I'd thought I could get away with it. The only thing that stopped me was the shame of getting caught.

"I don't mean to imply that I only stole that one time because I was hungry," Edan said. "I've done it a lot, honestly. Often because I was desperate. But sometimes just because it was convenient. It was both that night with Patrick."

"Is that why you're here?" I asked. "Turning over a new leaf?"

"Yeah. Well, that, and because it was Grayson. I wanted to help him. I owe him a lot."

"Why do you owe him?"

"He was always just a great friend," Edan said. "He's like my brother. I mean, he was kind of a rich asshole at first, but he couldn't help himself."

"How so?"

"He kept trying to get me to go home. I kept telling him, 'Dude, there's a reason I left.' He had a hard time understanding that I was better off on my own, even if certain things were more difficult."

I couldn't think of anything to say to that. I didn't want to ask why he was better off on his own, homeless, because I probably already knew. I could see what Edan meant when he called Grayson *a rich asshole*. It wasn't really an insult, just a way to describe a man who had never considered how bad life could get.

I certainly understood jumping into a dangerous situation just to get away from home. That made perfect sense to me.

A creak sounded from outside, and we both tensed.

"Maybe we shouldn't talk," I barely whispered.

"Agreed," Edan breathed.

Silence settled between us.

25

EDAN CHECKED ON THE SCRABS EVERY HOUR, UNTIL JUST AFTER midnight, when he carefully shut the door and said, "They're not moving. And most of them are underground."

"How well can you see them?"

"It's nearly a full moon, so somewhat well. But I don't think we should wait for daylight."

I shook my head. "I don't think so either." Scrabs, like us, couldn't see as well at night. We had a much better chance of sneaking away in the darkness.

"And I don't think we should run. They can feel vibrations in the ground, right?"

"Yeah, that's what they think."

"So let's walk. Carefully."

"OK."

He shifted, and his hair brushed against my forehead. Some part of his face bumped my cheek.

"Sorry," he said.

"It's fine."

The light of his phone filled the closet, and he started typing something. "I'm leaving Grayson a note on my phone. Just in case." He held it out to me. "Want to write a note to anyone? Who knows if it'll survive an attack, but you never know."

I looked down at the phone. Who did I have to say goodbye to? Laurence, maybe, but I didn't have anything left to say to him that hadn't already been said. Julian? Maybe I could tell him thank you, for helping me, for making me feel less lonely, but any way I turned the words over in my brain sounded cheesy. We'd barely started dating. A goodbye note would probably just make him feel weird.

I shook my head.

Edan slipped the phone back into his pocket. He took a deep breath and pushed the door open.

My muscles ached in protest as I stood. I grabbed my machete from where it was wedged by the wall and slipped it into the harness on my back.

We took a few careful steps away from the closet. It was dark, but I could just barely make out the shapes of the older furniture, of items scattered on the floor.

I followed Edan to the back door and carefully, silently, stepped outside. We walked slowly around the house and into the open. There was nothing but grass and a few trees around us. The road wasn't visible from this distance.

But I could see the scrabs.

There were about a dozen of them, piled together near holes in the ground like sleeping puppies. Six-foot puppies with sharp claws and cannibalistic instincts.

They were silent in sleep, which was terrifying. No snoring to alert people nearby of their presence.

I kept my eyes on them as I fell into step beside Edan. We moved as fast as we could without making much noise, slowly putting space between us and the scrabs. I couldn't see it yet, but we had to be getting closer to the road.

The ground gave way beneath my feet suddenly. I gasped, looking down in time to see my boot falling through a mess of twigs and leaves.

Edan's hand grabbed for mine, but I couldn't hold on. I reached desperately for something to stop my fall, but my feet hit the ground and I collapsed with a grunt. Thank god. Whatever hole I'd just fallen into wasn't that deep.

I stood slowly, testing my ankles to make sure I hadn't twisted them. Moonlight filtered in through the remaining branches above me, and I squinted at my surroundings.

I barely stopped myself from screaming.

Scrabs. Three fully grown ones, and at least two dozen tiny scrabs around them. Hairless, wrinkled, hideous baby scrabs. A nest.

A couple of the baby scrabs closest to me were stirring, shaking off the leaves I'd covered them in when I fell. The adult scrab next to them sighed. Its eyelids fluttered.

I took a tiny step back, pressing my back to the side of the hole. My heart pounded frantically in my chest. Was it dark enough in the shadows that the scrab couldn't see me?

The scrab's eyes opened.

I dug my fingers into the dirt behind me. *Please don't see me. Please don't see me.*

It blinked once and then rolled over. Something shiny and silver on its neck glinted in the moonlight as it moved, like it had gotten a piece of metal lodged there. The baby scrabs huddled in closer.

I let out a slow breath. I didn't know if I wanted to cry or vomit. Both, maybe.

I looked up to see Edan on his stomach, one arm reaching down into the hole. He opened and closed his fingers insistently, like he wanted me to hurry up.

I took a careful step toward him. A clump of dirt fell from the wall as I moved. A rock skittered across the ground.

I stopped, my eyes snapping to the scrabs. They were still motionless.

I reached up and wrapped my fingers around Edan's arm. There was no way he was going to be able to pull me up unless I helped, so I dug the fingers of my other hand into the dirt and tried to find a spot to hook my boot into the earth.

Something sharp pierced the ankle that was still on the ground, and I gasped, letting go of Edan's hand. I looked down.

One of the baby scrabs clung to my pants leg, its teeth in my ankle. I shook my leg, trying to dislodge it. That seemed to only make it angrier. It let out a soft cry and bit me again.

Edan stretched both arms into the hole. I threw a glance over my shoulder. Two of the adult scrabs stirred.

I dug my fingers into the dirt and launched myself up. Edan seized my arms, yanking me up until I could reach the edge of the hole. I crawled out, my breath coming in short, panicked gasps.

Edan grabbed me under the arms, helping me to my feet. The scrab on my ankle fell off as I stood.

It screamed.

I froze. Edan gripped my arm. I followed his gaze.

Several of the scrabs near the house were standing.

Staring at us.

Edan's eyes flashed to mine.

The scrabs dropped to all fours and began running.

We both broke into a sprint. We'd put some space between us and the scrabs, but not enough. Especially not if those three in the hole climbed out.

Edan skidded to a stop, grabbing my arm. I followed his gaze.

Dozens more scrabs were coming over the hill. They were just black shapes in the darkness, the pounding of their feet echoing across the area.

Edan's gaze caught mine again, and I saw my feelings mirrored there. We were well and truly screwed.

He grabbed my hand, and we broke into a sprint. We were headed in the direction of the road, I was pretty sure, but it was hard to tell in the dark.

And I was distracted by the fact that I was going to die.

I didn't look over my shoulder. I could hear the scrabs gaining, and I didn't want to see their faces.

I considered closing my eyes. I didn't want a scrab's face to be the last thing I saw before I died.

I looked at Edan, his face tight with fear and effort. He squeezed my hand. I squeezed it back.

The sound of an engine made me turn.

Three vans rounded the corner, headlights blazing. The first one veered onto the grass, bouncing as it sped toward us.

I nearly collapsed with relief. Beside me, Edan made a sound between a yell and a gasp.

The back doors of the van swung open as it screeched to a stop. A man dressed in all black held a sharpshooter rifle.

"Let's go!" he yelled, waving us forward.

Edan and I dove for the vehicle. Another man held out his hand and yanked me in. I landed in a heap on the cold metal floor. Edan collapsed next to me a moment later.

"Thank you," I gasped as I sat up. We started moving.

The overhead light was on, and there were three men in the van—the one driving, and two in the back with us. The sharpshooter had dark hair and olive skin; the other was white with gray-brown hair and a beard. I didn't recognize them from training.

"This is Webb with unit three, reporting from C site," the white man said. He had an American accent, and he was staring past my head, clearly talking into an earpiece. "We just picked up two idiots and—" He stopped abruptly as he focused on Edan. He grasped him by the shirt suddenly, bringing him closer so he could see the logo clearly. "Dammit, these are Grayson's people."

"What?" The sharpshooter stole a glance over his shoulder. "Seriously?"

"It's right there on their uniforms. Goddammit."

"Just toss 'em back out!" the driver called from the front. "Problem solved."

I went very still. The van slowed, like the driver thought this was a serious suggestion.

Who were these guys?

Webb stared at us like he was considering it. He pulled a pistol from his hip and clicked off the safety. Beside me, Edan took in a sharp breath.

"Sanchez, how many do we have out there?" Webb asked, without moving his gaze from us. His pistol was pointed at the floor of the van, but clearly ready to go.

"Three, four dozen?" Sanchez's eyes went big. "No, cancel that. At least a hundred, a hundred and fifty."

"No joke," Webb breathed. He grinned. "That's even more than—" His eyes cut to us, and he abruptly stopped talking.

"So. Many," Sanchez said, barely containing his glee. I'd never seen someone so excited about scrabs.

I leaned forward until I could see out the back of the van. A swarm of scrabs galloped over a hill, partially illuminated by the headlights of one of the other vans.

The van bounced dangerously and then evened out. The driver hit the gas. We were back on the road.

"I know we shouldn't have, but they're just kids. I thought they were locals." Webb was talking into his earpiece again. "Should we toss them out?" He listened for a moment. "No, we're leaving now. We're going to need serious backup for this." Another pause. "Well then, you need to get them out here because they're not going to stay here for long." He nodded. "Yeah. Got it." He touched his earpiece, ending the conversation.

The driver looked over his shoulder. "Are we throwing them out? Better do it before we get too far from those scrabs."

Edan and I glanced at each other. I saw my fear mirrored in his eyes.

"No, there's a chance they could evade them," Webb said. He scrutinized us. "A slim chance."

"Then, what?" Sanchez said as he pulled the van doors shut. "We can't take them with us."

"We can't let them go, not yet anyway." Webb clicked the safety back on and slid the gun back in its holster. "I didn't sign up to kill a couple kids." He fixed us with a hard stare. "So don't make me, OK?"

"What do we have to do to make sure that doesn't happen?" Edan asked. His voice was quiet, strained.

"You're going to sit there quietly. You're going to let us blindfold you—"

"Blindfold?" Sanchez asked, confused.

"They can see out that window." Webb pointed to the front of the van. "Do you really want them knowing where we're going?"

"Good point," Sanchez began rifling through a box. "I'll find something."

"You're going to sit tight for one night, and then you can carry on fighting scrabs with your fellow morons tomorrow or the next day." Webb leaned forward, addressing the driver. "Curtis, call ahead and ask them to secure the window in the upstairs room."

"Seriously?" Curtis twisted around to look at us. "I can just turn around. We'll toss them out and watch to make sure the scrabs get them."

Edan edged a little closer to me. I didn't know what to hope for. Was it better to stay in here with the armed men threatening to blindfold us or to face the scrabs again?

"Just make the call," Webb snapped. "It's not their fault they fell for Grayson's nonsense."

Grayson's *nonsense*? Did he know something that we didn't?

"Here," Sanchez said, handing Webb a white T-shirt and a bandana.

"Those'll work, I guess," Webb said. He rolled up the shirt and moved closer to Edan. "Lean forward, kid. Help me out here."

Edan didn't move. "Our team will miss us. If you just let us go, we—"

"Not happening," Webb interrupted. "You two can go back to waving around machetes like a bunch of idiots with a death wish tomorrow. But today, you're going to shut up and let me put this blindfold on. Or I'm going to shoot you. Those are your only two options."

Edan swallowed hard and leaned forward. Webb secured the shirt around his eyes, tucking in a piece so it didn't hang over his mouth. He moved on to me next, tying the bandana around my head tightly. I could see my feet through the crack at the bottom, but not out the window.

"I am not the bad guy here," said the man currently kidnapping and blindfolding us, "but I do have a job to do, and I can't afford to let you two screw it up." His shoes shifted away from us. "I'm not cuffing you as long as you don't touch the blindfolds. But I'm not moving from this spot, so don't try anything."

Edan's arm bumped mine as the van went over a hole. I reached out and slipped my hand into his. He squeezed it tightly.

26

THE VAN CAME TO A STOP ABOUT AN HOUR LATER. OR MAYBE TWO hours. It was hard to judge the time, given the blindfold and the darkness. My ankle was starting to hurt where the scrab had bit me, now that my panic was wearing off.

"Up," Webb said. "Don't take those blindfolds off, I'll help." I felt him tap a finger to my wrist. I was still holding Edan's hand.

I slipped my fingers from his and found the hand that Webb had extended. I got to my feet, keeping my head down so I could see the edge of the van. I jumped out.

Through the crack in the blindfold, I could see light flooding the ground from a source overhead, and two people standing nearby. Curtis and Sanchez, maybe. They wore matching dusty black boots.

It was noisy around me. Murmured voices and running footsteps. In the distance, someone called, *"In stall five, please!"* A cricket chirped.

"Whoops, sorry," I heard Edan say from behind me. "I can't see where I'm going. Could you just . . . thanks." I heard his feet hit the ground a moment later. His fingers brushed against my arm, like he was checking to make sure I was still there.

"Can we get a restroom?" I asked no one in particular. "We were locked in a closet for hours, and if you don't let me go soon, you're going to regret it."

"There's a toilet in the room," Webb replied. "Follow me."

"You're going to have to be more specific," Edan said dryly.

"Oh. Right. Grab your girlfriend's hand. I'll lead you in."

Edan's hand slipped into mine again. Webb yanked my other one, and I stumbled as he pulled me forward.

We crossed a threshold, and I saw a rug and wooden floors at my feet. A house, maybe?

Webb led us up the wooden stairs to the second floor. A door creaked as he opened it.

"Sit tight," Webb said. "You can take the blindfolds off, if you want." The door shut. I heard a lock click.

I yanked the bandana off. We were in a dark, totally empty room. A crack of light sliced across the floor from an ajar door to my left, and Edan pushed it open. The bathroom.

There was a small window on the other side of the room, but it was covered by something black from the outside. I rushed over to it and tried to find a way to push it open. There wasn't one. I could break it, but they would surely hear that. Not to mention that we'd just gone up stairs. We were on the second floor.

Edan disappeared into the bathroom, leaving me in darkness for a few minutes. When he reemerged, I ducked inside.

The bathroom was almost completely empty too. There was nothing but a toilet, bathtub, toilet paper, and a bar of soap by the sink. Not even a towel to dry my hands. I cleaned the bite mark on my ankle, which didn't look too bad. Luckily that thing didn't have many teeth yet.

Edan was standing by the window, examining it, when I stepped out of the bathroom.

"How's your leg?" I pointed to where blood was crusted to his pants.

"It feels OK. Yours?"

"Nothing serious."

He swallowed nervously. "I have to confess something."

I raised my eyebrows expectantly. He reached into his back pocket and pulled out a wallet.

I stared at it blankly for a moment before realizing. "That's not yours, is it?"

"It's Webb's."

"Why would you steal it? *How* did you steal it?"

"That shirt was a crappy blindfold. I could see if I tilted my head up a bit."

"I'm still waiting for the why."

"I thought it would tell us who these guys are. Honestly I was really hoping they were taking us to some high-tech facility and then I'd have his key card or something. And we'd just swipe it and go."

"That would have been helpful," I conceded. I glanced back at the door. "I mean, we could break down that door no problem. I've done it by myself before."

"Yeah, we—wait, what? You've broken down a door before?"

"Did you find out who he was?" I asked, ignoring the question.

He flipped the wallet open. Webb's picture was next to an MDG logo.

"What is the Monster Defense Group doing in France?" I asked.

"Well, they're doing something with those scrabs we just found, that's for sure." He closed the wallet, an abashed look crossing his face. "But I realized right after I took it that I was putting you in danger too, and . . ." He met my gaze. "I'm sorry. I wasn't thinking."

"It's fine," I said. At least he'd been trying to think of a way to get us out of here. I'd just gone along with it. "We should hide it, though. He'll probably just think he lost it somewhere. He's not going to suspect that you lifted his wallet when at least two other guys were watching while you were *blindfolded*."

He looked like he was trying very hard to hold back a laugh.

"What?" I asked.

"You accused me of being a bad criminal once. You seriously doubted my skills, you may remember."

"Oh my god." I rolled my eyes, but a smile spread across my face.

"I'm just saying." One side of his mouth lifted a little higher than the other when he grinned. "Blindfolded. And motion sick. And I had to pee, which was very distracting. And like you said, at least two other guys were watching."

"Fine, yes, you are the best pickpocket ever. I'll admit it."

"Thank you." He walked into the bathroom. "I'll put it in the toilet tank."

"Do you feel better now?" I asked. "The motion sickness?"

"I still feel a bit dizzy, but it'll pass," he called as the water turned on. He emerged a minute later, shaking out his wet arms. He wiped them on his pants and pulled out his phone.

"They didn't take your phone?" I asked.

"They sure didn't. I think this is their first kidnapping. There's room for improvement."

A laugh bubbled up in my chest. I realized suddenly how grateful I was to be with Edan, of all people, in this situation. I couldn't have handled a horde of scrabs or kidnapping amateurs with someone who defaulted to angry or hysterical in scary situations.

"Their Wi-Fi is password protected, though." Edan sighed and slid his phone back into his pocket.

The door opened, and I jumped at the sudden intrusion. Webb stood with one foot in the room, two rolled-up sleeping bags tucked under his arms. He tossed them on the floor.

"All right, kids, change of plans. You're going to need to sit tight here until we decide what to do with you."

My body went cold. "What to do with us?"

"You can't keep us here," Edan said.

"I can, and I will," Webb said. "The fewer morons we have running around making my job harder, the better. Stay quiet, and we won't have any problems, OK?"

We both just stared at him.

"With any luck, Grayson's teams will implode in the next couple days, and you guys can get out of my hair permanently." He stepped back, starting to pull the door closed. "We'll send up some food soon. And I mean it about being quiet. You start making trouble, and I can't be held responsible for what some of these guys will do." He looked at us seriously before pulling the door shut.

I took in a shaky breath and listened to his footsteps fade. "Why would they keep us here? How does that make any sense?"

"They were really excited about all those scrabs," Edan said. "I think they're worried that if they let us go, we'll tell Grayson about it."

"And, what? They want first crack at it? MDG doesn't even hunt scrabs, do they?"

"I have no idea. But I think we should try to get out of here. I don't want to wait around to see what they decide to do with us." He looked at me expectantly.

I hesitated. It sounded like Webb would let us go if we were patient. Of course, he'd also basically threatened to kill us if we made trouble, so maybe it was stupid to trust him.

"They're up to something with that nest," Edan said, when I didn't reply. "I want to get word to Grayson as soon as possible."

"Do you have a plan?"

"What's holding your bangs back right now?"

I put my hand on my hair, confused. "A bobby pin?"

"Perfect. Do you mind if I use it to pick that lock?" He jerked his head at the door.

"You know how to pick a lock?"

"What, in our time together, makes you think I *don't* know how to pick a lock?"

I laughed. "Good point." I reached for the pin.

"You can keep it for now. I can hear people in the house. Let's wait until tonight, see if it quiets down."

"You really think you can do it?"

"Absolutely." He held my gaze. "We're getting out of here."

27

I SAT ON MY SLEEPING BAG NEXT TO EDAN, OUR BACKS AGAINST the wall and our legs stretched out in front of us. The bathroom light cast a soft glow across the floor a few feet from us.

Downstairs, I could still hear murmured voices, even though it was late. We had no chance of escape if they didn't leave or sleep, and I'd had too much time to think. I was starting to worry about what Webb had planned for us if we didn't get out of here.

"Why did you break down the door last time?" Edan asked. We'd been quiet for a long time, yet somehow the question that picked up a conversation we had hours ago didn't seem out of place.

I couldn't think of a lie off the top of my head. I wasn't sure I wanted to lie, anyway.

"My dad locked me in my room when he found out I was coming here." I snuck a quick look at him, expecting horror, or at least surprise, but he just cocked his head, like he found this interesting.

"How'd you break it down?" he asked.

I almost laughed. Edan was so unflappable. It was nice to tell this story to someone who didn't immediately become uncomfortable and start pitying me.

"I just kicked it until I made a hole big enough to escape through. Made a run for it."

"Badass."

"And yet I'm right back here." Locked in a room by a dude who didn't trust me to make my own decisions.

"We're getting out of here," Edan said.

"But if we don't, you don't think they'll send us back, do you?"

"Send us back where?"

"Home. To the US."

"No. Why would they do that?"

"I don't know. It's just . . . I didn't have my parents' permission to come, and maybe they reported me missing or something." I glanced at him and then quickly away. "MDG has a lot of former military and law enforcement people working for them. You don't think they'd care, do you?"

"No," he said, but he sounded a little unsure this time. "I'm sure they don't care. And you got out of the country. If your parents could have stopped you, they probably would have back then."

"Right." I let out a breath. "That makes me feel better."

There was a long pause before he spoke again. "But . . . if something happens and you do end up back in the US, don't go back home. OK? Even if they say it will be better this time. Don't go."

I met his gaze, wondering what I'd said that made me so transparent. He understood, or he suspected, without me having to actually explain it.

"You didn't ask why," he said quietly. "When I said I left home, and I told you Grayson kept trying to get me to go back, you didn't ask why I wouldn't."

Right. Normal people probably asked why. Even if they

suspected, they asked, hoping for an answer that was better than what they were thinking. I didn't have that kind of hope.

"And you said your parents were assholes," he continued. "And your dad locked you in your room. Bedroom doors don't lock from the outside, so either he installed a special lock"—he pointed to the shiny new lock on the old door of our room—"or he did something to the door. Either way, it's not a normal thing to do."

"He used a rope," I said. "Tied it to the doorknob next to mine so it held it shut."

"Wow, that is some quick thinking." He did not say it like he was impressed.

"Yeah."

"My mom never would have locked me in my room. She really preferred it when I was gone, so that would have been counterproductive."

"Your mom . . ." I didn't know how to ask the question.

"Was the one to kick the shit out of me? Yes. Mostly." He'd said it easily, like he was used to telling the story to people. It was probably his way of coping with it, making it sound like it was no big deal anymore. It was how I'd always imagined Laurence would tell people about our dad.

"My dad did some too, before he left, but I was nine when that happened. Sometimes my mom's boyfriend got in on the action, though."

"Oh."

I'd never been on the other side of this conversation. But it didn't seem right to let him share that without offering something in return. It felt like a betrayal, to just say I was sorry and move on, while keeping the truth locked inside.

"It was always my dad," I said, the words a little strained as they got stuck in my throat. "My mom never did much to stop it, but my dad was the one who . . . kicked the shit out of us," I said, stumbling a little as I repeated his words.

"Were you there until you joined?" he asked. "Like, this was the first time you left?"

"Yeah. I never had anywhere else to go. Then this opportunity came up, and I guess getting killed by scrabs seemed preferable to getting killed by my dad."

"Yeah. Seriously." He said it like he totally agreed. Like it wasn't a crazy thing to do at all. "Your brother . . . he's older?"

"Yes. Three years older."

"Was he still around?"

"He was, but he left when I did. Dad went after him too sometimes," I said, knowing what Edan was getting at. "Not like me, because I was the bad one. But he got it some. And he tried to stop it some when he got older, but . . ." I shrugged. "Do you have siblings?"

"No. Not that I know of, anyway. Who knows what my dad did after he left. Maybe he's out there beating the shit out of a new family." He arched his back and checked his phone — 3:45 a.m.

"Did it make it easier?" he asked. "Having a brother to talk to?"

"Laurence isn't much of a talker. I think he mostly wanted to pretend like it wasn't happening. He and my mom were alike in that way. I'd think that things were going to change, that we'd finally acknowledge how bad he'd gotten, but the next morning it was like nothing happened."

"My mom did that to me all the time. She'd look at me all baffled, like she couldn't believe I was still upset. It made me feel like a crazy person. Like I was remembering things wrong."

"*Yes*," I said, my relief coming through in my voice. No one had ever voiced that exact thing to me before. "And you stop trusting your own memory, because maybe you actually are just overreacting or creating things in your head."

"It must have been worse for you, huh? Having a mom and brother also latch onto the lie. It seems lonelier, actually. Having people to talk to about it and being rejected."

"Maybe," I said quietly. "I think it's just bad either way."

"Yeah." He let out a long breath. "I've never talked to anyone about this before. It's weird."

"What?" I looked at him in surprise. "Really?"

"I mean, I've told a few people. Like Grayson. But it wasn't like this. He just got uncomfortable and told me how sorry he was. I meant I've never talked to someone else like this. Someone who understood."

"Me either. I'd never told anyone at all until Julian. And I only told him because I had to."

"You had to?"

"My dad was trying to make me come back home, and I'm only seventeen, so Julian was going to send me. I told him. Showed him the bruises on my arm."

He paused for a moment. "Did you feel like you needed proof?"

"Absolutely. Not because of anything Julian did," I added quickly. "We'd just met that day; I didn't know anything about the guy. But I've never felt like people would believe me just because I said so. Especially not strangers."

"I don't really feel that way. I think I did when I was younger, but not now. Why would I lie about that?"

"It's because I'm a girl. People are always suspicious of girls. Especially men."

"Oh. Shit. You're right. Jesus, that sucks."

I laughed softly. "It does."

We were both quiet for a moment. The voices downstairs had faded.

"Let's wait, like, half an hour," he said. "If it's still totally quiet then, we'll make a break for it."

"OK."

He shifted, adjusting the sleeping bag beneath him. "Does it not bother you?" he asked. "The sparring?"

"No. Why?" I turned to look at him, but his gaze was downcast. "Ohhhh. Is that why you avoid instead of engaging?"

"Yeah, I just . . . Part of me panics when someone tries to hit me. You can't tell?"

"I couldn't tell at all."

"That's good, I guess. I try to hide it. I spent a lot of time honing my flight response when I sensed danger, so I'm really fast. I'm basically having a mild panic attack every time we do sparring. It takes a lot of effort not to just run away."

I thought of how my heart would pound every time Dad would come home. Even if I knew he was in a good mood. Even if he was returning after a few weeks gone and I knew I'd have at least a few days before we slipped back into our normal routine. Every cell in my body went on high alert, regardless of how much I tried to reason with it.

"With scrabs too?" I asked.

"No, definitely not with scrabs. It's something about a fist coming at my face. I know I should work on it, but I'm paired with Gage now."

I winced. "That can't be helping."

"It's really not. I think Julian did it on purpose to torment me."

He was probably right. But surely Julian didn't know that Edan was *scared* of sparring. I didn't think he'd pair him with Gage if he knew that.

"What if we switch?" I asked. "I've been with Dorsey lately, and he'll have no problem sparring with Gage. We could work on it?"

"You don't mind?"

"Not at all."

"Thanks," he said, looking up at me with a smile. I returned it.

At four thirty a.m., Edan asked for my bobby pin.

He crept to the door and crouched in front of the knob, working almost silently.

Then he stood and turned to me with an expectant expression. It took me a moment to realize that the door was already cracked.

I wondered if he could see the surprise on my face in the dark. I'd believed he'd picked a lock before, but I thought maybe he'd popped open a jewelry box once. My hopes hadn't been high. They weren't even in the medium range.

A smile twitched at his lips, like he knew exactly why I was so taken aback. He tilted his head toward the door, indicating for me to follow him.

We stepped out of the room. The floors creaked quietly beneath our feet—there was no way to avoid it—but hopefully not loud enough to alert anyone of our presence.

Edan went left at the staircase. We slowly descended the steps. It was dark, the rooms on the first floor just shapes in the darkness. The front door loomed in front of us, and I scanned the wall next to it for an alarm system. I didn't see one. Which didn't mean it wasn't there.

We took the last step and crept to the door. Edan carefully unlocked the deadbolt. He grasped the knob and turned.

The door opened to silence. No alarm system. My shoulders sagged with relief.

We stepped onto the porch. We were on a farm. There were stables right across from us, and to my left was a large barn.

Edan sucked in a breath suddenly and grabbed my hand. I stole a glance over my shoulder as he pulled me off the porch. The property was gated, and an armed guard stood beneath a light in front of the gate.

We darted around the house. Edan dropped my hand as we pressed our backs to the wall.

"Did he see us?" I whispered.

"I don't think so."

I leaned forward, trying to see the back of the property. Was it gated all the way around? Were there more guards? All I could make out was the outline of another barn, and a smaller building in the distance.

Voices made my head snap back around. They were two male voices, coming from the front of the house. They were getting closer.

I took a quick glance left and right, and then darted for the barn in front of us. The door was cracked, so I pushed it open just enough to squeeze through. Edan followed.

"Oh my god," Edan breathed.

Scrabs. A whole row of them stretched out in front of us, locked in individual stalls. The building had probably been meant to hold livestock, but the stalls had been modified with steel bars to become cages.

And they were *silent*. Why weren't they growling? Roaring?

My eyes darted around the huge space. There were so many stalls — rows and rows of them. Several hundred scrabs could fit in here. *At least*.

I took a hesitant step forward and peered around the next row. Empty.

The following row was the same, two stalls in the middle completely mangled, like the scrab had torn the bars off. Red lights flickered on and off on the front of these cages, like they were malfunctioning.

"They escaped," Edan whispered. He touched the flickering light on the front of an empty cage. "Hundreds of them."

"Do you think—"

"That those are the scrabs we just ran into? Definitely. Some of them, at least. Did you see those things on their necks? I saw those same things on a few of the scrabs."

He walked back to the only remaining row of scrabs and pointed at one. It had a silver oval attached to each side of its neck, and three more across its forehead. Edan was right—I'd seen something just like that on one of the scrabs in the nest.

The scrab opened its mouth, and I tensed, waiting for the roar. Nothing came. Its face twisted with rage, mouth wide open, but its scream was nearly soundless. It was the same as the scrab that had almost killed Edan. Just a tiny squeak.

It turned to stalk farther into its cell, and I saw a third device, this one glowing red, at the base of its spine.

"Yeah, I'm just bringing him back now," a voice said. I heard the barn door slide open.

Edan and I darted to the next row and crouched behind the last empty stall. I snuck a peek around the corner.

Sanchez, one of the men who had picked us up in the van, was walking down the first row. He had a scrab on a leash, like a pet. It snarled up at Sanchez, ready to take a bite out of its owner.

"Hey," Sanchez said sharply. He was holding a black box in his hand, like a small remote control, and he aimed it at the scrab and pressed something. The scrab jerked, like it had just been electro-cuted, and collapsed onto its stomach.

Sanchez yanked roughly on its leash, forcing it to its feet. He stopped in front of an empty stall in the middle. He unlocked the cage.

"Sit," he said to the scrab.

The scrab sat.

I cast a baffled look at Edan.

"In," Sanchez said. The scrab stood and walked into the cage. Sanchez locked the door behind it.

I quickly ducked back behind the wall as he stepped away from the cage.

"He's in," Sanchez said. He must have been talking into an earpiece, because I didn't hear a reply. His footsteps faded as he walked away. I heard the barn door open again.

"What are they doing?" I whispered to Edan. "Why are they *training* them?"

"I have no idea," he said. "But let's get the hell out of here before they decide to stick *us* in those cages."

"There's another door over there." I pointed to a door in the corner of the barn.

We jogged across the barn. The scrabs in the first row turned to watch us as we ran.

I grasped the doorknob. It didn't budge. I fumbled with the cheap lock, realizing for the first time that my hands were shaking.

I finally freed the lock and pushed the door open. I practically launched myself out of it. I let out a relieved sigh as Edan shut the door behind us.

We stood in the dark, but a light shone over two vans parked in a patch of grass not far away. Behind them, I could see the wall surrounding the property. It was tall and topped with the messy, scary bundle of barbed wire that they used in prisons. Not the kind of wall we could climb.

I glanced at Edan. His face was tight as he looked from the wall to the front gate manned by the armed guard.

The guard was opening the gate, a black van like the others rolling through. The guard pulled the gate closed behind them.

"That gate doesn't look super strong, right?" Edan said. "They just latch it when they close it."

"I guess?"

"So we could probably drive a van right through it," he whispered. The van stopped next to the others beneath the light, and Edan's eyes followed the man who jumped out of the driver's seat. He walked into the nearby small shed.

"Do you know how to hotwire a car too?" I asked.

"No, I don't know how to drive. So that skill would be kinda useless."

"You don't know how to drive? How do you plan to bust a van out of here, then?"

He looked at me in surprise. "I assumed you could. Don't Texans drive everywhere?"

"Sure, but my dad never let me touch his car. My brother let me drive around a parking lot once, though." Like a year ago.

"That's one more time than me. You'll be fine. Assuming I can get those keys." He pointed to where the driver was coming out of the shed. "I think they keep them in there. He was swinging them when he went in, and now his hands are empty."

We waited until the man walked away before creeping through the dark to the shed.

"The door is probably locked, and it's too bright over there, anyway," Edan whispered. He pointed to a small window over his head. "Do you want to give me a boost, or do you want to climb in?"

"I'll give you the boost." I knelt down on one knee. He put a hand on my shoulder, using it for balance as he put his foot on my knee. He grabbed the edge of the window and pulled it open. His feet left my knee as he started to pull himself in.

"I see them! Hold my legs. I can grab them without going all the way in."

I wrapped my hands tightly around each of his ankles and glanced over my shoulder. We were still alone.

"OK, I'm coming out," he said, voice muffled. I moved my hands up to his calves, then his waist, as he slid out the window. He let go of the ledge, bumping against me as he hit the ground. I held tighter to his waist, steadying us both.

He whirled around, a grin on his face. Three sets of keys dangled from his fingers.

"All three of them, huh?" I almost laughed. Hope was blooming bigger in my chest.

"I don't know if they have others cars around here, but I wasn't going to just leave the keys there so they could jump in the other vans and chase us."

"Jesus, that's smart." I almost sounded annoyed. I'd been going for impressed.

His smile widened as he put a set of keys in my hand. "Don't press the Unlock button until we get close. I think we're going to need to make a run for it, but let's give ourselves time to get as close as possible."

"Got it." I gripped the keys.

We edged around the side of the shed. The immediate area surrounding the vans was empty, the light shining on empty grass. But a cluster of men stood outside the barn a few yards away.

I started toward the vans, Edan by my side. We were walking slowly, trying not to attract attention.

One of the men turned.

Then another.

We broke into a run.

"Hey!" a man yelled.

"It's the kids!" another called.

I pressed the Unlock button and the lights of the van on the left side flashed. I dove for it.

I yanked the driver's door open and jumped inside. Edan slid into the passenger's seat.

One of the men was racing toward me. "Stop!" he yelled. It was Webb.

I slammed the door shut. His hands hit the window. I pushed the Lock button.

My hands were shaking as I stuck the key in the ignition. I turned it, not entirely sure how long I was supposed to hold it. The car had already been running when I practiced with Laurence.

The engine roared to life, and I let go of the key. I examined the gear stick. It was an automatic, thank god. Edan and I hadn't considered what we'd do if it was a standard.

Through the windshield, I could see Webb yelling at someone, a furious expression on his face. A man stood at the door of the shed, shaking his head.

Webb looked back at us. Edan held up the two other sets of

keys, the best shit-eating grin I'd ever seen on his face. Webb cursed loudly.

I pressed what I thought was the brake. The engine revved. Apparently that one was the gas. I quickly switched to the brake and put the car in reverse.

I lifted my head to see Webb pointing his gun directly at my face.

I didn't bother checking the rearview mirror before hitting the gas. Bullets pelted the car. Edan yelped, ducking down in his seat. I yanked the wheel hard to the right. One of the back windows shattered as a bullet zipped through it.

I stomped on the brakes, sending Edan into the dashboard. He grunted. Outside, someone yelled. The gunfire stopped.

"You should probably put your seat belt on." I quickly took my own advice, and he clicked his into place.

I put the car in drive.

Something slammed into the side of the van. We nearly tipped over. Metal crunched.

A scrab stared at me through my window, its mouth open in a silent roar. A tiny light blinked on the side of its head.

"Go!" Edan yelled.

I pressed the gas and turned the wheel hard. We were facing the gate. Sanchez stood near it, another scrab at his side.

It just stood there, unmoving.

Sanchez had something shiny strapped to his wrist. He pressed his finger to it.

The scrab sprang into action. It galloped toward the van.

I floored the gas pedal, and we lurched forward. Something

hit the side of the van again, then I heard a thump. I looked in the rearview mirror to see one of the scrabs jumping up from the ground.

I turned my attention out the front windshield. The gate loomed ahead of us. The man guarding it dove out of the way.

I gripped the steering wheel, my heart pounding. The gate didn't look particularly strong, but maybe I was wrong. Maybe it wouldn't pop open, and we'd crash into it at high speed instead. Then those scrabs would jump through the back window and rip our throats out.

The car jerked as it hit the gate, the sound of metal hitting metal echoing through the van. We barreled straight through. Edan whooped.

I had to make a hard right onto the road, and I took it way too fast. The van veered into the grass. I jerked the wheel to the left, trying to straighten it. Edan clutched the dash.

"Sorry," I said as the van evened out.

"It's fine. You're doing great."

I glanced in the rearview mirror. A scrab skidded onto the road and then abruptly stopped. I hit the gas harder. The road was so dark I could barely see.

Headlights. Right. Turning those on would probably help. I fumbled with the knobs until the road in front of me came into view.

I let out a slow breath as we barreled away from the farm. My body was still buzzing with adrenaline, and part of me wanted to burst into tears.

"They were *controlling* those scrabs," I said. "Right? You saw that too?"

"They absolutely were."

"How? Why? *How?*" I couldn't wrap my mind around what exactly this meant. Was MDG building an army of scrabs? Who did they plan to use it against?

"My questions exactly." Edan's eyes were wide, his hair ruffling in the wind coming from the destroyed back window.

"Thank you." My voice shook.

"Thank you?" Edan repeated. "Me?"

I laughed, blinking back tears. "Yes, you. There's no one else in this car."

Edan twisted around in his seat like he just realized he should confirm that.

"For getting us out of there," I clarified. "Thank you."

"I didn't do it alone."

"Yeah, you mostly did."

"You saved me from getting eaten by a scrab, I saved you from a half-assed kidnapping . . . Does that make us even?"

"I think it does."

"I got the good end of that deal." Edan leaned his head back against the seat with a sigh. "I honestly didn't think they would shoot at us. I thought they were bluffing."

"They really were not."

"We need to find a phone. Or Wi-Fi. We need to call Grayson and tell him about that nest. They kept us because they didn't want us getting to it first."

"Because they wanted to capture them." My eyes widened. "Or *re*capture them."

"Holy hell. You're right." He pointed out the window. "Look, a house. Hopefully we're not too far from a town."

Twenty minutes later, the road curved and a huge cluster of lights appeared in the distance.

I glanced at the clock: 5:13 a.m. Nothing was going to be open at this hour.

I turned off the main road, and we drove slowly through deserted streets, searching for something that was open. Everything was dark and locked up tight.

"What do the French do when they want to make cookies at three a.m.?" Edan said. "If we were in New York, we would have passed, like, ten open stores by now."

"We would have seen at least one twenty-four-hour Walmart by now if we were in Texas." I peered past Edan at the stores on his side of his street. The word *boulangerie* popped out at me. I hit the brakes.

"Oof." Edan jerked in his seat.

"Sorry." I pointed. "But look. A bakery." The store front was dim, but I could see a hint of light in the back. "Bakers get up early."

"That's brilliant." He unhooked his seat belt. "Do you want to wait in the van while I run in?"

"Sure."

He climbed out, pausing to look back at me. "What's the French word for phone?"

"I have no idea."

"I'll figure something out." He shut the door and jogged to the bakery. He'd left the van window open, and I could hear as he banged on the door and yelled, "Excuse me!"

A man in a white apron appeared and spoke to Edan for a moment. He opened the door, and Edan disappeared inside.

Edan reemerged a few minutes later, smiling at the man and shaking his hand. He jogged back to the car and hopped inside.

"You talked to Grayson?" I asked.

"Yep. The French word for telephone is *téléphone,* by the way."

"Well, that seems . . . obvious."

"Grayson definitely thought we were dead. And he's pissed that I never bought a local SIM card. Apparently he's been calling every half hour." He held up a piece of paper with several lines scrawled on it. A map. "But I got directions once he calmed down."

"Where are we going?"

"Back to the scrabs."

28

THE SUN ROSE AS WE GOT CLOSER TO THE NEST. GRAYSON TOLD Edan that the teams were waiting until daylight to go back and search for us, but that they hadn't had much hope. Apparently the team members who'd been in the van with us had searched until they saw the scrabs outside the house and then were forced to hightail it out of there. I couldn't blame them.

I stopped the van on the side of the road. I couldn't see the house where we'd hidden from here, but I knew we were close.

I swallowed down a wave of fear as I looked out at the empty field. It had only been a few hours since Edan and I made a run for it, both of us convinced those minutes were our last. I sort of wished Grayson had told us to go back to Paris. I wanted a bed and a shower, not more scrab fighting.

A Jeep appeared on the road, followed by several more, and a long line of vans and trucks. About ten all-terrain vehicles zipped around them into the grass.

Grayson was in the passenger seat of the first Jeep, and he jumped out before it had completely come to a stop. Edan and I stepped out of the van.

Grayson rushed to Edan, almost knocking him over as he hugged him.

"You asshole," Grayson said as he released him. "I thought you were dead."

"I would have been, if it weren't for Clara." Edan smiled at me.

Several members of team seven jumped out of the Jeeps, and I was suddenly crushed between Patrick and Priya.

"You're not dead!" Priya exclaimed, jumping up and down with her arms around my waist.

"Not yet," I said with a laugh. I was actually sort of delighted by how happy Priya was that I wasn't dead.

The rest of the team stood a few steps away. Noah was grinning. Laila and Madison were laughing about something. Even Gage looked moderately happy to see us. Behind them, Naomi and the rest of UK team nine waved from their Jeep. I waved back.

"Julian?" I asked.

"Still in Paris," Noah said.

"We thought for sure you were dead when we saw all those scrabs over the hill," Laila said, leaning against the van. "Noah started video tributes that he was going to post after they notified your families."

"Oh god, you didn't notify my family, did you?" I asked Grayson.

He shook his head with a smile. "No. It's policy to wait forty-eight hours after you go missing to notify."

I let out a breath. "OK. Good."

"This is an MDG van?" Grayson laid his hand on the hood.

"Yeah," Edan said. "What should we do with it?"

"Just leave it here. I'm sure they'll be back to this area soon."

"Edan told you what we saw? The scrabs they were . . ." Training? Controlling? I didn't know what to call it.

"What?" Madison asked. "What did you see?" The rest of the team looked at us curiously.

"Let's deal with these scrabs first, and then we'll talk about it," Grayson said. "Team seven, will you go back to your Jeeps and get ready? Edan, Clara, grab some weapons. I need you two to lead us to the nest."

"They're hard to miss," Edan muttered. We walked to the second Jeep, where Laila was waiting with several weapons in hand. She gave both of us a machete.

"You guys can support me and Noah first," she said. "Noah and Madison came up with a plan to keep us mostly together, so you can squeeze into the Jeep with us."

I glanced over to where Noah and Madison were talking. *They came up with a plan?* Why hadn't Julian left Paris right away when he heard we were missing? Or when he'd heard there were scrabs? Grayson had said he was planning to come here this morning regardless, which meant Julian knew his team would be hunting this morning. Was Julian doing something important in Paris? Had he even cared that I was missing?

"What does *support* mean?" Edan asked. Patrick slid into the driver's seat of the Jeep, and Dorsey took the passenger's seat. A camera was mounted to the top of our vehicle. I noticed that several team members were also wearing the little cameras that Noah had recently received. Grayson had one on too.

"It means literally holding my legs while I shoot so I don't fall out of this thing," Noah said. He took one of the rifles Laila had in her hands and climbed into the Jeep. He stayed standing, pointing to the seat behind him. "Edan, you sit there."

Laila hopped up next to Noah, and I slid into the seat next to Edan. In front of us, Grayson's Jeep took off into the grass. Patrick hit the gas and followed.

"I hope they're still there," Noah said.

My thoughts were mirrored on Edan's face—I sort of hoped they'd left. Edan told Grayson how many scrabs we had seen, but I didn't know if he fully understood the sheer numbers out here.

On the other hand, I didn't want MDG to have the scrabs if they were going to lock them up and train them. I couldn't imagine what they wanted to train them for, but it would certainly be a disaster. They'd already let hundreds escape.

"There they are," Patrick said.

My head snapped forward. The patch of houses was straight ahead. I spotted the one where Edan and I had hid.

Two scrabs stood on their hind legs, watching us.

"Are you sure it's a nest?" Dorsey asked.

Another scrab climbed out of a hole. Then another. And another, and another, climbing out of holes all around the house.

"Never mind," Dorsey said.

"Get us a little closer," Laila said to Patrick. She and Noah had their rifles balanced on the frame of the Jeep. "Clara, hold my legs tight!"

I leaned forward and wrapped my arms firmly around her waist. Edan did the same to Noah. Around us, engines roared as vehicles zipped by.

Laila began firing. Dorsey shouted his approval as scrabs began screaming.

"Damn, you are good!" he said, twisting around to look at her. "They should have put you on a sharpshooter team."

I leaned to the side to peer around Laila at the scrabs in front of us. Two jerked as bullets pierced their flesh. They began scattering, running in every direction. Grayson's Jeep spewed dirt as tires spun. A scrab barreled straight for us.

"Hold on!" Patrick yelled.

I held Laila tighter as he jerked the wheel to the right. We barely swerved in time to miss hitting a scrab. Patrick spun the wheel again, turning us back around to face it. Noah and Laila fired.

We took off again, leaving the dead scrab in the dust.

"Patrick!" Dorsey yelled, pointing to the left.

Patrick hit the gas, but the scrab was already there. It crashed against the Jeep.

I tried to hold on to Laila, but the whole Jeep tilted violently to the right. The scrab slammed into the side again.

Someone screamed as we tipped over and crashed onto the ground. I fell on top of Edan and Noah. Laila fell on top of me.

"Ow," Edan said.

The scrab braced its claws against the frame of the Jeep, baring its teeth as it roared at us. Laila lifted her gun and shot directly into its mouth. Blood splattered across us as its head flew back. It collapsed.

"Gross," she said. She grabbed the frame and pulled herself out of the Jeep, then offered me her hand.

I stumbled out, grabbing my baton. Nearby, someone whooped. I heard gunfire.

I turned around. Two ATVs zipped past me, spraying dirt into the air. Jeeps and vans circled the area, picking off scrabs with bullets. Another van had crashed, and American team five ran on foot to a cluster of scrabs.

"Stand back," Laila said.

Five scrabs galloped straight toward us. Laila and Noah strode forward, guns aimed at them. Noah glanced to his left, then said something to Laila. They both lowered their guns.

A Jeep raced across the grass and skidded to a stop in front of them. It was the rest of team seven. Archer was driving, Priya in the seat next to him. Madison stood in the back with a gun, Gage and Zoe on the seats behind her. Archer stopped the Jeep between us and the scrabs. Madison began firing.

Laila and Noah ran to either side of the Jeep to help.

"Guys," Patrick said, pointing to my left. I whirled around. Three scrabs ran in our direction.

Gage and Zoe jumped out of their Jeep and ran to us. Gage flexed the fingers of his left hand. He wore brass knuckles with three-inch spikes attached. I hadn't seen that one amongst Grayson's weapons.

Gage darted forward as the first scrab approached. He swung the machete in his right hand high across its face and, with his left hand, drove his spikes directly under its chin. He punched the scrab with such force that its whole body jerked.

I winced, thinking of that punch hitting Edan's face.

The scrab stumbled back, and I leapt forward, sinking my blade into its neck. Gage nodded in approval.

Patrick and Zoe already had the second scrab on the ground,

and Dorsey was poised to drive his blade into the stomach of the third one as Edan distracted it.

Another scrab was headed in our direction. I gripped my baton.

"*Attention!*" I heard from behind me.

I quickly stepped back as an ATV whizzed by. The driver held one of the bladed clubs out to his side. It connected with the scrab, sending blood flying from its neck. I jumped forward, finishing it off with a quick stab to its stomach.

"Thank you!" I called as the ATV raced away.

"*De rien!*" the driver shouted over his shoulder.

Several members of team seven were attempting to right the Jeep. Patrick grimaced as they pushed it back up on its tires.

"Let's go!" he said, running around to the driver's side.

I climbed in behind Laila. She shot off a few more rounds as we took off, but dead scrabs littered the ground in every direction. A recruit in another Jeep lifted his arms in victory.

"Hey!" Grayson's Jeep sped up beside ours. Patrick slowed. "Where is the nest?"

"That house," I said, pointing to the house not far ahead. "On the side with the bushes."

"All right. Stay here." His Jeep took off. He jumped out as they approached the house. He peered into the hole and then stepped back, a huge grin on his face.

"Move back! Take cover!" he yelled.

Patrick put the Jeep in reverse.

"Keep us pointed at that," Noah said, looking up at the camera on the roof. Patrick stopped the Jeep.

Grayson tossed something in the hole and jumped in the Jeep. It sped away.

A blast rocked the earth. Fire and debris spewed out of the hole as it exploded. Recruits all around me cheered.

"Guys?" Patrick said. He pointed in the direction of the road. Three black vans like the one Edan and I had stolen veered into the grass and bounced toward us. The first one came to an abrupt stop, and Webb jumped out. His face was furious as he strode toward us. One hand rested on the gun at his hip.

"I don't think he's happy to see us," Edan said.

A Jeep rolled in front of us, blocking our view of Webb. Grayson hopped out, a grin on his face.

"Sorry guys, but we got them all. Better luck next time."

Webb grabbed his gun and aimed it at Grayson's chest.

29

"Seriously?" Grayson's voice was annoyed, not scared, like he knew Webb was bluffing. He lifted both hands in surrender. "You're going to shoot me?"

Webb hesitated for a beat, and then lowered the gun. He gave Grayson a venomous look.

Edan jumped out of the Jeep.

"Edan!" Noah grabbed for his shirt. "I don't think you should—"

Edan shrugged Noah off and strode to Grayson. "Hello again," he said to Webb.

Webb holstered his gun. Three men I didn't recognize exited the van and stood shoulder to shoulder with him. In front of me, Patrick and Noah exchanged a nervous look.

"What can I do for you guys?" Grayson asked. "If you came to thank us, that's really not necessary. We're always happy to kill some scrabs. That's why you're here, right? To destroy that nest?" His voice was too chipper.

Webb's eyes flicked to the scene behind Grayson—dozens of recruits around us, some of them edging closer, listening.

"Your kids stole a van from us," Webb said finally. He pointed to Edan and then to me.

"Borrowed," Edan corrected. Webb's jaw twitched.

"Do you want me to call the police?" Grayson asked. "You can tell them they stole your van, right after you kidnapped them and threatened to kill them. Oh, and then you shot at them. I'm sure the French police would love to hear all about the shooting. Amongst other things."

Webb's nostrils flared.

"And I'd appreciate it if you didn't detain my recruits again in the future. Ever. Again." Grayson's voice went hard with the last two words.

"No problem," Webb snarled. "Next time we'll just let the scrabs kill them."

"We had it under control." Edan glanced back at me. I cocked an eyebrow. "Mostly."

Webb stared at Edan. I got the impression Webb was barely holding himself back from lunging at him.

"The keys for the van?" he asked, practically spitting each word.

"We left them in the ignition," Edan said.

Webb jabbed an angry finger at him. "That is the last time I help a civilian in a scrab zone. I knew I should have just left you two idiots out there to die."

"That's for the best, because you're not that great at kidnapping," Edan said. "I have some notes, if you're interested."

A laugh bubbled up in my chest, despite my nerves. I pressed my lips together to keep it in.

Webb whirled around and stomped back to his van. The other men followed suit. Tires screeched as they raced back toward the road.

Grayson turned to Edan with an exasperated expression. "Did you really have to antagonize the men with guns?"

"Yes. It's like you don't know me at all."

I couldn't keep the laugh in this time. Edan grinned at me. There truly was no situation that could make him lose his cool.

"I have questions," Patrick said.

"So do I." Grayson beckoned for me to get out of the Jeep. "Clara, Edan, ride with me. You can tell me on the way."

Edan and I relayed what we saw to Grayson on the drive to camp. Edan sat in the front passenger's seat and did most of the talking. I was glad he had the energy to explain it. The lack of sleep was starting to catch up with me, and the events of the last twenty-four hours were a jumbled mess in my head.

"You seriously saw a guy controlling a scrab?" Grayson asked when Edan finished. Edan looked at me in the rearview mirror.

"Yeah. He told it where to go," I said. "He directed it to attack us. Have you ever heard about people doing this?"

"Not here." Grayson rubbed his left eyebrow with two fingers. "There were rumors that the Russians developed a scrab training program."

"Seriously?" Edan said.

"Yeah, but I figured they'd fail. I mean, it's crazy. These things can't be trained. They can't be reasoned with. Remember what happened to those Worshippers in Indiana?"

I did. They insisted the scrabs just wanted their own space and to be left alone. They put a few in a large, enclosed area and tried to leave. The scrabs promptly dug their way out and killed them all.

"Apparently MDG figured it out," Edan said.

"They didn't figure out how to keep them locked up, though," I said. "I think that entire nest was there because they let a bunch of them escape."

"It's so stupid." Grayson shook his head. "So unbelievably stupid."

"What are we going to do?" Edan asked. "People should know, right?"

"Yes. Definitely. I'll call the French police as soon as we get to camp. It's illegal to keep scrabs alive and confined here," Grayson said. "And I'm reaching out to some of my contacts back home. I'll let a few reporters know, see if they can do some digging. I'm already in touch with team leaders around the world, trying to find out if anyone has seen anything like this over there. I'm really worried about the UK."

"Because the scrabs are rumored to be smarter there?" Edan asked.

"Exactly. It's where I would go if I were looking for scrabs to train. And MDG will expect us to call the police, so they've probably already abandoned the farm site you were at."

"What about our team?" I asked. "And the other recruits. Do we tell them?"

"Let me try to get a handle on this first." Grayson's phone buzzed in his lap, and he took a quick glance down at it before returning his attention to the road. "I'm going to make some calls and find out what I can. I don't want people panicking and bombarding me with questions when I don't know any more than they do."

Grayson made a left, and the camp came into view. It consisted of several giant tents, some portable toilets, and lots of small tents on the outskirts of the area. The other Jeeps and ATVs were parked in the dirt in front of the camp, and a few more filled in around us as I stepped out. Noah pulled the camera off his Jeep and scurried toward a tent.

I leaned against the side of the Jeep with a sigh. "I need a nap."

"Me too." Edan looked down at his dirty clothes. "Maybe a shower first."

"Sorry, none of those here," Grayson said. "You can get cleaned up by the toilets, though. There's a hand washing station. And we have Wi-Fi out here, but I'm getting you a SIM card right away. Julian should have told me one of his team members didn't have cell service."

"Dorsey needs one too," Edan said.

Grayson sighed. "All right." He pointed to the tent in the middle of camp. Luggage was piled up outside of it. "Your bags are over there, if you want to change."

Edan and I found our bags in the pile and then headed over to the hand washing station. I had to change in one of the portable toilets, which was not easy (or fun), but I managed to wriggle into jeans and a clean T-shirt. When I was done, I found Edan shirtless at the sinks, splashing water on his arms.

I joined him, peeling off the old bandage on my arm that

covered claw marks. I was going to need a new dressing. I pressed down on the foot pedal to turn on the water.

I glanced up at Edan as I washed my hands. It was the first time I'd seen his full tattoos. He had one I'd never seen before —birds flying across his back and over his left shoulder. He caught me looking.

"Is it rude to ask about your tattoos?" I asked.

He turned off the water. "No, I don't mind. You mean, like, what they mean?"

"Yeah." I wiped off my hands on my shirt. "You're just eighteen, aren't you?"

"Yeah."

"Did you get them all recently?"

"No." He ran a hand through his hair, leaving droplets of water behind. "I was friends with a few artists. I started when I was . . . fifteen, I think." He pointed to his Hufflepuff tattoo. "That one was first. Puff pride."

"Sure," I said with a laugh.

He pointed to the words *way leads on to way* on his right forearm. "That one was second. It's from the Robert Frost poem. You know, 'The Road Not Taken'?"

"Oh, right," I said. "Doesn't everyone usually get something about the road less traveled tattooed on their bodies for that one? Way to be a rebel."

"Thank you. And yes. Everyone gets a 'road less traveled' tattoo because they don't actually understand what the poem is about. He's actually saying that the roads kind of look the same, and later he'll just put a spin on the story and say that he took the one less traveled. I, personally, always liked the part of that poem where he's saying you can't go back. You choose a road, and it takes you one place, which takes you somewhere else, and you just keep choosing and changing until you can't go back. Way leads on to way."

I almost said, *Wow, that was more profound than I was expecting,* and then realized it might be kind of rude.

But true. I'd clearly misjudged Edan. I got the feeling that Julian had done the same.

He flipped his left arm over to show me the tree. "That one was third, to cover the scar."

I touched his wrist lightly, leaning closer to see which scar he meant. A long, jagged scar ran through the tree. It almost looked like one of the limbs.

"My mom put my arm through a window," he said, before I could ask.

"And why a tree?" I asked quietly. I was worried that maybe it was too personal a question. Were Edan and I friends now? It felt like we were friends.

"A lot of reasons," he said, his gaze moving from the tattoo to meet mine. "I like that trees have roots you can't see. There's a whole hidden history there. You can only see what's above the ground, but it's what's underneath that's really making it strong. So when I decided to get a tattoo to cover up the scar, it just seemed fitting."

I looked back down at the tattoo, at the twisted roots, the

branches, the leaves. Everyone always mentioned regret when they talked about tattoos, but I couldn't see ever regretting this one.

He pulled his shirt on. "Hey, do you mind if we take a picture? For Instagram?" He reached into his pocket and pulled out his phone.

"Sure. Are you going to tell them we almost died?"

"I'll probably make us sound more badass than that."

"Perfect."

He stood next to me and held the phone up to take a selfie. He snapped a few and then scrolled through the photos. He angled the screen toward me.

"This one good?"

We were both smiling, my head tilted slightly in his direction. Any makeup I'd been wearing had long worn off, and we both looked exhausted, but it was actually a pretty nice picture. The morning sun cast a nice golden glow over our faces, and we looked relaxed, like we hadn't just had a terrifying experience.

"It's great," I said.

Madison appeared from around the side of a tent. Her eyes darted to me and then quickly to Edan. "Have you seen my brother?"

"He was headed to that big tent, last I saw," Edan said, pointing. "Hey—Madison."

She'd started to walk away, and she turned to look back at us.

"We didn't sleep at all last night. Is there somewhere we could take a nap?"

"Yeah. The tent I slept in last night is empty right now. This way." She led us around to the outskirts of the campsite, where a long row of smaller tents had been set up. She walked to a navy blue one and pulled back the flap. Four sleeping bags were laid out next to each other.

"Thanks," Edan said, ducking inside. He plopped down on the sleeping bag on the far right, so I took the one on the other side. Madison zipped up the tent and her footsteps faded as she walked away.

I stretched out and closed my eyes. I fell asleep to the sound of Edan breathing, the noises of the camp distant.

30

I JERKED AWAKE WITH A GASP, AND FOR A MOMENT I DIDN'T remember where I was. My hand fumbled for my weapons pack before I had even fully woken up.

The tent came into focus around me. I let out a sigh as I sat up. Right. I was safe. Relatively. I pulled the weapons pack a little closer.

Edan rolled over on his sleeping bag, rubbing his eyes.

"Sorry. I didn't mean to wake you." I pushed a hand over my head and discovered my ponytail was wildly out of place. I pulled the rubber from my hair and shook it out.

"I was just having a nightmare about being eaten, so I'd actually prefer to be awake." He stretched his arms over his head, revealing a patch of skin on his stomach.

"We're traumatized for life, aren't we?"

"I mean, we already were, so why not a little more?"

I barked out a laugh. "Sure. At least we did this one to ourselves, right?"

"That was exactly my logic for coming."

"Mine too." I tied my hair back again. "I don't know why some of our team came, honestly. When they talk about deferring college or missing their siblings' birthdays back home . . ." I shook my head. "Sometimes I want to be like, Noah, dude, what are you *doing* here?"

"He wants to help people. Plus he's awesome at this." He sat up, scrubbing a hand down his face. "But I know what you mean."

"Some of them are just way better people than I am."

"Lots of people are better than me," he said. "You get used to it."

I laughed again, but the way he said it made me think that he was sort of serious.

"Thanks for keeping me sane last night," I said, because I thought he should know that he had.

He looked at me in surprise. "Did I?"

"Yes. If I have to almost die again, I wouldn't mind having you around."

A smile spread across his face. "Same."

The zipper at the front of the tent moved suddenly, and Archer's face appeared at the flap.

"They sent me to wake you guys up," he said, and I tried not to look startled. Archer spoke so infrequently that I'd forgotten what his voice sounded like. "We're leaving."

"Where are we going?" Edan asked.

Archer shrugged and tossed me a phone. "Noah said that's yours."

"Thanks." I grabbed my weapons pack and crawled out of the tent. Archer handed me my backpack. "Did you see what Edan posted on Instagram?"

I shook my head.

"It's nice, what he said."

Edan smiled at Archer as he grabbed his bag. I opened

Instagram as I trailed behind them. Edan's post, the selfie we'd taken earlier, popped up on the top of my feed. It had thousands of likes and comments.

This girl has saved my ass like four times now. Clara risked her life to help me yesterday, and I'd be dead if she hadn't. And I'd be dead several times over if it weren't for the rest of team seven. Trust me, they're all just as awesome as they look on video. More so, even. I'm incredibly lucky to be surrounded by badasses like Clara.

I smiled, glancing up at Edan. He was already with the rest of the team, standing near the road with their luggage. They were all crowded around Madison and Noah, who were sitting on top of a suitcase. Noah had a tablet in his hands.

"Clara! Come see this!" Priya called.

"What is it?" I asked, walking over and standing on my toes to see over Dorsey's shoulder. A clip from an American news station was playing on the tablet. Noah scrolled back so that the video started over.

"We're getting reports that one of Grayson St. John's American teams scored a major victory today in France when they took out a breeding nest."

The footage switched to the side of the road where we'd just been. It was jumpy, disjointed footage, but I could clearly see Patrick landing a direct hit to a scrab. The bottom of the screen said *footage courtesy of Noah Cohen.*

"You already posted a video of this?" I asked.

"Yeah, Madison helped me comb through all the footage and we got it up as fast as possible." Noah held his fist out to her without looking up from the screen. She gave it a bump.

"The footage you're seeing is of American team seven, a team made up entirely of teenagers." The reporter said the last word like it was shocking. *"The team is already popular on social media, thanks to member Noah Cohen, who frequently posts videos on You-Tube of their training and missions."*

Dorsey nudged Noah with a grin. The footage cut to another scene, and I blinked as I realized it was me. It was the moment the guy on the ATV clubbed the scrab and I finished him off. When I turned to face the camera, I was smiling.

"Thanks for fighting right in front of the Jeep," Noah said. "That was really helpful for my video."

"Any time."

"All the American news stations are like this," Priya said. "Google *team seven.*"

Archer leaned close to her and said something that made her laugh. She rose up on her toes and kissed him.

What a strange couple. Priya must have known a completely different version of Archer, because I couldn't imagine Archer ever whispering anything to me that would make me laugh.

I pulled out my phone and searched *team seven.*

Teenage Team Defeats Scrabs in France

Grayson St. John's Fight Squads Score Major Victory

MDG Warns That Noah Cohen Video "Possibly Heavily Edited"

President Tweets About "Dangerous Kids with Weapons" After News of St. John Victory

"What do you mean it's gone? It's on *fire?*" I heard Grayson say, and I turned to see him standing not far away, phone pressed to his ear. "Yeah, OK. Call me back when you hear from the London teams."

I looked back down at Noah's screen. A blond man was seated with the reporter, the words *MDG Spokesman* on the screen.

"Videos like this may seem impressive from the outside, but in reality, these people are dangerous," he was saying. *"There are a lot of amateurs running around out there, armed to the teeth, and it's not safe. There's a real concern about lasting damage after they leave. Which will be soon, from what I hear. Recruit numbers are dropping."*

"Is that true?" Zoe asked.

"We always expected numbers to drop after the first month," Madison said. "We've actually retained more than we thought."

"Jake, we've just received word that French authorities have asked St. John to drastically scale back their operations there," the anchor said. *"Do you know what prompted this?"*

"Well, they've yet to produce any kind of good result in France," Jake said. *"And I understand there's been significant property damage. Teams in Paris keep running their vehicles into buildings. An American team chased a scrab into a restaurant yesterday and injured several civilians. And we've just heard about an abandoned farm that was destroyed recently."*

I looked at Edan quickly. "Is he talking about the farm we were just at?"

Grayson walked over to us. "Yeah, they torched it."

"I don't have confirmation yet," the man said. *"But I'm hearing that a couple of kids from Grayson's team were in the area."*

"Is he trying to pin that on us?" I asked, aghast.

"But you don't know for sure," the anchor was saying.

"I don't, but we have found some explosives, and they're the kind that the St. John teams use."

"He for sure is pinning that on you," Priya said.

"Dammit, I've never even gotten to use an explosive," Edan said. "If I'm getting blamed for this, I at least want to blow something up."

"Why didn't you take some pictures while you were there?" Gage asked, looking accusingly at Edan. "You had your phone on you, didn't you? You should have taken some pictures of the scrabs in the barn. Get some proof so this wouldn't happen."

"We were kind of busy escaping," Edan said.

"I'm just saying. If it were me, I would have thought to grab my phone and get some proof."

"Well, Gage, if you ever stumble across a barn full of angry scrabs while being kidnapped, I look forward to all your stunning photos. I'm sure you'll get that perfect selfie angle," Edan said. Gage sneered at him.

"Damn, Gage, do you really have to make it your full-time job to be a dick?" Dorsey asked. "Like, maybe you could be a part-time dick. What do you think?"

Laila's mouth rounded to an O, and she gave Dorsey a deeply impressed look. Edan stifled a laugh.

I braced myself for Gage's response, but he just turned red and looked at his feet.

"They can't prove anything," Grayson said. He sounded tired.

"Is it true that you're scaling back operations here?" Zoe asked. "What does that mean?"

"It's true," he said. "It means I'm moving all American teams to London. Some of the South American teams too, though a bunch of them are going to Spain. Only the African teams are staying in France. They're going to do their own thing."

"Their own thing," Zoe echoed. "Meaning they quit?"

"No, they'll still be fighting scrabs, and I've let them keep using my drones."

Zoe regarded him skeptically. I also got the feeling that he was sugarcoating some of this for us.

"This is an opportunity to do some good," Grayson continued. "They need help in London. And I'm worried that MDG is there. It's where I would go, if I wanted to capture scrabs. And they just torched their facility here."

"Plus France is kicking us out," Dorsey said.

"They're not kicking us out," Grayson said. "They asked that we take a break."

"A break always means they never want to see you again," Dorsey said. Grayson gave him a pained look. "What? It does. Every person I've dated who put me on a break never responded to my texts again. They're just letting you down easy before they ghost you."

"He's not wrong," Patrick said.

Grayson pinched the bridge of his nose with a sigh.

"But London is . . . it's bad, right?" Zoe asked, smacking her gum. "They, like, don't have enough police officers, right? Or they don't always show up?"

"They are overwhelmed, yes. And it is bad there. Worse than France. Worse than almost anywhere in the world, actually. Which is exactly why they need us," Grayson said. "But you're under no obligation to go. We're headed back to Paris now, to the train station, and you're welcome to go your separate ways once we get there. Just let me know if I should pull your luggage."

Around me, the team was silent.

"Good," Grayson said, pulling keys out of his pocket. "Let's go."

Part Four

KEEP CALM

31

It was night when we arrived in London. We took the subway from the train station, and exited into a busy intersection. It was chillier than in Paris, and I stuffed my hands into the pockets of my hoodie.

The streets were crowded, and several people were holding weapons—a woman walked by with a baseball bat, some people wore helmets, and one man had two long sticks strapped to his back.

"Is this normal?" I asked as we stepped onto a crosswalk. "Or are we in a scrab-heavy area?"

"The whole city is a scrab-heavy area." Grayson pointed to a convenience store. It had been demolished, glass and snacks spilling out onto the street. A dead scrab hung halfway out of the store. People barely glanced at it as they went by. A man was perched on a ledge in the middle of the mess, reading a magazine.

Grayson had secured us rooms in a hostel, which was mostly occupied by recruits. It was nestled between a Chinese restaurant and a bar with a patio packed full of people. Grayson waved at the patrons as he pulled open the door to the hostel, and several of them waved back. Recruits.

I spotted Julian in the middle of the hostel lobby, dressed in a black coat with a dramatic collar, arms crossed over his chest.

He was rubbing a finger across his bottom lip, his eyebrows drawn together. He looked anxious.

A smile spread across his face when he caught me watching him. He darted around Patrick and Noah, grabbing me as soon as I was within arm's reach and pulling me into a tight hug.

I tensed, very aware of the rest of team seven standing around us. I was pretty sure they all knew about our relationship, but it was still a little awkward to be hugging right in front of them.

"Are you OK?" he asked, holding me a little tighter. "They told me you were probably dead yesterday. I thought you were gone for . . . hours."

Some of my awkwardness melted away, and I pressed my palms into his back as I hugged him. It must have been terrible for him to think I was dead, but, selfishly, it was kind of nice to have someone care about me that much. The team had worried, sure, but I didn't think that anyone was more invested in my safe return than Julian.

"I'm OK," I said as I pulled away. "Why weren't you with the team?"

"I was in Paris, taking care of a few things. You heard about the recruits who ran a car into a restaurant? I just had to square some stuff away with the French police before I could leave."

"Thank you for that," Grayson said, appearing beside me. "I couldn't get you a private room here, but I figured you'd probably rather stay in the hotel across the street anyway."

"Yeah, I already grabbed a room," Julian said.

I gave him a surprised look. He wasn't staying with the team?

"I hate hostels," he explained.

"Did you get in touch with your dad?" Grayson asked.

Julian sighed. "Yes, briefly. He's coming here. Both my parents are."

Grayson's eyebrows shot up. "Here? To London?"

"Yes, unfortunately. They'll be here tomorrow."

He sounded tired. Julian still hadn't told me much about his parents, but it certainly didn't seem like their visit was welcome. I slipped my hand into his. He squeezed it.

"Grayson!" a voice yelled. It was a bearded recruit, standing at the door to the bar connected to the hostel. He walked across the lobby to Grayson. "Are you coming or what? We need to talk to you about your media strategy. MDG is making us look like idiots." He pointed to where most of team seven was standing together. "Is it true a couple of those kids blew up a farm in France? Are you sure you should be letting them use explosives?"

"No, that's not . . ." Grayson made an annoyed sound and steered the recruit back toward the bar, speaking quietly.

I looked up at Julian. "Why are your parents coming?"

"Just some business." He tugged on my hand. "Come outside with me for a sec?"

I let him lead me out the doors and onto the street. A light rain had started to fall, and we huddled together beneath the awning of the restaurant next door.

He wrapped his arms around my waist, pulling me close. "I missed you," he murmured, and then pressed a kiss to my lips.

"I missed you too."

"I may have to spend time with my parents while they're here, but I promise we'll hang out just the two of us after they leave."

"Is it coincidence that they have business here?" I asked. "Or did they come to see you?"

"They came to see me mostly." He sighed.

"You don't get along with them?" I couldn't help but pry. Julian had said so little about his family.

"My dad is . . . a lot. And he doesn't care about the teams, so he'll expect me to be at his beck and call while he's here."

"Did he support you doing this?"

"Not really, no. *Disorganized, naïve nonsense* were his exact words." His lips twitched in amusement. "He's not totally wrong."

My eyebrows shot up. "You're not thinking of leaving the teams, are you?" I didn't want him to leave. He was my best friend here and, besides Edan, the only person I'd ever really been honest with. This was supposed to be the beginning of my relationship with Julian, not the end.

"No, I didn't mean that. You just have to admit that Grayson is still working out some kinks."

I let out a relieved breath. "Good."

He put both hands on my cheeks. "I would never leave you behind. You know that, right?"

My breath caught in my throat. I did not know that. We'd only been together for a few weeks; I didn't think it was realistic to expect him to stick around if the teams fell apart.

"Listen, Clara." His face was close enough to mine to feel his breath. "I know that we didn't get to spend as much time together as we wanted the last couple weeks, but I feel like I should tell you that I think about you all the time. I wish that you were with me all the time."

I curled my fingers around his waist because I was suddenly very worried that I was going to melt into a happy puddle on the floor.

"I was so mad at myself for letting you go with the team to the campsite alone. I should have been there to protect you. I'm going to be here to protect you from now on." He said the last line so fiercely that I didn't have the heart to point out that I was able to protect myself. "No matter what happens, we'll figure it out together, OK? You and me. You're not alone."

My throat had closed, but I didn't have the words anyway. I was going to try for *thank you*, but he pulled me close, pressing his lips to mine, and I didn't have to say anything at all.

Team seven had just one room, a huge space with rows of bunk beds stacked three high, matching white sheets and blue blankets on each. I showered and changed, then climbed into my top bunk. I could already hear someone snoring, and the lights flipped off a few minutes later.

I tucked my phone against the wall and burrowed under the blankets. I tossed and turned for a while, listening to the sounds of breathing around me. Edan and I had only napped for a few hours, so I should have been exhausted, but my brain was being pulled in a million different directions—MDG, Julian, smarter UK scrabs. I sighed as I flopped over on my stomach.

In the bed across from me, Edan was also on his stomach, a book flat on his pillow. He was using his phone flashlight to see the pages.

He lifted his head from his book suddenly, catching me

watching him. He opened his mouth like he was going to speak, then seemed to think better of it. He flipped his phone over and began typing. Mine lit up a moment later.

Sorry, is the light keeping you up?

I typed a message. **No, I just can't sleep.**

Me either.

What are you reading?

Ancillary Justice. I put some books on my wish list thinking I'd just get a couple, but people got them all for me. Plus some more that they thought I would enjoy. So if you want to borrow a book I'm your guy.

I may take you up on that. I haven't read a book in a while. That's probably why I failed English.

Right after hitting Send, I realized how stupid that message made me sound. My cheeks flushed, and I was glad it was too dark for him to see.

He let out a quiet huff of air that was sort of like a laugh as he read it. He widened his eyes like he agreed.

God yes. Most of the books we read in English class made me want to stab myself in the eye.

I smiled, relieved, and typed a message. **Heart of Darkness? I definitely considered stabbing something or someone while reading that one.**

Never read it. I probably dropped out before having to be subjected to it.

Right. He'd said he dropped out his sophomore year. *I had better things to do,* he'd said.

That must have been when he left home. His *better things to do* was probably trying to find a place to sleep and a way to feed himself.

He sent another message. **Do you like graphic novels?**

I don't think I've ever read one.

I have a few issues of Saga. I think you'd like it. Want me to grab it for you tomorrow?

That would be great.

He looked up with a smile, which I returned. I mouthed *good night* and rolled over, closing my eyes and willing sleep to come.

32

Julian let us have a late start the next morning. We didn't have to be down in the lobby until ten, but I was still sluggish, yawning as I put on my uniform and grabbed my weapons pack.

Laurence had texted me in the middle of the night, responding to the message I'd sent him before I went to bed. I scrolled through them as I walked downstairs and into the lobby.

Glad you're OK. You didn't blow up a farm, did you? They're saying some kids from Grayson's teams got ahold of some explosives.

Also did you know that there are pictures of you and Julian kissing on Tumblr? It's kind of creepy.

"Everything OK?"

I looked up to see Julian standing in front of me. "Are there pictures of us kissing on Tumblr?"

He rolled his eyes. "Yes. Some weirdo took our picture."

"Last night?"

"Yeah. Noah has made you all into mini celebrities, whether you like it or not."

"It's a nice picture, though!" Priya called. She was standing nearby with Laila, looking at her phone.

"It is, I guess," Julian grumbled. "Why? Did someone say something?"

"My brother. He follows all the team seven stuff." I clicked over to Tumblr to look. It was a nice picture. Julian had his hands on my cheeks. We looked happy.

"Why do you keep in touch with your brother?"

I glanced up, surprised. "Why wouldn't I?"

He lowered his voice. "Because he didn't protect you. He's older, right?"

"He's twenty."

"Jesus. Yeah. He should have protected you."

I didn't think I agreed, but I wasn't going to get into it with half the team standing nearby.

"Oh, you're here," Madison said, striding up beside Julian. "I thought you might take the day off since your parents arrive today."

"Some of us actually take our responsibilities seriously, Madison," Julian snapped. His words dripped with disdain.

I reeled back, surprised, and a contrite look crossed Julian's face.

"Sorry," he said with a sigh. "I'm . . . stressed."

Madison just shot him an annoyed look and walked away.

"Have they arrived?" I asked. "Your parents?"

"They're probably landing now." He tugged on his lower lip. "I'm kind of on edge about it. My dad is . . . difficult."

"I understand," I said, reaching for his hand.

He smiled. "How are you feeling? I can give you the day off, you know. It's no trouble if you need to recover. You can hide in my hotel room for the day, if you want. It's just across the street."

I shook my head. "I don't need it."

He looked like he might argue, but the rest of the team arrived in the lobby, a sudden whirlwind of noise and laughter.

Julian stepped away from me. "All right, guys," he called, addressing the whole team. "We're headed to a gym a few blocks away. We're meeting a UK team there to discuss next steps." He led us out the door and onto the sidewalk.

We walked for about ten minutes and then turned into an alley. To the left was a sign that said MONSTER ATTACK CLUB, above a doorway lined in red. The words BOXING CLUB were stamped into the wall. It must have been a boxing gym before the scrabs.

Julian reached for the door. A scream sounded from behind us.

I whirled around, already reaching for the machete on my back, but I saw nothing.

"Come on," Julian said pushing past us and breaking into a jog.

We headed back to the street and around a corner in the direction the scream had come from. We all came to a sudden stop.

"I stabbed it in its fucking eye, and it's still not good enough!" The yell came from an auburn-haired boy dressed in a black St. John uniform. He was in the street with four other team members —two girls and two boys.

Two scrabs were directly in front of them. They were both on the smaller side, maybe six feet tall, but with some of the longest claws I'd ever seen. They curved at the ends, almost reaching the ground even when the scrabs were standing on only two legs.

One of them collapsed suddenly. Blood poured out of a wound on its chest. The other had a spear sticking out of its neck. One of its super-long claws had broken off and was lying in the street.

The one-eyed scrab staggered forward, in the direction of the auburn-haired boy. His expression was annoyed, not scared.

"Connor!" one of the girls yelled, dark braid flying as she ran toward him.

"Sorry, no, I've had enough," Connor said. He had both hands on his hips, apparently unconcerned about the approaching scrab. His eyes caught on us and lit up. "Americans!" he yelled, pointing. The scrab spun to face us. "Yes, perfect, attack the Americans."

"*Connor*," the girl with the braid said again, exasperated. She caught the scrab by surprise from the side, shoving a long machete into its neck. She quickly stepped back as it fell to the ground with a loud thump. She turned to us and smiled. She was maybe a few years older than me, with brown skin and wide, pretty eyes.

"Sorry," she said. She had a British accent, like Connor. "We were at the gym, but we heard screams, so we came to help. I'm Saira. I'm the team thirteen leader."

"The famous team seven!" a tall sandy-haired boy with a wide smile called, sidestepping a scrab body as he walked to us.

"I know you," Noah said, pointing. "You're Thomas Clarke."

"That's me," Thomas said.

"YouTuber," Noah explained to us.

"Oh, right, I follow you," Madison said. Thomas's grin widened.

"Anyway, this is thirteen—Thomas, Harry, Connor, and Mia," Saira said, pointing to each member as she said their names. Thomas waved enthusiastically. Mia, a curvy blond girl, just squinted at us. Connor was still annoyed. Harry said something that I couldn't understand.

"What did he say? What is that accent?" Zoe whispered.

"Scottish," Madison said.

He spoke again, this time to his team members. Again, it sounded like a different language.

"Is that English?" Zoe asked. "Don't Scottish people speak English?"

"I think . . . he said something about shorts?" Madison frowned as she surveyed the team. "Wait, no. No one's wearing shorts."

Harry and Mia laughed.

"You guys only have five people on your team?" Priya asked Saira.

"We had ten," Saira replied. "They died."

"Oh." Priya obviously wished she hadn't asked.

"There you are!" a voice called.

We all turned. Grayson was jogging down the street, bloody machete in hand. He slid it back into its holster as he stopped in front of us.

"I chased a few scrabs a couple blocks over," he explained. He was breathing heavily, his eyes bright with excitement. "Did you tell them?" he asked Saira.

"I didn't," she replied. "Are they coming with us?"

"Yeah, I think that's best. These two"—Grayson gestured to me and Edan—"Clara and Edan, they're the ones who saw the farm in France. And Noah's got cameras on half the team."

Saira's eyes flicked to the cameras on the chests of several team members. She appeared impressed.

"What's going on?" Julian asked.

"Saira has a lead on a possible MDG facility," Grayson said.

"Connor got it, technically," Saira said. "Friend of his in North London keeps seeing dodgy-looking men going in and out of a self-storage facility across the street from his flat."

"Self-storage?" Gage said skeptically. "Do you really think they'd put scrabs in a storage facility?"

"Why not?" Grayson asked. "The ones Edan and Clara saw had their vocal cords cut, so it's not like they're making noise. And that area has been almost demolished by scrabs in the last year or so. It's a ghost town."

Saira nodded in agreement.

"Did you tell the police?" Julian asked.

"I told them, but they said they can't get to it right away," Grayson said.

"That means bugger off and stop bothering us," Connor translated.

"We get that response a lot," Saira added.

"They did send an officer to do a quick drive-by, and she said she saw nothing. But it's best if I check it out myself anyway," Grayson said. "The police can only poke around so much without a warrant. Besides, my police contact practically told me to go for it."

"I'll bet he did," Connor said.

"You seriously want to go break into a random storage facility?" Julian asked.

"It's not random, we have a tip. And I wouldn't say *break in*," Grayson said. "Explore the area. Maybe stumble across an unlocked door. Or a mostly unlocked door." He grinned.

"I've been a bad influence on you," Edan said with a laugh.

"We're not here to chase after MDG," Julian said. "We're supposed to be helping people."

"We are helping people. By figuring out what MDG is doing with those trained scrabs," Grayson said.

Julian's jaw twitched. "I'm not getting arrested for breaking into a storage facility. That's stupid."

"Tell us how you really feel, Julian," Edan said dryly. Julian shot him a contemptuous glare.

Grayson and Madison exchanged a look I couldn't read. They could communicate with just their eyes, apparently. I couldn't imagine having a relationship like that with my brother.

"It takes the police at least an hour to respond to calls in that area, if they come at all," Saira said. "Trust me, you're not getting arrested."

"And you're free to go back to your hotel, if you want," Grayson said calmly. "Any of you can opt out of this assignment." He pointed at the end of the street. "Vans should be waiting. Let's go."

The team began to move in that direction, but fingers closed around my wrist, keeping me in place. I looked at Julian curiously.

"Let's get out of here." He said the words softly, but Noah and Madison obviously heard them as they walked by. They both shot us disapproving looks. I'd never seen such scorn on Noah's face, actually.

"Great team leadership as usual, Julian," Noah said. My eyebrows shot up. Did Noah dislike Julian? Maybe Madison had been badmouthing him to Noah.

"Sticking your nose where it doesn't belong as usual, Noah,"

Julian snapped back. "I told you that if I wanted your opinion on my training methods, I'd ask for it."

Or maybe Julian totally deserved that look Noah was giving him.

I drew my arm from Julian's grasp as Madison and Noah walked away.

"This isn't what we signed up for," Julian said, returning his attention to me. "Let's get out of here and let Grayson be an idiot by himself."

"We can't abandon the team," I said, exasperation in my voice.

He shrugged. "It's their choice to go."

"Julian . . ." I frowned at him. It wouldn't kill him to show a little concern for his team. "I'm going. I've seen an MDG facility before, maybe I can help. And I think you should go too."

He let out a deeply annoyed sigh. "Fine." He looked like he was going to reach for my hand, but I really didn't want to hold his hand right now. I turned and quickly walked away.

33

THE RIDE ACROSS LONDON WAS TENSE, AND SILENT. JULIAN scowled the whole way, and I didn't think that Grayson was accustomed to driving on the left side of the road, or to driving a standard, because the trip was full of jerks and sudden stops. Edan practically fell out of the car when we finally stopped.

"Oh god," he said, bracing his hands against his thighs and doubling over like he was going to puke. Gage and Zoe edged away from him.

We were on a street corner between an apartment building and a wall covered in graffiti. The street was mostly empty, except for two men in the distance. They turned a corner and disappeared.

"The storage facility is two blocks that way," Grayson said, pointing. "Saira's taking her team to Connor's friend's apartment first. Apparently he has a pretty good view. I'm going to get closer with Edan and Noah. Everyone else stick with the teammate I assigned you."

Madison appeared beside me. "We're together," she said with a sigh, probably to let me know just how much she appreciated that. "Grayson put us into teams of two while you were talking to Julian."

"Maddie and Clara, you guys follow me for about a block and then wait. Patrick and Dorsey, go one street over and wait there.

Laila and Gage, you do the same," Grayson said. "And everyone remember to stick close to your teammate. No splitting up. Julian, stay here with the rest of your team. I'll text you a position when I get closer."

Julian's eyes darted to me, and then to Madison. He looked like he might say something, so I quickly walked away. I didn't want Julian suggesting we desert the team again, especially in front of everyone.

We followed Grayson until he made a motion for us to stop, and then watched as he continued down the street with Edan and Noah. I could see the storage facility now, a green and white building next door to what was left of an apartment complex. The entire building had cratered in, probably after an underground scrab attack damaged the structure.

We stood in silence for so long that I began to hope that a scrab would shoot up from the ground. I always ended up hoping for that when I was alone with Madison.

"This is why Grayson made the rule about not dating team leaders," she said suddenly.

I looked at her, surprised. "What?"

She gestured between us. "This. The weirdness. That's why he made the rule."

"So the weirdness is all my fault, and not because you've been super rude to both of us?"

"I mean . . ." She twirled her hair around her finger as she considered. "Maybe." She paused again and then shook her head. "Nah, it's all your fault."

I was pretty sure she was kidding, but it was hard to tell, and my eyes caught movement behind her suddenly. It was a black van at the end of the road, a block away, driving in the direction of the storage facility.

"Madison." I pointed. "That looks like an MDG van."

She turned, but it had disappeared.

"Let's go see," I said.

She pulled her phone out of her pocket. "I'll text Gray."

We jogged to the end of the block. The van had pulled into an open garage door at the back of the storage facility, and a man jumped out of the driver's side and headed deeper into the garage.

"Come on," I said, breaking into a run.

"What are we doing?" Madison whispered.

"Seeing what's in that van. It didn't look like he locked it."

"Probably because he's coming right back."

"Then we should definitely hurry. Your camera is on, right?" I stopped as we approached the garage, taking a moment to peek around the corner. It was empty.

"Of course it's on. I'm not wearing it because it looks cute." She adjusted the camera on her chest.

I darted to the van and grasped the back handle. I pulled the door open.

A scrab lunged at me.

Madison gasped. I stumbled back, barely escaping a swipe of claws. The scrab—no *scrabs*, plural, there were two of them —were chained to the van. Their legs were free, but each arm had a silver cuff and a short chain that was bolted to the floor.

The scrab closest to Madison lunged again, yanking on its

chain. The bolt began to pull away from the floor of the van. It wasn't going to keep the scrab contained much longer.

Madison pulled out her machete. I grabbed mine as well.

"How many times have I told you not to leave them unattended?" a voice called. "And why is this door still open?"

The garage door began to close. I darted toward it, but it was moving too fast, and I could hear footsteps approaching from the other side of the van.

Madison and I scrambled to the front of the vehicle and crouched down in front of the headlights. I slid my machete back into its sheath and peeked around the side of the van to see a man dressed in a suit standing near the roaring scrabs.

"Oh, come on, Kavanaugh! They even opened the door! You should have at least checked on them before walking away."

Footsteps pounded the pavement. "Jesus, they've almost pulled those chains out," a second male voice said. They both had American accents.

"We need to rethink the restraints we're using. I'm bringing it up with investors." He sighed. "Come on, let's send a sedation team to deal with this. There's a retrieval van leaving now. They've picked up significant scrab movement a few miles away."

"Yeah?" The second guy sounded excited.

Retrieval van? That sounded like they were capturing more scrabs. I looked at Madison. She was already typing a message out on her phone.

A door opened and then closed. The van rocked on its wheels as the scrabs roared.

Madison stood. "Let's get out of here before—"

The door slammed open, and she quickly crouched down beside me again. Heavy footsteps pounded against the garage floor.

Too heavy. Those didn't sound like human footsteps.

I peered around the front bumper. Scrabs. Five of them. They were big ones—broad and bulky, with claws that looked so sharp I wondered if someone had filed them to a point. They all had the same silver things on their heads that I'd seen at the farm in France. Three ovals across their foreheads, and one on either side of their necks.

"Subdue," a voice said. I crept around the van until I could see where it was coming from.

It was a blond woman, dressed in the usual black MDG uniform. She stood at the top of the steps in front of the door that led into the building. She held a tablet in her hand, her attention focused on it.

She glanced up. "Good."

I ducked back down, scrambling to join Madison on the other side of the van and see what was *good*. The trained scrabs had the two new ones free from the chains. They held the growling scrabs by either arm.

"Steady," the woman said. She lifted a strange-looking gun and fired.

Two darts shot out in quick succession and sank into the angry scrab's neck. The woman fired two more into the other one. They both slumped to the ground.

A man dressed in a suit appeared behind the woman.

"I heard these are the good ones," he said, peering at the still-standing scrabs. They were stiff and motionless, like they were waiting for instructions.

"Not just good, the *best*," the woman said. "These can take verbal commands. We've taught them twenty-seven different commands, and there's no reason they can't do more. Watch." She swiped at the tablet and then looked back up. "Retrieve."

Two of the scrabs immediately began moving. They knelt down and each grabbed the arms of the scrabs that had been darted.

"Bring," the woman commanded.

The scrabs marched forward, dragging their motionless friends with them.

"Why did only those two obey?" the man asked.

She angled the tablet screen toward him. "I gave the others a shock that keeps them in place. We haven't been successful giving commands individually yet. We tried giving them names, but they didn't seem to understand it. They're pack animals. They want to work together."

The man smiled. "I'm sure you'll figure it out. This is impressive work. I assume these five are going out with the first shipment?"

"Oh, definitely." She stepped aside as the scrabs approached her, letting them drag the unconscious ones into the building. She was so close to them that they could have easily swiped their claws across her throat. She didn't seem the least bit worried.

A phone buzzed, and the man pulled it out of his pocket and then looked at the woman. "It's the Dust Storm facility. Do you have a minute? The guys there have some questions for you about the scrab shipment. They want to make sure they're prepared to take them all in."

"Of course."

The man glanced at the three scrabs still waiting in the garage. "Do you need to do something about them?"

"They're fine for a few minutes. They won't move until given another signal." She punched a code into the pad on the door and pushed it open. It slammed shut behind them. Silence descended on the garage.

I looked at Madison. She was crouched on the ground, machete clutched in hand. Her eyes were wide when they met mine. She opened her mouth like she was going to speak.

I put a finger to my lips. She snapped her mouth shut.

I crawled closer to her and peered around the edge of the bumper. The door into the building was locked, but there had to be a button in here that opened the garage door.

Two of the scrabs stood side by side near the front bumper. The other one had been in the corner before, but I couldn't see it from this angle.

That woman said that the scrabs wouldn't move again until she commanded it, but would that still be true if they spotted us? It didn't seem worth the risk. We should wait for them to retrieve the scrabs and then make a run for it.

I turned back to Madison. I gasped.

The third scrab was standing on the other side of the van. It was maybe five feet away from us. Motionless.

Madison followed my gaze. She shot to her feet, her eyes wide and her machete poised in front of her. The scrab still didn't move.

"What is it doing?" she whispered.

I reached behind my head to grab the machete in my weapons pack. My hand hit something slimy.

I screamed, spinning around to see a scrab standing right behind me. My weapons pack ripped off my back. It dangled from the scrab's claw. I scrambled closer to Madison, but the second scrab was just as motionless as the first.

"What are they doing?" Madison gasped again. We were backed into the wall, trapped by the scrab on either side and the van in front of us. "Did it just take your weapons pack on purpose? Grab something from mine."

Mine was still dangling from the scrab's claw. I opened her pack with shaking hands and grabbed the baton sword. The scrabs didn't move.

"Do you think they can hear us in the building if we scream?" she asked.

"I don't know. But they may just set the scrabs on us if they find us. Do we want to risk it?"

The scrab tossed my weapons pack to the other side of the garage.

"Let's risk it," she said.

We screamed.

The scrabs lunged.

I had the baton sword ready, but it only took half a second to realize that there was no possible way I could fight a scrab while cornered. It was one of the things we learned in training—scrabs always had the advantage in a small space.

I dove for the ground and scrambled under the van. Madison did the same.

The third scrab slid under the van. It snarled. Its claws scratched against the floor as it crawled toward us.

My hands were shaking so violently I almost dropped my sword. I gripped it tighter, thrusting it forward as hard as I could. It sank into the scrab's eye.

The scrab made a squeaking sound, its claws skittering across the floor as it retreated. I crawled out behind it, my breath coming in short, panicked gasps. I dove forward to yank the sword from the scrab's eye. It squeaked again, claws swiping wildly at me.

I drove the blade into its neck and darted to the side as it fell.

There was a glowing red light behind it. The button to open the garage door.

I leapt across the garage and slammed my hand against the button. The door began to open. I grabbed my weapons pack from the floor.

"Clara!"

I whirled around to see Madison on the ground, halfway out from under the van. One of the scrabs was flailing around the garage, a machete stuck through its hand. I couldn't see the other one, but the van rocked violently, like the scrab had just crawled under it.

I grabbed Madison's arms and helped pull her to her feet. Blood dripped from her pants leg. We sprinted for the door.

I ran smack into Grayson.

"Oh thank god," I gasped. Noah and Edan were beside him, weapons out.

I pointed a finger at the garage. "Scrabs. Trained. Really smart. One of them grabbed my weapons pack."

Grayson unsheathed his machete. The scrab Madison had impaled finally got the blade out of its hand and moved toward the garage door. The other one crawled out from under the van and stood shoulder to shoulder with its buddy.

"What is—" The woman from before appeared at the door. Her eyes widened as she took in the dead scrab and the other two, now stalking toward us. She fumbled with her tablet. "Halt!" she called.

Both scrabs froze, a jolt going through them like they'd just been shocked.

Grayson marched forward, blade pointed at them.

"Stop!" the woman yelled. "Don't you dare—"

Grayson slashed his blade across the neck of the first scrab and then the second. He was incredibly quick with the weapon and knew exactly how much pressure to put behind the blade to kill quickly. Both scrabs fell to the ground.

The woman gasped as she ran down the steps. "I just told you to stop!"

Grayson lifted an eyebrow as he pulled his phone from his pocket. He swiped at it and then lifted it to his ear. "Hi. I'd like to report some scrabs being kept alive in north London."

The woman turned on her heel and darted up the stairs.

"Did you get my text?" Madison asked Grayson. "Did you see a van leaving?"

"Julian and Saira went after it with the teams," Grayson said, sliding his phone back into his pocket. "I've got Patrick and Dorsey waiting with the other van, but I think we should stay here until —" He cut himself off, body going rigid. He swept his arm out, pushing me behind him.

Three men stood in front of the garage, guns aimed at us.

"We're going," Grayson said, lifting his arms. "All right? We're leaving." He motioned for us to go, and we all broke into a run.

We ran to the end of the street, where the van was waiting. Patrick was in the driver's seat, Dorsey in the seat beside him.

"Maybe we should stay and wait for the cops," Madison said, looking back in the direction of the storage facility. The men appeared at the end of the road. I was suddenly very aware of how deserted this area was.

"No," Grayson said. "Get in the van. We'll go meet the rest of the team."

Patrick opened the door and started to step out.

"Grayson, no offense, but you are terrible at driving a stick," Edan said. "Please let Patrick drive."

Grayson waved for Patrick to get back in. "I'll navigate. I'm tracking Saira's phone."

I slid into the back row of the van with Edan and Noah. Grayson and Madison took the seats in front of us. Patrick hit the gas.

"Just straight for a couple miles," Grayson said, and then twisted around to look at me and Madison. "Did you guys hear anything else in there?"

"Did you get any video?" Noah asked.

"I don't know," Madison said. "It was on, but you'll have to see what it picked up. We heard something about a *Dust Storm* facility."

"And a shipment," I added. "They were sending out some scrabs with the first shipment, and it sounded like they were going to this Dust Storm facility."

"Dust Storm facility . . ." Edan looked at Grayson. "Arizona? New Mexico?"

"It would be incredibly difficult to get scrabs into the US," Grayson said. "My guess would be the Middle East."

"Most countries in the Middle East don't have a scrab problem," Dorsey said.

"Not yet," Madison said. "But if MDG ships some in and loses control of them . . ."

"Well, that's typical," Patrick grumbled.

"We just killed three that they were going to send," I said. "That woman said they were some of the best."

"And they were pretty terrifying," Madison said. "They were, like . . . toying with us. They cornered us and grabbed Clara's weapons pack. I've never seen scrabs like that." Her gaze shifted to meet mine.

"Is your leg OK?" I asked.

"It's fine. Thanks," she added. That expression on her face looked almost like a smile.

"Turn right at the next light," Grayson said to Patrick. "You should see the van a few blocks down." He glanced at his phone. "And Saira said the scrab siren just went off. We should be able to hear it soon."

We drove for several minutes, until the faint wail of the siren filled the car. The streets here were a little more crowded, and everyone was running in the opposite direction we were driving.

Patrick pulled over to the side of the road, and Grayson opened the door to reveal Julian's anxious face. He reached a hand into the van, and I took it as I climbed out.

"Are you OK? Are you hurt? They told me you guys got caught in an MDG garage!" He had to shout to be heard over the siren.

"I'm fine. Madison too," I added, even though he hadn't asked.

"Why were you in that garage, anyway?" He frowned at Madison. I couldn't tell if he was mad, or just yelling to be heard.

"It was my fault," I said. "I wanted to see what was in the van."

He sighed. "I should have made you stay with me."

He should have *made* me stay with him? Did Julian think I couldn't take care of myself?

"It was a smart idea." Madison's tone was sharp, almost angry. "We heard some stuff that might be useful, and I may have even gotten some footage that we can share."

"Julian, can we do this later?" Grayson stood nearby with the rest of the team. Saira and team thirteen were a few paces away, weapons drawn. "Where is the MDG van?"

Saira pointed. The black van was parked at the end of the block. "They haven't moved for a few minutes!" she called.

"They must see us," Grayson said.

The ground began to rumble. I grabbed my machete.

Julian grabbed my wrist, dragging me to him. "Stay close, OK?" he said softly.

"Uh . . ." I didn't think I could keep track of him *and* fight scrabs. Why was he suddenly acting like he had to protect me?

Screeching tires saved me from having to answer. Several black SUVs hurtled down the street, passing the first van and heading straight toward us.

Julian's hand tightened painfully around my wrist. I yelped, surprised.

"Oh god, I'm sorry," he said, letting go of my wrist and grabbing my hand instead. He cast a worried look at me. "I think this was a bad idea."

The earth split. A scrab roared onto the street about half a block from where we stood. Several more poured out after it, shaking dirt from their thick hides. Their black eyes found us. A flash of teeth.

Grayson made a move toward them, but the SUVs weaved around the scrabs and skidded to a stop on the street, blocking our path. I caught a glimpse of two men as they raced out of the van. They had the same dart guns I'd seen the woman use earlier.

The passenger-side window of the closest SUV rolled down. The man was wearing sunglasses, but I recognized the smile he shot at us right away. Webb.

Edan and I traded a glance. Grayson muttered something so rude I was surprised it hadn't come out of Madison's mouth instead.

The door of another SUV opened, just barely. A hand dropped three silver canisters in quick succession. They rolled toward us.

"Oh sh—" Grayson's words were cut off by a loud *pop pop pop* noise. White smoke filled the air. My eyes began to burn.

Through the smoke, I could just barely see Webb stick a gun out the window. He fired.

Grayson's body jerked and he crumpled to the ground.

34

GRAYSON MOANED AS HE ROLLED OVER ON THE COUCH. "DID I fall asleep again?"

"Yeah, you keep going in and out," Madison said, setting a cup of coffee on the table next to him. "Which is impressive, given the volume in here."

We were huddled around the couch in the corner of the hostel lounge with UK team thirteen. We were surrounded by at least a hundred other recruits, all of them speculating about MDG at full volume. Word had gotten around about our run-in with MDG after recruits saw us carry an unconscious Grayson through the hostel lobby, our eyes red and our faces splotchy from the tear gas.

"That was one hell of a tranquilizer." Grayson slowly sat up and grabbed the coffee. He looked at Noah, who was on the floor with his back to the couch, laptop open. He'd been combing through videos from our team's uniform cams, looking for proof that MDG was capturing and controlling scrabs. "Are you done looking through the videos? Did you get anything?"

"Not yet," Noah murmured. "But we got nothing from Maddie's camera in the garage, unfortunately."

"Why not?"

"Too dark, and even when there is light, there's nothing helpful. There's a brief shot of the scrabs in the van, but you actually can't see where they're chained up. So it just looks like two angry scrabs, same as usual."

Madison and I glanced at each other. There was no audio on the uniform cameras, and without any video proof, all we had was our word. Which was good enough for the team, but not the rest of the world.

"What about on the street? Did you get anything of them capturing those scrabs?" Grayson asked.

"Still looking," Noah said.

"How many did they get?" Grayson asked.

"It was hard to tell," Julian said. He was sitting on the floor next to me, his expression tight. He'd looked worried since the moment Grayson collapsed. "We hightailed it out of there as fast as we could after you were shot."

"And it was tough to see with the smoke," Saira added. "But I think at least ten."

"Maybe closer to fifteen or twenty," Connor said. "I saw more coming up as we left."

"Should have called a backup team," Grayson grumbled.

"I'm sorry I was too busy making sure you weren't dead to call a backup team," Julian snapped. "And I wasn't exactly eager to send another one of our teams into danger."

"Julian, I meant that *I* should have called a backup team," Grayson said. "When we headed over there. I wasn't blaming you."

"Sorry." Julian sighed and closed his eyes for a moment. "Sorry. I'm on edge." He glanced at me, and I quickly looked away. I was still annoyed with him for being rude to the team earlier. And for acting like he had to protect me.

"What are they going to do with the scrabs?" Zoe asked. "MDG protects, like, celebrities and politicians and stuff. Are they going to use them as bodyguards against other scrabs?"

"I doubt they'd need this many if they were just planning to use them for their celebrity clients," Grayson said. "They had a few hundred at that farm in France before they let them escape. And that was just that one location."

"Then . . . what?" Zoe asked.

"And why are they sending them to this Dust Storm facility? Are they building an army? For what?" Madison asked.

"Exactly. For what." Grayson leaned back, his gaze on the ceiling. "The potential is terrifying. The advantage we've always had over scrabs is our intellect — they're just not as smart as us. But with training, and a person controlling them . . ." He shook his head. "They could potentially have the most powerful army in the world."

"But is that so bad?" Gage asked. "They're an American company. The US already has one of the most powerful militaries in the world. Maybe this is just the next step."

"First of all, that's horrifying. I do not want my government using these things against anyone," Grayson said. "Secondly, you're assuming that MDG is going to hand over this technology to the government. They're a private company."

"And you're assuming they'd hand it over to the US government," Laila said. "Just because they're Americans doesn't mean they won't turn around and sell it to the highest bidder. They can just take their piles of cash and go hide on an island in the Caribbean with all the other rich people. We still don't know where this Dust Storm facility is, but it's probably not in the US."

Gage blanched.

"This is all just speculation," Julian said.

The woman who often worked the front desk appeared in the doorway, hands on her hips. The noise level in the lounge had reached a roar.

She cupped her hands around her mouth. "Can you please keep it down?"

No one obeyed, if they'd even heard her. She tried once more, and then muttered something I couldn't hear and walked away. Julian cast a concerned glance from her to Grayson.

Noah cursed and closed his laptop. "Nothing. I got nothing."

"You checked all the cameras?" Zoe asked.

"Yes. All of them. Everything is obstructed by the SUVs or the gas."

"It's fine," Grayson said. "We'll keep working on it, and I'll keep passing info to my contacts. Saira's working on getting leads on more storage facilities. We think they may have several around town."

"Grayson, they just shot you." Julian sounded exasperated.

"With a tranquilizer gun," Grayson said. "I'm fine. Just a little woozy."

"You were in the middle of the street, surrounded by cameras. These guys had no problem setting scrabs on Clara and Edan. There's no telling what they'll do if they get you alone." Julian's hand brushed against mine. I moved it away. "And what about everyone else? You're fine putting everyone in danger?"

Worry flashed across Grayson's face.

"We're already in danger," Laila said.

"And what are we supposed to do, just forget about all of this?" Noah said. "These guys might be building an army, and we're just going to let them keep capturing scrabs and shipping them to god knows where?"

"Julian does have a point, though," Grayson said. "This might put a target on our backs."

Edan shrugged. "I think it's already there, Grayson. They know we've seen all sorts of things."

Grayson looked at Julian like he thought Edan had a point.

"I don't know. Just make sure you're honest with everyone about the risks." Julian's phone buzzed, and he sighed as he read what was on the screen. He closed his eyes for a moment, like he was gathering his strength. "My parents are here. I need to go say hi." He stood and extended his hand to me. "Will you walk with me?"

"Yeah." I ignored the hand and got to my feet.

I followed Julian out of the lounge, through the lobby, and to the street. He stopped and turned to me as the door swung shut behind us.

"We might give you guys the day off tomorrow," he said. "I'd been hoping to spend it with you, but I think I'm going to have to hang out with my parents."

I crossed my arms over my chest. "Why were you like that today?"

His eyebrows drew together. "Like what?"

"Rude. Why were you rude to Noah? And Grayson."

"Noah does not take this seriously enough."

"He's the best one on the team. And just because he posts videos on YouTube doesn't mean he's not taking it seriously."

"He spends all his time talking to his phone, and then turns around and judges my training methods. Just because he's the best doesn't mean that he can do any better. Would you like it if you had someone constantly making snarky remarks about your job?"

"No," I admitted.

"Are you really judging me for this?" His tone softened a little. He sounded hurt.

"I didn't mean that," I said. "But I think that the stress of trying to keep everyone safe is getting to you. Why were you mad about me going into the garage? You said that you should have *made* me stay with you, which is insulting, frankly. I'm trained to fight these things."

"I know you are, but . . ." He looked uncomfortable.

"What?"

"You're just one of the weakest ones on the team. I don't say that as a criticism," he added quickly. "I know you're working hard, but I'd be lying if I said I didn't worry about you. I let you out of my sight for a few hours in Paris, and you nearly got killed. Then I do it again today, and you end up trapped in a garage full of scrabs. I'm just trying to make sure you're safe."

I flushed. He wasn't wrong—I *was* one of the weaker team members. But I hadn't thought I was that far behind Dorsey, or Priya, or Zoe. Maybe I was wrong.

"It's not your fault," he continued. "Grayson should have spent more time on training. I told him that, but he wouldn't listen." He blew out an annoyed breath and glanced at where an incredibly fancy black car pulled up to the curb.

The car door opened, and I could actually see Julian's shoulders tense. A man stepped out. He had the same handsome face and the same dark hair as Julian. But his hair was streaked with gray, and his face was twisted into a snarl.

"Of all the fucking stupid things to say," he spat at the woman climbing out behind him.

"I'm sorry, I just thought—" Julian's mom had her purse clasped to her chest, and she abruptly cut herself off when she spotted me. "Oh. Hello."

"Mom, Dad, this is Clara," Julian said. "She's on my team."

Julian's dad rolled his eyes and muttered something I couldn't understand.

"And she's my girlfriend," Julian added. His father had no reaction to that.

"Nice to meet you, Clara," his mom said. She was a small woman with a neat blond bob and a worried expression. "I actually saw your picture online, with Julian."

"Mom, I told you to stop reading those gossip sites." Julian's tone was annoyed.

"Why? Everyone loves you two."

Julian's dad walked away, headed for the crosswalk that led to Julian's hotel. It seemed he was done talking to us.

"It was nice to meet you, Clara," his mom said, and scurried after him.

"I'll see you later," Julian said, planting a kiss on my forehead.

"Then why did you come?" I heard Julian's dad say loudly to his wife. A passing couple appeared startled.

I looked from Julian to his dad. I had a bad feeling, the kind I got when Dad came home. I knew that pleading expression his mom had. She was trying to keep him happy.

"Is everything OK?" I asked Julian, catching his hand before he could follow them.

"Yeah, he's always like this." He rolled his eyes and squeezed my hand before letting it go. "Sleep well. Enjoy your day off tomorrow." He turned to follow his parents.

35

I SPENT THE NEXT MORNING IN BED. GRAYSON GAVE US THE DAY off to follow a lead and formulate a strategy to track MDG, and Julian was with his parents, so I wasn't sure what to do with this sudden free time.

I was still annoyed with Julian, but I sort of wished he'd texted or called me today. I was a little worried about him after meeting his dad. I glanced down at my phone again and sighed. I needed to find something to do to take my mind off it.

I rolled over and looked across to where Edan was stretched out in his bunk, a book propped up on his chest.

"Hey," I said.

He tilted his head back and then rolled over on his stomach, putting the book aside.

"You don't drink, do you?" I asked.

"No." He glanced around the empty room. "Everyone else is downstairs drinking, aren't they?"

"Yes. The bartender is serving all recruits. Even at noon, apparently."

"Patrick did mention something about day drinking."

"Do you want to go to the gym?"

He propped his head up on his hand and gave me an amused look. "You want to go to the gym on our day off?"

"I thought we could practice sparring. Without everyone around judging us." Julian's words kept running through my head —was I really that much worse than the rest of the team? I needed to take every opportunity to practice.

"Yeah, OK." Edan ducked as he scooted out of his bunk and climbed down the stairs. "Can we get fish and chips after, though? I feel like that's what you're supposed to do in London, and I don't know when I'll get another chance."

"Sure."

I jumped out of my bunk and walked across the room to my locker, spun the dial and opened it. We'd received two stipends so far, and I had a small stash of cash. I pulled a few bills out and tucked them into my pocket, and then grabbed my weapons pack.

Connor and Mia were in the lobby, and they waved when they spotted us.

"We heard from the police about the storage facility," Mia said. "They found nothing."

"I'm shocked, I tell you," Connor said. "*Shocked.*"

"It probably took them so long to get there that MDG was long gone," Mia said.

"They may not even be all that motivated to catch MDG," Connor said. "If you know what I mean."

Edan and I looked at each other, confused.

"Connor's always going on about conspiracy theories," Mia said with an eye roll. She gestured at the door to the bar. "Are you coming?"

"No, we're headed to the gym," Edan said. "We'll see you guys later."

They headed into the bar, and I followed Edan outside. "Is there a reason?" I asked. "For not drinking?"

"My mom's an alcoholic," he said. It was sunny, but still a bit cool, and he wore a red hoodie with his black track pants. His hair was soft, not shaped into its usual perfectly messy style. It made him look younger than usual. "And I only have a few memories of my dad, but they all involve alcohol, so I'm guessing he was not about the moderation."

"So you just avoid it totally."

"For now. Maybe that'll change in the future, but for now it feels like something I can control. It's my choice. People sometimes act like you're doomed to be exactly like your parents. I felt that way for a while."

"Yeah?"

"Yeah. Like how people always talk about the cycle of abuse and how kids who are abused are likely to become abusers themselves. And how you're more likely to be an alcoholic if your parents are. That felt sort of terrifying to me a few years ago. But after I left home . . ." He shrugged. "It's all my choice, you know? I'm not going to wake up tomorrow and start beating the shit out of people. I think my mom's parents were even worse to her than she was to me, but it just feels like an excuse. If anything, you should be *less* likely to hit your kids, because you know firsthand how it feels."

"True," I said quietly. I wondered if Laurence felt that way. I'd worried about becoming like Mom sometimes, too forgiving of Dad's behavior, too willing to pretend like everything was fine when it wasn't. Did Laurence worry about becoming like Dad?

We turned into the alley and walked through the gym doors. The woman at the front desk waved for us to go through.

The gym was nearly empty, except for a couple guys working with a scrab dummy in one of the smaller rooms. The gym consisted of three rooms—the big one in the middle with a boxing ring, and two smaller ones with scrab dummies and other fake weapons. We grabbed gloves and headed into the ring.

"I need to work on my uppercut," I said. "Julian says mine is weak. How do you feel about that?"

"Fine."

"You sure?"

"Yeah. He's right, you should work on it. Noah can throw an uppercut that knocks a scrab off its feet. Gage can do some serious damage with his uppercut and those spiked knuckles of his." His eyes lit up. "Oh! We had a heart-to-heart, by the way."

"You had a heart-to-heart with *Gage?*"

"I told him that I did not appreciate him using my face as a punching bag during sparring practice, because my parents were abusive. He was weirdly nice about it. He apologized and said that he was so terrified when we started training in Paris that the only way he could deal was by yelling and punching people."

I gaped at him. "Seriously?"

"Yeah. And now he feels bad because everyone hates him. Except Zoe. I think they're sort of a thing."

"Ew."

"Agreed."

"But he really just told you that? He said he was terrified?"

"He sure did. It was like he felt like he had to tell me something personal because I'd confided in him. It was kind of nice, in an awkward way."

"And you don't mind? That he knows? I wouldn't trust Gage with secrets."

"Eh, it's not a secret. It's too much work to lie about it. For me, anyway."

"I guess," I said. It all felt like work, honestly. "Uh, let's get started, then." I avoided his gaze and raised my gloves. "Move a little slower for me?"

"Sure. Can I make a request?"

"Of course."

"Don't pull your punches *too* much."

"Seriously?"

"Don't hit me with your full strength, but I think it'll help if you knock me around a little. I trust you."

I trusted him too, I realized. I trusted several members of team seven—Patrick, Laila, Priya, Noah—and I was a little surprised to find that he fit firmly on that list.

"Gentle knocking around. You got it." I smiled at him. "Let's go."

Edan shrugged on his hoodie as we walked out of the gym a couple hours later. "You cool with taking the subway out a bit? Or—the Tube. Connor made fun of me yesterday for calling it the subway. I found a good place a few stops away."

"Sure. As long as you know how to get there." We walked down the steps of the Underground entrance. "You did really good today.

We should try to get Julian to pair you with someone other than Gage. You'd kill it with a partner like Madison or Noah. Someone fast."

"You're pretty fast," he said as we tapped our cards and walked to the crowded platform. "And you're getting faster. You're going to give me a run for my money soon."

"Yeah?" I smiled. "That's nice to hear. I was always considered pretty good in my high school combat classes, but Grayson's training is so much more intense. I always feel like I'm failing at it."

"You're definitely not failing at it. But my high school combat classes were a joke. We mostly just sat around and talked. When I went, anyway. Which wasn't often."

"Why'd you drop out?"

"I got a job that was offering a lot of hours, and at the time it seemed smarter to do that. And I hated school, honestly. It all seemed so pointless — sitting around doing nothing in combat class, or memorizing crap so I could regurgitate it on a test later. I figured I could just memorize stuff for one test and be done with it. Which I did."

"You already took a GED?"

"Yeah, a few months ago."

"How was it? I'm going to have to take it eventually."

"I thought it was pretty easy, except for math. I've always been terrible at math. But I just bought a book and studied a little before. You'll be fine."

"Maybe. I'm not, like, the smartest person in the room," I said to my feet.

"Just because you weren't good in school doesn't mean you're not smart." He laughed. "I mean, that's always been my hope. Otherwise I'm a real dumbass."

"I don't think you're a dumbass, if that makes you feel better."

"It does, thank you." He leaned forward, peering down the track. Lights were approaching.

We squeezed into the packed subway car, and I ended up standing over the seats, squished in between Edan and a guy who developed an instant fascination with my boobs. I turned so I was facing Edan instead.

The guy in the seat just below me leaned back, phone poised like he was taking a picture. It was pointed in our direction.

Edan was staring over my head, and I leaned closer to him, rising up on my toes so I could whisper in his ear.

"Is that guy taking a picture of us?" I asked.

Edan waited a moment before discreetly glancing over, and then looked at me in amusement.

"I think he is?"

"Why?"

"He's probably impressed by my good looks."

I rolled my eyes. "That must be it."

The train went around a curve and I stumbled, lurching into Edan. I grabbed a fistful of his hoodie, and he circled an arm around my waist.

"Sorry," I said. He dropped his arm as I regained my balance.

We got off two stops later, and I glanced back at the guy who took our picture as I stepped off the train. He grinned and waved. I gave him a confused look.

We climbed the stairs up to the street, and Edan pointed to my left.

"It should be right—"

His words cut off as the sound of glass shattering echoed down the street. A scrab flew out the front window of a convenience store and landed on the street with a roar. It was much smaller than most scrabs I'd seen, at maybe four feet tall. It probably wasn't even fully grown yet. Its dragged its short, sharp claws across gravel and snarled.

"Not even one day off, huh?" Edan said, reaching into his pack for a weapon.

"Apparently not." I pulled my baton sword out of my pack, unsheathed it, and screwed the sheath to the bottom of the baton.

The scrab stood on all fours in the middle of the street, nearly motionless as it observed the scene around it. People ran in all directions—into stores, toward me and Edan, away from us. Everyone moved quickly but without panic. Business as usual.

Edan and I broke into a run, dodging the crowd. The scrab lowered its head and bared its teeth at us.

Edan got to the scrab first. He ducked as it swung at him, thrusting his stun gun into its side. The scrab roared.

I tightened my fingers around my baton and aimed it at the scrab's neck. It swiped it away with such force that I lost my balance and hit the ground. *Thud thud thud*. The scrab was running away.

I scrambled to my feet and broke into a sprint behind Edan.

The scrab galloped toward a group of teenage boys in school uniforms. One had his phone out, and his eyes went round as he realized that the scrab was headed for him. He cursed and turned to run.

Edan stunned the scrab in the leg. It howled and screeched to a stop. The boys scurried into a restaurant.

The scrab lunged at Edan, who ducked and scrambled away just in time. He stunned it in the side.

I skidded to a stop in front of the scrab. Its eyes were full of fury as it looked up at me. Both clawed hands were headed straight for me.

I drove my baton straight up into the scrab's neck. It jerked, a squeaking noise escaping its throat. Blood dripped onto my arms, and I leaned back, trying to avoid getting it on my face. Wetness splashed onto my neck. Gross.

The scrab stumbled backward and collapsed on the ground.

Edan lifted his arms in triumph. The crowd at the end of the street burst into applause.

"Yeah!" one of the boys in the restaurant yelled. All four of them were standing in front of the glass front window, phones out and pointed at us. Sirens sounded in the distance.

I shook my arms, blood flying through the air.

"Here," Edan said, jogging over to me and unzipping his pack. "I have some wipes." He tugged a few free and handed them to me.

"Thanks." I wiped my arms down until they were clean. "Do I have any on my face?"

"Just on your neck. I'll get it." Edan grabbed a wipe and swiped it down my neck a few times. "Badass as usual."

"You too," I said with a smile.

He stepped back, taking the bloody wipes from me and tossing them into a trashcan. Behind him, two police cars stopped near the scrab.

"So," he said. "Still hungry?"

36

WE HAD INSTRUCTIONS TO MEET JULIAN AT THE GYM THE NEXT morning, and I walked over with Edan. Most of the team was already there, and they all turned and stared at us. Noah's face broke into a huge grin.

"Oh hey, guys. What have you two been up to?" He said it like he knew exactly what we'd been up to. Beside him, Madison raised her eyebrows. Priya looked delighted. Patrick cocked his head and squinted.

Edan and I traded confused glances.

"Your adventures yesterday made the news," Noah said. "Well, the Tumblr and Twitter news." He swiped his phone a few times and then held it up so we could see. It was open to Tumblr.

GUYS YOUR SHIP IS SAILING, the top of the post read. Below it were several pictures of Edan and me on the subway. We were standing side by side in the first one, smiling at each other in the second one, and appeared to be cuddling in the last one. Edan's arm was around my waist, and I was gripping the back of his hoodie. My face was in his chest, and his was tilted down to look at me, almost like he was getting ready to kiss me.

"OK, that picture is wildly misleading," Edan said. "The train was crowded, and Clara just bumped into me."

"Uh-huh," Priya said, mischief in her smile. "Why were you guys out together just the two of you, anyway?"

"We came here to do some sparring practice, and then Edan wanted some fish and chips, so we decided to get lunch. He picked a place with a scrab attack," I said.

"But they gave us free fish and chips for killing the scrab," Edan said. "So really I chose well."

"There are pictures of that too," Noah said, handing his phone to Edan. "Scroll down."

"You started your date with exercise?" Priya scrunched up her face. "You guys are weird."

"It wasn't a date," I said.

Edan scrolled to the pictures and videos of us fighting scrabs. They came from several different angles, but the boys in the restaurant had clearly gotten the best shots. They had one of me at the moment I'd stuck the blade in the scrab's neck, my face turned away as blood splattered on my arms. The series ended with a picture of Edan wiping down my neck, each of us smiling at the other.

They are the cutest, the first person who had reblogged the picture said.

The second one said, *She's cheating on Julian??????*

Edan glanced at me, and then quickly away. He avoided my gaze as he handed the phone back to Noah.

Heat rose up my neck. The pictures told a story that wasn't entirely true, but it suddenly put the afternoon in a different perspective. Someone had cobbled together a narrative for us from only a few images. I didn't have any images to counter the story, just a memory of an afternoon that had felt like two friends hanging out. This new spin felt intrusive and confusing.

"Sorry to disappoint Tumblr, but we were not doing anything nearly as romantic as those pictures suggest," Edan said. He was obviously trying to keep his voice light and only half succeeding.

"I'm not sure that picture of you wiping blood off of me even qualifies as romantic," I said with a grimace. "I think Tumblr needs to reevaluate that one."

Edan laughed. Our eyes met, and he widened his, like he was annoyed by the situation.

"Julian's not going to like this," Madison said.

"When does Julian like anything?" Noah grumbled.

I bristled. "Not going to like what?"

"These photos of you and Edan. You guys hanging out behind his back."

"It was not *behind his back*," I said, my words sharp. Priya eyed us warily, and I stepped closer to Madison and lowered my voice. "I was just hanging out with a teammate."

"Did you tell him beforehand?"

"No, it was a last-minute thing."

She lifted her eyebrows as if to say that I'd just proved her point.

The door opened, and Julian walked in, staring at his phone. He wore his high-collared jacket, the one that made him look like he belonged on the pages of a magazine.

Madison was wrong. She was just jealous. Julian wouldn't get mad without at least talking to me first.

Julian glanced up from his phone, his gaze catching on mine. He clenched his jaw so hard I could see it.

My chest tightened. Madison hadn't been wrong.

UK team thirteen walked in with Grayson, snagging Julian's attention away.

"All right, guys, I'm splitting some of you up today," Grayson said. "Clara?" He beckoned me over.

I walked to him. Julian stood beside him, intently avoiding my gaze.

Maybe it was stupid to think he wouldn't be mad. I'd be upset if I saw pictures of him hugging another girl. Sure, I'd want the whole story, but I wouldn't be able to control my initial reaction.

"Julian wants you with him on a special assignment today," Grayson said. "Is that OK?"

"Sure," I said. "What is it?"

"We got a huge shipment of stuff in from people's lists, and we need someone to go through it."

"Can you spare Julian for that?" I asked.

"I mean, I'd rather not, but . . ." Grayson was resigned, like they'd already fought about this.

"It's fine," Julian said, his voice clipped. "We'll get it done by this evening and then we can resume your wild goose chase."

Grayson turned his back to Julian. "You are welcome to stay with the rest of the team, if you'd rather not hang out with this jerk. We're following some leads on MDG movement in the area."

I actually didn't want to desert the team, but I couldn't decline to spend the day with Julian, especially when he was upset. I clearly needed to talk to him about those pictures.

"I'll help Julian. It'll go faster with the two of us." I gave Julian a smile that he didn't return.

"OK." Grayson seemed like he wanted to say more, but he closed his mouth and walked across the gym.

Julian strode toward the door without saying a word. I hurried to catch up with him, catching the door before it closed. "Julian!" I called.

He stopped on the sidewalk and turned to me. His mouth was set in a hard line, anger radiating off the stiff set of his shoulders.

"Are you mad about those pictures with Edan?" My words came out in a rush. "Because it's not what it looks like. Someone took a photo right when I bumped into him. You can tell, can't you? That they're misleading."

"Not really," he said, voice rising. "I saw photos of the two of you, away from the rest of the team, apparently having a great time."

"We were just sparring, and then—"

"Just the two of you."

"Well, yeah, he was the only one around, and you said I needed to work—"

"Now it's my fault?" He let out a humorless laugh.

"No, I didn't say that. I just—"

"Why wouldn't you call me and tell me about Edan? Because you felt guilty about it, right?"

"No, I didn't think it was a big—"

"You would have told me if it wasn't a big deal. We texted last night, and you didn't say a word."

"I said I went to the gym!" A lump had formed in my throat, and the words came out shrill.

"And you conveniently left out the part about who you went with. And your little lunch date after. How would you have felt if there were photos of me and Madison cozying up on the subway? Alone?"

"Not great," I said quietly. "I'm—I'm sorry. I should have told you that I went with Edan. But it wouldn't kill you to trust me a little."

"We've barely been dating for a few weeks. You haven't earned any trust."

I blinked. I had to *earn* trust?

His expression softened slightly. "And trust is not my strong suit," he said, quieter.

"Well, it's not mine either, but I'm trying."

He nodded, then closed his eyes for a moment and let out a breath. "Please just don't hang out with Edan alone again."

"We're just friends," I said.

"You may think that, but I wouldn't put it past Edan to be working an angle."

"I think you've gotten the wrong impression of Edan," I said.

He gave me a look that clearly said now was *not* the time to be discussing Edan's good qualities.

"I don't think it's too much to ask that my girlfriend not go on dates with other guys," he said.

"Of course I won't go on dates with other guys," I said. "But Edan's my friend."

"And you really need to hang out, just the two of you? Even though it makes me uncomfortable?"

"Well, no, I don't want to make you uncomfortable, but—"

"Then don't do it. I hate the guy. If you're using him to torment me, then congratulations, it's working."

"God, Julian, no, I would never do that."

"Then what? Why would the two of you need to hang out alone?"

"No, we don't," I said. "I just . . . I mean . . ." I was confused now. I didn't *need* to hang out alone with Edan, especially if it upset him this much.

He let out a giant sigh. "Listen, just go do the packages. There's another recruit waiting back at the hostel with instructions."

"You're not coming? I thought we were doing it together."

"No, I have to meet my parents. I'll come find you later, though."

"Julian, I only agreed to do this because I thought you needed my help. If you're not even going to come, I should probably just go back to the team and—"

"Would you just go back to the hostel?" Julian's voice was loud, almost a yell, and I took a startled step back. "I got you an easy assignment today. It wouldn't kill you to show a little appreciation."

"I—um . . ." My heart was pounding too hard to form words. I grasped my wrist, pressing both arms to my chest.

Julian took a deep breath. "I'm sorry. I just need you to go do this assignment, OK? We'll talk later."

I nodded mutely. He turned and stomped away.

\\|/|

Julian hadn't been exaggerating—there really were a lot of packages. It took me most of the day to sort through them all and transport them to the various hostels and hotels around London where the recruits were staying.

Julian texted me just after I'd finished, asking me to meet him in front of his hotel. I found him standing on the sidewalk, hands stuffed in his pocket, a contrite look on his face.

"Hey," he said softly as I approached.

"Hey." The word came out as I meant it—suspicious. I'd spent most of the day replaying our conversation in my head, and I wasn't sure that I actually had anything to be sorry for. Sure, Julian didn't like Edan, but I still had a right to be friends with him. The fact that Julian didn't trust me was his problem, not mine.

"I'm sorry," he said. "For getting mad earlier. I'm having a rough time lately. My parents . . ." He let his voice trail off.

"What about your parents?"

He pinched the bridge of his nose. "It's nothing. My dad is just stressed, as usual. And *I'm* stressed. I can't convince Grayson to back off of MDG."

"Why should he?"

"Because he's going to get himself killed! And probably take a few of you with him."

"Don't you want to know what they're using those trained scrabs for?" I asked. "It's terrifying, what they're doing."

Julian just shrugged, not meeting my gaze. He didn't seem at all interested in what MDG was doing with trained scrabs.

Across the street, several vans stopped in front of the hostel. Some of the teams were back.

"Do you want to go inside?" Julian asked, jerking his thumb at the hotel. "The hotel restaurant is pretty good."

"What?" I stared at him with mounting confusion. "No. We should go check on the team." I pointed to the vans. "Have you heard from Grayson about how their day went yet?"

"No," Julian said, his gaze fixed somewhere over my shoulder.

Why wouldn't he want to go check on his team? Why was he so against Grayson investigating MDG? I quickly turned away before my face betrayed my suspicion.

I crossed the street and walked into the hostel, Julian behind me. A wall of noise greeted us.

I froze. Recruits were crowded into the lobby, everyone shouting. One of the women working the front desk was arguing with a team leader, and the other was pressed into a corner, arms crossed over her chest as she frowned at the scene around her. Team seven and UK team thirteen were in the middle of it all, covered in blood and grime.

I pushed through the crowd to them. Edan spotted me first. He had shallow claw marks across his neck and blood that probably wasn't his splattered heavily across the front of his uniform.

"Clara," he said, relief in his voice. He managed a weak smile.

"What happened?" I asked.

"MDG happened," Laila said, wiping blood off the camera on her chest.

"The tip was good," Saira said. "They were definitely there. And they were ready. They sent their trained scrabs after us."

Priya pushed her hair out of her face, leaving a streak of dirt across her cheek. Beside her, Thomas's eyes were red-rimmed. I realized suddenly that Mia wasn't with them.

Guilt unfurled in my stomach. I should have been there. Both Julian and I should have been there.

I glanced at him, expecting to see my expression mirrored there, but his face betrayed no emotion.

"Are you sure?" Grayson said to Noah. "You don't have to come."

"I want to," Noah said. He was reattaching his camera to his chest.

"Where are you going?" I asked.

"Saira had one more lead we didn't get to today. A really promising one. So I'm headed back there now."

"Seriously?" Julian snapped. He looked at Noah. "You are not going with him. None of my team is. You all almost just died. Mia *did* just die."

Grayson's jaw clenched. "The fact that they just tried to kill us is even more reason to go. Why are they so desperate to capture scrabs? And keep it a secret? They used smoke bombs again today to ensure we couldn't get any footage."

"I'm just worried—" Julian began.

"Oh, *now* you're worried about your team?" Noah interrupted. "You deserted us entirely today, but now you're worried?"

"You know what? Go with him," Julian said, sweeping his arm out. "Go with Grayson and get yourself killed. I don't even care."

"Thanks for the support, Julian," Madison said dryly. She cut a quick glance at me before looping her arm through Noah's. "I'm going too."

"I can go also," Edan said.

Julian's hand closed around my wrist, tight and insistent. I shook him off.

"No, that's all right," Grayson said, throwing Edan a grateful smile. "I don't want a bunch of us there for this. We're going for stealth on this one."

Julian rolled his eyes. I stared at him, a heavy weight settling at the bottom of my stomach. It was almost as if he was *protecting* MDG.

"Why don't you go get that cut cleaned?" Grayson said to Edan. He fixed Julian with a hard stare. "Maybe now's a good time to check on your team's injuries?"

"We're fine," Priya said quickly, like she didn't want Julian's help. "Come on, Edan, I'll do it. Archer, you have a full first aid kit, don't you?" He nodded.

I watched them go, followed by the rest of team seven. Grayson left with Noah and Madison. Around us, the crowd thinned as recruits headed to their rooms. I was left with just Julian.

I realized, with a sinking feeling, that I didn't want to be alone with him. It was only a couple days ago that I'd felt a rush of relief every time I saw him. I'd felt like I belonged with him. Like everything would be OK if Julian was around.

Part of me desperately wanted to push down the sinking feeling in my gut so I could get back to that feeling. I wanted to cling to the sweet, generous version of Julian I knew.

"This is getting ridiculous," Julian muttered. "I give all the teams another week, max."

I reeled back, alarmed. "What?"

His face softened when he caught my expression. "We'll be fine. Don't worry, OK?"

I stared at him, waiting for more, but he just stepped away.

"I'll see you tomorrow," he said. "Have a good night."

I watched as he walked through the door and disappeared.

It sounded like he'd already given up on the teams. And coupled with what he'd said about MDG . . . None of it felt right.

Plus Julian hadn't even seemed upset that his team had such a bad day. He hadn't asked about any of their injuries.

He'd never shown much concern for them, now that I thought about it. He'd always been worried about me, but he'd never had much interest in the rest of them.

I took a shaky breath as I trudged upstairs and into our room. Priya was smoothing a bandage over the scratches on Edan's neck. Laila, Patrick, and Dorsey sat on the floor, talking softly.

"You OK?" Priya asked. Silence followed, and I realized with a start that she was talking to me.

"Oh, me? Yeah. I'm fine."

She seemed skeptical. My face must have given something away.

"How are you guys?" I asked, glancing at Edan. He was also giving me a look like he could read every emotion on my face.

"Tired," Priya said. She pulled her dirty shirt away from her chest and wrinkled her nose. "I'm going to change and go to bed."

I grabbed my pajamas and followed her to the bathroom down the hall. The lights were off when we returned. Priya flopped down onto her bunk.

I climbed into mine. Edan was on his stomach, the light of his phone illuminating his face. I had a text from him.

You look like someone killed your puppy.

I winced and typed out a reply. **I've always hated that expression. Who kills puppies??**

He smiled as he read the message. **Sorry. You look like someone was very rude to your puppy.**

I just feel bad that I wasn't there with you guys today. It was true, even though it wasn't why I looked like someone had been rude to my puppy.

It's not your fault Julian sent you on a different assignment.

I looked up at him and nodded.

Another message from him popped up a minute later. **Is everything OK? Julian looked kind of pissed this morning. Was it about those Tumblr pictures?**

Yeah, he saw them. I explained, but he was still mad about it.

He hates me, so I'm sure he preferred it when you hated me too.

I didn't HATE you.

You certainly didn't like me.

Well the feeling was mutual.

I mostly didn't like you because you didn't like me. Everyone likes me. I'm charming and witty.

And so modest.

That too. He grinned at me, then looked down to type another message. But seriously, it's shitty of him to get angry at you about those pictures. Madison told me that Julian was probably going to be mad that we were hanging out at all. We sort of had a fight about it.

My eyebrows shot up. **You had a fight with Madison?**

Yeah. I told her that she made it seem like you were to blame if Julian got jealous. She said she hadn't meant for it to come out like that. I think she felt bad, just FYI.

There was a pause before his next message.

But I think I got mad at her because she made it seem normal. Like it was OK that Julian got jealous.

He typed for a long time, so long that I might have thought he was doing something else if it weren't for the dots beneath his last message. Finally he made an annoyed sound and tossed the phone aside.

He scooted to the edge of his bed, closer to me, and then reached out, bracing his hands against the bottom of my bunk. I pushed my phone aside and leaned closer to him.

"I just want you to know that it's not normal." His voice was so quiet that I had to scoot closer, until our faces were only inches apart. "I don't know if you need to hear that. I'm not even sure if *I'm* overreacting or not. But the jealousy and the short temper and the way he acted the other day when you snuck into the MDG garage—it feels bad."

His gaze held mine, his expression serious. I couldn't breathe.

"So if you need someone to say it, I'm saying it," he whispered. "It's not normal."

37

"Hey, guys. Wake up. WAKE UP."

I blinked at the sound of Noah's voice and rose up on my elbow. Gray early morning light flooded the room, and Noah stood in the doorway. There were dark circles under his eyes, and he still wore the same bloodied uniform he'd had on last night.

"Grayson was arrested," he said. "And the hostel is kicking us out. Get dressed and pack your bags."

"Wait, what?" Patrick stood, squinting in the light. "Grayson was *arrested?*"

"The cops caught him trying to break into a warehouse we thought was owned by MDG. It wasn't."

"Madison?" Edan asked.

"She's downstairs. We were on the other side of the building when the police came. We managed to sneak away. But seriously, guys, they're kicking us out, like, *now*. Get dressed."

I climbed out of bed. "Where are we going to go?"

But Noah had already disappeared.

We all ran to the restrooms and changed as fast as we could. No one else was bothering with a uniform, so I threw on jeans and a T-shirt and stuffed everything else I owned into my backpack. I slung it over my shoulder with my weapons pack, my gaze snagging on Edan's as I straightened. He quickly looked away and walked out the door.

OK. It was all I said last night, after he leaned over into my bunk and whispered that Julian's jealousy wasn't normal. I couldn't think of any other response. Between Edan calling out Julian's jealousy and my worries about his involvement with MDG, I was pretty sure that I couldn't speak without bursting into tears.

I took a shaky breath as I walked out of the room and downstairs.

It was chaos. Recruits were packed into the lobby and streaming out onto the sidewalk. Madison was yelling at a red-faced man at the reception desk.

Noah appeared in front of me, his expression dark. "Can I talk to you a minute?"

I followed him out of the lobby and onto the street. Recruits were all around us — I spotted Edan and Dorsey a few paces away — and Noah lowered his voice when he spoke.

"Did you see Julian last night? After we left, I mean."

I shook my head. "No, why?"

"He caught up with us before we left. Grayson told him where we were going."

I looked at him expectantly. "So . . ."

Anger flitted across Noah's tired face. "So no one else knew. The tip we were following, it was from Saira's team, and she came with us. Julian stopped us to find out where we were going, and then the cops show up? Do you think that's a coincidence?"

My stomach clenched. "Why would Julian do that? Why would he want Grayson arrested?"

"Yeah. That's my question exactly."

The hostel door swung open, and a dozen angry recruits streamed out, dragging their luggage behind them.

Noah watched them go. "Someone put pressure on the company that owns the hostel to toss us out. Doesn't Julian's family own some hotels? Do we know which ones?"

"I . . . I don't know," I stuttered.

"Speaking of," Noah muttered. He jerked his chin at something behind me.

Julian was walking across the street, hands stuffed into his coat, gaze downcast.

"Maybe you should talk to him." Noah pressed the palms of both hands to his eyes. "I don't have the patience for Julian today, and he'll never admit to anything if I scream at him."

My chest tightened. "Yeah, go back inside. I'll talk to him. I really don't think he had anything to do with this." The words sounded like a lie.

Noah lowered his hands and gave me a suspicious look. "I hope you're right." He pulled the door open and disappeared into the hostel.

Julian crossed to my side of the street. He hadn't spotted me yet. He was walking very fast, making a beeline for something. I followed his gaze. Edan and Dorsey.

Edan noticed him first, turning with a slightly pained expression. "Hey, Jul—"

Julian punched him in the face.

I gasped as Edan went down. Dorsey dove in between the two of them, but Julian was already taking a step back. He pointed a furious finger down at Edan.

"I know exactly what you're doing, and it needs to stop," Julian spat. Edan, still on the ground, blood pouring from his nose, was clearly baffled. "Don't talk to her, don't look at her, don't text her. You got it?"

My body went cold, and then numb. This was about *me?*

Edan's gaze shifted to me. Julian turned. His jaw twitched.

I couldn't move. I was rooted to the ground. *Don't text her,* Julian had said.

My phone—*his* phone—was suddenly heavy in my pocket.

Dorsey helped Edan up from the sidewalk and steered him toward the door of the hostel. Edan hesitated, his eyes meeting mine. Blood trickled down his chin.

"Dude, you're bleeding everywhere," Dorsey said. His lip curled as he cast a glance at Julian. "Come on."

I nodded, telling Edan to go. The world felt like it was moving in slow motion. Edan let Dorsey push him inside.

Julian grabbed my arm. "Let's get out of here."

We'd taken several steps before my brain kicked in. I twisted my arm out of his grasp. He stopped short and reached for me again, but then seemed to think better of it.

"What are you doing?" My words came out as a gasp.

"We need to go," he said, ignoring my question. His gaze flicked to my backpack. "Do you have all your stuff?"

"Are you . . . What is . . . ?" I'd lost my ability to form words.

The dread uncoiling slowly in my stomach was swallowing up every ounce of sense that I had.

Julian's lips were thin. He was obviously trying to keep his temper in check. I took in a slow breath.

"Why did you just do that?" I asked.

He looked away and said nothing.

"Did you read my texts? Last night, with Edan? Is that why you're so mad?"

His expression was icy. "I told you that was a team phone when I gave it to you. It shouldn't be a surprise that I monitor what goes on with it."

My back hit brick, and I leaned into it, grateful I had something to hold me up.

He *had* said it was a team phone.

He had not told me he would *monitoring* it.

"You should have told me if you were going to be reading my text messages," I said, my voice shaky.

"I wouldn't have had to if you'd been honest with me!" Julian took a step closer to me, his tone low but furious.

"Honest with you about what?"

"About Edan! You said you would stop being friends with him. And then you *immediately* broke your word. Not even twenty-four hours later. I can't trust you, so this is what happens."

"How can I trust you, when you're the one reading my texts?" I shot back.

"Do you want to see my texts? Fine." He grabbed his phone from his pocket and shoved it at me. "Take a look. You won't find any secret midnight text sessions with some other girl. You won't find *me* discussing our relationship with a girl I know you hate."

I tried to swallow around the lump lodged in my throat. He sort of had a point about that. The tiny sliver of doubt felt like relief, like I could excuse him violating my privacy in a pretty horrible way and forget he'd just assaulted Edan. It would be easier, to forgive him and carry on thinking he was the guy I wanted him to be.

But he wasn't.

I looked down at the phone he still held between us and then back up to him. The words *this is over* were on the tip of my tongue. I wanted to throw the phone he'd given me in his face and stomp away dramatically.

But Noah's angry face flashed through my mind. There were more important things happening here besides my relationship with Julian. I took a deep breath.

"OK," I said. "Open it. Let me see your calls and texts from last night."

He blinked, clearly taken aback. "What?"

"Show me everything you did last night and this morning. Everyone you called, emailed, texted. Let's see it."

"Why?"

"You just said I could."

"I was making a point."

"Do you have something to hide?"

Neither of us spoke for a moment. He did not open his phone.

"Did you hear Grayson was arrested?" I asked.

"Yes."

"I heard you stopped them before they left and asked where they were going."

He was silent.

"And then the cops showed up. Is that a coincidence?"

He looked away from me. For all of Julian's talents, lying was not one of them.

"And *I'm* the one who can't be trusted? What did you do, Julian? Why are your parents here? Did you have something to do with us being kicked out of the hostel? Why are you so against Grayson going after MDG?"

He shushed me, casting a glance over his shoulder at the recruits loitering on the sidewalk a few yards away. None of them were watching us.

He stepped back, jerking his chin to indicate I should follow him. He walked around the corner and into the alley. I went slowly, part of me reluctant to leave the safety of the street.

He moved close to me as soon as I rounded the corner, so near our chests were nearly touching. "It's complicated," he said quietly.

"You did it, then? You called the cops on Grayson?"

"I did it for his own good. These MDG guys have no qualms about killing him if he gets in their way. I *saved* him."

"How do you know what MDG was going to do?"

"Like I said, it's complicated."

"How is it complicated?"

"I know some things because of my dad's association with MDG."

My brain started buzzing. "Your dad is part of MDG? Did you know that the team was walking into a trap yesterday? Is that why you pulled me out?"

He said nothing.

"Julian, they could have been killed. Mia *was* killed," I whispered, horrified.

"Clara, listen," he said in a rush, putting a hand on my neck. "Grayson doesn't fully understand what MDG is doing. He doesn't get the scope of it. We want to be on their side." His eyes burned into mine. "*Trust me.*"

I jerked away. "What does that mean? Why would you betray your best friend like that?"

He rolled his eyes. "Don't be so dramatic. I didn't *betray* him."

"You betrayed the whole team. You let them walk straight into MDG's trained scrabs. What is MDG doing that made you feel OK about that?"

He grabbed my arm, his fingers tight around my wrist. "Why don't you calm down first? Then we can talk about it."

I tried to twist out of his grasp, but he held firm.

"Julian, let go." My heart pounded in my ears.

Danger, danger, danger.

"Would you just listen to me for a second?" His voice was raised, full of frustration. "You're getting hysterical without even listening to me."

"Let go of me!" I'd meant to yell, but it came out hoarse and pathetic. A choked sob escaped my lips as I finally wrenched my arm free. His fingernails scratched my skin. I barely felt it.

I took a few hurried, clumsy steps until I was around the

corner and back onto the safety of the street. Julian immediately blocked my path. He reached for me again. He put a gentle hand on my shoulder.

"Move," I said shakily, trying to sidestep him. "Don't touch me."

"Clara, would you stop being ridicu—"

An arm shot between us, muscling Julian out of the way. Madison. She fixed Julian with a hard stare.

"She said, don't touch her," she said slowly.

Julian took a step back, rolling his eyes. He actually looked *amused*.

He lifted his hands in surrender. "Can we stop it with the dramatics?"

Madison made a noise between a laugh and a scream, like she'd heard this before.

"Just go, Julian."

"Fine." He peered past her, his expression soft when it landed on me. "Call me when you calm down OK? I'm not mad."

"Wonderful. Thanks for letting us know. We were all so concerned," Madison said. Her arm was still stretched out in front of me.

Julian shot Madison a withering look and then strode quickly away. I watched him go.

Madison finally dropped her arm and turned to face me. My heart was beating too fast, tears clouding my vision.

"Are you all right?" she asked. "What was that about?"

I drew in a ragged breath. I needed to tell her about Julian calling the cops on Grayson, and that he apparently had information about MDG, but the words wouldn't come out. My whole relationship with Julian had been upended in a matter of minutes, and I couldn't make my brain or my mouth work.

My gaze snagged on my arm, on three shallow scratches where Julian's fingernails had left a mark. I pressed my own fingertips to the edge of each one. A hysterical laugh escaped my lips.

"Do you want to go inside? Find a bathroom? I like to have my panic attacks in bathrooms," Madison said.

That struck me as wildly funny. I laughed until tears streaked down my cheeks. If Madison was alarmed by this, she didn't show it. She just watched me, head cocked to one side.

"I'm sorry," I gasped. "I'm just . . ." I took in a deep breath, trying to calm down. It didn't work. I made a strangled noise that was kind of like a scream.

"Are we yelling now? Oh, I can get behind that." She balled both her hands into fists and let out a truly impressive scream.

I laughed, wiping a hand across my wet eyes. I screamed.

A passing man jumped, startled, and gave us a disapproving look.

"Fuck you, keep walking," Madison said, pointing at him. "We're having a bad day."

He grumbled something and hurried down the sidewalk.

I wiped my cheeks again as I leaned back against the wall. I was crying harder than I'd realized. My brain couldn't fully process what had just happened, so apparently all my emotions were going to leak out my eyes instead.

"Thank you," I said with a sniff. I opened my mouth to

apologize, to say I was stupid for not listening to her about Julian, but my gaze caught on someone behind her. She turned.

Edan had just emerged from the hostel, a tissue pressed to his nose. His worried expression deepened when he caught sight of us.

"I should tell you guys something about Julian," I said.

38

THE STAFF AT THE HOSTEL CALLED THE POLICE TO GET THE LIN-gering recruits out of the lobby. The remaining team leaders stood in the street and argued about where to go until Madison announced that she'd convinced the owner of the gym to let us stay there for the night. A few of the team leaders looked a little taken aback that she'd solved the problem so easily. I didn't think people expected much of Madison.

We followed her down the street and into the gym. Every-one immediately broke into groups, staking out sections for them-selves. Team seven huddled in the corner of the main room, and I relayed what had happened with Julian.

Well, I relayed the part about how he'd called the cops on Grayson. And about how his parents were working with MDG, and it seemed that Julian was now too.

I had to sit on my hands because they were shaking. I under-stood that the important thing here was that Julian was working with MDG, and that he'd let his team march straight into a dan-gerous trap yesterday.

But my brain was stupidly screaming about everything *but* Julian's MDG ties. I was thinking about eating macarons with him outside the training complex in Paris. About kissing him in the train station after he told me that he wouldn't leave me.

About how I'd ignored his temper, and his jealousy, because I liked how I felt when I was with him.

"Why would he do that?" Patrick asked. I focused on him and tried to look like I wasn't screaming on the inside. "Was he with MDG this whole time, or did he recently switch over? Does it have something to do with his parents coming into town?"

"I don't know," I said.

"His parents just got here a couple days ago," Madison said. "It doesn't seem likely that Julian changed his mind since then. He must have known something all along."

She was right. My throat closed, and I just shrugged.

"He didn't explain exactly why he's helping them?" Priya asked.

"N-no, we didn't get a chance to . . ." I took a deep breath. "We didn't get into that."

"Are you guys seeing Twitter today?" Noah asked, swiping at his phone. "Some of the recruits have spilled the beans about MDG's trained scrabs."

"What's the reaction?" Madison asked.

"Mixed. Some people are freaking out. Most don't seem to believe it, though."

Patrick turned back to me. "Julian said that Grayson didn't understand the scope of what MDG is doing. What does that mean?"

"I don't know."

"Why wouldn't you ask?" Gage demanded. "That would have been helpful information."

"Gage," Edan said sharply. Several members of the team regarded Edan with surprise. "Lay off."

"I'm just saying," Gage said, but his tone softened a little. "And why did Julian punch you?"

Edan's eyes darted to mine. "He's always hated me."

"He was jealous," I said quietly. "He thought Edan and I had something going on."

"Do you?" Zoe asked.

"No," Edan said at the same time Madison snapped, "Irrelevant."

Madison's phone rang. "I'll be back. I think this is about Grayson." She stood and walked across the gym, weaving through recruits sprawled out on the floor.

The lump in my throat grew bigger. Gage was right. I should have asked Julian more questions. I should have put the teams first. Instead I'd gotten hysterical and focused on our relationship. If I'd kept calm for a few minutes, I could have gotten information out of him. Helpful information.

Tears threatened to spill over again, and I quickly got to my feet. The back door was propped open, so I escaped through it and down the narrow alleyway. It was empty, save for two guys smoking near the street.

I crouched down, running both hands into my hair. I had taken stupid to new levels. I'd looked stupid in the face, laughed, and run right past it.

I'd had an easy way to pump Julian for information, and I'd blown it.

Madison had warned me about Julian, and I hadn't listened.

My entire life I'd said I'd never be like Mom, and here I was. Just like her. I'd made excuses for Julian, just like Mom. I'd said that *I* knew the real Julian, just like Mom had always claimed with Dad. The anger, the temper, that wasn't the *real* Julian.

Footsteps drew close to me and stopped. I glanced up. Edan stared down at me, his expression tight and unreadable.

I sat on the concrete, even though it was dirty and gross. I was too exhausted to care. Edan lowered down beside me.

"I'm sorry," I said. "That he hit you."

"That is in no way your fault."

"He was reading my text messages. That's why he was so mad today. Because he saw what we said last night."

"That is deeply screwed up."

"Yes." And yet I felt like I should have expected it. "Thank you. For what you said last night. I did need to hear it."

"I'm sorry I didn't say it earlier. I meant to. I wanted to. When we were at the farm, I kept thinking I should say, *Hey, Julian is a real ass, and his temper scares me.*"

"I'd seen his temper," I said. "I'm responsible for my own choices."

"That's . . . yeah, that's a really good point," he said with a soft laugh. I managed a small smile. "But, still, I'm sorry. I wanted to be honest with you, but we'd just become friends, and I didn't want to screw it up."

"It probably wouldn't have changed anything," I said. "I was determined to be as stupid as possible. Still am, apparently. Gage is right. I should have asked Julian more questions. I was so mad about him selling you guys out, and then he grabbed me, and I panicked."

Edan turned to me quickly. "He grabbed you?"

"It wasn't a big deal, I just didn't handle it well because . . . well, you know."

His pointed to the scratches on my arm. "Did he do that? I think it's a big deal."

My phone buzzed in my pocket, and I pulled it out. I had a text from Julian.

Will you please come to my hotel so we can talk? Or I'll meet you somewhere. Please, Clara. Let me explain.

A second message popped up.

I didn't mean to scare you today. I'm so sorry.

"Julian's apologizing," I said softly. "He says he wants to explain."

"Explain what? That he's an asshole? We got it, thanks."

I'm so sorry. I stared at the words. He always apologized after yelling. He would apologize and make an excuse—*sorry, I'm stressed; sorry, I'm on edge; sorry, I'm just trying to keep you safe.* You weren't actually sorry if you kept doing the exact thing you claimed to feel bad about. I knew that better than anyone.

And yet part of me wanted to believe it. I almost wanted to march over there and hear him out and find that version of Julian I'd met on the floor of a hotel ballroom in Atlanta. At least then I'd find out why he suddenly decided to betray his best friend and join MDG.

"Wait." I sat up straight as a thought occurred to me. "I should let him explain."

"What?" Edan looked alarmed. "Clara, no, that guy is—"

"No, no, not like actually—" I cut myself off as I jumped to my feet. "Come on."

I rushed back inside. Team seven was still in the same spot,

Madison plopping down next to Priya. I hurried to them, Edan on my heels.

"I have an idea," I said. "Julian just texted me asking me to come over. Let me go and try to get some answers about MDG."

"*Just* to get answers about MDG?" Madison asked, her brow creased with worry. It was an expression shared by several other members of the team.

"Yes, just to get answers," I said, exasperated. "I'm not an idiot. I mean, I *am* an idiot, I'm a total moron, but—"

"You are not a moron," Edan said.

"Whatever. My point is, I'm not going over there to reconcile with Julian. I'll just let him think that, and maybe I can find out some stuff."

"Like what stuff?" Priya asked. "Do we need answers that badly?"

"They're capturing and training scrabs for a completely unknown purpose," Noah said, looking up from his phone. "And shipping them to that Dust Storm facility, which we still don't know anything about. Maybe they already sent them there. Plus I don't know about you guys, but that thing Grayson told us about other countries also training scrabs is giving me anxiety. Why did Julian jump over to their side so quickly? What does it mean that we don't know the scope of what MDG is doing? And—" He cut himself off abruptly and took a deep breath. "Sorry. I'm calm. I'm fine." Madison patted his arm.

"It couldn't hurt for me to try to find out more information," I said. "If only to help Noah's anxiety." I tried for a lighthearted tone, but I was pretty sure everyone could hear how much I wanted to do this. It was the only thing I *could* do. I would lose my mind if I had to sit here and dissect every moment of my relationship with Julian.

"I have medication to help my anxiety, but I appreciate the offer," Noah said.

"Just let me go back to Julian and apologize and say that I was wrong," I said. "Maybe I can find something out."

"Why would he tell you anything?" Priya asked. "He's going to be suspicious if you suddenly start asking lots of questions."

"I can be subtle about it. And he just texted me." I turned the phone so they could see. "Look. He's sorry. I know exactly how to handle a guy when he's pretending he's sorry."

Edan's eyes met mine. His expression was pained.

"You know I'm right," I said.

"Why does he know you're ri—" Patrick abruptly stopped talking as Laila elbowed him and Priya shot him a look.

My suspicions about them figuring it out had been correct. Girls always knew things.

"My dad was always sorry after beating the shit out of us," I said, working hard to keep my voice steady. "I can handle myself, I promise."

Patrick blanched. Several pairs of eyes dropped to the ground.

"It's your decision," Madison said softly.

I looked down at the phone in my hand. "Does someone have a phone I can borrow? I want to call my brother, but Julian's been tracking everything I do on this phone."

Madison held her phone out to me. "You can use mine. It's

probably best I have his number in case something happens, actually."

"Thank you."

"You're seriously doing this?" Edan asked.

"I'm doing this," I said firmly.

I waited until evening to call Laurence. I told myself it was because of the time change, and I knew he slept in late on weekends, but really I was just nervous. I had to rehearse the conversation several times in my head.

I went outside to call him, and found Gage and Zoe standing near the door. He had a cigarette between his lips, and she was batting a cloud of smoke away from her face with a laugh.

I walked to the other end of the alley and leaned against the brick wall as I dialed Laurence's number.

He answered on the third ring, his tone cautious. "Hello?"

"Hey. It's me."

"Clara?" He sounded stunned.

"Yeah."

"Is something wrong?" he asked. "Are you OK?"

"I'm fine," I lied, before remembering that this was a call for truth. I was so used to brushing past things with Laurence. "I mean, I'm not hurt or anything."

"Where are you right now?"

"London. Are you still in Oklahoma?"

"Yeah, for now. Is . . . How are you guys doing? The teams, I mean. Did Grayson really get arrested?"

"He did. But he's getting out soon. It's fine."

"Oh."

"I was just calling . . . um, I guess because I wanted to talk to you before I go do this thing that's kind of dangerous. And now Madison will have your number, in case something happens."

"More dangerous than usual?" He sounded worried now.

"Maybe not. I'm probably overreacting. But I don't want them calling Mom and Dad, which I told them, so it's just you."

There was a brief pause. "Does your team know . . ."

"About Dad? Yeah. Recently, actually."

Another pause. And then, "That's good."

"You think so?"

"Yeah. You should tell anyone you want. I always wondered why you didn't—" He cut himself off abruptly.

"You wondered why I didn't tell anyone about Dad," I finished.

"I didn't mean for that to sound like it was your fault," he said quickly. "I guess I understood, in a way. I mean, I know why I didn't say anything."

"Why?" I asked.

"I . . ." It took him a long time to find the words. I waited. "When I tell someone, I also have to tell them that I didn't do anything to stop it. Someone recently asked me why you joined, and I just froze. What was I supposed to say? My little sister ran off to fight scrabs because it was better than living with our dad?"

"It's not entirely true that you didn't do anything to stop it. You stepped in a bunch of times."

"And usually just made it worse."

"Well."

"I don't need you to make me feel better about this. I don't want you to, I mean."

"OK," I said quietly.

"Why didn't you tell anyone? Was it just to protect Mom?"

"A little," I said. "Or a lot, maybe. But the hell I was used to seemed safer than the unknown hell. Like Mom always says, things could be worse."

"She does say that a lot."

"And I guess I thought she was right. Dad was better than starving. He was better than a group home or foster care. He was better than having no family at all."

"Yeah," Laurence said, a little sadly.

"Can I ask you a question?"

"Sure."

"Do you worry about being like Dad?"

"All the time."

I blinked, surprised by the immediate honesty. "Really?"

"Of course. Everyone says that abusers were often abused themselves. Sometimes I feel like a ticking time bomb, waiting to explode rage all over everyone."

"Laurence, you barely show any emotion at all, much less *rage*."

"I guess I went too far in the other direction."

"God, that's depressing," I said.

"What? Do you worry about being like Dad?"

"No. Not at all. I worry about being like Mom." I closed my eyes for a moment. "I *am* like Mom."

"How?"

"I got involved with this guy who turned out to be . . . not great. And it seems so obvious, looking back on it now. The flashing warning signs. But I did exactly what Mom did. I made excuses."

"What guy?" he asked. "Julian? Or Edan?"

"Julian," I said. "I forgot that you look at Tumblr and know these things. Edan is just a friend. Those pictures are wildly misleading."

"It's weird that strangers are speculating about your love life."

"It really is."

"He didn't hurt you, did he? Julian?"

"No, he didn't hurt me. We'd only been dating a few weeks, but I could just see it, you know? That I was headed down that exact same path, and I didn't even realize it at first."

"But you did realize it. Mom and Dad have been married for, what? Twenty-five years? You might have missed the warning signs at first, but you saw them pretty quick. You should give yourself credit for that."

I blew my bangs out of my eyes. "I don't feel like giving myself any credit, honestly. I feel like a dumbass."

"You're not a dumbass, Clara," he said softly. "No matter how many times Dad said it, you're not."

I swallowed around the sudden lump in my throat. "Have you been drinking?"

"What?" he asked with a startled laugh.

"This is the most talkative I've ever heard you. Like, in my entire life. I thought maybe you were drunk or something."

"No, I'm not drunk. Honestly, I'm worried you're calling me because you think you're about to die. You don't think you're about to die, do you?"

"God, I hope not."

"That does not make me feel better."

"It was nice of you to get talkative because you think it's the last time we'll ever talk, though. I appreciate it."

He laughed again, and then was quiet for a long moment. "I appreciate you calling. I wasn't sure I would ever hear from you again after you left. I was really surprised when you left me that message about your ashes." He paused. "And a little freaked out at the prospect of being sent them."

"Sorry. But someone has to get them. And you're kind of . . . it in the family department."

"Yeah," he said, his voice barely a whisper.

I swallowed down the lump in my throat. "I'll text you when I can, OK?"

"OK. Thanks."

"Bye, Laurence."

"Bye, Clara."

I ended the call and took a few deep breaths before walking back into the gym. It was quieter now, some of the recruits gone to find their own housing for the night. Or never coming back.

I found Madison in a corner, flat on her back on one of the many sleeping bags that had appeared during my conversation with Laurence. I sat next to her.

"Thank you," I said, passing her the phone. "I saved his number under Laurence Pratt, if you need to call him."

She took the phone and rested it on her stomach. "Got it." Her gaze remained on the ceiling.

"You all right?"

"Yeah. I took a Xanax. I'm waiting for it to kick in." She turned to look at me. "You want one?"

"No, thanks. I've never taken a Xanax before. I'm not sure that now is the time to start."

"Or it's the *perfect* time to start."

I flopped down on my back. "Any news about Grayson?"

"He's getting out tomorrow. Wait to text Julian until after we talk to him, OK?"

"OK."

"I'm going to get you one of his phones too. So you have a way to keep in touch with us without Julian monitoring it."

"Thank you," I said. "And I'm sorry."

"For what?"

"For not listening to you about Julian. You were just trying to warn me about him, and I accused you of being jealous."

"I was absolutely jealous," she said. "I did not have one hundred percent noble intentions when we had that conversation."

"No?"

"No. I did want to warn you, and I tried to convince myself that was all it was, but I was totally jealous. And I can't even explain *why*. I didn't want Julian. I knew he was a jerk."

"You just didn't want to see him with someone else?" I suggested.

"I guess. He was my first love. In a way. Maybe *love* is the wrong word. He was the first guy I was super into." She stared at the ceiling again. "He was older, and he was always around because he was friends with Grayson. The three of us had this weird worship thing going on. Grayson is three years older than

Julian, and Julian idolized him when he was young. And Julian is two years older than me, and I was the same way with him. I had the biggest crush on him, and he knew it."

"Have you guys ever actually been a couple?" I asked.

She made a *so-so* motion with her hand. "We sort of started something when I was fourteen. We'd just sneak away and make out. But he got weird about it because he thought I was too young, and he was probably right. There's kind of a big difference between fourteen and sixteen. So we broke up, and he basically told me to wait. After we'd made out a lot, it should be mentioned. But he decided that we couldn't officially be together until I was older, so we ended it. And started things up again right after I turned seventeen, almost a year ago."

"Is it almost your birthday?" I asked.

"Yep, two weeks. Julian and I actually got together on my seventeenth birthday. Like that was the age he'd decided on or something. I don't know. But we were barely together. It lasts maybe three weeks before he finds out that I'm not a virgin and totally loses it. When he told me to *wait*, he meant in every way." She looked at me, eyebrows raised. "Keep in mind that Julian is not a virgin."

"But he's mad that you're not."

"Yep. He gets so mad, calls me a slut and all these other names. And I get upset, but I refuse to apologize, which is what he wants. He keeps telling me to admit to my mistakes and maybe he can forgive me. And I'm like, dude, forgive me for what? I had sex and I enjoyed it. I have no regrets, and I'm not apologizing for it. So he yells a few more insults at me, and that's it."

"Jesus," I said. "That's horrible. How did you even stay friends with him after?"

"I didn't want to make things awkward between him and Grayson. Which was stupid, because things were already awkward between the two of them. Julian's worship turned into full-blown jealousy. I honestly think that's the only reason he even liked me. It was a sort of twisted way to get to Grayson."

I covered my face with my hands. I didn't know whether to cry or laugh hysterically. Both, maybe. "I'm an idiot," I said softly.

"Let's take a moment to appreciate the fact that I was jealous of you being with him, even after all that. If we're giving out stupid awards, I think the first one goes to me."

"Let's take a moment to appreciate the fact that I grew up with a controlling, short-tempered father who terrorized us, and I didn't even see the similarities." I dropped my hands from my face.

Madison looked over at me. "Does Julian remind you of your dad?"

"Yeah, now that I think about it. Dad's jealous and controlling. Short-tempered. Mean when he's angry. I don't mean to imply that Julian's going to start beating on his girlfriends — I hope not — but he certainly has all the other aspects of my dad's personality."

"It makes sense now, why you're so secretive and closed off. I sort of thought you were just a bitch and had no interest in being friends with any of us."

I laughed, startled by her honesty. "Don't hold back. Tell me what you really think."

A smile spread across her face. "I usually tell people what I think." Her smile faded. "I do wish I'd told you the whole story about Julian, though. I should have, but I wanted to hate you, and part of me almost felt smug, like you'd get what you deserved when he turned on you." She laughed at my expression, which was probably a mix of amusement and horror. "Too honest?"

"No, please go on," I said with a laugh. "I don't think anyone's ever been this honest with me in my life."

"OK, well, if we're being honest, can I also say that I'm jealous of your boobs?"

I let out a big, genuine laugh that made me feel better than I had in days.

"Seriously," she said. "When you tried on those horrible sports bras that Grayson ordered, I almost told you that your underboob looked really good. Like, celebrities try to do that on purpose. You should reconsider that sports bra, is what I'm saying. Especially if you're looking to attract every guy in the room."

"God no," I said, my voice still amused. "I'm never dating again."

"I always say that, and it always lasts, like, three days." Her gaze cut to something and then back to me. "Besides, a certain tattooed member of our team has been making puppy dog eyes at you all day."

I followed her gaze across the room, to Edan. He was sitting with Patrick and Noah, laughing, and decidedly not making puppy dog eyes at anyone.

"He has not," I said, returning my attention to her. "He just feels weird because Tumblr is shipping us and Julian freaked out about us being friends."

"Sure," Madison said, in a way that meant she didn't believe me at all.

"It's true. And like I said, never dating again. Or at least not until I'm thirty."

"Right."

"I'm not."

"Uh-huh."

Part Five

ALIVE

39

"How about your bra? Can you fit a knife in between your boobs?" Madison peered into my cleavage.

"Madison, I have my weapons pack, and Edan just strapped a foldable ax and pepper spray to my leg. I don't think I need a knife in my boobs as well." I gave her an amused look as I slung my weapons pack over my shoulder. We were in the lobby of the gym with Edan and Grayson, who wore matching nervous expressions.

"I'm still not sure this is a great idea," Grayson said. "Maybe I should just go talk to Julian."

"Has he answered a single one of those text messages you keep sending him?" Madison asked, eyebrow cocked.

"No." He gazed at his phone sadly.

I held up the phone Julian had given me. "He's texted me three times this morning."

"Do you really think he knew what MDG was doing all along?" Grayson asked. "He couldn't, right?" He seemed to want to convince himself more than me.

"I'll try to find out," I said gently.

"You know what you're going to say?" Madison asked.

"I figure I'll act scared. Tell him we're a mess and we're getting kicked out of the gym today and I have nowhere to go."

"That's actually true," Grayson said. "I haven't found hotel rooms yet. We don't have anywhere to go."

"Text us as often as you can," Edan said. "You have one of Grayson's phones?"

"Yeah, it's in my bag. Are we good? I should walk over to his hotel by myself."

Madison nodded. I typed out a text to Julian.

Are you at your hotel?

A response came immediately.

Yes. Are you here?

I can be there in ten minutes. Is that ok?

Yes! I'll meet you in the lobby.

I released a breath and slid his phone back into my pocket. "OK, he told me to come over." I sounded calmer than I felt.

I pushed open the door and walked outside. Madison followed me.

"You can't follow me all the way to the hotel, you know," I said, smiling to hide my nerves.

She rolled her eyes. "I know." She swallowed, the annoyed façade she'd been wearing slipping away. "Be careful, OK?"

"I will."

"Should we hug? I feel like we should hug."

I laughed, my nerves easing a little. "We should definitely hug."

We embraced briefly before I turned and began walking. It was gray and raining, and I stopped after a few blocks to pull my sweatshirt out of my backpack. I yanked it on, my arm hitting a passing woman.

"Sorry," I said. She didn't acknowledge that she'd heard.

I shrugged on my backpack as I trudged forward. The streets were clogged with people, but I was suddenly aware of how alone I was. I'd never gone outside in Paris or London by myself. I'd always been with at least one team member.

But now there was no one. Even when I met up with Julian, I'd still be alone. He didn't count anymore. He'd shifted from safe to scary.

His hotel came into view. Maybe this had been a bad idea.

The ground rumbled suddenly. I froze. The man next to me broke into a sprint and disappeared around the corner.

The scrab roared up from the ground and landed so hard the ground trembled. It shook its body, sending dirt flying through the air. I lifted my arm to shield my eyes.

It grabbed for a nearby woman, who whirled around and smashed a baseball bat against its paw. She took off.

And now I was alone for this. I'd never fought a scrab without the team before, and like Julian said, I was the weakest member. I needed someone there to watch my back.

But I realized, too late, that everyone around me had taken off at least five seconds ago, leaving me alone on the sidewalk. The scrab dropped onto all four paws and fixed its gaze on me. It had blood splattered across its snout. From its last kill, I guessed.

I ripped open my backpack and pulled out the machete and baton sword. I scrambled away from the sidewalk and into the street. I knew how bad it was when you let a scrab corner you.

It swung around to face me. It leapt forward, teeth bared, and I stood my ground, fingers tightening around the baton. If I moved too soon, it would have time to change course. Scrabs weren't nearly as agile as we were—once they started running, it took them an extra second to get their bodies moving in a different direction.

I darted out of the way just before its claws reached me. I raised the baton over my head, jabbing it into the side of its neck.

It roared, stumbling back. I slashed my machete across its stomach, and then scrambled back as blood poured onto the street. The scrab collapsed.

Cheers rose up from behind me, and I turned to see a crowd down the block. People started down the sidewalks again, business as usual now that the scrab was taken care of.

"That was brilliant," a young guy said, shooting me a smile as he passed.

I returned the smile. Why had I doubted that I could take down *one* scrab by myself? Even if I wasn't the best on the team, I still knew how to fight these things. I was even *good* at fighting these things.

I yanked my sword baton from the scrab's neck and shook off some of the blood before retracting it and putting it back in my weapons pack with my machete.

"Clara!"

I looked up at the frantic voice. It was Julian, weaving around people as he raced down the street. He skidded to a stop in front of me, looking from me to the scrab.

"Oh god. Are you OK?" He put his hands on my cheeks, and I tensed, barely resisting the urge to jerk my head away. "I'm so sorry. I should have come to get you, not make you walk over here by yourself. I don't know what I was thinking."

I stared at him. Julian didn't know me at all, and I wasn't sure if that was his fault or mine. Maybe I'd let him think I was fragile and scared. I guessed that was the version of me that he'd met that evening in the Atlanta. He'd seen a desperate, crying girl who needed help, and I'd seen a kind, generous boy who was more than willing to give it. We'd both been wrong, but I was the only one willing to look beyond their first impression.

"I'm OK," I said quietly. Tears welled in my eyes. I wasn't even entirely sure why. I was exhausted, and disappointed, and angry.

"I'm sorry." He pulled me into a hug. "I'm so sorry about yesterday. I just got so mad about Edan, and my parents being in town is totally stressing me out . . ." He stepped back, keeping his hands on my arms. "Where did you go last night? Why didn't you answer my texts?"

"We slept at the gym." I took a step back so that his hands fell off my arms. "And I didn't text back because you acted like an ass, Julian. You were trying to force me to go with you without explaining what was going on."

"I wasn't trying to *force* you," he said. "I wanted to explain, but you didn't give me a chance."

"Go ahead. Explain."

"Do we have to do this in the middle of the street?" His phone buzzed, and he pulled it out of his pocket and sighed as he looked at the screen. "Shit. I need to go, actually. Do you want to wait for me in my hotel room? I may be a while . . ." He tugged on his bottom lip.

"Where are you going?"

"To . . . see my parents," he said haltingly. He really was a terrible liar.

And if he didn't want me to know where he was going, that was exactly where I wanted to be.

"You're the one who texted me, wanting to talk." I didn't have to fake my annoyance. "I'm not going to go wait in your hotel room. I need to find a hostel and figure out what to do next."

He frowned. "What do you mean, find a hostel? Isn't Grayson finding the teams a place to stay?"

"I'm sure he is, eventually, but I don't want to spend another night sleeping on a gym floor. I don't want to do this at all anymore." I gestured to the dead scrab, the lies coming easily. Julian would never confide in me if he thought I was still part of the team. "You know I just joined to get away from my dad, and I'm away. I'll figure something out."

"By yourself?" He looked horrified.

"Apparently." I dug his phone out of my pocket and held it out to him. "Here. This is yours." His horror intensified, as I'd predicted. Without the phone, he'd never be able to find me again. I was barely even on social media. And if I'd learned one thing about Julian, it was that he was very invested in keeping track of me.

"No." He shook his head and took a step closer to me. "You're not alone, remember? You don't have to figure out everything by yourself." His phone buzzed again, and he made an annoyed sound. "I really do have to go." He considered for a moment. "It's a long drive, though. Do you want to come with me? We can talk on the way."

I tried not to look too pleased with myself. "Yeah. OK."

Julian led me back to his hotel, where a fancy rich-people car was waiting. The driver held the door open for me, and I slid onto the white leather seat. The inside of the car was huge and pristine, with a small screen in front of each seat and a clear partition separating the back from the front. Water bottles waited in the center console.

"Jesus," I murmured.

Julian laughed and pressed a button that turned the clear partition opaque. "We can talk privately in here."

The car began moving, so smoothly and quietly that I wouldn't have realized we were in the middle of London if I couldn't see it for myself out the window.

It hit me suddenly that I was trapped with him. I hadn't even asked where we were going. He said we could talk *privately*, implying that the partition was soundproof. Would the driver even be able to hear me scream?

I took a slow, steady breath. I had Grayson's phone in my bag. I had weapons. I could do this.

"So," I said, staring out the window in case my face betrayed my fear. "Are you going to tell me why you let your team walk into a trap?"

"It wasn't a trap," he said softly. "Grayson kept following MDG, so they retaliated."

I looked at him. "But you knew that they'd retaliate with trained scrabs?"

"I was warned that there would be consequences, yes. But they were just trying to scare Grayson off their tail. None of this would have happened if he'd left them alone."

"He won't leave them alone because he wants to know what they're doing," I said. "Can you blame him? They're training scrabs and using them against people. That's terrifying."

"I know it can seem scary, from the outside. But you've heard about how the Russians might be training scrabs?"

"Grayson mentioned that rumor."

"It's more than a rumor. And the intelligence community is pretty sure that the North Koreans have a program too. My dad told me."

"How? There have never been scrabs in the Korean peninsula."

"There have never been scrabs in *South* Korea. North Korea has one of the largest militaries in the world, and the entire country is smaller than Florida. They could have easily gotten their scrab problem under control before a single one made it to the southern border, and just lied about it."

"How does that relate to MDG?" I asked.

"They've just been preparing for the worst possible outcome. What if Russia or North Korea succeeds? That's how this all started. MDG wanted to keep us safe, and they tried to get a defense contract so that we could develop a training program in the US, but no one would go for it. They said it was too high risk. So they found private investors instead."

"They're training them for defense purposes? Like to work with the military?"

"That was the initial goal, yes."

"What's their goal now?"

He hesitated, considering his words for a moment. "Defense is still the main goal."

I cocked an eyebrow. "Why is it a secret, then? They've clearly made serious strides with the training program. Why not brag about it? Try to get that defense contract again?"

"Government isn't always super open to new ideas," he said. "And MDG feels like they can be more effective in the private sector."

"How are they going to make money? Investors generally expect something in return."

He looked a bit startled by that question, like it was more than he expected from me. "I can't answer all these questions. My dad told me some stuff in confidence."

"You must understand why I'm scared, though, Julian. Where are these scrabs going to end up? Who's going to buy them?"

"They're not for sale. MDG has plans for them."

I looked at him expectantly. "Like?"

"Well, MDG's parent company does a lot of private security work in Iraq and Afghanistan. Imagine how helpful scrabs would be there, even just as bodyguards. You can't even shoot at these things without the bullets ricocheting back at you. And private prisons, maybe, one day. There's always a prison guard shortage." He smiled at me, apparently unaware of my mounting horror. "You're safe. I promise. Especially now that you're with me."

I had to beat down the urge to scream, *What is wrong with you?* Transporting scrabs to countries that had never had a scrab problem was a horrible, irresponsible thing to do, but I got the feeling that he really didn't care.

"Is that their main purpose, then? Sending them with private contractors to war zones?" I asked.

"Why do you care so much what MDG is doing?" he asked, suspicion creeping into his voice.

"Julian." I gave him a baffled look. "They've used them against me. I've seen firsthand how scary that can be. Why *wouldn't* I care?"

He sighed, tugging on his lower lip for a moment before answering. "To tell you the truth, I don't actually know the full extent of what they're doing. My dad has shared some stuff, but he can't tell me everything. Or he won't. Not yet, anyway."

"But you still trust them?"

"I trust my dad, yeah. And I think that what MDG is doing is smart. Private police and security forces will be the norm in most countries soon." He gestured at me. "You know that. You're part of one right now. Grayson and MDG are basically doing the same thing, MDG is just doing it better. And if I'm going to choose a side, it's going to be the side with the scrab army."

He laughed. I tried not to look horrified.

"Listen," he continued. "You have to promise me that you'll keep all of this a secret. My dad only let me join Grayson's teams because I promised not to tell anyone what I knew about MDG."

"Wait—what? You knew about this the whole time?"

He nodded.

"Why would you help Grayson do this if you were working with MDG? Were you spying on him?"

"No, not really. Most of what Grayson does is out in the open; there's no need to spy. Honestly, I was mostly keeping him safe. And all of you."

"How?"

"Grayson goes wild when he gets an idea in his head. He wanted to kick the teams into high gear six months ago, when we were barely prepared. I slowed him down, which benefited everyone."

"Because MDG needed time to capture scrabs over here," I said slowly as it clicked into place.

"And Grayson needed time to build an effective training plan so he wouldn't get all of you killed." He rolled his eyes. "Everyone worships fucking Grayson, but do you know who they should actually be thanking? *Me*. Most of you are still alive because I made him take his time."

Was he serious? I tried to keep an incredulous look off my face, but I wasn't sure I succeeded. Luckily Julian wasn't paying attention to me.

"Grayson never appreciates what I do for him," he continued, talking faster as he got angry. "He still treats me like I'm that little kid who followed him around everywhere. He thought that these stupid teams were such a great idea, but we are, like, fifteen steps ahead of him." He smirked. "He can carry on with his little scrab fighting teams if he wants. It doesn't matter after tonight. They're getting the last of the scrabs out of here."

"Out of here?" I repeated, fighting to keep my voice steady. "Where are they sending them?"

"To their US facilities for further training. But you *really* can't tell anyone that. My dad would be pissed if he knew I told you."

My eyes widened. They were shipping scrabs to the US?

Tonight? I touched my backpack, where I'd hidden Grayson's phone. I needed to find a way to text him.

"Don't worry," Julian said, clearly catching the horror in my expression. "The facilities are state-of-the-art, according to my dad. They've had to improvise temporary solutions here, which caused some problems, as you saw. They'll have a much better handle on things in the US facilities."

"Are you—we—going back to the US?"

"Don't worry," he said with a chuckle. "We'll be safe, even if we do go back. I promise."

He actually thought I'd be OK with this appalling plan just because *I'd* be safe. He really didn't know me at all.

"I may want to go back to New York for a while, but not right away."

"Is that where the facilities are? New York?"

"No. They're out in the middle of nowhere." He waved his hand. "Not important. I was actually thinking we could escape to Barbados for a bit, after my parents and I wrap things up here. We have a house there, and I can probably take a couple weeks off."

"Sure," I said faintly.

He took my hand. I forced down a wave of nausea.

"Everything will be fine, Clara. Trust me."

40

WE DROVE FOR AN HOUR BEFORE THE CAR TURNED INTO THE driveway of a massive house. It was red brick with white pillars in front, its expansive windows uncovered and providing a partial view of an impressive interior.

The driver stopped, jumped out, and opened Julian's door.

"Why don't you wait here for a minute?" Julian asked, unbuckling his seat belt. "I'm just picking up some stuff from my dad, so I shouldn't be long."

"OK," I said, trying not to sound too happy about it. Once he left, I could text Grayson.

And I desperately wanted Julian as far away from me as possible.

He jumped out, and the driver closed the door behind him and wandered to the front of the car. I leaned back, watching through the back window until Julian disappeared through the front door.

I grabbed Grayson's phone from my backpack and typed out a text to him and Madison.

It's really bad. They're shipping the scrabs back to the US. They have facilities there for training. Julian knew the whole time.

Grayson's responded immediately. **What???**

Julian took me to a house like an hour outside the city. I'm sending you the location. I dropped a pin and sent it to them.

The door opened suddenly, and I jumped, the phone falling into my lap. Julian's mom leaned down, peering at me with a smile.

"Clara, right?" She wore perfectly pressed white pants and a light-green silk shirt. "I met you with Julian a couple days ago?"

"Yes. Clara. That's me." I slipped the phone into my backpack with trembling hands.

"Come on out of there. It's so rude that Julian left you in the car."

"Uh, OK." I grabbed my backpack and climbed out, taking a quick survey of my surroundings. The driveway curved around the back of the property, and several black vans were lined up there.

Julian's mom extended a hand to me. "I'm Faye." She had smooth, clear skin and meticulously applied makeup. Her blond bob was perfect. I wouldn't have guessed she was old enough to have a nineteen-year-old son.

"Nice to meet you," I said, shaking her hand.

"Come on in. Julian will only be a minute, but you don't have to wait in the car." She steered me to the front door.

It was cold and quiet inside. The floors and walls were white, the kind of house that was too scary to touch anything for fear of leaving a smudge. There was a staircase directly in front of me, and a hallway behind it that led further into the house.

To the right was a sitting room, a tray of cheese and fruit on the table in front of the floral couch. There were several empty wineglasses as well, but no people.

"Please, sit," Faye said, and I followed her into the room. "Are you hungry? A few friends just left, but there's still plenty of food, as you can see."

"I'm fine, thanks." I already felt sick; I didn't need to add any food to my stomach.

She sat on the couch, patting the spot next to her. I eased down next to her, dropping my backpack by my feet.

"Julian told me a bit about you." She smiled like he'd said good things. "In fact, he told me last night that the two of you were thinking of going to Barbados."

I tried to hide my surprise. *Last night?* Julian sure had a lot of faith that I'd forgive him. I hadn't even answered any of his texts last night. He *really* didn't know me at all.

"We are," I said. "Thinking about it."

"I'm so glad to hear it," she said. "I've been trying to get him to go for a while. You've been a good influence on him. I could tell, every time we talked on the phone. He seemed happier, more relaxed. Julian needs someone to help him loosen up a bit."

"Does he?" I shifted uncomfortably.

"He's a lot like his father. Both of them so serious and focused. Boys need someone to save them from themselves, you know?"

I nodded like I agreed. I did not. I was not here to save Julian. I was still trying to save myself.

"But you'll love Barbados. So beautiful and peaceful. Have you ever been?"

"No." Despite my mounting panic, I said the word with a trace of amusement.

"Where are you from?"

"Texas."

"Ah." She didn't sound like she approved of Texas.

Her eyes caught on something, and a smile spread across her face. "Julian! Over here, hon. I found her in the car."

Julian was standing at the front door, hand on the knob. He peered at us in surprise. I stood, trying my best not to look like I was freaking out.

But I was. I absolutely was. I needed to find a way out of here.

No. They were shipping scrabs *tonight*. If anything, I needed to stay and figure out where those scrabs were. I forced a smile.

"You shouldn't have made her wait out there," Faye said.

"Oh, I just . . ." Julian cast a worried look over his shoulder. His father strode into the foyer, his gaze immediately catching on me. He shot his son a look of utter contempt.

"Julian, a word," He grabbed Julian roughly by the arm and pulled him into the hallway. I could see Mr. Montgomery jabbing a finger into Julian's chest as he spoke.

"Don't mind my husband," Faye whispered to me. "He just has a lot on his mind."

I bit back a hysterical laugh. I would have said the same thing about Julian a few days ago.

Mr. Montgomery took a step closer to Julian. He was clearly trying to intimidate his son. My stomach twisted.

Julian nodded, and then he and his dad walked back into the foyer. Julian widened his eyes at me slightly as he approached. He was trying to smile, but he was obviously shaken.

His mom looked between the two of us, like she'd just caught that subtle interaction. She placed a light hand on my arm, briefly. I resisted the urge to swat it away.

"Clara." His dad said my name with disapproval. "Julian tells me you've left Grayson's teams."

"I did," I said.

"Are you going home?" Mr. Montgomery asked. "Where is home?"

"Texas," Faye said cheerfully.

"No, I'm not going back to Texas," I said.

"We're thinking of going to Barbados," Julian said. "Just for a quick vacation."

"Do you really have time for a vacation?" Mr. Montgomery asked snidely. "You helped create this mess we're in."

"Grayson made the mess, not me," Julian muttered.

"You helped him along. You certainly exaggerated your ability to keep Grayson under control."

Julian flushed but said nothing.

Mr. Montgomery leveled an intense stare at me. He was trying to intimidate me. I couldn't bring myself to pretend it was working.

"Hon, I was going to go say goodbye to the guys before we left. Why don't you come with me?" Faye took her husband by the arm and steered him back into the hallway.

"Sorry," Julian said, once they were out of earshot. "He's a bit much, right?"

"He's horrible," I said.

He seemed taken aback. "He gets riled up sometimes. He means well."

"Does he? He was pretty harsh."

"It's just how he is." He said the words heavily. Like he'd once hoped his dad would change but had learned better. "And he's upset right now because I couldn't stop Grayson from chasing after MDG. I can't blame him."

I could blame him.

Julian fished a card key out of his pocket and handed it to me. "Listen, there was a change of plans. Take the car and go to my hotel. I'll be back later tonight." He picked up my backpack and handed it to me.

"Where are you going?"

"Dad needs me to supervise the stuff going on tonight. I may be kind of late."

The *stuff* was absolutely the scrab shipment.

"Why don't I just stay? I don't mind waiting. I mean, you brought me all the way out here." I tried not to sound as desperate as I felt.

He shook his head. "I can't. Dad's super pissed that I brought you here, and I don't want to make him even angrier. Go back. Order some room service. Get a movie if you want." He planted a quick kiss on my cheek, and then pulled the door open for me.

I walked through, my heart pounding as I shot him a smile. I couldn't just *leave*. I needed to find a way to follow him and find those scrabs before they were shipped.

The door shut behind me. I walked around to the other side of the car and discreetly pulled Grayson's phone out of my backpack. I typed out a message to Grayson and Madison, taking a quick glance up to make sure Julian hadn't reappeared.

Do you have anyone nearby that could follow Julian? I think he's going to wherever the scrab shipment is.

Grayson replied immediately. Is he leaving soon? I just headed out with your team. We're coming to the location you sent us.

I don't know, I replied.

The driver opened the passenger side door for me. "Are we waiting for Mr. Montgomery, or should we head out now?"

"Actually, Julian sent me out here to let you know you're done for the night. We'll be staying here." I held my breath. I had no idea if Julian had given him other instructions.

He just smiled and closed the door. "Have a good evening."

I darted out of the driveway as he pulled away. The last thing I needed was for Julian to see me standing around as the car left.

I crept around the side of the house, in the direction of the vans I'd seen earlier. I stopped when I heard voices, and then carefully peered around to the back of the house. My hands were shaking, and I folded my arms against my chest, willing my body to calm down.

Mr. Montgomery stood with a red-haired man and Julian near the vans. A stocky man was loading boxes into the back.

"Yeah, Julian's going to take the van," Mr. Montgomery was saying. "I'm headed out to the docks to check on the transport."

"Then you're out of here?" the other man asked.

"Yes, thank god," Mr. Montgomery muttered. He squinted up at the overcast sky. "I hate London." He began to turn, and I quickly ducked behind the corner again.

When I peeked back out, Mr. Montgomery and Julian had

disappeared. The man was loading the last of the boxes into it. He closed the doors and headed back to the house.

"All set!" he called. I heard a distant reply.

There was definitely no time to wait for Grayson. I needed to get in that van.

I took a cautious step forward, until I could see the back doors of the house. Julian and his dad stood in front of them. The vans had been backed into their spots, the rears facing away from them.

Julian's dad walked inside. Julian stepped off the porch.

I grabbed his phone from my pocket, almost dropping it as I desperately pressed the message button.

I should have told you that I missed you, I typed frantically.

We were so close that I could hear his phone buzz after I sent it. He stopped several yards from the van, his face breaking into a smile as he read my message.

I darted to the back of the van and tried the door. It had to be unlocked. I hadn't seen the man lock anything before he walked away. It *had* to be.

The door clicked open. My phone buzzed. Julian's footsteps got closer.

I slipped into the van and softly shut the door behind me. It was full of boxes, but there was enough room for me to hide amongst them. I pushed a few aside and wedged myself in between them.

A door opened and then closed. The van started.

Julian let out a sigh. I heard his shoes hit the ground as he stepped out.

The back door opened.

I stayed perfectly still.

It slammed shut again.

I let out a slow breath as I listened to Julian walk back to the driver's seat. The van jerked forward.

Oh god. I was really doing this. I had jumped into the back of this van bound for some MDG location, and I had no plan. What was I going to do when we arrived?

I held my phone up with shaking hands.

I missed you too. So much, Julian had written back.

I did not think he was going to take it well if he discovered me in the back of this van.

I typed out a message to Grayson and Madison. **Ok I did something.**

Madison replied immediately. **That sounds bad.**

Grayson: **What did you do?**

Clara: **I'm in the van with Julian. Hiding, I mean. I jumped in when he wasn't looking.**

Madison: **CLARA THAT'S BAD.**

Clara: **We can't let them ship those scrabs. Can you track this phone?**

Grayson: **Yes!**

I bit back a curse as I typed out my next message.

Clara: **I should have just put the phone in the van. I'm a dumbass.**

Grayson: **No you're not! You're brilliant. We're held up in traffic, so we might be too late anyway. Take photos. And video. If it's safe.**

I'll try. I may have been a total dumbass, but at least I was surrounded by people who would make equally stupid choices, if given the opportunity.

Madison: **Edan wants to know if you have your weapons.**

Clara: **Yes.**

Madison: **Good. Also the whole team is here, and they say you're** a badass. I concur.

I smiled despite the terror still coursing down my spine. **Thanks.**

41

It was nearly an hour before the van stopped. My heart stopped with it, and I froze, listening to the sounds of Julian sliding out of his seat. The door slammed shut.

I waited a full minute before slowly sitting up. I couldn't hear voices or footsteps. He hadn't opened the back door to unload the boxes.

I carefully crawled to the rear of the van and tried the handle. The door creaked open. I pushed it slowly and peeked out at my surroundings.

The van was parked in front of a small two-story wooden house. The windows were all dark, even though the last wisps of sunlight were almost gone.

I edged out of the van and quietly pushed the door closed. Julian was nowhere to be seen. There was a thick row of trees to my left, and I couldn't see neighbors. We were definitely out of the city. On a farm, maybe.

No, an equestrian facility. The iron fence at the front of the property had two horses on it, and there was a three-rail fenced area to my right that had obviously been used to exercise horses in the past. Now it was overgrown and deserted, since you'd have to be insane to keep horses this close to a highly populated area.

To the right, set a bit back from the house, I could see the edge of a large wooden structure. A barn or stables. The area between the house and the structure was just a grassy field.

To the left of the house was a smaller, square building, like a shed or a guesthouse. Past that was a truck carrying a large blue shipping container, muddy track marks showing its path through the grass.

I followed the tracks back out to the narrow road. Two more trucks. These were even bigger. The container on the grass could hold maybe fifty scrabs, if they were tightly packed, but the ones on the street could easily hold at least a hundred. I snapped a quick picture, but it was very dark, the containers barely visible.

I pulled out my phone and texted Madison and Grayson.

There are three shipping containers here. I think they're planning to ship scrabs by boat.

A reply came a moment later. Grayson wants to know if you can get a license plate number. And a description of the shipping containers.

No license plate. The containers are blue. It's hard to see anything.

One of the trucks began moving, slowly rolling down the street.

One truck is leaving, I texted. **Headed south on Dalten St.**

Are the scrabs already loaded in that one?

I don't know.

We're sending UK team thirteen to follow it. The police should be on it as well.

I heard voices from behind me, and I scrambled to hide behind the van.

"Yeah, I'll show you," a voice said. "Come on."

Footsteps headed away from me, and I peered around the side of the vehicle. I couldn't see anyone.

I crept across the lawn, staying low to the ground. I realized as I rounded the corner of the house that there were actually *four* shipping containers. There was one sitting in the grass just past the large barn. Its doors were open, waiting to be loaded.

Two men walked toward the barn. I knew them both: Julian and Webb, the MDG guy who had kidnapped Edan and me in Paris.

They both had their backs to me, so I ran silently across the grass to the large barn. I stood at the corner of it, peering around at them. They were maybe twenty yards away, studying a small tablet in Webb's hand.

"So SAC control is pretty basic," Webb said to Julian. "You just—"

"Are we seriously calling them that?" Julian asked. "SACs?"

"Yes," Webb sighed wearily. "They're convinced people will warm up to them faster if we rename them." He turned his attention back to the tablet. "Anyway. These are numbered, silent scrabs. You heard anything about them?"

Julian shook his head.

"Hey, let me get one out here!" Webb called into the barn. "Any one will work."

A man emerged from the barn a moment later, a leashed scrab following behind him. It had a red 5 painted on its chest.

"You can drop him," Webb said. The other man let go of the leash. The scrab remained motionless.

"The first thing you have to do is activate the number you want," Webb said. "See this row of numbers on the side here?"

"Yeah," Julian said.

"Press the number, and it activates the scrab. Watch." Webb tapped the tablet. The scrab straightened and looked left and right. "You can activate a bunch at once and give them all the same command. These scrabs have a device in their ears that's connected to the tablet, so you don't need to shout a command, you just press the button on the tablet and the earpiece gives them the command." He tapped the tablet, and the scrab galloped forward. He tapped again, and the scrab stopped.

"Wow," Julian said.

"Good, right?" Webb said. "It's how we're working around their pack instincts. And these scrabs also understand hand signals, so you can point them in specific directions, or at specific people. Works well with the attack button, so you can sic them on certain people. Usually."

"Usually?" Julian repeated.

"We still get a few that break off and do their own thing every now and then. Loud noises confuse them, get them all agitated. Something with the earpiece, I think. We're working on it." He pointed to the tablet. "But that's what the red button is for. This big one at the top? It will shock all the scrabs that are currently activated. Should make them all stop what they're doing."

Julian said nothing. I couldn't see the expression on his face, but it made Webb laugh. He clapped Julian on the shoulder.

"You'll be fine. This whole shipment is high-level SACs, and you'll have some other guys with you. I'm just going to show you how to control them in case of an emergency. Better safe than sorry, right?" He gestured for the man to take the scrab back into the barn.

"Yeah," Julian muttered, taking out his phone.

"You know you can't take pictures, right?"

I grabbed my phone from my pocket. *I should have been taking pictures.* I held up the phone and started recording.

"Why would I take pictures?" Julian's tone was deeply annoyed.

"That squad of yours chronicles every single moment of their life. I can't turn on the news without seeing one of their selfies."

"I'm not taking selfies with the scrabs. I'm not an idiot."

"All right, no need to get testy. Just keep in mind that your dad threatened to kill me if anyone gets proof of MDG's involvement in this, and I think he was half serious. He's a scary guy, your dad."

Julian shrugged. "Are we almost ready?"

"Still loading."

I ducked out of view, pressing Stop on the video. I switched to my messages and started a message to Grayson.

There are actually four containers, they're still loa

"Clara?"

The voice made me jump. It was Julian, standing only a few yards away, and staring at me with mounting confusion.

"What are you doing here? Did you—" He strode closer to me, his expression baffled. "Did you follow me here?" He looked down at my phone. The phone that was very obviously not the one he gave me.

"Uhhh . . ." I quickly pressed Send on that partial last message and fumbled for the button to lock it.

I wasn't fast enough. He snatched it out of my hand and read what was on the screen. I dove for it, but he spun away and swiped through messages, his face contorting with rage as he read.

"Are you serious?" he hissed, turning to face me. His eyes had gone black. "Were you spying on me?"

I said nothing. I was searching for an escape route. If I just took off, I might be able to outrun him.

He grabbed my arm. I'd missed my opportunity.

"What was this, then?" His voice rose with every word until he was shouting. "When you came back to me, you were *lying?*"

I took a deep breath. The only option here was to try and keep Julian calm. "I was just — I was just scared and confused, and I —"

"You lying *bitch*," he spat. "You ungrateful, lying bitch! What the fuck is wrong with you?"

I froze. I should have tried to twist out of his grasp — he was hurting me — but my brain wouldn't listen.

Danger.

"I saved you!" he yelled. "You would have been back on a bus to Dallas if it weren't for me. And this is how you repay me?"

He was nearly shaking with rage. My breath started coming in short, panicked gasps.

"I trusted you! I told you . . ." He trailed off, eyes widening. He grabbed my other wrist, yanking me closer so he could scream in my face. "You stupid, worthless piece of — I can't believe I ever thought I was in love with you. You're fucking pathetic, you know that?"

"Julian, please let me go." My voice wobbled. I was suddenly replaying every moment of our training in my head. He was incredibly strong and fast, and I didn't think I could hold my own against him, even if I managed to grab a weapon from my backpack. A scrab I could handle, but Julian? Julian was scary as hell.

"Let you go," he scoffed. "You really are a moron, you know that? You think I'm just going to let you walk out of here?"

He yanked on my arm and began walking. I dug my heels in, desperately trying to twist out of his grasp. But he held firm, pulling so hard on my wrist that I stumbled and hit the ground.

He tore my backpack off, tossed it out of reach, and then grasped the back of my shirt. The fabric pulled tight around my neck as he began dragging me.

"Julian," I wheezed, my feet kicking up dirt. "You're choking me."

"Too damn bad!" he yelled. "This is what you get for picking Grayson over me. You brought this on yourself!"

He walked faster, heading toward the smaller stables in the distance. I desperately tried to pull my shirt away from my neck, tears welling in my eyes. My vision started to go black.

He dropped me suddenly. I hit my knees, gasping for air.

The world began to come back into focus, and I scrambled to my feet. We were in the stables. Julian grabbed my wrist again.

I screamed for help. I'd take my chances with one of the MDG guys.

A familiar man ran into the barn. It was Webb, eyes wide. "What the hell is going on?"

"Don't worry about it," Julian said, roughly spinning me around.

The stables were made up of stalls like the ones I'd seen in France, though these were wooden, with just simple locks on the doors. Inside, handcuffs dangled from the walls.

Julian shoved me toward the closest stall and then threw me inside. I stumbled and hit the ground. The door slammed shut. The lock clicked.

"Isn't that one of Grayson's people?" Webb asked. "What is she doing here?"

"I'm taking care of it," Julian said sharply. "We need to get the scrabs out of here now. Grayson and some other idiots are on their way. Maybe the police too."

"Are you kidding me? I've got fifty SACs to load still, and every single one has to be secured properly."

I slowly got to my feet. My legs were shaking.

"I don't care," Julian said. "Just throw them in there."

"Kid, I cannot just *throw them in there*," Webb said, clearly exasperated. "These things get antsy in their crates."

"Just do it!" Julian yelled. "My dad will kill me if I don't get this shipment out, and I don't know how long we have."

"Don't panic," Webb said. "We can fix this. We loaded all the best SACs first. We can spare some to help us take care of this."

"What do you mean?" Julian asked.

"We've got fifty that still need to be loaded, and about thirty that were rejected from the program that we need to kill and dump tonight anyway. Let's put 'em to use instead. Hey—Drew?" He paused. There was no response that I could hear. He must have been talking on the phone. "Have you finished securing the SACs in container two?" He paused. "No, that's fine. You can finish in a minute. Do me a favor and grab those reject scrabs and put them at the north and south checkpoints. Half on each side. Just let 'em loose on whoever tries to get through."

"Julian, don't let him do that!" I yelled. "You're seriously going to sic scrabs on your own team? On Grayson?"

"The dude wants to kill scrabs," Webb said. "Let him do it! Hey —and Drew? Put, like, three good SACs at the front of the house, just in case. Don't activate them yet." He paused. "What are you going to do about her?"

"I'll take care of her in a minute," Julian said.

I swallowed down a wave of panic.

"What does that . . . ." Webb trailed off. "You know what? Never mind. I don't want to know. I'm just going to go mind my own business." His footsteps faded as he walked away.

The door of my stall shook, like Julian had kicked it, and then I heard his footsteps recede as well.

I pressed my back to the wall, closing my eyes as I let out a slow breath. I was almost five thousand miles from home, and I'd managed to end up in the exact same place. Locked in a room.

The anger and panic rose up so suddenly that I had to crouch down and bury my head in my knees. Tears slid down my cheeks. Outside, the voices grew distant and then faded. I was alone.

42

THE SILENCE WAS STRANGE. I'D BEEN SURROUNDED BY PEOPLE, constantly, for weeks. Silence reminded me of home, of tiptoeing around in the morning so I wouldn't wake Dad. It reminded me of sitting on the porch that last night in Dallas, watching Laurence lug the painting across the yard.

It felt different, though. I'd felt so helpless, so trapped in that silence at home. It hadn't occurred to me until now how rarely I'd felt helpless since joining the teams.

I stood, wiping the tears off my cheeks. I had to get out. Julian was coming back, and he mostly likely planned to feed me to a scrab. And the team would be here soon. I wasn't going to just curl into a ball and cry while they fought off thirty scrabs.

I kicked the door, but it was far sturdier than the one in my bedroom. I wasn't going to be able to just a kick a hole through it. I stood back, considering for a minute.

The ax strapped to my calf tickled my skin.

Right. I had weapons this time. I said a silent thank you to Edan.

I grabbed the ax, unfolded it and locked the handle. I swung it at the door.

It lodged in the wood, and I had to pull hard to free it. I swung again. And again, and again.

I heard a yell from outside.

I swung faster.

I finally made a hole big enough to stick my hand through, and I fumbled around, searching for the lock. I twisted it free. The door swung open.

I launched out of the stall, tripping on the door frame and almost face-planting in the dirt. I found my balance, ax still gripped in my hand. It was the only good weapon I had at the moment.

I burst through the door of the stables. The field in front of me was empty, the shipping container next to the barn now closed. The sun was completely gone. There were lights on either end of the barns and at the back of the house, but they cast only a faint glow over the area.

I broke into a run.

A scream sounded from the front of the house. My feet pounded the grass harder.

I raced past the barn, to the house, and skidded to a stop. Two police cars were on the street behind the truck, doors ajar. The bodies of four officers littered the front lawn. Two scrabs stood nearby rigidly. Another was next to one of the bodies, breathing heavily and snarling.

Julian stood on the porch, tablet in hand. He was completely still, staring at the scene in front of him.

"What did you do?" Webb yelled. He burst out of the house,

staring at the dead officers. "Did you order them to attack the cops?"

"They had guns!" Julian's voice was shrill, panicked. "They were yelling at me, and—"

"They had scrab Tasers, you moron!" Webb shouted. "The police here don't carry guns!"

Julian's face was oddly blank, and he hadn't noticed me standing to his left. "They saw the scrabs." His voice was calm as he pointed to where ten scrabs stood in front of one of the trucks. "So I think the words you're looking for right now are *thank you.*"

Webb reeled back a little. "Damn, kid."

"Stop calling me that," Julian snapped.

A hand landed on my shoulder, and I jumped, a gasp escaping my mouth. I whirled around to find Madison.

She tugged me to the side of the house before Julian saw us. I squeezed her hand, nearly weak with relief.

"Where's the rest of the team?" I asked.

"They're here. We didn't think it was a good idea to just roll up to the front door. Are you OK? What happened? Did they lose control of the scrabs?"

I shook my head, tears welling up in my eyes. I wasn't even sure why I was crying. I felt overwhelmed. "Julian did that. He sent the scrabs after those officers."

"Christ," Madison muttered. She lifted her phone to her ear. "Yeah, Grayson? I've got her. You're clear."

"What's he doing?" I asked.

"Explosives. He's blowing up those transports. He wanted to make sure you weren't nearby first."

"They're releasing some scrabs at north and south checkpoints, wherever that is."

Madison's fingers flew over her screen as she typed. "OK. I'm letting everyone know. UK team thirteen went for the other truck, and we've got another American team close behind, but that's all we could get on short notice." She read something on her screen and cursed. "They've got scrabs on either end of the street. Those must be the checkpoints. American team four is getting slammed."

Movement caught my eye. Laila was jogging toward us, machete in one hand, a weapons pack in the other. She tossed it to me. "Come on. Grayson's handling the explosives. He wants us to get out of here and go help the team down the street."

I grabbed a machete and my sword baton out of the weapons pack, and then strapped it to my back as we ran.

"Hey!" The hoarse, angry scream belonged to Julian. I dared a glance over my shoulder. I stopped.

Julian was running away from the house, furious gaze on something across the field. Edan. He was backing out of the big barn, his phone in front of him like he was taking a video. He shoved the phone into his pocket and took off, machete swinging in one hand. Gage and Dorsey were behind him, slower but right on his heels.

I skidded to a halt. My heart thumped in my ears.

Julian stopped and jabbed at the tablet. He pointed across the field, directing the scrabs.

They galloped straight for Edan, Gage, and Dorsey.

"Julian, no!" I sprinted toward them. Madison's and Laila's footsteps were right behind me.

All three boys drew their weapons as the scrabs lunged at them. Archer and Zoe darted out from behind the barn.

I swung my machete as soon as I was close enough to hit flesh. The scrab turned on me, teeth bared. I slashed my blade across its throat.

Archer leapt for a scrab with his weapon, but it skidded away. It headed straight for Julian. He punched at his tablet. Nothing happened.

"You said these stupid scrabs or SACs or whatever were trained!" He reached into his waistband and pulled out a gun. He held it straight in front of him, waiting until the scrab was close enough for a good shot. The *bang* echoed across the field. The scrab collapsed, twitching.

"Julian!" Webb dashed out the back door of the house. "Julian, no, put that—"

Julian shot the scrab again, drowning out the rest of Webb's words. It stopped twitching.

"Stop!" Webb yelled. "Gunfire confuses them, we haven't figured out—"

Two of the scrabs who'd been headed for us cut left, making a beeline for Webb, and he abruptly stopped talking. He pulled a Taser from his belt and aimed it at the scrab. It convulsed as it went down.

Edan yanked his machete out of a scrab as it fell to the ground. His chest heaved up and down, blood streaking his arms.

Bang.

Bang.

Bang.

The noise came from the large container next to the big barn.

You can't just throw them in there, Webb had said.

The container tipped over. A claw ripped apart the metal door.

Scrabs poured out. Webb still had his Taser, and he stuck a couple scrabs with it. They went down twitching.

"Julian! A little help here?" he yelled.

Julian had his back to Webb. He was staring at me.

Two scrabs slammed into Webb at once. He screamed as he disappeared beneath them.

Julian began slamming his finger repeatedly into the tablet. Most of the scrabs stiffened. A couple kept running and disappeared into the trees behind Julian. From somewhere nearby, Priya screamed. Dorsey and Laila immediately took off in the direction of the sound.

Grayson sprinted away from the truck parked in the grass, sidestepping Webb's body.

The container on the truck exploded. Grayson covered his head with his arms as flaming pieces of it went everywhere.

He hurled something at the scrabs standing rigid near the trees. It sailed through the air and landed on the ground, bouncing once.

It exploded.

Both Edan and I jumped. Scrab parts went flying. Julian hit the ground, covering his head with his hands.

Grayson cut right, jumping in to help Dorsey fight a scrab that was on fire. Laila and Priya were standing over three dead ones nearby.

I heard yelling, and I turned to see a few guys running toward the road. MDG guys, probably. I squinted, searching for Julian.

He appeared from behind the house, his stride quick and even. His eyes caught on something, and fury flashed in them. It was Noah, adjusting his uniform camera so it was aimed straight at Julian.

Julian took off toward the barn. He wrenched the door open.

"Julian, no!" I yelled.

He ignored me, disappearing inside the barn. Dorsey and Gage were right behind him.

They both shot out of the barn as quickly as they'd gone in. A scrab burst out of the door behind them. More poured out after it, teeth bared, silent except for the thud of their paws on the ground.

"Hey!" Noah sprinted toward the scrabs, frantically waving his arms. Patrick and the rest of the team followed close behind him. "Over here!" Several of the scrabs veered in their direction.

Dorsey reeled around to fight the closest scrab. He tripped on something I couldn't see, his machete flying out of his hand. The scrab lunged.

Gage shot in front of Dorsey, swinging his spiked knuckles at the scrab. They lodged in its throat.

The scrab opened its mouth in a silent scream. It drove all ten of its claws into Gage's chest.

Dorsey yelled something. I clapped a hand over my mouth, squeezing my eyes shut. When I opened them a moment later, I saw Gage crumpled on the ground and Dorsey a few steps away, desperately fighting off another scrab. Every member of the team was engaged in all-out battle.

I ran forward, catching a glimpse of Julian out of the corner of my eye. He was in front of the barn with his tablet. Grayson was inching closer to him, taking down scrab after scrab, but Julian kept releasing a new one every few seconds.

A second scrab was headed straight for Zoe, and I cut it off, using my machete to whack it across the face. I sliced my blade across its neck and it fell to the ground.

I turned to find Zoe letting out a relieved sigh as her scrab went down. She gave me a half-smile as she wiped a hand across her brow. I gasped as I caught movement behind her.

"Zoe, look—"

The scrab behind her took her off her feet as it sank its teeth into her neck. I dove forward, sticking my machete into its side, but it was too late. Zoe's eyes were blank as she hit the ground.

A strangled cry caught in my throat. I whirled around, desperately searching for the rest of the team. Most of them were still fighting, but I didn't see Noah or Madison.

A blur of movement caught my eye. It was Edan, shooting across the field. He sidestepped a scrab and slammed into Julian, knocking him into the barn door. Julian ducked away, throwing a punch so hard it knocked Edan off his feet. He hit the dirt.

Julian stepped into the barn for only a second. A scrab roared out; this one's vocal cords still worked perfectly well. It grabbed ahold of Edan's leg and yanked him into the barn. Edan clawed desperately as he disappeared.

I was running before I realized it. My feet pounded the earth, my breath coming in gasps.

Grayson leapt out of the darkness and tackled Julian. They fell to the dirt, a mess of limbs. Julian snarled something I couldn't understand.

A scrab blocked my path, and I barely got my machete up in time. My hands were shaking, but I hit my target. The scrab fell, giving me a view to the barn.

Julian slammed his foot into Grayson's stomach. Grayson doubled over with a wheeze. Julian took off.

I ran, skidding to a stop in front of the barn door. I braced my hands on either side of the door, suddenly too scared to go inside.

Edan limped out of the darkness, and I almost collapsed with relief. I grabbed his arms, searching his body for injuries. His face was twisted in pain, the leg of his jeans torn open and bloody.

"Always the legs," he said with a wince.

He took both my hands and flipped them over.

"DAMMIT, EDAN!"

I glanced over my shoulder. Julian was patting his pockets, searching for something.

I looked back down at my hands, where Edan had just placed the tablet.

"You know how to use this thing?" Edan asked.

I meant to smile, but a sob escaped my lips. "Yes."

I took a step away from him, letting my free hand grasp his as we started to part. "Stay here, OK? You can barely walk." The image of a scrab dragging him screaming into the barn was still playing on repeat in my head. I was painfully aware of the fact that I still had no idea where Madison and Noah were. I didn't want to lose another friend tonight.

He nodded, his fingers gripping mine a little tighter.

As I turned, I caught Julian's gaze. He was staring at our hands, his expression twisted into the most monstrous expression I'd ever seen. Our eyes met.

Danger.

Danger.

Danger.

I pressed the red button as I walked to him. There were only two scrabs left on the field, and they both went rigid as I shocked them. Patrick leapt forward, killing the one closest to him.

I took in a tiny breath as I drew closer to Julian. There were at least ten scrabs just around the corner of the barn, waiting at attention. He'd obviously been holding those for the next wave.

"Give me that before you hurt yourself," he snapped. He held out his hand.

I realized too late that his other hand was reaching into his waistband. He lifted the gun and pointed it over my shoulder.

I dove for him, but it was too late. Two quick shots rang out, Julian's arm jerking as he fired. I tackled him. He grunted as we toppled to the ground.

I heard the familiar pounding of heavy running footsteps. The gunshot had sent the remaining ten scrabs in every direction.

"No!" Edan yelled from behind me. "No, no, no. Grayson?"

Julian shoved me off of him, flying into a sitting position. He aimed the gun straight at Edan and didn't hesitate. He squeezed the trigger.

It clicked. He squeezed again. Another click. He was out of bullets, or it was jammed. He let out a yell of frustration.

Edan, kneeling over Grayson with his hands pressed to his bloody chest, gave Julian a truly horrified look.

Julian's eyes were wild as he turned to me. He lunged for the tablet.

I shot up and broke into a run. Half the scrabs were headed for the team, one alarmingly close to Laila. I pressed the red button just before it reached her. Every scrab I could see came to a halt, mouth open in a silent scream.

Julian was gaining on me, and I ran faster, speeding into the darkness beside the barn. A hand seized the back of my shirt, yanking it so violently that I was airborne for a moment before I hit the ground, hard. My weapons pack flew off and skittered across the ground.

I rolled over, cradling the tablet to my chest. I stumbled as I tried to get up. He reached for me again, and I smacked his hand away as I shot to my feet.

He swung. I saw it coming a half second before his fist landed on my cheek.

It knocked me on my ass, stars dancing in my vision.

"Oh god," Julian's voice was a strangled sob. "I didn't mean to do that. Oh my god, I didn't mean to do that, Clara. You know I didn't mean to do that, right?"

I looked up at him, baffled. He had both hands in his hair, eyes wild, cheeks wet with tears.

Why was *he* crying?

I should get up. I knew this, and yet my legs wouldn't move. My cheek stung. It felt like something had come loose in my brain.

"Why did you do this?" Julian was screaming and crying at

the same time. It was truly a sight, watching a man who had just killed several people feel sorry for himself. "Why did you make me do this?"

In the distance, someone screamed.

I still had the tablet.

My brain clicked back into place. I jumped to my feet, repeatedly pressing the red button. I had no idea if it did anything. I ran back toward the field.

"Why are you running away from me?" Julian screamed. He was following me. "All I ever did was try to help you. I was going to give you *everything,* and you spit it back in my face! Do you want to get yourself killed, Clara? Because that's what's going to happen! You're going to fucking die!"

He grabbed me around the waist so suddenly that I gasped. He yanked me against him.

I rammed my elbow into his side. He cursed. His grip on me loosened.

I pulled free of him and spun around. He had his fists raised again.

But I saw it coming this time. I ducked and let his arm sail over my head. I smashed my fist into his chin. He hit the ground.

I gasped for breath. "Still alive, asshole."

43

I TOOK OFF, LEAVING JULIAN IN THE DIRT.

My knuckles throbbed, and I almost dropped the tablet twice as I ran back to the field. I was on the verge of total panic, too terrified to look over my shoulder to see if Julian was following me.

Dead scrabs littered the ground. Patrick and Dorsey were fighting one off. Laila and Priya sprinted to help.

"Clara." Madison came to a stop beside me. "Thank god you're OK. Have you seen Noah? We were in the trees, but—"

Her face paled. She raced to where Edan was sitting next to a motionless Grayson. I pressed my hand to my mouth, tears welling in my eyes.

"I'm sorry," Edan said, roughly wiping tears from his cheeks. "He jumped in front of me when Julian shot at me."

Madison laughed. She clapped a hand to her mouth, a second hysterical laugh escaping before she dissolved into tears.

Edan's eyes caught on something behind me, and he closed them, looking away. I turned.

Noah was dragging Archer's body out from beneath a dead scrab. I gasped, the tears I'd been holding back streaming down my cheeks. Noah pulled until Archer was completely free, and then stepped back and glanced at us. A single claw had ripped a huge gash down the right side of his face, and the entire area was covered in blood.

"Jesus, Noah." Dorsey rushed forward, ripping open his weapons pack. He produced his first aid kit.

Sirens wailed in the distance, and Noah shook his head, putting his hand on Dorsey's.

"It's all right. They'll . . ." He gestured vaguely in the direction of the sirens, apparently unable to finish the sentence. His shoulders sagged heavily. Dorsey pressed white gauze into his hand anyway.

I wanted to sink down beside Madison and sob, but I was still clutching the tablet in my hand, and I needed to make sure there weren't scrabs waiting to pounce. I wiped my eyes and walked to the barn door.

There were several rows of scrabs still in cages. One snarled.

Priya stepped inside. Her eyes were red, and dirt and blood was smeared down her arms, but her expression was all relief as she looked at the scrabs.

"MDG didn't get any of them out," she said, leaning back against the wall with a sigh. "All the containers and trucks are still here, except for the one you saw leave earlier. Team thirteen is going after that one."

"That's good," I said quietly. Had we won? This didn't feel like winning.

Priya wiped her cheeks with a sniffle. "Where is Julian?"

"Oh. I—I left him on the other side of the barn." I stepped toward the door. "I should go—"

She put a soft hand on my arm, shaking her head. "Don't

worry about it. The police will grab him if he's still nearby." She managed to almost smile. "I hope you punched him a few times."

Dorsey, Patrick, and Laila walked through the barn door. Laila wrapped an arm around Priya. Patrick reached for my hand and gave it a squeeze. Noah followed close behind them, holding a bloody white bandage to his face.

"Madison wanted a minute alone with Grayson," Noah said quietly.

I glanced at the door. Where was Edan?

"He's around back," Patrick whispered, even though I hadn't asked.

I squeezed his hand again before slipping out the door. Madison was sitting cross-legged next to Grayson's body, and she didn't look up as I edged around the barn and then walked quickly to the back. Tears welled in my eyes again. I took a shuddering breath.

Edan was crouched on the ground beneath a soft yellow spotlight, arms wrapped around his legs, head lowered to his knees.

He shot up at the sound of my footsteps, hand fumbling for his machete. His eyes focused on me, and he let out a sigh, shoulders slumping as he dropped his hand.

"Sorry," I whispered.

"No, it's fine." He wiped both palms across his cheeks. "I just didn't want to fall apart in front of Maddie. I think she needs everyone to stay calm for a minute. Or she just wants be alone so she can have a breakdown in private. I don't know."

"Do you want me to go so you can have a breakdown in private?" I asked. I wondered if he could hear that I wanted the answer to be *no*.

He pressed his lips together for a moment, hands on his hips. When he spoke, the words were wobbly. "I really don't."

I was shaking as I stepped forward and pulled him into a hug. He wrapped his arms around my waist and lowered his head onto my shoulder. He held me tightly.

"I'm sorry," I whispered. "I'm so sorry."

It took a moment before he responded, his voice quavering. "Julian's the only one who should be apologizing."

"I don't think that's ever going to happen." I closed my eyes as I pressed my hands to his back. The full horror of what had just happened was starting to settle in, and I was worried that I might collapse if I let go.

We stood in silence for a long time before I found words again. "I'm so glad you're OK," I whispered.

He put one hand on the back of my head, his lips close to my ear. "I'm so glad you're OK too."

Julian was gone by the time the police showed up. I gave them a statement about everything, from MDG's plan to build a scrab army to Julian shooting Grayson and trying to kill Edan as well.

Grayson had booked the teams' hotel rooms earlier in the day, and all eight of us crowded into one. I'd taken a shower and changed, which had only momentarily made me feel better. The image of Grayson's body jerking as he was shot was on replay in my mind. Noah dragging Archer's body. The scrab snatching Zoe. I closed my eyes, blinking back tears.

Noah and Madison sat on the ground near the window, laptops in front of them. They were searching the team's uniform camera footage, trying to find proof of anything that had happened tonight. The right side of Noah's face was bandaged. He'd keep the eye, but he was going to have a scar. *An impressive scar,* the doctor had said, obviously trying to put a positive spin on it.

I was sitting on the ground against one of the beds between Patrick and Edan. Laila and Dorsey were on the bed behind us, Priya on her stomach on the other one. The news played on the television. So far, nothing about MDG or what had happened tonight.

"Anything?" Priya asked Noah and Madison softly.

"Not yet," Noah said. "It's too dark. I'm about to check Patrick's camera, though."

"The *New York Times* just broke the news of Grayson's death," Laila said, eyes on her phone.

Madison's eyes snapped up. "What does it say?"

"It just says that he died in London this evening, more details to come."

Noah's phone rang. "It's Saira," he said, and swiped at the screen. "Hey, Saira? You're on speaker with the team."

"No, it's Connor," the voice on the other end said. *"Saira's getting Thomas checked out of hospital, and she asked me to call."*

"Is the rest of team thirteen OK?" Priya asked. "Harry, I mean?" She winced. UK team thirteen was down to four members.

"Yeah, he's fine, thanks. But I've got bad news. That truck that Clara saw leave before anyone got there? The one we followed? It was empty."

"Empty?" I repeated.

"Yeah, we lost track of it, so we called it in to the police. Don't

know if it was always empty or if they unloaded it after hearing about what happened. But it was totally empty by the time the police stopped them."

"Does it really matter, though?" Noah asked. "There were shipping containers full of scrabs. They were locked in a barn. The police saw all of that."

"Yeah, they did, but Saira's just heard that there's nothing tying MDG to any of it. There's one dead MDG employee there—uh, Webb, I think was his name—and apparently they're denying any knowledge of what he was doing. Everyone else took off."

"There must be something there that leads back to MDG," Madison said, frowning. "The equipment, the vans, something."

"Maybe," Connor said. "I imagine it will be days before they sort through it all. But that's not the worst part."

Noah's eyes flicked from his laptop to the phone. "What's the worst part?"

"We just heard that Julian gave the police a statement. He said that Webb killed Grayson. He completely denied everything Clara told them. Said she was just trying to get back at him for breaking up with her."

"Seriously?" Priya practically yelled.

"The American news stations are picking it up," Dorsey said, staring at his phone. "Are you seeing Twitter?"

Edan glanced at his phone. "Julian leaked his statement. TMZ is saying Grayson was killed by a rogue MDG agent, that Webb guy. And—" He cut himself off, leaning his head back and closing his eyes.

"What?" I asked.

"There's also a story about you," Priya said. "But no reputable news site has it," she added in a rush. "It's mostly just on Twitter."

"What story?" I tried to grab for Edan's phone, but he moved it away, giving me a pained look.

"It says you cheated on Julian, got really mad when he broke up with you, and stalked him." Madison said the words furiously, reading them from her phone. "Apparently there's a source who said you showed up at a friend's house and made a scene in front of his mom."

"He's just trying to discredit you," Noah said. "Get his story out there first."

"The crazy-bitch defense," Madison said bitterly. "A classic."

I pressed both hands to my forehead, a humorless laugh escaping my mouth. I'd take a scrab or a SAC or whatever you wanted to call them any day over Julian. All these monsters couldn't compare to him.

"*Did you get any proof from your uniform cameras?*" Connor asked. "*You were wearing them, weren't you?*"

"Still looking," Noah said. "Let me call you back when we know, OK?"

"*Yeah. Talk to you later.*"

No one spoke for several minutes as Noah and Madison combed through video footage. I pressed my arms to my chest and said a silent prayer that we captured something that would incriminate Julian. I desperately wanted him to pay for killing Grayson, and Zoe, and Gage, and Archer. He may not have shot them, but he released the scrabs that killed them.

"It was too fucking dark." Madison pushed her computer off her lap and gripped her hair with both hands. I got the feeling that searching the camera footage had been the only thing keeping her from bursting into tears. "He shot Grayson, and there's absolutely no proof of it."

"Noah?" Edan asked.

Noah shook his head sadly. "I've got nothing. These cameras aren't good in low light, and they don't have audio. We've got some footage of scrabs in the barn from Edan's phone, but not when Julian is in there with them. Everything else is just total darkness or jumpy footage where you can't see what's happening."

"So we have nothing." Priya moaned in frustration.

"Not exactly," Edan said quietly. He looked at me. "We have Clara."

"What do you mean?" I asked.

"You could tell the truth," Edan said. "Julian's out there lying because he's scared you'll tell the truth. He told you everything, and he's terrified."

"Why would anyone believe me?" I asked.

"Why *wouldn't* they believe you?" Dorsey asked.

"Because it's just my word against Julian's. And apparently everyone is already listening to him."

"Some people won't believe you," Edan conceded. "But some will."

"Dorsey, hand me my camera," Noah said. Dorsey grabbed it from the side of the bed. "We could film a video right now. I can get it up immediately."

I hesitated. Could I even be coherent talking about what had happened? Where would I even start? MDG's plan to build a scrab army was so wild that *I* still had trouble believing it.

"You don't have to," Madison said quietly. She swallowed hard, blinking back tears. "You already talked to the cops. You told them the truth. And I'm sure American law enforcement will be talking to you soon."

"But Julian's lying about her!" Priya said. "Everyone's going to think she's making it all up. I think it's a good idea to tell the whole story before Julian twists everything around. And the Montgomery family hires an army of lawyers."

"Is it worth the risk?" Patrick asked. "Putting yourself out there when you know people are just going to hurl abuse at you?"

I let out a short laugh. Madison looked startled. The rest of team looked at me worriedly, except for Edan, who gave me a tragic smile that mirrored my own.

"Men keep hurling abuse at me, no matter what I do, so I might as well put it to good use. Let's do it," I said.

"Well, that's depressing," Noah said, getting to his feet. "After we're done, I'm going to go have a nice long cry. Who's in?"

"I am definitely in," Madison said. She leaned her head back against the wall, her eyes meeting mine. *Thank you*, she mouthed. I nodded.

I smoothed down my hair. It was still wet from my shower. A bruise was blooming on my cheek from where Julian had punched me, but I didn't want to put on makeup. It felt like protecting him, to cover it up.

"Do you want us to leave while you do this?" Edan asked.

"No, stay." I smiled at him. "It'll be easier with friends nearby."

Noah perched the camera on a chair. "Ready when you are."

I let out a long breath. I looked straight at the camera.

"Hi. I'm Clara Pratt. And I'm here to tell you the truth."

Acknowledgments

It took five years for *All These Monsters* to go from idea to published book, and I couldn't have done it without the help of so many people. Thank you to:

My editor, Emilia Rhodes, for believing in this book not once, but twice, and for helping me make it so much better.

My agent, Emmanuelle Morgen, for working hard to make sure this book (and all the others!) ended up in the right hands.

The entire team at HMH for giving this book a beautiful package and working hard to get it into reader's hands.

Shannon Messenger for the notes on early pages of this book, and for being an all-around great friend. I'm so glad I awkwardly introduced myself to you at a book festival back when we were both newbie authors.

Kate Johnston for organizing a writing retreat that helped keep me sane at just the right time.

Maurene Goo for recommending I watch *Coffee Prince,* a Korean drama, which, in a roundabout way, partially inspired this book.

Chelsea Moore and all the instructors at Ro Fitness for giving me a place to row out my writing frustrations.

My family, especially my mom, for putting up with my writer mood swings and always being so supportive.

My sister, Laura, for reading several drafts of this book and never getting tired of it. Thank you for never getting tired of reading my books.

And to all the readers who picked up this book or any of my others—thank you so much.

DON'T MISS THE
THRILLING CONCLUSION

ALL
THESE
WARRIORS

SUMMER 2021